*For Gay,
with best wishes*

Sheila Finch

June 2017.

A VILLA FAR FROM ROME

Sheila Finch

A VILLA FAR FROM ROME
Copyright © 2016 by Sheila Finch
All rights reserved. This book, and any portions thereof, may not be reproduced without written permission except in the case of brief quotes embedded in critical articles and reviews. For more information, contact Hadley Rille Books.

ISBN-13   978-0-9971188-3-4

Ebook Edition also available.

Cover art © Yana Dhyana
Published by
Hadley Rille Books
Olathe, KS 66062 USA

www.hrbpress.com
contact@hadleyrillebooks.com

For my niece, Caroline Scallan.

ACKNOWLEDGMENTS

As usual, my gratitude to the members of the Asilomar Writers Consortium who have supported, guided, encouraged and celebrated with me over the years. In particular: Rose Hamilton Gottlieb, Jon Russ, Daniel Davila Houston, Grant Farley, David and Mary Putnam, Barry Slater, Kendall Evans, Harry Lowther, Samantha Henderson, Lydia Bird, and Deborah Kolodji.

PROLOGUE

[Pyrgi, near Rome, AD 61]

FATHER SAID SHE WAS TOO YOUNG to go to the chariot races at the new stadium her family built, though her three brothers were allowed to go, Titus younger than she. Father said she was too young to attend the banquet where the emperor would sit at their table.

She watched them return, late afternoon sun streaming over her brothers' shoulders, laughing, their faces red, sweat plastering their hair in tight curls, their new tunics dusty. Talk spilled out of her brothers' mouths: Chariots tangling – the crowd roaring – horses lying on their sides, shrieking, legs beating uselessly in the air – the charioteers slashing the harness with their short swords. And the emperor, driving through a gap in the middle of the chaos, winning the laurels. Valentinus punching Julius in his excitement at the telling. Julius shoving Titus to the floor because he was older, bigger. All three wild with laughter.

Only Father wasn't laughing. His face stern, he'd gone straight to his study, summoning his Greek secretary. Mother went to her chamber, proclaiming a headache from the sun. The slaves and the freed servants they'd brought with them from their house in Rome rushed to and fro readying the banqueting chamber. The smell of meat and fish roasting with garlic already filling the house. More dishes being prepared than she had ever seen before – she had no name for most of them. More servants hired to serve them. Musicians! Dancers! Even a juggler to entertain the royal guest. The emperor would arrive and the banquet begin when the sun was fully down. The emperor, who right now was bathing, his slaves preparing clean robes in the guest chambers Father had built especially for him on the side of their house that had the best view over the valley and the family's grapevines to the dark sea.

She hadn't seen the emperor yet, but the silly house slaves who'd been allowed to witness his coming that she'd been denied – confined to her chamber with her nurse like a child! – prattled of his fine features. His glorious curls gilded by the summer sun. His piercing eyes. His witty talk. He was so young, they said. And strong, brave, godlike.

Her heart fluttered like one of her caged birds. Why were they denying her this great celebration? Soon the house would fill with guests from town – it wasn't often that the emperor came so far from Rome to their small town. Even Titus would be allowed to be there! Why was she banned from feasting her eyes on the emperor too?

She would defy her father and watch from behind a column in the great chamber where the painted Muses danced on one wall and the Fates spun their thread on another. Once the banquet started and the wine was flowing, no one would think to look for her. It was dangerous to defy Father, his anger flashing like lightning over the family. She would bribe old Cassia – her nurse had a weakness for sweet figs dripping honey – to let her peek for just for a moment. She was not an infant to be sent to bed early when guests arrived for fear she'd embarrass her parents.

She was almost grown up now – a young woman.

Later, while her old nurse slept, gorged on honeyed figs steeped in wine, she crept through the flickering shadows of the wall torches, the noise of the hired musicians, the servants hurrying to and from the kitchen carrying amphoras full of wine, the best of the harvest. She hid herself behind the thick columns. Across the hall, the emperor reclined on his couch, the slaves filling and refilling his cup. Her brothers slumped, loose muscled as if they not the emperor had taken part in the races earlier. Her father, his back to where she hid, sat stiff as a statue. She could not see her mother.

And the emperor – every bit as beautiful as a young god as everyone had said, a carving of the young Apollo wreathed in golden curls – looked up, his eyes lit with inner fire, catching her gaze. Silence filled the hall, all motion seemed to stop. Heat flooded her face, her breath tangled in her chest, but she could not tear her gaze free of him.

He raised his cup to her and drank.

How scary it was to lurk here where she had been forbidden! At any moment her father could turn and see her. Heart pounding, she crept away, back to her room where old Cassia lay snoring on the floor at the foot of her sleeping couch. Trembling, she slipped out of her robe and lay down, knowing sleep would not come now.

She had looked upon the face of a god.

The candles burned low. The small window that looked out to the low hills was still dark when he came in. She saw him in shadow, unloosening the brooch that held his toga, She felt the weight of his body slumping on top of hers, his hand clamping her mouth shut, the rhythm of his hips grinding against her, his teeth catching her brow, her cheek, the hiss of his peppermint-scented breath in her ear, *My little slave girl, my pretty little slave!*

The pain that ripped through her like fire.

Afterwards, he left as silently as he had entered, and she lay in the tangled bed linens, feeling the warmth of blood on her thighs as the rising sun slid through the window across the still sleeping nurse. Her body ached. Her mouth tasted of peppermint

She would not allow herself to cry.

She had just turned twelve years old.

CHAPTER ONE

[Noviomagus, Britannia, AD 66]

"I DON'T LIKE THIS AT ALL," Breca said for the third time. "He's far too young."

"I was hardly much older than Amminus, my heart, when my father sent me to live with the emperor. I survived, didn't I?" Togidubnus patted his wife's arm as he passed through the room.

"But Rome is so far away!"

"No further than it was when I was there."

"Don't make jokes, Togi," she said. "We know nothing about this emperor."

"What's there to know?"

He stopped in the doorway to his study where he had been assembling documents recounting his memories of the most recent campaign against the rebel queen Boudicca that he wished to present to the emperor. The small house was quiet in the early spring afternoon; seagulls heading back to the channel waters from foraging expeditions to the chalk hill country were the only sound from outside. He loved this little house his father had built, sheltering them like a mother hen with her brood below the Downs and so close to the sea.

"Please, Togi," Breca said. "I beg you. Don't take the boy."

He'd heard rumors that Rome was losing its taste for the wilder parts of its far-flung empire; the cost of retaining the legions based in Britannia was an increasingly unpopular expense. The emperor, so the gossips said, was considering pulling the legions out. In Togidubnus's view, that would be a disaster for both Rome and the people of these islands. It was

A VILLA FAR FROM ROME

important to secure ties with Rome.

"It's only a year. One year to teach him the ways of a ruler."

"A Roman."

"We are all Romans now, my heart."

"They will never think of us as anything but barbarians. Surely you see that? I have a very bad feeling about this."

"What's to fear? It'll make a man of him."

Sending the boy to the Roman court was a good idea. He himself had benefitted immensely from spending a year of his adolescence under the tutelage of Emperor Claudius, a man who'd been – he thought – unfairly judged by his own mother as a "monstrous specimen" due to his physical infirmities. At Claudius's court, he'd become proficient in Latin – and there was no way to succeed without speaking the Mother Tongue of the Romans, no matter how much his wife wanted to cling to the old ways and words. He'd gained protection and favor shown in the name he'd returned with: Tiberius Claudius Togidubnus. The world from now on was going to be Roman. His oldest boy would do well to grow up Roman. But Breca was a princess of the Regni, and a descendant of a long line of Druid priests, and not as comfortable as he with Roman rule.

Voices outside the long, unshuttered windows drew his attention. His two sons were playing with a young brown-and-white dog; twelve year-old Amminus – but the emperor would have something to say about that name if he liked the boy! – throwing a hunk of bone for the dog. Catuarus, four-years younger, stood laughing under an oak, grabbing the bone away from the panting dog as fast as she retrieved it. Sunshine flooded the river meadow with soft gold, the scent of the nearby sea drifted inside, white butterflies swooped among the spring flowers. The weather was good for traveling the long distance from the little harbor of Noviomagus Regnorum to Rome's port at Ostia.

"Remember, Breca, I met this emperor while I was at Claudius's court. He was a young boy. I seem to remember him excelling in sport, especially with horses."

"That tells me nothing. Many a monster has been good with horses."

"Enough!" he said sharply.

She came to him, contritely, and laid her head on his breast. His put his arms around her. They remained in each other's embrace for a moment listening to the sound of the boys at play.

He wouldn't speak to her of his own ambitions. He was a princeling, a chief, as his father had been, of the Catuvellauni, rewarded with this house in the territory of a related tribe for their long service to the Romans. He'd taken Breca to be his wife. The Regni had been without a king for several years; if their council of Elders could be brought to see that closer relations with Rome were beneficial for the tribe, the election next Beltane could go his way. And some day, his oldest son would need this Roman education to lead the land and its people.

"I have such fears, Togi," she said, her voice muffled by the fold of his tunic.

He stroked her hair, soothing her. "He'll be all right, my heart. The emperor will make a warrior of him. And one day he'll be a fine leader in my place."

"Sulis grant the truth of that!"

He kissed the top of her head. "You must remember to call her Minerva. Someday, I'll build a temple dedicated to her for you."

"It's only the ramblings of a foolish woman who loves her husband and dreads his absence."

"Never foolish. Tell me, descendent of a long line of Druids, shall I return triumphantly from Rome?"

A shadow passed across her face and she turned away from him. "I see you return in good health. The rest is darkness."

"A night journey! With my beloved wife holding a lamp, lighting the way to our bedchamber, no doubt."

She slapped his arm, but he saw the smile she tried to hide from him.

The two boys tumbled into the room, punching each other's shoulders, grabbing at ears and hair, laughing. The older of his sons was tall, pale of face and hair, and very thin, bones sticking up in awkward places as if he were the son of an impoverished iron smelter instead of the

A VILLA FAR FROM ROME

chief of the Regni. Yes, Amminus would benefit from the discipline of Rome. He was too much devoted to books. In Rome, they'd put flesh on his bones with martial exercise such as only the Romans knew, make him stand up straight, like a man, instead of slouching like an untaught girl.

"Are you prepared for the journey, Amminus?" he asked.

The boy nodded, avoiding eye contact with his father. "I didn't have much to pack."

"Why so glum-faced? The sea journey alone should make you happy. You boys have grown up in boats and on the water since you were babes."

"I'll go instead!" The younger son was sturdily built, muscular, copper haired and dark eyed like the ancestor he was named for, his cheeks flushed with good health. He'd make a good warrior some day. Time enough for that later. There'd been a girl between them, but she hadn't lived to see her fourth birthday. His wife had compensated by spoiling the boys and over-protecting them, especially Amminus.

"He's right," Breca said. "It's a very long journey. And why must you travel by sea the whole way? Wouldn't it be better to take the land roads to Rome? Amminus has a weak stomach. If you encounter storms, he'll suffer."

"Bandits by land!" The younger boy slashed about him with an imaginary sword.

"I've made my decision. I've arranged passage with a merchant leaving on the high tide tonight, and we'll take it. No more arguments!"

* * *

A full moon rose over the little harbor as the family made their way down to the merchant's ship, Amminus holding his mother's arm, Catuarus skipping ahead. The salt smell of the tide, high and about to turn, filled his nose. An owl glided silently over his head. Minerva's bird; a good sign.

"Be more cheerful, my heart." They'd reached the lamp-lit quay where two house servants waited for them with a chest filled with clothes for Amminus to wear during a year in the emperor's house. "I'll return before you know I'm gone. I'll bring you treasure from Rome."

Breca pulled her wool cloak tighter round her shoulders, but said nothing. He saw the glint of tears in the moonlight. There was nothing to fear. She'd foreseen his return and her second sight was never wrong.

"Don't forget to tell the emperor how you defeated that bad Queen Boudicca!" Catuarus said. "Tell him about the battles and the blood and how you killed –"

"Don't be foolish!" Amminus interrupted.

"No quarreling now. That would be a most unfortunate memory to take with us. Amminus, take your leave of your mother. The next time she sees you, you will be a man."

Breca embraced her older son and whispered in his ear as the younger one leaped about them in excitement. She let Amminus go and he made his way cautiously aboard the rocking ship. The boat's master stood with the mooring rope in his hands, eager to be off on the tide.

"Breca – " He took her in his arms.

But she put her fingers over his lips, silencing him. "No need for talk. I shall pray night and day until you return."

"A very long prayer indeed! But thank you. I will keep your memory safe in mine."

He kissed her, then boarded the boat without looking back.

CHAPTER TWO

[Rome, AD 66]

ROME WAS MUCH LARGER – and noisier and dirtier – than Antonia had imagined. She had few memories of the city she hadn't visited since she was ten, but she'd grown up believing it must be paradise from the way her mother lamented its loss. And the streets! Instead of the careful, clean lines of Pyrgi, the little town on the Tuscan coast where their country villa stood, the city's jumbled streets, some new, some obviously in blackened ruins, seemed intended as a vast labyrinth. On both sides of a narrow, rubble strewn passage, tall new buildings shut out the sun. Stopping to catch her breath, she eased the sack containing a little bread and everything she still owned off her back. Once, the family had owned a house here in Rome. Lost along with the villa in Pyrgi after her father had gone bankrupt.

The buildings on this block were new but hardly attractive, so crowded together. None were less than two storeys in height, some more than four, all apartments, stacked on top of each other the way a child might stack blocks. She couldn't imagine living like that. They faced inward, presenting blank, white walls against which a variety of merchants and hucksters spread their wares, shoddy leather goods and cheap trinkets, flagons of wine of such inferior harvest her father would not have given it to the servants. Here and there, the blank walls were broken by open shop fronts where flies swarmed over the hanging carcasses of sheep and goats and the stinking piles of fish.

"We would do well to find a room to spend the night," Nikolaos said. The Greek who had been her father's secretary shifted the sleeping child from his left shoulder to his right. "It's been an arduous journey, and you need to rest."

They had been traveling for the better part of a week, sometimes on foot, sometimes given a ride by a farmer with an oxcart who took pity on them. Though it was still early in the year, the city was already as hot as an oven preparing to bake bread, She ached all over, but they couldn't stop now.

"Time to rest after I speak with the emperor!"

It had taken her years to find the strength to make this decision to confront the emperor, years filled with tears and recrimination, her mother's lamentations, her brothers' scorn, the servants' whispered spite, all overshadowed at last by the family's decline into bankruptcy, the auctioning off of the family estate, her father's eventual suicide. Years in which she was forced to grow up too soon into womanhood and reluctant motherhood. The father must acknowledge his child.

"I doubt we could gain access to the palace at this late hour," Nikolaos said.

"Must you strike down all my plans? Why did you insist on coming with me anyway?"

He looked at her sternly as a tutor might look at a lazy scholar. "You know very well that a Roman woman doesn't travel alone anywhere, especially Rome."

He was right, of course, though it irked her. Everything in her cried out for confrontation with the emperor. For the last year, that had been all she could think about. Her brothers had scoffed at her plan. Even old Cassia, her nursemaid, one of the few freedmen and slaves still kept on by the family, shook her head. Her mother, filled with grief for her daughter, feared for her safety if she so much as reminded the emperor she was alive. Why were they so certain he wouldn't welcome her – and his child? Only the Greek, freed by her father before his death, elected to go with her to Rome.

She looked at the crowded street, and a wave of tiredness and nausea swept over her. "How will we find lodging?"

"The man who sold us bread at our last stop mentioned a place."

They had come to a halt outside one of the small shops, a place of

A VILLA FAR FROM ROME

cheap leather belts and dusty boots, sandals even old Cassia would have disdained, piled in unappetizing disarray outside its door. The result looked more as if it had been swept outside like trash rather than goods hoping to entice buyers. But there was a stone stool, apparently for the convenience of customers trying on shoes. Nikolaos helped her sit and lowered the sleeping child into her arms. The sack that represented all that was left of her previous life lay by her feet.

"Hey!" The shoemaker came running out, waving his arms. "No public loitering!"

Nikolaos tossed a small coin. The man's hand snaked out and seized it before it fell.

"Don't stay there all day!" the shoemaker grumbled, disappearing back into the darkness inside.

The Greek strode away.

Without his presence, she felt suddenly vulnerable, conscious of the stares and the rude gestures aimed her way. The child whimpered and thrashed in her sleep. Antonia held her tighter, her own heart racing. Late afternoon, but the city retained the oppressive heat, and the smells of putrid vegetables and rotten meat were making her feel faint. This was not how she'd remembered Rome. All those years she'd dreamed of a city built of gleaming marble, with wide streets down which bronze-decked chariots dashed, drawn by white horses, beautiful people in their white togas, off to attend banquets and gladiator competitions. And at the end of one of those fine streets would be the emperor's palace.

At first she'd been lost in a welter of emotions, confused, ashamed, hurting by turn. Believing the emperor would send for her helped save her from destroying herself once she found out she was with child. Her father blamed her for everything, the child, the debt they had incurred from the emperor's visit, their own deteriorating future. He'd kept her away from Rome as she grew into girlhood, he told her, for fear something like this would happen. The child was fretful, demanding constant care. The family grew poorer, the vineyards were sold, the servants let go, even the slaves sold off.

"What's your price?"

Startled, she looked up into the red, bloated face of a middle-aged man above a torn and grimy-looking toga.

"I said, what's your price? You charging extra for the child?"

She felt her the heat rising in her cheeks. He leaned over her, blocking her escape. His breath was sour with cheap wine and onions. And behind him she saw three other ragged men, leering, waiting their turn. She screamed. The little girl woke and added her voice to her mother's.

The shoemaker hurried out, waving his arms. "No whoring on my premises! Be gone!"

"I'm no whore – "

"No gentlewoman either!" the shoemaker snarled. "What lady travels by foot, alone–"

One of the ragged men dragged her to her feet, another pulled the wriggling child out of her arms. The fear vanished and something else, something raw flooded through her. Her mind emptied of thought, her body acted by its own will. She snatched up the sack still lying at her feet, swung it – brought it to connect hard with the first man's head.

The man screamed, clutching at his eye. "Bitch!"

Nikolaos was back, pushing the men out of her way. "There will be no more of this!"

"Traveling with an escaped slave, no doubt!" the man in the soiled toga said.

"I am a freed man," Nikolaos said.

"Show proof, Greek! Where's your cap?"

Niko pulled the freedman's cap out of his tunic and slapped it carelessly on his head.

"Niko..." But the combined effect of the fear, the anger and the rank smells of the city got her, doubling her over to vomit on the cobblestones.

The men backed away in exaggerated disgust.

Nikolaos gave Antonia his cloak to wipe the mess off her mouth and chin.

"No man sets hand on me without permission!" She was still

A VILLA FAR FROM ROME

trembling with shock and anger. "My brothers taught me that. Especially Valentinus. When we were young, he used to wrestle with me – and sometimes I beat him, too."

He lifted the child from the street where the man had set her. "We need to get away from here."

The room he had found for them in a nearby inn was tiny and dark, up two narrow, rickety flights of wooden stairs. It smelled of candle smoke and the sweat of its previous occupant. The one bed was hardly more than a pallet, scarcely room for herself let alone the child. She was so tired she felt she could sleep standing up. She judged it was the tenth hour from what she remembered of the way the shadows fell outside in the street.

"I'll sleep on the floor by the door," Nikolaos said.

The proprietor of the inn had given them an oil lamp to light their way. In its sputtering light, she looked at the Greek who had assumed the role of her protector. He was the same age as her father, tall and olive skinned, with a face whose lines suggested sculpture. He'd been an athlete in his youth, a long distance runner, before the Romans took him captive. But the years of hardship had taken their toll on him as well; she was aware for the first time of the stoop that was slowly conquering his proud posture.

"You'll be cold, Niko."

"I have my cloak." He'd rinsed it in one of the many public taps with running water in the city. In the heat, it had dried almost instantly.

The child was weeping now, begging for food. She searched through the sack, already knowing there was little left but dry crusts. Nikolaos left the room. She sat on the uncomfortable bed and took the child into her lap, thinking. How far down the malicious Fates had brought her since the long ago night she'd made the unwise decision to defy her father and spy on the emperor at supper!

Nikolaos came back, carrying a rough platter with a hunk of fresh bread and some olives, a small jug of wine. She broke off pieces of the bread, dipped them in the wine, and fed them to the child. The Greek took a few olives, a sip of wine. She herself had lost all appetite.

"There's a public bath house nearby," Nikolaos said. "We'll visit it in the morning."

She hadn't had the chance to bathe since leaving home, Odd though it would seem to have to share the process with strangers, she would be grateful for the warm water.

"Good. I'll bathe and put on my clean tunic to see the emperor."

"He has a strange reputation." Niko looked as if he was trying to think how to make something simple for her to understand, something bad.

"I'm no child, Niko."

"Of course not. But I hear the talk about him in the marketplace. They say he's unpredictable. A god in the morning, a demon at night."

"Well, so are many men."

"Keep your wits about, you. Don't trust too quickly."

"You worry too much."

Later, lying in the darkness, the child beside her, she listened to the sounds of the inn's other guests quarreling. Something crashed and the walls shook. Someone cried out – a woman's voice.

She felt the resolve hardening in her heart. No matter what it took, she'd persuade the emperor to acknowledge his child.

CHAPTER THREE

Neptune's temple, when Togidubnus found it, was disappointingly small, at least by comparison with the temple consecrated to Jupiter Capitolinus he'd just passed. A long room with an arched roof supported on stone pillars, elegantly decorated with friezes of sea horses pulling shell chariots, and dolphins sacred to the god of the sea. The colors and gilding the craftsmen had used were admirable. But he was frustrated; he'd expected something much grander. As a resident of an island, a man who'd gone to sea in a fishing boat when he was little more than a tiny lad, he was conscious of the importance of a sea god in a way the citizens of this teeming city were not.

He shaded his eyes against the dazzling noon sun, measuring the temple's marble proportions in his head, thinking of the monument he'd like to erect in Noviomagus Regnorum someday. He felt the trickle of sweat under his tunic; he'd forgotten how unbearably hot Rome could be, even in late spring. He exchanged a few small coins with a merchant in the courtyard for a bird to sacrifice and looked around for a priest to perform the ceremony.

The temple he would build should be sacred to both Neptune and Minerva, in honor of his wife's allegiance to the old goddess, Sulis, known to the Romans as Minerva. Thinking of Breca, he was suddenly swept with homesickness. He'd been here less than a week and already he yearned for the cool breezes and summer showers of his homeland. Breca wasn't happy with this new world order under Rome's thumb. He saw it in the way she clung to the old ways, the old names. He respected her for it, even though he felt she was wrong. Her faithfulness was only one of the qualities that made him love her.

SHEILA FINCH

The other disturbing matter was that he hadn't seen his son since they'd arrived in Rome several days ago, and he missed the boy's company. The emperor had been quite taken with the shy, scholarly boy, but he'd sent Amminus off with two other sons of noble families and a tutor. Foolish father! he chided himself. Amminus wasn't the first son of a tribal chief to be educated in Rome. He too had spent time here when he was a boy – and emerged the better for it, hadn't he? It was more important today than ever that a boy who would someday be a chief in Britannia become a true Roman.

Across the courtyard he saw a priest and hailed him. The priest came slowly, folds of his white toga draped over his head to form a hood, every step proclaiming his importance and the low estate of the petitioner waiting with the dove fluttering in his hands. Togidubnus held his impatience in check.

"For my son's well-being."

The priest took the bird from him with a gesture that suggested he was disdainful of the small size of the offering. As if the whole ceremony bored him, the priest deftly wrung the bird's neck and fed the still body to the flames in a bronze bowl on a minor altar at the foot of the great steps. He recited the sacred words in a rush.

This casual observance offended him, even though he didn't consider himself a pious man. He understood how small and unimportant his tribe was to the Roman Empire. Here he was as poor as any country simpleton come to gawk at the emperor, and he must get used to being treated as such. Once he'd had a chance to lay out his plans for the emperor, things would change for himself and the Britanni.

He stepped past the priest and mounted the steps to enter the almost deserted temple and light incense at the high altar. Gazing up at the twice life-size statue of the sea god holding his trident aloft, his beard a tangle of kelp, he felt grounded again. He lifted his arms in prayer for a good outcome for his son. It never hurt the outcome of anything to pray to the gods, even when one was not much of a believer.

That done, he stepped out of the temple's shade and back into oppressive heat. A flock of pigeons, grey as the stones that littered the

A VILLA FAR FROM ROME

Downs outside Noviomagus, clattered up from the steps as he descended to the cobblestone street. In the fierce sun, the flowering trees and shrubs that spilled over low walls glowed scarlet and gold. Shading his eyes with his hand, he squinted up the street to see which way he should go. Surely he should remember the city better than this? It was different from the memory he carried of his days here as a boy at Augustus's court. An obviously new and unfinished building caught his eye.

Of course. He'd heard about the devastating fire that had consumed a large part of the city two years ago. Malicious gossip said the emperor had set fire to his own city so he could have the glory of rebuilding it. He refused to give credence to such vile rumors.

Two men, their togas disheveled as if hastily donned, emerged from a doorway next to the temple. They were laughing and weaving, obviously drunk so early in the day; one bumped against him. He opened his mouth to complain and became aware of the establishment they had just left. A brothel. He didn't remember Rome having such lax sexual mores – or was it that he'd been too much the raw young provincial to notice? When he'd first planned this journey to the emperor's court, he hadn't expected to be yearning for home so quickly. What did that portend for Amminus in this loose city? He consoled himself: They boy would be blessedly oblivious, just as he had been.

A small animal, bones protruding from dirty matted fur covered in dust, streaked across the street, narrowly missing his foot. Cat? he wondered. Too big for a rat. But surely, in a city as big as Rome, a cat could find prey to hunt. Breca would have taken it in and fed it scraps. He smiled at the thought.

After a while, his mood lifted. The city itself charmed him again, as it had years ago. He loved the new white temples, the tall buildings housing apartments and inns, the wide straight streets, the bustle and country smells of the markets – ripe cheese, garlic, sausage – the aqueducts bringing fresh mountain water to the city's flowing fountains, the marble statues and monuments he'd admired as a boy. This is what he wanted for his beloved Britannia: prosperity and the rule of law, Roman law. This was a goal worth giving up some of the old ways.

A little way past the temple, the road widened into another market square. Next to a stall selling books and leather goods on one side, and one selling meat on the other, he saw a small shop where the owner displayed jewelry, silver brooches and rings, bracelets, hair ornaments for a lady, and he remembered his promise to his wife. He shouldered his way through a throng of customers, many of them slaves shopping for their masters, and studied the glittering array. He thought of Breca's long hair, still thick and dark, how it ran like silk through his fingers, more precious to him than gold.

"How much?" He held up his selection, a tiny silver comb inlaid with small motifs of mother-of-pearl.

The price the shopkeeper asked was more than double the amount he had to spare. Lodging was not cheap in Rome, and he couldn't be certain how many more days he would need to stay here. He'd like to have enough left over to give Amminus a trifle to spend – he remembered well how it was to be a boy in such city! He shook his head and moved on. Two more shops offering trinkets also were out of his range. The pricking of homesickness he'd felt earlier grew into an ache. He grew tired of the heat and the pushing, shoving crowds, and if he didn't get back to the palace soon there'd be no time to bathe before the emperor's banquet.

Two of the city's professional whores passed by, one deliberately leaning in and brushing against his arm and laughing at his discomfort. He didn't see the large man with the tray of trinkets suspended around his neck until he collided with him.

"Watch your step, barbarian!" the man growled

He studied the peddler. "My apology, citizen. My eyes were obviously dazzled."

The man who appeared to be older than Togidubnus, had obviously been a strong brute in his day. Even now, the muscles were the first thing Togidubnus noticed, and the incongruity of cheap leather cuffs on both wrists of hands holding a tray of silver pieces. He wore a grimy tunic, no toga, and battered sandals. He took in the man's broken, badly set nose.

A VILLA FAR FROM ROME

And the piercing blue eyes.

"I seem to know you – but that can't be."

The old man squinted at him. "The little Britanni? Came back with us from the Fourteenth Gemina – When was it now? Too long!"

"Gallus?" Memory flooded back. The winter journey over angry seas with the legion returning to Rome after the defeat of Caratacus that had convinced his own father to throw in the family's lot with Rome, the start of his stay at the court of Augustus. "I thought an old war horse like you would be dead by now!"

The old man laughed. "The life of a peddler isn't much better! But is it truly you? Little Fox, we called you, on account of your cunning habit of stealing food from the camp."

"I was always hungry as a boy. And you were full of tricks to take your companions' coins away from them. It's a wonder nobody killed you!"

Gallus snorted. "Most people are too stupid to notice they're being conned. But not such a little Britanni now – You've grown long in the limb."

"What are you doing now, old friend?"

The legionary took his elbow, steering him out of the crowd. "Selling trinkets to peasants from the country buys me a cup of cheap wine at the end of the day. What wouldn't I give for a taste of the honest barley beer your Britanni brewed!"

"No family?" But he knew the answer. The life of a legionary left little time for a wife and children, even had they been allowed, though Gallus had probably found women enough and maybe left bastards. He thought of all the warriors he'd known, Roman or Britanni, and how hard it was for them to give up the military life when they were too old to march and fight.

"What brings you to Rome?" Gallus asked.

"I hope to persuade the emperor of the importance of that tiny corner of his empire that I was born in. I want him to see how it can become the jewel in his crown."

Gallus laughed. "Good luck with that! Well, have to keep moving. I haven't sold much today. Glad to have seen you again, Little Fox."

"Wait." The old man was obviously in need, and he still had to find a gift for Breca. "Let me look at what you're selling."

"Trash. Not fit for the son and grandson of a chief – Isn't that what you are?"

"A poor man too, I'm afraid. That piece there –" He pointed out a large, shiny brooch set with pearls. "For my wife. How much?"

"Not that one. It's a cheap fake." Gallus pushed the gaudy brooch to the back of the tray. He touched a finger to a small silver comb with a tiny sliver of amber in it. "This one's genuine."

"How much?"

"My gift in return for a pleasant memory."

He gazed at the old man, obviously poor and maybe homeless too. But the man's spine was straight and the old eyes still burned with pride. He wouldn't insult him by insisting on paying.

"Come with me back to Britannia." The words were out of his mouth before he had a chance to realize his intention. But why not? There was always work to do, in the fields, in Noviomagus itself, and warm places to sleep. He wasn't so poor a chief he couldn't take care of an old friend.

"You meant that, Little Fox."

"Indeed I did. A bed. And lots of barley beer! I leave Rome in a couple of days. Meet me at the port."

"And in return, what would I have to give?"

He didn't need to think. "Stories of the glory days of the legions!" He wasn't going to tell him that the Second Augusta had been soundly thrashed by the rebel Queen Boudicca before her eventual defeat.

Gallus blinked rapidly. He walked away without speaking.

Togidubnus turned towards the palace, thinking about the speech he hoped to make tonight. The rebel queen, Boudicca, was a remote kinswoman, and part of him understood her deep distrust of the conquerors. But as he saw it, the advantages of Roman protection outweighed the negative effects of occupation. And the emperor must see the advantages to Rome of treating Britannia well; he must be convinced by the plan.

A VILLA FAR FROM ROME

He'd known the young boy at Augustus's court as Lucius Domitius Ahenobarbus. Now he rehearsed the name the Emperor Claudius had given the boy upon adopting him: Claudius Caesar Augustus Germanicus.
Nero.

CHAPTER FOUR

Antonia was up before the dawn light pushed in through the window, shuttered against insects as well as the night's two-legged prowlers. She hadn't been able to sleep for long. The child tossed and turned, whimpering in hunger and discomfort that – the gods allow! – would be no more after today. The Greek still slept on the floor by the door.

She needed to bathe before coming into the emperor's presence. Her only experience of him had been that evening in her father's villa in Pyrgi, but she instinctively knew he would expect those around him to maintain the appearances of courtly society. Anything less would be perceived as disrespect. Even though it was his excessive expectations as a guest in her father's home that had ruined the family, she must not come to him as a pauper.

Opening the shutters, she smelled the night's rain. Puddles dotted the inn's small courtyard, shiny as coins tossed for beggars. That meant the streets would be muddy, but there weren't enough coins left in her purse to hire a carriage to keep the hem of her tunic clean on the way to the palace. Jupiter Pluvius, she thought, be kind to me today.

"The *thermae* aren't open this early," Nikolaos told her.

She turned to see him arranging the leftover bread and olives on a small table.

"I dreamed last night of my wedding."

"Put no trust in dreams. The god responsible for dreaming is a trickster."

"Oh, you and your stupid Greek superstitions! I don't intend to marry the emperor, Niko. Besides, he is already married to another."

"For the moment, I believe."

A VILLA FAR FROM ROME

She smiled at him. "Perhaps I can use that to my advantage."

The Greek didn't smile in return. "The wise man steps cautiously into the lion's den."

"Aha! But the wily woman has a plan to handle this lion!"

Nikolaos shook his head. "Always an answer. Some day, you may have one answer too many."

An hour later, she hesitated in the entranceway to the *thermae*. She was used to sharing the baths with men, both sexes naked. But that had been the family experience in the villa her father built on the hillside overlooking the Tuscan Sea. This public bath was enormous, mosaiced rooms for undressing, heated rooms where slaves waited to anoint the body with perfumed oils to draw out poison from the skin, huge pools of cold water under an open roof to follow the heat, rooms where more slaves patted the visitors dry and anointed them again. The baths were crowded. It overwhelmed her senses. But the baths were free, a gift of the emperor to his citizens, like the fresh water pouring from the city's fountains, and the spectacle of the circus.

With the encouragement of last night's dream still vivid in her memory, she ignored the stares or the occasional lewd comment and thought only of her coming meeting with Lucia's father.

* * *

"Stop! You may not enter here!"

The palace guard was dressed like a legionary in a woolen tunic dyed red, and hobnailed leather sandals – like her oldest brother who'd joined the legion just before she left home – but no helmet. He held his sword across the door blocking Antonia's way into the vast atrium. Behind him, she glimpsed the enormous vestibule with a glittering, more-than-life-size statue that she guessed was meant to be the emperor himself.

She stood straight, shoulders back, remembering her brothers playing at war. Appearance was persuasive. "By whose command?"

"The emperor's."

"Then tell the emperor that the daughter of his old friend Gaius

SHEILA FINCH

Antonius Plautinus stands at his gate."

After bathing, she'd put on her one remaining good tunic, and she'd marched proudly through the streets, avoiding the puddles, holding her little daughter's hand, Nikolaos a few paces behind. This was the day she would come into her own. No more worrying about where the next meal would come from, or how to find a new cloak for Lucia before winter came. Head high, she had ignored the stares and the comments. The new palace, still under construction on a little hill near the center of the city after it burned down, had been easy enough to find. Every citizen of Rome had a story to tell about the lavish new residence, known as the Golden House, the artificial lake and well-tended parklands, the shining, gold and jewel bedecked statues, the woods, the parklands the vineyards that surrounded the glorious house itself. Their taxes had been raised to build it.

The guard still hesitated. "Ah – Lady, you see –"

"Good fellow," another voice said. "Lower your sword and let a gentlewoman enter out of the sun."

She turned to see a very short man, not even as tall as herself, a dwarf, swarthy and small-eyed, but exquisitely dressed in a fine linen toga and wearing silver armbands on both arms. He smiled at her in friendly fashion. The guard obviously recognized the newcomer and lowered the sword.

"Please," the small man said. "Come in with me out of the sun."

She stepped past the guard whose gaze was now fixed on the far distance, pulling the child with her; she was grateful for the man's intervention. The cool anteroom smelled of fresh cut herbs. The little man led Antonia through the vestibule to a vast triple colonnade that stretched as far as her eye could see and into one of several buildings clustered around an artificial lake. Nikolaos waited just inside the arched marble doorway.

"Your name interests me," the man said. "Was this the Antonius Plautinus who built the new stadium a few years back, up the coast in Pyrgi?"

"That was my father." Her eyes adjusted to the gloom inside the building and she gazed at him. "But I'm afraid I don't know who you are."

A VILLA FAR FROM ROME

"Of course not. You must have been a child at the time the emperor visited for the chariot races –" He broke off and stared at the little girl who was fingering a carved stone bird that sat on a little pedestal.

"This is my daughter, Lucia. She's four."

"Lucia?" His face lost color. His eyes rolled up till she could only see the whites, He appeared to be calculating something. "Four. And at the time – You would've been about fourteen?"

"Twelve."

"Ah. He likes them young." There was an awkward moment of silence. "Why have you come here?"

"To see the emperor. I know he's in Rome."

"He's here. But you can't see him. And certainly not with this child!"

"Why not? I am a citizen. Who will prevent me from audience with my emperor?"

He clapped a hand over his mouth as if he'd said too much. "You must return to your father's home immediately!"

"My father is dead. Our home and our vineyards lost to us. The child and I have nothing to return to."

"I'm sorry. I'll find money for you. But you must go. Right away. Trust me. Your lives will be in danger if the emperor so much as senses your presence here."

"Just *what* will happen if I learn about it?" A man whose brow was wreathed with laurel came through an inner, curtained archway. Two older senators were with him. "Satrias, who are these people?"

The little man bowed. She was close enough to see that the dwarf was shaking. "Citizens, Great Caesar. But they're just about to leave!"

The emperor flopped unceremoniously down on a stone bench; he elaborately arranged the folds of his purple-hemmed toga as if to make up for the casualness. She knew enough about cloth and weaving to know it was a very fine toga that fell into such elegant folds. He narrowed his eyes to study her. Was he short-sighted now? She stared back at him, determined not to let him see fear or awe in her. He looked older, of course, but also heavier, less the athlete of his early days, cheeks showing the red puffiness of a heavy drinker. The dark gold curls she remembered were longer and carelessly tumbled as if he'd just left his bed, but the eyes, dark and bright as a bird's, were the ones that had caught her hiding at the banquet.

"Name yourself," he ordered, and she heard Satrias moan softly.

She stood tall, unafraid of him. "Antonia Plautina."

The emperor yawned. "I don't recognize the name."

"From the country, Great Caesar," Satrias put in hastily. "And they're just leaving!"

"Go away!" The emperor snapped his fingers at the dwarf who hastily backed out of the room.

"My father was Gaius Antonius Plautinus, once the owner of a villa in Pyrgi. And this is my daughter, Lucia."

He leaned forward and gazed at the child, still absorbed with the stone bird. Antonia's heart raced; he didn't seem to remember her. He sat back and without looking at them, flicked his fingers in dismissal at the two senators.

When they were alone, the emperor said, "Now tell me why you have come to me."

She smelled remembered peppermint on his breath. "You were a guest in my father's house, four years ago, after the races. I was still a child."

He was silent for a moment. The he nodded. "A pretty one at that, and rebellious, if I remember. A child who peered at me as I dined.. Tell me why you came here."

"You left me with a child."

He stared at her. "Why should I believe that?"

"Look at her. See her eyes, her hair. She is yours."

"So is my shit. But I don't need to look at it."

His vulgarity shocked her. "Lucia is your blood."

He turned his gaze on the little girl, studying her. "Why did you give her that name?"

"At birth you were named Lucius Domitius Ahenonbarbus –"

A VILLA FAR FROM ROME

"I know my own names!" he said petulantly. "I prefer Nero."

"As you wish, my lord. But the girl is yours."

"Apparently you aren't aware of the opinion of those good Romans who say I'm incapable of fathering a child that will live. How touching!" He gazed at the child. "A pretty one at that. A pity my wife can't produce one like her."

Seeing the dissolute wreck of his once-athletic body, banished the last fragments of her childhood fantasies. But she'd made this difficult trip all the way to Rome to find justice, and was not about to meekly go away without it. "You left me with the child, but no estate or fortune to raise her. Great Caesar, you are spoken of far and wide as a just and benevolent ruler – without your help, how will she avoid ending up on the streets of Rome like a common whore?

"Your parents?"

"My father took his own life in disgrace after the villa and the farm were sold."

Nero frowned, turning back to look at her. "My child, you say?"

"Lucia is your daughter."

Nero stood up, agitated. "Don't say that so loudly! You must not say that name here."

She put a hand on Lucia's shoulder, turning her face toward him. "She inherited your hair."

"Pity she's not a boy. I might've adopted her. But you don't understand. I can't acknowledge a bastard. I don't wish to have her blood on my hands. And it *will* come to that if my enemies learn of her existence."

Her heart pounded so loudly she feared he would hear it in the quiet room. "Please, my lord –"

He shook his head violently, curls bouncing. "Intrigues– conspiracies – I'm surrounded by enemies. At court. In the senate. Any one of whom would like to bring me down."

She didn't see what that had to do with herself or the child. "Without your help, she'll starve, or be forced to walk the streets of this city – "

"– and you would give them a weapon – "

"Is it right that your noble blood should be so abused?"

She couldn't guess the angry thoughts that darted behind his eyes. Had she pushed him too far?

His expression relaxed. He stood up and adjusted his toga with a flick of a heavily-ringed hand. "You were a pretty little piece. And the child has your looks as well as mine. I'll find a solution. Attend my banquet tonight. Keep the child out of sight."

Nero went away through the curtained arch where the senators waited. She heard the murmur of their voices fading.

Trembling, exhausted as if she'd been riding wild horses with her brothers, she turned to go. Nikolaos stepped through the outer archway. He didn't speak, but lifted the child to his shoulder. She couldn't say if she'd won a concession from the emperor or whether some worse fate waited for her and the child. It was out of her hands.

CHAPTER FIVE

THE OPPRESSIVE HEAT SAPPED HIS ENERGY and dulled his brain, reminding him his bones were aging. Small obstacles and impediments loomed large enough to undermine his good humor. Worse, they scuttled his plans to cement his relationship with the emperor for the good of Britannia. Days of evasions, postponements and excuses from Nero's secretaries; he had yet to have private time with the emperor to discuss his ideas.

The emperor's new palace where he was a guest, was dubbed the Golden House, but it was far more than a mere house. A whole village of the Regni could be housed on the grounds and still there would be room for more! Inside the walls there were forests, vineyards, a fair-sized lake – but what took his breath away at first were the interior walls covered in fine marble and alabaster, and even gold and jewels, enough to buy food for his tribe for an entire year. Breca would be horrified at the waste. Yet it was not finished! He could see the walls of chambers still under construction, stretching away into the unbelievable distance.

It was just as well Breca did not see it. He must mind his words when telling her about this.

He prided himself on being a practical man; while he was here, he would take advantage of the opportunity to bathe properly and prepare himself for the coming banquet. He emerged from the *frigidarium* which had closed his pores opened by a plunge in the enormous heated pool in the *calidarium*, refreshed but oddly ill at ease. The cloying luxury of Nero's palace offended him, but there was more to his unease. If Breca were here, she'd tease out the cause; his wife had equal parts counselor and seer in her, qualities he cherished.

SHEILA FINCH

A slave appeared, carrying fresh clothes for him to put on.

Tonight, he intended to summon all his ability to get his message across to Nero in conversation at the banquet; he'd have not only the emperor but several important senators as audience. Important diplomatic decisions often were made over shared food and wine in this city. Nero would see the wisdom of what he urged for Britannia and agree with his counsel! Then he could go home to his own misty corner of the Roman empire.

But as the slave led him into the *triclinium* and indicated the couch where he should recline, he saw how difficult his task was going to be. The banquet hall was gigantic and covered by a great revolving dome that cast alternating light and shadows on the guests below. The grand marble table was at least double the length of the longest one he'd ever seen, and his place was close to the far end. Along two sides, senators and their wives had taken their places on the waiting couches, jewels glittering in the light of massed oil lamps. The third, shorter side, was reserved for the emperor himself; two sets of cushions in different colors were at this end which was at present empty.

He made a mental note to describe for Breca the statues lining the walls, how the men wore their hair in elaborate curls on top of their heads, oiled and perfumed, how the women wore delicate braids threaded with shiny beads. He would be careful what he described, but there was so much to tell her about the city and its customs. No doubt she'd find these elaborate fashions amusing, probably foolish. He would have to agree that this new palace, Nero's Golden House, overwhelmed the eye with its display of wealth to a degree that his predecessors, Augustus and Claudius, would have found ostentatious even in their most ambitious moments.

Amminus was nowhere to be seen. For a moment, he felt the cold touch of anxiety. He dismissed it. The boy would be with the emperor, certainly, and would enter when he did.

He was aware of several sidelong glances from guests, but nobody spoke to him. He supposed that even in a city like Rome, so full of people of different races from all corners of the empire, his Celtic looks still stood out. A slave with an ewer approached and poured wine into a fine glass

A VILLA FAR FROM ROME

beaker. The tableware too was better than he'd come to know in the court of Augustus, both spoon and knife polished to a high sheen, their handles engraved in intricate patterns. Dishes of mushrooms, olives, and oysters were passed from guest to guest as appetizers.

Halfway down the table opposite his seat, he became aware of a thin young woman, hardly more than a girl, sitting alone, The guests on either side of her ignored her presence, a sign he recognized as indicating her low status. A group of slaves entered and began to play flutes and cymbals. He found himself nodding to the pleasant rhythms.

A guest reclining beside him, a portly man with dark, oily curls and a red-scratched chin betraying a recent visit to an inept barber, leaned toward him. "Let us hope our great and honored host doesn't add to the entertainment tonight."

He didn't know how to answer this, but was saved from the trouble by the fat man nudging him in the ribs and fluttering his eyelids in comical fashion.

"The emperor sings, you know. Such a voice!"

He was profoundly out of place, a country hare surrounded by city dogs. Yet part of him relished the grandeur of it all. A little touch of this pomp and ceremony would be fine at home – though he'd have a hard time persuading Breca.

A trumpet sounded and the emperor himself accompanied by two officials, one a dwarf, joined his guests. Nero's golden curls were piled high on his head in almost female fashion, and bound by a golden wreath; he took mincing little steps toward his place at the head of the tables, as if he were dancing. He realized that Nero had hardly grown any taller than when they were both boys at Augustus's court, while he himself had added at least a *pes*. And there was Amminus! He saw his white-robed boy, looking serious and rather out-of-place, led by a slave to take a seat to one side of the emperor's couch at the head table. He was proud and nervous at the same time. The other two boys, sons of Roman senators who were to be his son's co-students, were absent.

SHEILA FINCH

The emperor stopped before he reached his place of honor. He gazed down at Togidubnus who tried to scramble to his feet in the imperial presence. Nero's hand on his shoulder pushed him down again.

"No, no, Tiberius, old friend of my boyhood," Nero said, smiling broadly as if at some delicious secret. "Loyal ally!" He turned to the dwarf who stood scowling beside him. "Satrias, you must remind me to reward my dear friend for his service in our defeat of the notorious rebel queen – whatever her name was."

"Boudicca," the dwarf muttered.

Encouraged, he began. "Great Caesar, I would discuss my plans –"

He stopped short, aware Nero's smile had faded. "I meant, my *humble suggestions* –"

But the emperor walked past him and was now reclining on his couch, the servants bustling around him, arranging his toga, making him comfortable, the dwarf filling his wine cup.

Once the emperor was seated, the feast began. More food than he'd ever seen in any one meal: venison, wild boar, suckling pig, goat, duck and pheasants, one overloaded dish followed another – even a peacock arrayed tail and all – and all of it to be washed down with flagon after flagon of heavy wine. Caesar Augustus had been miserly in his treatment of guests by comparison. But very little fish other than the oysters, he noted, disappointed. In his island home, fish was usually the main dish on the table, and he preferred it. Too much rich meat slowed his thoughts, and he was going to need to be mentally nimble later tonight.

The noise in the room from the musicians and the roar of conversation combined to bring on a headache. The heavily spiced smell of the food that kept coming – wave after wave of steaming platters – started to make him nauseous, and the heat from so many guests under one roof was stifling. He felt a trickle of sweat sliding down from his hair and surreptitiously wiped it. Nobody was paying him attention, anyway. Adding to his dismay was the growing conviction that his well-planned speech was not going to find anybody sober as an audience tonight, let alone the emperor. How naive to ever think it would!

Hours passed. His limbs ached with the strain of reclining in what to

A VILLA FAR FROM ROME

him was an awkward position. His eyes smarted from the effects of too much wine and the smoke from the oil lamps. There was a momentary lull when one of his neighbors suddenly fell off his bench, victim of too much wine. Two slaves removed him. The noise resumed. Across the table, another man vomited, but nobody paid attention. One thought pushed its way into his pounding head; Breca would not approve of this decadent Roman way of entertaining guests.

Now the slaves were bringing honey-sweetened cakes and fruit, and bowls of warm, scented water for the guests to wash their meat-sticky fingers. And more wine. Above the table, the ceiling opened up and rose petals rained down on the guests with cloying perfume. He closed his tired eyes and gave up on his intention to speak of the importance of Britannia to Rome. Indeed, he doubted his wine-thickened tongue could find the words. All he desired was that the interminable feast would end, the morning would come quickly, and he would be on his way home.

He had almost drifted into sleep when a loud trumpet burst startled him. The emperor was standing on his couch, a silver chalice in one hand, a slave propping him up at his elbow. He heard a low grumbling around him as the guests were forced to stand too in respect, a task some found almost impossible after such indulging.

"My friends, my countrymen!" Nero's voice emerged high and squeaky. "My guests!"

The room hushed. A little late in the proceedings for a toast, he thought. He reached reluctantly for his fine glass beaker which the slaves had refilled. His hand was unsteady and he succeeded only in knocking the beaker over and spilling the wine across the table, splashing the toga of a man who hardly noticed, his attention fixed elsewhere. When he looked up from this disaster, he saw the emperor beckoning to a guest to come and stand beside him. Togidubnus followed the direction of the other guests' gaze and saw the young woman he'd noticed earlier walking slowly – reluctantly, and accompanied by two slaves – to the head table.

Nero stretched one hand down and seized the girl's wrist, holding it over her head.

"Antonia Plautina," Nero announced. "Daughter of the respected senator and my dearest friend, Gaius Antonius Plautinus – deceased!"

The emperor paused to make his face a mask of suffering that would've made actors proud. He was embarrassed for the emperor, but the guests clapped in approval.

Nero continued, "A treasured friend whose hospitality I have so enjoyed in the past."

A tear appeared at the corner of his eye, and the emperor allowed it to make its way down his cheek. A moment's hesitation, and the guests applauded again.

Aware he was being observed by the guest who'd commented on Nero's singing, he made the motions too. A quick glance at his son, beside the emperor, revealed that the boy kept his eyes on the plate before him. Wise boy, he thought with pride.

"But away with sorrow! Tonight it is time for happiness and rejoicing." Nero lifted his chalice. "We are here to celebrate Antonia's marriage."

The young woman's face indicated anything but happiness, he saw, and wondered what was going on. None of this drama was his business. One more thing to endure before the night was over and he could return home. The other guests cheered loudly. A servant appeared behind her and placed a wreath of orange blossom on her head. Slaves hurried to refill the cups emptied in the toast to the bride-to-be.

"Where, you may be wondering, is the bridegroom?" Nero said, his voice climbing in his excitement. "Ah! I see him, shyly waiting his time to claim his bride!"

There was some raucous laughter at that, and he caught a few lewd suggestions. He was startled when two slaves appeared and took hold of his arms, urging him to move towards the emperor's couch. They jostled him into position beside the young woman. He caught the sweet scent of orange blossom.

But this wasn't right. "There's some mistake –"

Nero smiled down, small eyes glittering fiercely.

A VILLA FAR FROM ROME

"I give you Tiberius Claudius Togidubnus, chief of the Regni – a very small tribe in our Britannic territory!"

There was laughter at that, but Nero held up his free hand and it subsided. "From this day, I shall name Tiberius Claudius Togidubnus, *king* of his tribe!"

No! he wanted to say. *You can't do this! The Elders must vote* –

"And now he'll be the worthy bridegroom of my dearest friend's daughter."

The room erupted in a wave of cheers and hoots, but he felt as if he were engulfed in ice, unable to speak for the sudden realization of what was happening.

"Great Caesar – I am already married – I have a wife in Britannia."

"A wife in Britannia!" Nero giggled, swaying drunkenly on his perch. The dwarf stood hurriedly to support him. "But I am the emperor, am I not? I make the laws that govern this empire, isn't that true? And I can break them. Away with such feeble impediments! I divorce you, Tiberius Claudius Togidubnus. You are no longer married to the wife in Britannia."

He was aware of two things: the young woman's sullen face – obviously this was not her plan – and Amminus, whose face was as white as his toga, his mouth a silent rictus of horror.

Nero's eyes narrowed. He handed his chalice to one of the men supporting him, and reached down to grasp the boy's shoulder. "Your boy shall be witness to this marriage, King Tiberius."

He saw the tears on his son's cheeks and his heart pounded. "Don't do this, Caesar. I beg you."

In response, Nero nodded to a guard. The soldier stepped forward and took the woman's hand as Nero released it, then made a grab for Togidubnus's hand. He took a step back, but he was aware as he did so of Nero's tight grip on the boy's shoulder. His son shook with fear. Defeated, he let the soldier lift his hand and join it with the girl's.

"Where's the auger?" a drunken voice shouted from halfway down the table. "We need an augury!"

SHEILA FINCH

"What do we need with augurs examining entrails?" Nero said. "I make the laws here! Tiberius Claudius Togidubnus and Antonia Plautina, I declare you married under my Roman law."

The assembled guests roared their approval again. Drunk as they were, did they even understand what Nero was doing? In the midst of his pain, he knew they had as little choice in the matter as he.

"And as proof that in Rome all things are done lawfully," Nero said, "I'll have this divorce and marriage written out and signed, and you shall take it with you. And now, to bed!"

Nero scrambled down from his perch with the help of the dwarf, his hand still firmly grasping Amminus's shoulder, the wild glitter gone from his eyes. He spoke softly so few other than Togidubnus could hear. "Remember, Tiberius, take care of your wife, and I will take care of your son."

The last glimpse he had of Amminus was the tear-stained face glancing back at him as the emperor's party left the banquet chamber.

His vision suffused with blood. Wild, brutish thoughts tumbled through his mind. He would chase Nero down and throttle him – stab him with one of the many knives on the table – kill him – spill his blood over the marble floors of his palace –

"Whatever you're thinking," a sullen voice said. "It won't work. He has many guards, you're just one man."

He looked down into the young woman's face, ugly with anger. She was hardly more than a girl. "My son – "

"You've lost the battle. Just like I have. Don't think I'm happy to be married off to an old barbarian!"

The guests were leaving the banquet chamber now, many of them stumbling or leaning on slaves. He stood, still in the jaws of a nightmare.

Someone touched his arm, a Greek freedman by the look of him. "The emperor has given orders that you both leave for Britannia tomorrow. I'll go with you. There's nothing in Rome for me."

The woman turned to the Greek and collapsed sobbing into his arms.

"There will be time later," the Greek said to him over her head. "But not tonight."

CHAPTER SIX

THE BAD WEATHER BEGAN the moment the ship left the dock at Ostia at the mouth of the Tiber. An early storm hit them two days out, and the trireme lurched and rolled in shoulder-high waves that washed over the deck, drenching Togidubnus and the sailors trying to keep the ship on course. The smell of salt, usually a welcome perfume he'd known since childhood, was bitter in his nose. He could have gone down inside, into the shelter of a small cabin, but the Roman girl was there, vomiting from the sea malady. The Greek was with her, taking care of her and the child.

He pulled his cloak up higher on his neck to keep out the driving rain; the storm was fierce for so early in the year. He crouched in the bow, staring into the black water. Above his head the canvas snapped and ropes beat against the mast; the song of the wind in the rigging was high and terrifying. Sailors rushed about, shouting orders to each other and to the rowers whose strength at the oars couldn't compete with the fierce determination of the sea to overturn the ship and drown them all.

Neptune preserve me! And if Neptune saw fit to grant his prayer, how was he going to deal with this situation when he arrived back in Noviomagus? His stomach knotted.

How could he ever explain this Roman girl and the child to Breca?

What choice did he have but to accept the emperor's command, since he was a Roman and sworn to obey Roman law?

And Amminus was a hostage. Breca hadn't wanted him to take Amminus to Rome. He'd been so certain what he was doing was right.

Why had he not seen the treachery of Nero ahead of time? How could he have ever believed he was going to discuss matters of state like equals – and not see the peril he was putting his son in? He'd been a fool to assume this court would be a safe space for Amminus to learn Roman statesmanship, as he'd done at the court of Claudius. There were no answers, but the questions continued to torture him.

"Here. Some bread, a piece of fish – you must eat something."

He looked up at the old legionary, heavy cloak draped over his head, offering a plate. "I'm not hungry."

Gallus had joined the party on the dock. The old warrior spent most of his time gaming with sailors if they weren't working, or lending a hand with the ship's lines when they were. Togidubnus took the plate but had no appetite for food or conversation; every man on board had heard of his failed dealings with Nero and his forced "wedding" with the Roman girl. He would have found their sympathy as toxic as their mockery. The bitter irony was that he was unshakeable in his belief in the superiority of Roman law – and it had dealt with him like this.

"Not wise sleeping out here, Little Fox," Gallus observed.

"Gallus, I was never your commander in the legion, but I'm commanding you now. Leave me in peace!"

"Leave you to wallow in self-pity, you mean."

"How can you know what I feel?"

"Everybody knows!" the old man said sharply. "The emperor needed to get his bastard away before his enemies discovered her. You were just a convenience. Grieving over what's done doesn't help."

"What does?"

"You're making too much of this. A Roman thinks nothing of having a wife and taking a concubine –"

"I took an oath!"

The wind tore the old man's reply to shreds and he went away.

A bedraggled gull, swept onto the bow by the force of the wind, eyed the bread hungrily. He tossed both fish and bread into the air and the bird gulped them down.

Breca's reaction to his news would only be the beginning. The Council of Elders wouldn't be happy that Nero had pre-empted their choice of king. He couldn't see his way forward.

Later, he awoke to find himself shrouded in layers of heavy cloaks and

A VILLA FAR FROM ROME

leather hides. Someone had tried to protect him from the weather. He had no sense of how much time had passed, just a fleeting memory of being forced to eat a few bites of cheese and bread at one point – Gallus again entreating him to go below – the rain stinging his face – the bitter cold in his bones. For the most part, the sailors had respected his misery and left him alone.

The sky was full of fast-moving clouds and patches of intense blue. The sea was wrinkled, sparkling under flashes of sun. Overhead, the sails were stiff with wind, racing over the water to make up for storm-lost time. In the distance, the Pillars of Hercules loomed. A few hours and they would pass through the gap and out into the open sea.

His mind felt as clear as the air this morning. All life was a risk, a gamble like old Gallus wagering on the roll of a dice. Nero too had much to lose in this game if he played him false. It wasn't a pretty game, and there'd be no winners. But it might equally be true that he could work it so there'd be no losers.

He was a warrior still. He'd find a way to deal with the fate the gods had given him.

* * *

It was evening, several days later, when the ship skirted the island of Vectis and came in sight of the south coast of Britannia with its many bays and inlets that he knew so well. The land was already shadowed, but the sun slipping down the western sky still sparked the water into a million shining coins. A cool breeze sprang up as the shadows lengthened. The tide ran high and a strong current carried them to shore. A flock of shorebirds swooped over the ship, turned in an instant and swerved back toward land. Below them, a dolphin leaped, another. The smells of land reached him now, pine, and the subtler smell of gorse, the first summer apples ripening on the trees; his heart swelled in recognition. He'd been away several weeks and the seasons had changed.

The ship's master guided the ship past the channel that led to the old port of Hengistbury Head that even before the Romans came had been always busy, then smoothly into the channel leading to Noviomagus Regnorum. Now he could make out the gleam of lanterns lit to guide fishermen home. He knew this channel well, the deeps and the sand bars, the very run of the waves. He'd fished these waters as boy with his father, flounder and eels and plaice, and sometimes dab driven down from the northern coast. The dock that served his small house lay just at the edge of his vision now.

"So that's to be my place of exile."

The Roman girl had come to stand beside him, clutching a blanket tightly around her. Her face was grey, her eyes as lusterless as one who'd lain abed many days with fever. She looked very young and very scared. In spite of his fury at what had happened, he sensed that she was as much a victim of Nero's cunning as he, though the reason that lay behind it was not clear to him.

"That's my home."

"A land of barbarians –"

Annoyed, he cut her off. "Neither you nor I asked for this. But since we have no power to alter our destiny, I suggest we face it with civility."

"I will never give up till my child gains her rightful place in Rome."

Her voice shook. In the dusk, she seemed smaller and thinner than he remembered from that terrible night he'd been forced to take her as his wife. Hardly more than a child, and only a few years older than Amminus – A jolt of fire raced through him at the thought.

Sailors came up to the bow, mooring ropes in hand, and he had to step aside as they made preparations for docking. The girl went away.

And now – there, on the dock in the flickering light of the lanterns – he could see the tiny figures of Brcca and his younger son, Catuarus, waving. Light caught the glint of silver from the torc she wore round her neck, eight strands of copper and silver twisted to a delicate chain. He'd given it to her on their handfasting day, token of his love. Someday, he'd give her a better one, made of gold.

The ship bumped the dock, people crowded on deck, sailors threw ropes, others on land caught them, made them fast – He was home.

"Togi, I knew you would come today! I read it this morning in the

A VILLA FAR FROM ROME

omens. Thank Sulis for her protection!" Laughing, tears of joy streaming down her cheeks, Breca ran towards him as he stepped down onto the dock. She threw herself into his arms. "Welcome – Oh, welcome home!"

Her familiar smell, woodsmoke and lavender, filled his nose. He closed his eyes against the ache that suddenly assaulted him and embraced the wife of his heart.

"Catuarus, come." Breca pulled out of his embrace. "Greet your father!"

He opened his eyes and saw his son hanging back, staring at the scene on the dock. Through the turmoil of Roman sailors unloading boxes and chests, barrels of wine some local dignitary had ordered, and Regni scurrying to take up the burden, he saw Gallus helping the Roman girl step over the side of the boat onto the dock; the Greek waited his turn, carrying the child.. He felt as if he'd turned into a statue on the Via Appia: *Togidubnus the Trapped.* There was no good way to handle this.

"Togi?" Breca said.

The Roman girl stood between the legionary and the Greek, her face a sullen mask. The child sucked on her thumb. Nobody spoke.

"The emperor wishes us to have guests. The Lady Antonia Plautina and her daughter." He switched to the Old Tongue of his childhood and spoke low enough that only she could hear. "Please, Breca, accept this for now. I will explain it later."

She turned her gaze on him, her eyes that he knew from all their years together could read his soul. There were no secrets between them. A long moment passed. She held out her hands to the newcomers. When she spoke, her voice was cool, her Latin precise. "Be welcome in my house."

Antonia glanced from one to the other of them. She ignored the outstretched hands of his wife and walked up to Togidubnus. She slipped her arm through his, her eyes burning him. He was astounded by this open challenge and couldn't think fast enough of a way to respond that wouldn't make the situation worse.

Catching hold of Breca's hand, he led the way over the bridge across the little stream, aware of how stiff his beloved wife's body felt next to his

* * *

One battle did not need to be fought that night.

"I will need a large room to retire in," the Roman girl announced, when they stood in the atrium. "With space for my child, and an anteroom for my servant."

Breca's eyes widened, but she made no comment. His chest tightened in anticipation of the task to come, explaining political necessity which could not be adequately condoned..

Grateful for the reprieve, he summoned a serving woman who led them away. Alone, he followed Breca into their private quarters. The room was dimly lit from one oil lamp; in its light he saw the familiar wall hangings and the bed where she'd conceived both his sons. His love for Breca and his love for his home ran together like a torrent of spring-melt and swept his heart away. He reached for her to take her into his arms, but she evaded him, moving to and fro in the bed chamber, carrying blankets, re-arranging heaps of clothes.

She'd said nothing since greeting the Roman party, deliberately avoiding him, busying herself first with her son's preparations for bed, then her own. He was exhausted from the voyage and would prefer to have this conversation with her in the morning, but he saw now that it would not wait.

Begin with the emperor, he thought, rehearsing the explanation that would explain nothing. *Nero's powerful – But Rome is far away and we can –*

She was too wise for him to coat this with honey. When the silence had lasted longer than he could bear, he caught her as she passed and drew her to him. He stroked her beautiful, long loose hair. She would not meet his eyes.

"I brought a gift," he said, retrieving the hair ornament from the small leather purse in which he'd carried it. He held it out to her on the palm of his hand.

She glanced at the silver comb with its amber chip, taking it reluctantly. He sat on a wooden bench and drew her onto his lap. "We must talk now, Breca."

A VILLA FAR FROM ROME

"I listen, Husband."

Something in the way she said the word confirmed his fears. He was never able to keep the dark things from her, even had he thought it possible to shield her from this one. Long moments passed in the dim room while he weighed how to make the truth less harmful, or whether all of it could be told at all.

In the end, he chose simplicity.

"For reasons of his own – " Better not right now to go into what Gallus had told him on the ship. "– the emperor decided I must marry this girl, Antonia, and bring her and the child to live here with me."

"How can that be, when you are married to me?"

He considered for a moment the decree of divorce and remarriage that Nero had caused to be drawn up, but she didn't read Latin and he knew it wouldn't persuade her to accept this injustice. "You know, my heart, you are and always will be my one true wife." He realized his voice was shaking and she who knew him better than he knew himself must notice that. "But the emperor rules us both. Antonia too. He decreed that you and I are no longer married."

"And you accept that? The mother of your sons is no longer your wife because Caesar decrees a Roman marriage?"

"I had no choice. I am a Roman citizen."

"You married me under our sacred law of handfasting. Can you so easily toss this aside?"

Because he has Amminus! "We'll find a way to work with this, my heart. In the morning we'll talk more." No good, he realized at once.

"And Amminus? What of our son, left in the care of such an emperor?" She freed herself from his arms and stood up.

"I have his promise he'll take care of Amminus if we take care of the girl and her child."

"You believe this?"

Of course he didn't trust Nero! But how could he add to her anguish by admitting that he'd been outmaneuvered into leaving their son in possible danger?

"It's only for a short while, Breca, I swear to you. A year."

"What are you not saying to me, Togi? What threat will you not speak to me?"

"We can do this. Once our son is home --"

"And until then you expect me to be a concubine in my own home?"

Her anger battered at him and he stood with his head lowered, not answering for fear she'd pursue the safety of their son, knowing he deserved far more than her anger.

"I'll sleep in Catuarus's room, tonight."

"Breca –"

Without looking at him again, she left the sleeping chamber they'd shared since before Amminus was born.

Still clothed, he lay on the bed, one arm over his eyes, in too much pain to sleep until the first light of dawn crept through the shuttered window.

Rising in haste, he narrowly missed stepping on the silver comb which lay on the floor.

Catuarus's room, when he reached it, was empty.

CHAPTER SEVEN

[Noviomagus, AD 66]

"Wake up!"

Lucia squatted beside the man who was still asleep, wrapped in his cloak on a pallet outside the door. She poked his shoulder with one finger. "Niko! Wake up."

She'd pulled her tunic on before she'd left the bed she'd shared with her mother, but it was getting too short for her now and only reached her knees; she'd left her sandals off, preferring to be barefoot whenever her mother wasn't around to catch her. She was glad to be off the boat – although the boat ride would've been better if Ma had let her go up with the sailors. She'd wanted to look at the waves and the birds, and she didn't like the smell because Ma was sick all the time. This house was colder than the one she remembered as home, but the garden she could see through the archway at the end of the corridor looked interesting.

"Niko!"

He fidgeted at that and grunted. She poked him again, harder this time, and he sat up, pulling the cloak around his shoulders.

"Wanna eat," she said.

"I want to eat," he corrected, saying the words slowly in precise Latin so she could catch every bit.

She wasn't interested in learning this morning. "Get up!"

"Lucia, this isn't our house. We'll have to be patient," Niko said.

"Now."

"Your mother –"

SHEILA FINCH

"She's asleep!"

Niko sighed and got to his feet. "Stay here till I get back. Don't wander off."

"Promise."

But as soon as he'd walked off – in bare feet too, she noticed, leaving his sandals on the floor where he'd been lying – she saw something flash outside past the archway. Curious, she went to find out what it was.

The garden wasn't nearly as tidy as the one where she'd lived in Pyrgi. Instead of paths between neatly clipped bushes and statues where she'd played "catch me" with the younger slaves, there was nothing here but sloping land covered in grass and trees. But she noticed a spider web, like a silver net with little crystals sparkling in the sun. She hadn't liked spiders ever since one of the children from the village who came to play with her at her grandfather's house, dropped one down her neck. But she did like to see their pretty webs. There weren't as many flowers in this garden, and the ones she could see were turning brown and shriveling up. She stopped to sniff, but they were past the time of scent. And it was much colder than that other garden. She was disappointed.

She saw the flash again – brown and white fur. A dog!

Laughing, she forgot all about cold air or breakfast and chased after the dog. It was too fast for her to catch. Her hair came loose from its clip and floated on the air behind her as she ran.

The dog led her over the rough turf towards a shallow stream full of water grass where ducks were hunting for breakfast. Just as she reached it, the dog plunged in, water splashing up in a big rainbow arc in the pale morning sun, the ducks quacking in alarm and flapping their wings, the dog barking. Enchanted, she hitched up her tunic and followed the dog into the stream. The water wasn't very deep, but it was very cold and full of bubbles that tickled her bare legs.

The brown and white dog was almost at the other bank, half walking, half dog paddling.

"Come back, doggie!" she called, wading after it.

She couldn't move as fast as the dog did and it soon scrambled out. The bed of the stream was made of small, smooth stones, slick with the

A VILLA FAR FROM ROME

fast-moving water, and suddenly her foot slid out from under her and she went down.

"Niko! Niko! Help me up!"

But of course, Niko couldn't help her. He was back in the house where he'd told her to stay. Somehow, she managed to get back on her feet and grabbed at a clump of reeds along the far bank. She pushed her dripping hair back out of her eyes and found herself eye to eye with a boy, a few years older than she was. He knelt on the bank, his hand holding the wet dog by its neck ruff.

"Who are you?" she demanded. Boys weren't supposed to just wander about like that. If Niko saw him, he'd scold!

"You're the one who should give a name," the boy said. "This is *my* home."

He had a very strange way of saying the words – she could hardly understand him. Even Niko, who had a funny way of saying things, spoke clearer than this boy. He had dark eyes and odd colored hair too, red like autumn leaves, not black or dark brown like hair was supposed to be. Even yellow.

"Is this your dog?"

The boy nodded. "We had to leave last night and I couldn't find her. I came back for her."

"Her? I didn't know dogs could be girls."

"Silly!" He grinned at her, showing gaps where he'd lost teeth. "This is Beech. We call her that because she was born under a beech tree. She's a year old."

"I'm four," she told him. "How old are you?"

"Eight, I think. I don't remember when my birthday is."

She stared at him. What an odd thing to say! A birthday was a great celebration, a feast day. Perhaps she hadn't understood him.

"Better get out of the water before you catch cold." He held a hand out to her and she took hold,

"Are there dolphins in this water?"

"Dolphins? Of course not! They swim in the sea, not in the little streams."

"Niko showed me some. They were swimming next to the big boat." Niko had taken her out of the smelly cabin where Ma was being sick and took her up on deck. He'd pointed to five big grey shapes swimming beside the boat. One came up and looked right at her! It had started raining again and she had to go back inside.

"They do that sometimes." He let go of the dog and held his other hand out to her. "My name is Catuarus."

"That's a funny name. I don't know anybody called that name."

"Of course not, it's my name! And what's yours?"

"Lucia."

"That's pretty. Now, come on. Get out of the water."

She took his hand and climbed out of the stream. The dog licked her hands, her bare legs where the wet tunic had bunched up, and tried to reach her face. The air was warm and she felt her skin drying.

"Beech likes you," the boy said.

Shyness came over her and she looked down at her feet. She tangled her fingers in the young dog's fur. They all three stood silently for a moment.

"This stream goes down to the sea," the boy said after a moment. "You can catch fish there."

"I've never caught a fish!"

"I suppose I could teach you sometime – if you want."

In the distance, she heard Niko's voice calling her name.

"Somebody's looking for you. You'd better go. Will you get a whipping for being wet?"

She looked up at him, surprised. "Only slaves get whipped! My Mater is Antonia Plautina."

"Well I've never heard of her!"

"We live in a big house in Pyrgi –" She flung her arms wide to describe how big it was, then broke off. They didn't live there any more.

"Don't start crying. That's for babies."

She whispered, "I don't know where I live now."

A VILLA FAR FROM ROME

The boy dropped her hand and stepped away. "Maybe you've come to live in my house!"

Niko's voice was closer now. She could hear him crashing through the bushes on the other side of the stream.

"You're the reason my mother and I had to leave last night."

"No! I was asleep." She felt the start of tears again at his harsh words.

The dog stood on its hind legs to lick her cheek. She buried her face in its still-wet fur that smelled clean and fresh like the wind.

"Well," he said slowly, watching the dog. "Maybe it isn't you exactly that did it."

Niko came out from a thicket of leaves. "There you are! You need to come back in the house before your mother notices you're missing."

He took two big steps across the stream. One more and he reached the other bank. The dog growled.

"Beech!" She and the boy said it at the same time. The dog sat down and began to scratch its ear.

"Look how wet you are!" Niko swung her up onto his shoulder and turned to cross back over the stream.

She looked back at the boy and the dog on the far bank. "Will you come back and play with me sometime?"

"Maybe," he said.

CHAPTER EIGHT

Antonia slept until midday, the first good sleep she'd had since leaving Rome. She sat up, disoriented at first, staring around the small, spare room, wondering where she was. It all came back in a rush.

Exiled.

Worse – married off to a barbarian. Bad as life had become, those last years in her father's villa when the free servants left one by one because Pater couldn't afford to pay them any more, and all their friends turned away from them, she could never have imagined this. She'd been so certain the emperor would embrace his daughter once he knew. How would she survive – how would her young daughter survive – in such an alien place? The emperor couldn't have meant for this to be a punishment. She had done nothing to deserve it.

Shortly before the boat had set sail from the port at Ostia, the dwarf, Satrias, had found her. "You have to understand his fear of assassins," he'd said. "Look at this as his way of protecting you and the child." In misery, she'd stared at him. "How can you believe that?" The dwarf shook his head. "The court is full of enemies. Hide the child!"

She slipped her legs over the edge of the bed. The tiled floor was cold to her feet.

"Niko!"

The Greek appeared in the doorway immediately, as if he'd been awaiting her summons. "I hope you slept well? Do you think you could keep food down now?"

"Yes, to both your questions. A little food," she said. "But first I need to bathe. Ugh! I smell! This place – primitive though it is – must have a bath?"

A VILLA FAR FROM ROME

"Indeed." Niko opened one of the wood chests that the emperor's dwarf had sent with them on the voyage and took out a fresh tunic and undergarments for her. "Primitive, by the standards of Rome. But adequate."

She shuddered. "I can't stay here, Niko. I must go back to Rome soon."

"Are you certain of that?"

"Yes! I know what the emperor said – but he didn't mean that. He's pleased to have a child – I'm certain he is! – but he can't acknowledge her just yet."

"Forcing you to marry a barbarian and go into exile is a strange way to show his pleasure."

His scepticism made her angry. "You think I'm still a child, don't you?"

"Not a child, but the years in Pyrgi sheltered you from the evil in the world."

"Sheltered? After what happened to me – and my family! How can you say that?"

"You've seen the face of evil, but you still don't understand it."

"You may not be a slave now, Niko, but you're still a servant. I won't listen to any more." But the dwarf's words echoed in her mind. Going back wouldn't be so simple.

Niko led her out of the bedchamber along a short colonnade open to a simple garden, lacking the elaborate lawns and bushes, the groves of olive trees at her father's villa. It was a very small house, Roman in design, but unattractive. This passage connected the rooms she'd glimpsed last night and where she'd slept, and those in another building a short distance away. Some of the walls were of simple wattle and daub construction, but she saw through an archway that at least one room had walls painted red and white.

A female barbarian scurried past with an armload of woolen cloaks.

"Wait!"

The woman stared at her for moment, her expression slack.

"Do you understand Latin? I need more covers for my bed. It was cold last night."

The woman shrugged, miming her lack of understanding.

"You should try to learn their tongue," Niko said.

"I certainly will not! Here —" she snatched a cloak off the pile and thrust it at him. "Keep that for me."

The woman uttered a stream of words she didn't understand, and ran away down the length of the colonnade.

Another servant, an older man, crossing the garden, digging tools in hand, stopped to watch what was happening. Aware of Antonia's eye on him, he made a gesture as if he were warding off evil and hurried out of sight.

"Why don't they like me? They know nothing about me."

"News travels fast," the Greek observed.

"What does that mean?"

"I expect we'll find out."

"Barbarians!"

"*Keltoi,*" he said. "A Greek word."

"Celt. Is that their name for themselves?"

"This tribe call themselves Regni."

At some point there would have to be a discussion with the owner of this crude house – her husband! her gorge rose at the thought – about the behavior of the servants towards her. More than that, they needed to establish the rules of their cohabitation – the implications of that term terrified her – until she could return to Rome.

The sky was clouding over, and raindrops pattered against the paving stones of the pathways, raising the scent of wet earth. At the far end of the colonnade – not far at all, the house was very small – Niko ushered her into the empty bath chamber. He clapped his hands twice and a young boy scrambled through the doorway.

The facilities consisted of a tiny, cramped *caldarium* with a heated floor and a bench covered by towels where she lay while the boy anointed her with perfumed oils and scraped the soil from her body. To one side of the room was a modest pool of cold water to cool off after the slave was done.

A VILLA FAR FROM ROME

Adequate, as Niko had judged it, but a far cry from what most citizens had access to in Rome.

Later, cleansed of the foul stickiness of the long days at sea and her own sickness, she let the boy dress her in the clean tunic and drape the *palla* over her shoulders. He fumbled with the lacing of her sandals, and growing impatient, she slapped his hands away. If only old Cassia had been here to help her! Her nurse would've dressed her quickly and efficiently –

A wave of homesickness and grief crashed over her; memories of childhood flooded back. Her legs gave way and she had to sit down. She longed to feel her mother's hands in the lamplight, brushing her hair at bedtime again – to see her father, singing as he saddled the horses in the sunny courtyard in Pyrgi – even to experience her brothers' teasing, the backdrop of her childhood. If only she could go back to the time before this nightmare began!

She recovered her composure and nodded at the boy. He opened the door to the garden. Niko was waiting outside under the colonnade's tiled roof, holding Lucia's hand. Behind them, grey rain sleeted down; she heard the sound of the run-off roaring along the drainage ditch that skirted the colonnade.

She was an exile. She was a mother herself. She must make the best of it.

* * *

It didn't take long to make a survey of the house. It was pitifully small and spare and had very few servants to take care of it. Just what she might've expected of barbarians, even if they were playing at being Roman like her new "husband." She stood at the end of the building where the servant's quarters were and the kitchen. Together, they weren't even the size of the kitchen in her father's villa. The rain had let up, but heavy clouds warned it could return at any minute, and water dripped from the eaves. Summer was obviously over. But somewhere, a bird was still singing. Like her, it was making the best of things.

Lucia stomped her way through puddles in the garden, splashing herself and Niko who was trying to catch her. Children made themselves happy anywhere, especially with a servant as devoted as Niko to shield them from trouble.

She thought about that. When her father freed his Greek secretary, Niko could have left. There was no reason why he should have stayed, let alone chosen to accompany her on her journey to Rome, or on this exile. She gazed at him as he chased her daughter through the puddles. He was almost as old as her father. What could have prevented him from returning to his native land once he was a free man?

"Niko."

He looked over at her and the child promptly ran away through the puddles.

"Why are you here? I want to know."

"Because you and the child need me."

"My father gave you your freedom. You can't care that much about us."

"I cared for your father – he was an honorable man. And I swore an oath to stay with you as long as you and the little one needed me."

"And then?"

He shrugged. "I'll decide when the time comes."

A thought occurred to her. "Were you with him when he – Did you know?"

"Yes."

"You didn't stop him."

"No."

She gazed at him but he didn't elaborate. She tried another way. "You're a handsome man, Niko. You should return to Greece and seek a wife."

He didn't reply to that either. Just as well, she needed him as a tutor for Lucia, so the child wouldn't forget her Roman heritage.

Across the sodden turf, she saw the outbuildings that obviously housed the stables; rain dripped off the red tile roof. The woody scent of some herb she didn't recognize reached her. No olive trees or vines, no fruit trees, nothing useful at all. And as for the house's owner himself, she

A VILLA FAR FROM ROME

hadn't seen him since their arrival last night.

She needed a plan.

Last night, the barbarian woman had looked about as happy to hear her husband had a new wife as the new wife herself had been. Might there be an opportunity in that? Could she be persuaded to become an ally, helping her go back to Rome? Unable to see for the moment how she might work that, she stored it away in her mind for later.

At the far edge of the untidy garden, the land dropped off low cliffs into the sea. She stood under the shelter of a short colonnade from which the rainwater dripped. Behind her, the land rose slowly to a long line of hills, so tame, compared to her memory of wild rocky walls rising straight along the coast where the family's villa stood, the waves crashing below it, the vineyards and olive orchards terraced above it. Even in rain, how beautiful, compared to this tame scene! How would she ever get used to it?

Coming towards them from the direction of the stables was a figure she recognized, Gallus, the former legionary. Another one who came to this bleak place without being forced to. The only true Roman here, if she didn't count Romanized barbarians like her new husband. Surely he would be an ally. Seeing her, Gallus raised his arm in greeting.

"Plenty of room for improvement here," the old man said, as if he'd been reading her mind.

"Why did you choose to come here, Gallus?"

He blinked at her blunt question. "Beats life on the streets of Rome."

"Couldn't you – a Roman – have made a life in the countryside at home, instead of this barbaric place?"

He turned abruptly in the direction of the servants' quarters.

"Wait. Please. I didn't mean to offend."

At the edge of her gaze she saw Niko glance in her direction.

Gallus stopped and faced her again. "Little Fox is my friend."

She stepped back from his barely controlled anger. A gust of wind blew a sheet of water off the overhanging roof, drenching her shoulder. She shivered at the cold touch and shrugged her mantle closer.

"Are there any other –" She hesitated, afraid she might offend him again. "Are than any Romans anywhere near here?"

"There's a garrison up the way, just outside the town. A few women, camp followers. A couple of government officials and their wives. This isn't the headquarters of the legion."

She was chilled by the coldness of his tone. "You don't like me."

"I think you're going to be trouble for Little Fox. And I'll be very unhappy to see that."

A sudden gust of wind shook raindrops off the boughs of a nearby tree. Clouds scudded over the sky and the sun disappeared again. The last thing she needed was to make an enemy out of the man who might be her only link to Romans for miles around. The realization brought tears to her eyes.

"I think we should all go in now." Niko stood behind her. He hoisted Lucia onto his shoulders.

"Ma!" the little girl said.

Shaking, she didn't trust herself to speak.

"Mater," Niko corrected as they walked back to the house.

"Mater! I made a friend today! Two friends, because one is a doggie."

CHAPTER NINE

TOGIDUBNUS WAITED TWO DAYS to give Breca the dignity of her anger. He deserved it. There should have been something he could do rather than bring another woman into Breca's home – even if he'd been forced to do it. But his last sight of his son with Nero's hand on his shoulder filled his mind again, and he almost broke apart with grief and rage. Until he had Amminus safely home, he was in a trap. So many rumors he'd heard about Nero while he was in Rome; some of them probably true. Better not think about them if he wanted to keep his wits. The thought of what might happen to his boy if Nero thought Togidubnus was disobedient buckled his knees. One year, just one year.

Why did Nero want the girl so far away from Rome? Gallus had suggested the child was the emperor's own, but the old legionary was full of gamey talk like that. He didn't think it worth much. But what if it were true? More important, what difference did it make to himself and his plans? The effect on his union with Breca was devastating. That had to be resolved as soon as possible,

One thing he would've sworn at Neptune's altar if he'd still been a believer: He would not take the Roman girl to bed. He had one wife in his heart, no matter what the emperor said – and thank Neptune for the small mercy that Nero had been too drunk to insist the marriage be consummated on the first night as was customary! Even if he must be celibate for months. He had married Breca in a Druid ceremony when they were both only a year or two older than Amminus was now. Even though he no longer believed in the old gods and the old ways, he would never violate that oath of handfasting.

Early on the second morning, he called the stable boy and ordered a horse be prepared for him. He wasn't going so far that he couldn't have walked, but riding would be quicker and he was impatient to talk to Breca. He stood in the colonnade under the small overhanging roof, watching a light rain patter on the garden. The flowers were almost all gone in the suddenly cold autumn weather, the leaves turning brown and gold. Breca always loved this time of year, the time of apples ripening and berries on the bushes along the winding paths, harvests being gathered in –

He shook the melancholy thoughts away.

Yawning, the boy led out a roan mare with a white mark on her face. The stallion, her stable mate, thought himself too good to be ridden on social calls, especially in the rain. The mare could be persuaded if he spoke kindly, and today she was content to go, she knew where they were going. One thing he knew, horses couldn't be driven around like sheep or cattle; they had to be coaxed and persuaded. He mounted the mare and patted her neck.

He knew where Breca would've gone. Knowing his wife, he was certain she wouldn't have looked for shelter in town; the bustle and clutter of Noviomagus didn't appeal to her. What would she have thought of Rome that could have swallowed ten of this town and not had a stomach ache? She had family west of here, ten miles as the Romans counted, on a marshy island in the channel where her uncle, Arto, a Druid, lived.

He turned the mare's head in that direction and became aware of the small figure in a bedraggled tunic, standing in the rain close to the horse's head – almost under its hooves. The child stared up at him trustingly.

"Be glad that Snowmark is a gentle horse," he said sternly to the Roman girl's daughter. "And a wise one."

"I like horses," the little girl said. "My Uncle Valentinus let me ride with him when we lived at home."

Poor child, he thought, she too was at Nero's mercy, whatever her parentage. Did no one pay attention to her? He'd seen her yesterday too, unaccompanied.

"Will you let me ride with you sometime?"

He wasn't ready to answer her yet. He kicked Snowmark's side lightly and rode away.

A VILLA FAR FROM ROME

* * *

The autumn sun had reached its highest point in the cloudless sky before the track he followed turned to cross a shallow channel that separated the marshy island from the flat lands at the foot of the hills. The tide was running out, and he waited patiently till it was safe to ford the channel. Anxiety set his thoughts churning. What right had Breca to desert him like this? When had he ever broken his trust to her? Together, they could plan their way forward. Running away from him was the worst thing to do. But he could never hold his anger against her for very long.

The ground beneath Snowmark's hooves was spongy, covered in wild grasses, sweet-smelling marjoram and thyme, and bird's foot trefoil, criss-crossed by streams as thin as one of Breca's ribbons. Quail gathered a last meal or two from the grasses before flying south for the winter, and the shrike, hunter of small prey, took up residence in their stead. Ahead, a pipit flew straight up, squeaking its alarm at the horse's approach. As he rode, a patter of rain moved in from the sea, then let up, and sun dappled the chalk hills behind him again, throwing into sharp relief the centuries old burial mounds high up on the slopes. The air was sharp as crystal; he could see all the way across the bay to the island of Vectis, a bright line on the horizon. Below, and to the south, the breeze blew the incoming waves into froth as they curled over grey pebbles, mirroring the wind-torn clouds overhead.

He watched a rabbit dash away from his horse's hooves in a blur of brown body and white tail. This was his people's land, and he loved it above everything except Breca and his sons. Somewhere nearby, he remembered, there was an ancient shrine to Sulis; no-one, not even Breca's uncle, knew when it had been built.

Now he could see several of his people's timber-framed roundhouses scattered about, smoke curling lazily through the opening at the apex of the thatched roofs. Pigs and fowl rooted for food amongst them. In several doorways, faces peered out, their expressions a mixture of respect – he was their chief – and disapproval – he had wronged Breca. Nothing stayed secret in such a small community for long.

A small figure draped in a fisherman's grey and blue checkered wool cloak stood in the doorway of the largest house. Togidubnus dismounted and turned the mare loose; she wouldn't go far. The boy avoided meeting his eyes.

"Good day to you, my son," he said. "I've come to talk with your mother."

The boy shook his head. "She may not want to talk with you."

Behind Catuarus, Breca appeared in the doorway, unsmiling. She put a hand on the boy's shoulder.

Seeing her there emptied his heart of all its anger. She wore no jewelry, her hair loose today, and he saw how it began to turn silver like leaves on a tree preparing for winter. Had it been that color before he left for Rome? He'd thought he knew his wife so well, but he couldn't remember a detail like that.

"My heart. Please let's talk."

She spoke in a low voice to the boy, and Catuarus went back inside the roundhouse. He held his hand out to her and she took it. A shudder passed over him at the sudden familiar smell of her, and he felt the tears rise. But a warrior didn't weep. They followed one of the paths away from the cluster of houses; the way wound between the sturdy grey trunks of a small stand of young oaks and beeches. Neither spoke.

He could hear the sea's sighing breath under the wild cries of the gulls and cormorants. The tide was fully out now, and he smelled the exposed kelp beds, dark and green. He imagined the girls and women, just out of sight, harvesting the mussels and cockles that were now exposed, and the tasty oysters that were this bay's treasure. Sea and land were kind to the Regni. There was something here Rome could never match, no matter how useful her gifts.

"Do you remember how often we walked these paths when we were young?" He used the Old Tongue, the syllables sliding like clear rainwater over his lips. "In summer, with the moon rising – until your uncle came after me with a switch!"

She stopped and looked up at him. "I thought we would walk together for ever."

A VILLA FAR FROM ROME

"And so we shall!"

She shook her head. "I can't agree to it."

"Your Druid family suspected me of wooing you because you were a princess of the Regni, a tribe that I, as a Catuvellauni had been given to rule."

"Even then, I knew that was not true."

Hand in hand, they walked further into the trees. Hidden in this grove of old oaks and willows, the ancient shrine stood, a low three-sided hut of limestone boulders, brought from far away in the west to house the Maiden's altar. In his memory, it had been larger and grander, but that was because he'd been a young man giddy with love.

"You remember?" she asked.

"Do you doubt that?"

Breca let go of his hand and stepped over the threshold. The little altar was covered in dry leaves a recent wind had brought inside. She brushed them carefully off the stone. Under them, he saw a knot of wildflowers someone had left as an offering, dry now. And a pile of smooth river stones, Sulis's emblem.

"This isn't of my choosing," he said. "I had no power to refuse the emperor."

"Our son is a hostage, Togi? Is that what you fear to tell me?"

"Mo more and no less than the Roman girl, Antonia ."

"A hostage."

"I promise you –"

She put a finger on his lips silencing him. "It's not wise to take oaths in Sulis's house. Oaths you cannot keep."

Again, his heart churned. How unfair it was of her to put it like that! As if he'd had a choice! But as swiftly as the resentment came over him, it went away.

"As Sulis is my witness, one thing I can promise you. I will never take the Roman girl to bed. No one can force me to betray my vow to you. You alone have my heart."

She sighed. "The world itself has changed, Togi. You told me I must remember. The Maiden's name is Minerva now."

There was something he could do to distract her from dark thoughts of Amminus in Rome. "I'll build that temple for you in Noviomagus that I promised – a large and beautiful one. Together we'll dedicate it to Minerva-Sulis. And to Neptune, ruler of the sea, our father."

"A Roman temple means nothing to me. Once you would've known, Togi."

He fumbled in the pocket in his tunic and drew out the silver hair comb she'd dropped on the night he'd returned from Rome.

"I wanted you to know I kept you in my heart when I was away."

She looked at the trinket on the palm of his hand, touched it with one finger. "Amber for peace," she said softly. "Patience, too."

"Have patience with me, Breca."

"No good will come of your desire to please Rome above all else. Don't you see that?"

"I'll find a way –"

"I keep thinking of Amminus."

"It's for Amminus that I'm doing this! Can't you accept that?"

She turned and walked out of the shrine. In the space of a moment, he couldn't see her among the tall grasses.

He glanced at the silver comb, still in his hand. He put it on Sulis's stone and went to find his horse.

CHAPTER TEN

RAIN HAD TURNED THE LITTLE GARDEN INTO A LAKE today, or she would've walked her frustration off outside. The weather was yet another burden of her exile. She'd been here a little more than two weeks already, but it felt like a lifetime! Why couldn't it just storm and be done? This all-day drizzle was depressing.

With nothing better to do, she visited the kitchen – cramped and inefficient, like everything else. The cook either was too stupid to understand Latin, or truculent, and it still took far too long to get her to prepare a sparse but proper Roman meal.

But this was where she was going to have to live for now. It was the first time she could ever remember being on her own, to make her own decisions, no father or brother to overrule her. The old barbarian didn't count, and he didn't seem interested in her anyway. So whether she wanted to be here or not, she needed to claim her own power in this house.

The first problem was that her mother had taught her some things, but she hadn't taught her how to control a household. But surely it couldn't be that difficult! The first thing to do was teach the cook how to prepare food the Roman way, and that she knew. That rabbit there, on the stone cutting slab, the old woman was sawing at it as if it were a tree! She seized the knife out of the woman's grasp and ran a finger down the blade. Too blunt, it needed sharpening. She didn't see a whet stone nearby, but she did see a gleaming knife with a sharper blade.

"Now, pay attention and I'll teach you how it's done." She was no stranger to knives and kitchens. "There. See where I made the first cut to remove the pelt? It comes off easier now."

But either the old woman was too stupid to get anything right, or too cunning. If they'd been in Rome, her mother would've had the slave whipped. She swept the cut pieces off the board into the waiting stew pot and added beans and chopped cabbage leaves, olive oil, leeks and garlic for seasoning the bland flesh. The old cook looked at her, then added a small handful of oysters still in their shells, and a little wine. There was something defiant in that action, as if the woman resented the cooking lesson she'd just been given.

She had just sat down at the table with Lucia and Nikolaos when she heard a horse whinny. She glanced out the unshuttered window and saw her husband dismount from the horse and hand the reins over to the stable lad. He'd been gone all day again. She was certain he was avoiding her, for which she was grateful, but it only postponed the discussion they must soon have. She'd spent long hours – days! – thinking over what had to happen to make this intolerable situation bearable. The time was overdue for her to lay out the terms under which she'd live here peacefully until she could plan her return to Rome.

Patchy sunlight slanted through the open door, laying a path of brightness across her table. He filled the doorway with his tall frame and blocked it. With his back to the light, she couldn't read his expression, but she saw the slumping shoulders. She wondered what he did every day. *An old barbarian*, she'd called him, that first day she'd set eyes on him in Nero's palace, and so he was.

"We are about to eat." She was careful to keep her tone neutral. "Join us."

He stared at her for a moment as if he'd forgotten who she was or how she'd come to be in his house. He nodded and came to the table, bringing the smell of rain with him.

She clapped her hands to summon one of the kitchen servers. No one came except Lucia followed by Niko. Her husband – she'd better get used to the word for the time being -- sat patiently at the table, avoiding her eyes.

"Niko, will you please serve Tiberius."

He appeared surprised to hear her use his Roman name. She certainly wasn't going to call him by that barbaric Britanni mouthful! The Greek set the bowl in front of him and let him serve himself.

A VILLA FAR FROM ROME

"Tiber! Tiber!" Lucia chanted. "Are you a river?"

"Lucia!"

"Well, Tiber's a river. Niko told me."

"But *Tiberius* was an emperor," the Greek said, pouring water mixed with honey and a little wine for the child.

"I have to call him *something.*"

"The Tiber is a very fine river," Tiberius said. "Bigger than the ones we have around here."

"Show me rivers around here?"

She was astounded to see that rather than appear offended by the child's forwardness, Tiberius smiled at her. This rare display of friendliness made her uncomfortable. She didn't want them all to be friendly together. She wanted to go home.

"Eat your meal and go to bed!" For a moment, she wished she could accompany the child to bed, but knew she wouldn't sleep.

Niko took Lucia away. She wasn't planning on staying here, but she did need to find a female slave. It wasn't proper for Niko to do it all. Besides, the Greek showed obvious displeasure when she asked him to play a servant's role. A heavy woman of middle years entered with a lamp, put it on the table, scowled at both Tiberius and Antonia. Pools of yellow light pushed the gathering darkness to the edges of the room; shadows jumped across the table, and Tiberius's face became suddenly ancient and deeply lined. The servant refilled their wine cups and took away the empty food plates.

"Your slaves aren't well-trained, Tiberius. In fact, they are most rude."

He busied himself with his cup, moving it around on the table as if he were planning a battle and the cup represented his army.

"I've been here for several days now, and still they can't follow my orders. Why is that?"

"They have their own opinions."

"I don't understand. They're *slaves*. Slaves don't have opinions."

"No. They're freemen. Servants."

"I would've thought —"

"What you might've thought in Rome doesn't count here."

The hardness of his tone caught her like a slap on the cheek. "I'm going back to Rome as soon as I can! But until then, I expect those who serve me to behave according to their status."

"What makes you think you can go back, when the emperor himself sent you away?"

She stared at him. "He was inebriated. He'll come to his senses and welcome me back."

He shook his head.

The rest of the meal passed in silence. Tiberius ate very little, and her own appetite had shrunk since her bout with the sea malady. The room was growing chilly; she wished she'd put on a palla. In the silence, she heard the patter of rain begin again.

"This house is cramped and cold and uncomfortable. You can't expect me to stay here."

He had an odd way of raising his bushy eyebrows when he was surprised. "What do you intend to do about it?"

"I can't believe the emperor meant for me to raise Lucia here."

The window showed a quick flicker of lightning, storm approaching. The oil lamp was sputtering, not burning true, and she could smell the sooty smoke. Couldn't they even get oil lamps right in this damp island? She thought of the pleasant evenings when the warmth of the day lingered over her father's vineyards where the grapes would almost be ready for harvest, stars shining in a cloudless, indigo sky. The villa in Pyrgi – gone forever. And her father dead by his own hand. The frustrations and anxiety of the last few days overwhelmed her. The rough wine she'd drunk didn't help. Tears welled up again – she cried altogether too much these days. She was so tired! But they had to have this conversation and get it over with. Thunder boomed; she felt the vibration in her bones.

"You know the emperor is the child's father?"

"I'd heard rumors." His tone was neutral. He busied himself with his food, avoiding her eyes.

"He would acknowledge her immediately if it weren't for his

A VILLA FAR FROM ROME

enemies."

"Ah."

"You don't have the right to know any more than that – even if you are my husband! At least, you're my husband for the time being."

She wanted to fight him, to shout and berate, but he was obviously not going to argue. She took a deep breath. "I'm willing to make a pact with you. I'll live civilly with you until I can go back to Rome. You will treat me with the respect and comfort due a wife. But I won't consummate this false marriage. Don't you even imagine for one moment that I will!"

"Of course not!" He looked surprised. "An acceptable contract. Thank you."

She looked away from him. It didn't help that he was being reasonable.

Thunder shook the house. The sound of the rain on the roof and the colonnade outside was deafening. Tiberius stood up and looked out the door. Beyond him, she saw a sheet of water pouring down from the overhang, lit by another lightning flash like a temple trick performed by an unscrupulous priest to suggest Jupiter's presence.

He waited for the next roll of thunder to pass. "This is typical sea weather. It won't last for long. I was expecting it. I saw gulls flying far inland. They always know what's coming."

She was so homesick for her warm, sunny Roman countryside in that moment. "I hate this rain!"

"It rains in Italia too."

"Not like this! I don't want to be here."

"Do you think I want you here?" he replied sharply.

Her control gave way and she put her hands on her face and sobbed. "At home...it doesn't... I wish...." She couldn't finish the thought.

After a moment he got up from the table. He stood stiffly, not looking at her. "I'm going to Noviomagus in a couple of days. You should come with me."

"Why would I want to see where barbarians live?"

He gazed at her for a moment and she was afraid she'd gone too far.

"I – I didn't mean that."

"I know a Roman lady you would enjoy visiting. Would that please you?"

She wiped tears off her cheeks. "It might."

He nodded to her before he left. "Good night, Antonia."

A Roman woman to visit – someone who'd understand her longing to go home. It was a little comfort, but sometimes, her father used to say, a very small log is enough to save a drowning sailor.

CHAPTER ELEVEN

THE STORM HAD WASHED OUT PART OF THE ROAD between the house and Noviomagus and blown down several small trees, compelling the horses to pick their way through the mud. It had been an unusually strong storm; Togidubnus wondered if that portended anything about weather in the season to come. Large puddles were another hazard. Gallus, who refused to ride, claiming the legion lived on its feet, took Snowmark's reins and led the Roman girl around the largest of them. Antonia huddled on the mare's back, wrapped in two cloaks, her own and one of his; she suffered unusually from the chilly weather. Yet today the sky was clear, and overhead crows swooped and danced in joy, their raucous laughter cascading down the sky.

Taking the Roman girl — he refused to think of her as his "wife" — with him to Noviomagus had seemed a good idea. She was a problem he couldn't solve, and she acted as if she thought he was the cause of it. Gods willing, a visit to the Roman town and other Romans would take the edge off her sharp tongue.

He was overdue for visit to the basilica, the new building almost completed now where the Regni's Council of Elders met and the tribe's justice was dispensed. Had they heard about the girl? Surely they had! Gossip spread fast, especially something they'd consider disgraceful. Add that to the fact that his previous attempts to use superior Roman laws and techniques to better the life of his folk were frequently misunderstood as a betrayal of the old ways. As if he were less Regni because he wanted to better their lives. What they did not understand was that the old times were gone and wouldn't come back. The Romans were here to stay. They were all Romans now.

But once he had Amminus back he'd find a way to put Antonia out of his life and get his family together again.

They passed the short stretch of wall that the Second Augusta had begun years ago when the Romans had planned to make Noviomagus a strong fort, but so far the walls remained unfinished, a mix of hard-packed earth and mortared stones. He remembered those days from his childhood, when his own house had been little more than a granary and stable for the legionaries, favored because of its closeness to the sea and the little supply port.

The basilica he needed to visit lay at the crossing of the two main arteries, the boundary road *Cardo Maximus* and the *Decumanus Maximus*, the road that marked the edge of the military garrison. The roads were noisy and cluttered with horse-drawn carts rumbling over the cobblestones, and peddlers on foot, their wares dangling from yokes slung over their shoulders. Four legionaries marched past, escorting a shackled fifth on his way to punishment; the prisoner's face was bloody.

From the center of the town, streets of merchants and residents followed an orderly grid, a small imitation of a Roman city. Very small! Noviomagus would hardly count as more than a village compared to Rome itself. A couple of officials who had family with them lived in houses in Noviomagus. If Minerva smiled on his mission today, he'd find someone at home and willing to entertain Antonia. A little further on, past this central intersection, there was a narrow street of finely built houses, one of which housed the family of Marcus Favonius, the centurion who commanded the region's troops. He stopped the horses at the entrance, marked by a banner displaying the Second Augusta's Pegasus emblem, and waited. Soon an old Regni man came out and took the reins. He dismounted. Gallus helped Antonia.

A female slave appeared – Celt, by the look of her, but not one of his own Regni – and showed them through the arch into the atrium; Gallus waited outside. He hadn't been here for a while, and the owners had added several features, one of them a marble fountain, a dolphin spewing water

A VILLA FAR FROM ROME

into a basin that Breca would like, when he could see clearly how he could afford to make improvements to his house –

"Tiberius!"

A plump, round-faced Roman matron swept towards them, arms outstretched. Her dark hair was held back with an elaborate silver comb; more silver, laced with amber beads, circled her neck. She wore a white linen tunic, edged with green and gold, so fine that only the warmth of her house made it possible to wear on such a chilly day. A very small girl child clutched at her leg. Legally she wasn't the centurion's wife, for centurions like the legionaries they commanded were forbidden to marry, but she might as well have been in this far corner of the empire. She would be the last person to scorn him for his own marital problems.

"Why have you made us wait so long for your visit?" she asked, but didn't pause for his reply. "Marcus will be disappointed to miss you. He's on training exercises with some of the men. Will you stay and dine with us? The slaves are about to serve the cena but they're so slow! Actually, the only one who knows what she's doing is sick today."

"Gracila –"

She ignored the interruption. "Our son is accompanying his father today – never too young to learn the ways of the legion, Marcus says. Oh, Tiberius, there's so much to tell! Did you know, they finished building the new arena while you were gone? You'll have to bring your family into town to see the exciting gladiator fights!"

She was a chatterer, but exceedingly friendly, and he felt at ease with her. She wouldn't be so quick to judge; her own status was not without stain. He tried again, holding up a hand to interrupt the flow of talk.

"Gracila, I've brought a visitor, a guest in my home." He laid a hand on Antonia's shoulder and felt her muscles stiffen under his touch. "Antonia Plautina, from Pyrgi."

"Ah, so the gossips were right! You know how fast news travels here. I heard you'd brought a guest back with you." She stopped, and he saw her blush as she realized the thorny ground she was about to tread on. She gave a tiny laugh and continued, "But Pyrgi? Oh my dear one! My grandmother came from that area! I grew up farther down the coast – Pompeii."

She embraced Antonia, smothering the girl's attempt at a reply. The child at her hem, caught in the embrace too, shrieked.

"Unfortunately, Gracila, I have business –"

Gracila released Antonia from her embrace. "I heard that too. You're a *king* now, aren't you?"

He heard the faint tone of mockery in her voice. Romans – even kind ones like Gracila – had scant respect for client kings. "I'll leave Antonia with you. You'll find lots to talk about." At least one of them would, he thought.

Gracila held Antonia at arm's length and inspected her. "You're not feeding this child properly, Tiberius. Look how thin she is! Well, my cook will soon remedy that."

Impatient to get away from the torrent of words, he went back outside to where Gallus waited.

"Like old times." Gallus nodded toward a couple of soldiers walking by. "Off duty and on their way to the tavern."

"Why don't you join them?"

"I intend to. I came to Britannia for the beer, remember?"

"And to win at dice, separating poor soldiers from their pay." He glanced at the servant still holding the horses. "See to the horses for me. I'll walk."

* * *

The dozen or so aging members of the Council, governing body of the Regni, who happened to be in the basilica today were enough to keep proceedings droning on through the afternoon. Some of the old men had adopted Roman togas and cloaks and were clean-shaven, a sign of their willingness to appropriate the benefits of the occupying power, but not necessarily the Roman philosophy of advance and improvement. The rest of them wore their braids and beards and traditional robes with an air of defiance, although most of them were Roman citizens by necessity if not by choice. Some of the Elders frowned over tablets bearing notice of tax disputes, neighbors' quarrels and boundary issues. He doubted all of them

A VILLA FAR FROM ROME

could read Latin. Nor were all of them disposed to be friendly to him. Boudicaa's cause had found many supporters here as elsewhere.

He'd known these men since his father's day; he knew which ones were willing to take a bribe and which were not. They were capable of melding Roman law with Regni practice, governing without the input of a chief. Occasionally, a matter came before them for which the ultimate punishment was death, and the chief would have the final say. Nothing like that came up today.

But this was the body that also controlled public works, and he needed their approval – and funds – if his proposal for a temple was to become reality. He wanted it for Breca's sake, but it would also be a symbol of his power as chief of the Regni. He reined in his impatience and considered which of the old men he could count on to be on his side, and which he'd have to win over, and at what price. He'd chosen not to take his official seat but sat on a bench that ran along one wall where several petitioners sat waiting their turn. Their rough clothing smelled of smoke and earth and onions, reminding him of his family's own humble beginnings.

At last, the final complaint was settled and the old men prepared to go home. He stood.

"A moment more." He used the Old Tongue to avoid stirring up the minority among them who regarded Latin as an abomination.

Some of the old men acknowledged him with a nod, others looked annoyed at being delayed. Two appeared to have just woken out of sleep. And one, the Chief Elder of the Council, a large man with hooded eyes and a small mouth, he knew instantly was no friend.

"Noviomagus grows and prospers. Fish and crops are abundant. Our mines flow with copper and silver. We are at peace with our neighbors. Our Folk, renowned throughout the south, grow too, and with this our need for monuments to mark our devotion to the gods who reward us. I propose that we build a worthy temple to honor Neptune and Minerva."

He could almost hear the sound of coins being counted in the old heads as they considered the cost of this.

A small man shook his head, braids flying. "A very fine idea – if we had the money to do it!"

"How big a cost is too large to honor the gods that protect us?"

The Chief Elder, Epilus, looked up from the tablet he'd been studying. "This council has larger matters to dispose of than the cost of a temple."

It was a challenge thrown at his feet. The chamber fell silent. He was suddenly aware of the distant sounds of the town outside this building, the rumble of carts, the shouts of tradesmen. These were his people. He must be strong for them now. The old men stared at him, waiting. He knew what was coming; he'd expected it. He had to hold firm, let them see the righteousness of his claim to lead the tribe no matter how it had been decided..

"Let us begin with these large matters." He stood tall before them, a warrior, willing himself to show no expression.

"You have proclaimed yourself king in violation of our laws," the Chief Elder said. "It is our custom for the Council to elect a king after a study of the eligible."

"My father Cunobelinus was a king. I've proved myself in battle with the best of the legions."

"One princeling among several," a very old man put in.

"Nevertheless," Epilus said, "You took it upon yourself to usurp this Council's right to make the choice."

"I heard that Caesar had something to do with it," a man he didn't know, with a narrow, scarred face said slyly.

Several of the Council murmured at this. For some of them, that was worse than if he'd seized the kingship by himself. But there was also the other matter of the Roman wife Caesar had thrust on him; they hadn't mentioned that yet, but he knew they were thinking of it. Lesser affairs had split a tribe before. Though he understood the justness of their argument, what had been done was done.

"The proper ceremonies were never performed." Epilus said.. "You have not been consecrated."

A VILLA FAR FROM ROME

He let the words hang there; there was no answer he could give to them. In his mind, the Regni must move forward, leaving the old ways in the past. But he knew he was in the minority in this chamber.

A man, bearded, with long grey locks braided in the old style, who hadn't spoken up yet, said, "It may prove that having a king who is Caesar's friend will be of benefit to the Regni."

Togidubnus was aware of the ripple of disapproval that ran through the Council. The Regni, like other tribes, had no choice but accept the authority of their Roman conquerors, and on the whole they understood the benefits of the situation. But being a friend of Caesar had a smell to it like two day-old fish. Trying to explain or excuse would make it worse. He held his words.

"What Caesar has done we can't undo," the grey-braided man said. "But, surely, the son of Cunobelinus was a worthy candidate, and one we might have selected by ourselves. I see no harm done."

"Has the Praetor been consulted about this proposed building of a temple?" another man asked suddenly, jolting the discussion away from the dangerous ground it had been occupying. "Governor of the province, his approval surely is necessary?"

He knew he hadn't escaped their anger entirely. He heard the scorn underlying the man's words. He had to let their resentment take its course.

"And when was the last time the Praetor was in Noviomagus?" The youngest member of the Council, scarcely beyond his middle years, spoke up. "Does the Praetor give a fig for what we build?"

"A little caution!" Epilus rapped on the long table, bouncing the writing tablets. "Remember we have Caesar's friend here!"

He read the waves of both pro- and anti-Roman feeling in the chamber, no better and no worse than they had ever been since the days of Boudicca's rebellion.

"How long would this take to plan?" a man asked.

"I've made preliminary sketches, based on the temple to Neptune in Rome."

"A formidable model, no doubt," the Chief Elder said. "But why Neptune and Minerva and not Jupiter? Won't a temple in their honor and not his draw his wrath on us?"

"We're dependent on Neptune's protection of our island. And Minerva –"

"Is the new name for an old goddess of our ancestors," the man with braids said smoothly. "I say we should build a temple to Sulis here."

He marked that one as a friend. "We have no shortage of craftsmen and builders in Noviomagus."

Committing the large amount of money that would be needed to build a big temple was a serious matter. Some of these men would never forgive him for fighting against Boudicca, necessary though that had been. On the other hand, offending a chief selected by Rome by vetoing his project wasn't a good idea either. He let them consider their dilemma.

"We need time to think this over," the Chief Elder said. "Such a large undertaking...."

"So large indeed!" The small man who'd first questioned the project shook his head.

Angered, he abandoned his resolve to stay calm. "We can't continue to live in the past! We must move forward, taking the best from Rome and marrying it to the best from our ancestors."

He stopped, aware that his unfortunate choice of image had not gone unnoticed. His stomach clenched and heat rose into his face.

"Ah," the Chief Elder said, his tone silky. "We've heard about that too."

"Where would you build this temple?" the man with the braids asked.

He was grateful to the man for deflecting their spite. "Where the old sanctuary to Sulis once stood."

The man nodded solemnly. "That's hallowed ground. It so happens that I own that land."

He gazed at the man. He'd thought he might count that one as an ally. Had he been mistaken?

The man smiled. "I shall donate the land for this noble cause."

A VILLA FAR FROM ROME

No one offered any further argument, The Elders filed out of the building, but the one with traditional braids remained.

"You have an enemy in the Council," he commented. "Epilus doesn't like ideas he didn't think of first."

"I haven't sought an enemy. But I won't hide from one who chooses to make himself such."

"You don't remember who I am, do you? I'm Pudens, son of Pudentinus. I knew you when you were hardly more than a young lad following your father around and carrying a Roman sword that was too big for you."

"A sword I learned to put to use! But I don't play the warrior any more." Not since the campaign against Boudicca where he'd been torn between family ties and the sense that Britannia's future lay with Rome. "I'm a man of peace now, a builder of temples."

"A fine occupation," Pudens said. "Alas, I am only a merchant."

"A little more than that?" he guessed, since the man had land in Noviomagus to donate.

Pudens chuckled. "I've found a new occupation, supplying the garrison with its needs – whatever they might be. I'm rewarded well enough."

* * *

Once he retrieved her from Gracila's non-stop chatter, Antonia was ready to talk.

"You can't imagine what a relief it was to be in a comfortable *Roman* house!" she told him as they mounted the horses .

Gallus was nowhere to be found, and they left without him. As the horses plodded their way through the remaining puddles out of Noviomagus, he became aware of the clusters of men and women on the streets– two here, four there, another outside the inn – staring at them as they passed. The faces turned towards his were grim, accusing. This was not the reception he was used to as a prince of the Regni. But he knew what they were seeing: Their leader riding with his new wife, a public insult to Breca. He wanted to explain – but there were no words to excuse his actions in their eyes.

"It was actually *warm!*" Antonia said. "They have a functioning hypocaust, and not just for the baths. You should have one built."

Luxuries like that had never been high on Breca's list, though she might enjoy it if he installed it. If she came back to him.

When she came back to him. He was not ready to give up hope.

CHAPTER TWELVE

THERE WAS NOTHING TO DO. She'd explored everything. The servants went away because they didn't like Romans, Ma said. Ma said she and Lucia were Romans. There was no one left to play with her.

Ma said Niko was her tutor now, and what that meant was Niko didn't have time to play with her any more. They had to spend the whole day doing lessons. She liked learning to read! But the book Niko had was all about kings and emperors, no children in it once they'd got past the story of the twins and the mother wolf.

The rain had stopped and the clouds raced across the sky, looking as if something was chasing them. The air was so cold she could see her breath even indoors. Making clouds with her mouth was boring after a while too.

The boy with the odd name might come back with his dog.

She pulled on her tunic, hitching it up at the waist with her belt so it left her lower legs free, grabbed a palla and wrapped it around her shoulders, not bothering to fasten it. She left her sandals inside because the grass was going to be wet and Ma would scold if she ruined them. If only she had a dog, like that boy, it would come running after her and they could play in the meadow where Niko wouldn't see them and call them back inside.

No one else was awake in the villa, not even the stable boy who had to get up early to feed the horses. Some day, she'd like to help him. She stopped under a stand of trees. They'd lost most of their leaves – didn't they feel cold? She listened, hoping to hear a dog bark. A strong wind whipped the bare branches about, but the only sound was birds, crows mostly, and house sparrows chirping. All the ones with pretty songs had already flown south, Niko said. Ma had added, *To Rome, probably!* Wasn't that a very long way for little birds to fly?

The stream where she'd met the boy and the dog was a short walk. But this morning she thought of something else. She could see the pathway to the dock where they'd landed when they'd come to live with Tiber. She hadn't liked the sea much when they were on it, but that was because Ma kept her down in the cabin where she was being sick, and the smell had almost made Lucia sick too. She could have a quick look before Ma and Niko were awake. No one would know.

Pulling her palla tight about her shoulders, she ran as fast as she could across the damp turf that led to the wooden dock. Out of breath, she stopped on the slick, wet planks and stared at the water. To one side, the dock was wide where the boats tied up. The other side sloped down to a stony beach.

Waves crashed against the dock, and the water was a dull grey color with sparkles here and there when the sun came out. The waves had foamy white tops that looked like lambs' wool. Seagulls flew circles over the water, screeching, their heads turning this way and that. She saw a small black dot on the grey water, a little boat. Maybe it was a fisherman, catching the fish she'd eat for cena. Niko told her that Britanni girls and women hunted for shellfish and oysters here along the rocks at the edge of the sea. She'd like to see that too – maybe help -- but nobody was doing that today.

The air was very cold and the sea spray smelled grey-green like kelp. Niko called this an inlet from the real sea. Like the mouth of the River Tiber, he'd explained, only the other way around.

Something jumped in the water – Something big and dark. Two somethings.

Her heart raced

Dolphins.

She recognized them immediately. They were close enough to shore that she could see their smiling faces poking up above the surface, looking at her. She waved, but they had gone under the water again.

She jumped off the dock onto a narrow stretch of sand and ran along at the edge of the water, dodging the incoming waves. If only they'd stay

A VILLA FAR FROM ROME

near shore long enough for her to get closer to them!

A wave caught her as it broke on the shore, and the edge of her tunic was soon wet. How cold the water was! She remembered a pool in her grandparent's garden. That water was never cold. Her toe stubbed against something and she looked down. A little pile of shells the storm had swept in, most of them broken but one or two whole. Forgetting the dolphins, she bent to pick them up. Another wave came in. This one drenched her from the shoulders down. This wasn't a good idea. She liked water – Uncle Valentinus had taught her to swim a little bit in that pool – but that water was warm, not nasty cold like this. She remembered her uncles, laughing and shouting out, their hair streaming wet over their shoulders. Swimming looked like so much fun.

She put her wet fingers in her mouth. They tasted salty. She took a step closer to look. A wave hit her in the face. She gasped, losing her breath in the wind. She needed to sit down and catch her breath. Between the narrow beach and the turf there were some large rocks with flat tops. She dragged her feet through the water that now swelled about her ankles. The rock's sides were slick. Something slimy and grey grew on them. Her fingers scratched and scraped; getting a firm hold of the rock was difficult. She was shivering now and couldn't stop.

Just as she got her fingers in a crevice near the top of the rock and started to pull herself up, the biggest wave of all splashed over her head, knocking her hands off. She slid back down, powerless in the strong pull of out-rushing water. Her knees grazed against the rock. Terrified, she screamed, but water filled her mouth and choked her. She was off the rock and bobbing in the churning water, her palla still around her neck. She had to do something! Uncle Valentinus had told her never to go swimming with clothes on. But she hadn't meant to go swimming! What should she do? She scrabbled at the palla – fingers so cold she could barely feel – and it floated free.

She was going to drown. Niko would be very angry because he'd warned her that the sea could drown her.

SHEILA FINCH

A thought popped into her head. The first day her uncle took her into that pool at home, she'd been scared of the water and started crying. Uncle Valentinus had told her to turn on her back and spread her arms. She could float like that for ever, he'd said. She wouldn't drown. She tried to remember what his face looked like to help her, turned onto her back, and looked up at the grey sky. The water was calmer out here, but she was being carried far out.

A swell jostled her and she went under again.

When she opened her eyes below the waves, the light was green, and bubbles raced past her face. She needed to breathe, but when she opened her mouth the salt water rushed in and she gagged. She thrashed her arms and legs trying to get to the top again, and for a moment her head did break the surface. She took in a huge gulp of air. How far away the dock looked! *I'm going to do it! I won't give up!*

A wave knocked her under again. This time, everything was a blur. Her heart hammered and her chest was a big lump of hurt.

Something nudged her shoulder, her leg. Something grabbed her tunic, dragging her –

Her head burst out of the water again and she gasped for air. For a moment, she bobbed in the water, throat burning and eyes tight shut against the stinging, too shocked to think.

Hands grabbed her shoulder – pulled her up.

"Here," a man's voice said in broken Latin. "Not fight me now! Let me get you into the boat."

Her hips scraped the edge of the boat as he dragged her aboard. She lay choking on the bottom. Hands turned her over onto her stomach and she vomited sea water.

"Better."

She rolled onto her back and opened her eyes. An old man with white hair down to his shoulders and a very wrinkled face like an apple left in the barrel too long looked down at her. He had a lot of long hair under his nose too, just above his lip and curling out from his face. She'd never seen anything like it! It waggled when he talked. His eyes were the same grey color as the sky.

A VILLA FAR FROM ROME

"Not good day for swimming," the old man said.

She didn't like being scolded by someone who didn't speak very good Latin. "I didn't mean to go swimming! I'm not good at it yet."

"Truly?"

His voice sounded like laughing. She scowled at him.

He handed her a heavy wool cloak, grey patterned with green and blue diamond shapes. "Put this around you."

As she took the cloak, she saw his bare arms – they looked as if somebody had scribbled all over them in blue ink, whorls and scrolls and curly bits. She wanted to ask who'd done such a thing to him, but was afraid he'd be angry.

The boat rocked violently and tipped to one side. She screamed and grabbed at the man. He leaned over the edge, reaching for something. A rush of something dark and furry fell into the boat. It scrambled to its feet and shook itself in a cloud of drops. A dog.

"She saved your life," the old man said.

"Beech!"

The dog lunged at her and began licking her face. She shrieked with joy and hugged the animal.

"You know my great-nephew's dog?" the old man asked.

Something hard had come into his voice. He leaned closer to her, screwing up his eyes as if he had trouble seeing her clearly. She'd offended him. Maybe he'd throw her back into the sea. Beech licked her nose.

Then the man did something frightening. His head lolled back and his eyes seemed to roll up into his skull. She clutched the dog.

Whatever had just happened didn't last long. His eyes came back to their proper place and he looked at her for a moment, saying nothing.

"I – I'm Lucia Plautina," she said in a small voice. My mother's name is Antonia Plautina. We live in that house –"

He picked up the oars and started rowing. The boat fought the rolling sea, turning and heading in to shore.

Tiber stood on the dock, and Niko was with him. They were both frowning. They grabbed the rope the old man threw to them and pulled the boat in till it bumped against the wood, then fastened it. Niko reached down and lifted her, crooning into her ear that she was safe now and that everything was all right. The old man and the dog stayed in the boat.

"Arto," Tiber said. He looked as if he was going to say something, but he shut his mouth.

The old man who'd rescued her spoke words in a language she didn't understand, but she saw from Tiber's face that he'd understood, and he didn't like it.

CHAPTER THIRTEEN

"SULIS WAS KIND TO THIS ONE," Breca's uncle said in the Old Tongue. "This child's children shall inherit your kingdom."

Angered, Togidubnus turned his back on the old man in the fishing boat and strode away. The Druid's prophesying was unwelcome. The "kingdom" belonged to whoever the Council of Elders elected – and he intended for that to be Amminus, when the boy was old enough. The emperor had taken a lot away from him, but he couldn't take that. Not now, since Boudicca's uprising had shown how easily the tribes could be stirred up against Rome. The days when Julius Caesar could crush the tribes of Gaul with a couple of legions were long gone.

The wind was cold enough for snow, though it was far too early for that. He wished he'd stopped to grab a cloak when he'd realized the child was missing. A line of crows, breast feathers fluttering in the wind, cawed at him from the roof of the colonnade. They were clever birds, smart enough to make fun of events humans found important. Some of the old people believed their presence on the roof was a bad omen for a household, but he'd never believed tales like that.

Gallus came out of the house. The old legionary hadn't returned from Noviomagus until well into the evening of the next day; then he'd come back reeling like a drunken pig. Gallus needed something to occupy his time. He'd taken the old man away from his life as a peddler on the streets of Rome and what had he offered in its place? Idleness. Doing nothing was not good for any man.

"Two men to see you, " Gallus said.. "They seem to think you want to build something?"

"A temple."

He'd been prepared for arguments with the Council of Elders, the exchange of favors, threats, bribes both open and subtle. But they'd put up little opposition in the days since his visit. What did their approval mean? Could he trust it?

Gallus laughed. "Little Fox building a temple! To Bacchus, I hope?"

In the black mood he was in this morning, he found this irritating. But a thought occurred to him. "When you were with the Fourteenth Gemina, did you have much experience building?"

"You know right well we did! We built roads and walls and forts for Vespasian. More than we fought, we built. Why're you bringing that up now?"

"I might need your good sense as my overseer."

"You want me to build a temple in Noviomagus?" Gallus sounded skeptical.

"I'll draw up the plans. I'd want you to be in charge of construction. Acquiring the materials. Hiring the men. Seeing to it that they give an honest day's work."

"You're serious about this temple."

"Yes." Something tightened in his chest and he didn't want to talk about it. But he'd known Gallus a long time; the Roman was probably the only friend he had. "I'm building a temple to Neptune and Minerva. For Breca."

"I can do it," Gallus clapped Togidubnus on the shoulder. "You got a bad roll of the dice, Little Fox. But a warrior plays it."

* * *

The elder of the two men who were waiting for him in the small room he used as an audience chamber had obviously worked so long with clay that the white dust had seeped into his pores. The skin of his hands and face was a chalky grey, giving him a corpse-like appearance. The younger one resembled an ox, broad-shouldered, heavily muscled and red-faced. Their presence filled the cold room with a faint odor of brick dust. Both men ducked their heads respectfully as Togidubnus entered.

He got straight to the point, asking in the Old Tongue. "How much

A VILLA FAR FROM ROME

experience have you had building such a large structure as this one will be?"

"I built the temple to Sulis Minerva in Aquaesulis," the older one said.

"You're a long way from home."

The man shrugged. "My wife is Regni. So is this lad – my son."

"This temple will honor Sulis too."

"You have a drawing of what you want me to build?"

"Rough sketches for now, but I'll have more details within the week. I know what I want." He gestured to Gallus and switched to Latin. "This man has experience building for the Emperor Vespasian. He'll oversee the work for me."

The builder answered in heavily accented Latin, "And who shall see we get paid for this?"

"The Council of Elders and I will share the cost."

He looked ahead to the day when Amminus's schooling in Rome came to an end; once the boy was safely home, he'd petition Nero to undo what he'd done that night of the drunken feast and take Antonia back. He made a silent vow that the first ceremony to take place in this new temple he was building would be dedicated to the reunion of his family.

"How long do you expect this will take?" Gallus asked.

"Give me the sketches," the builder said. "Then we'll know. We'll start to lay the foundation right away. After that, the gods will decide by whatever weather they send."

* * *

He'd just left the audience chamber when he heard the clatter of horse hooves on the gravel path that veered off the Roman road to cross his land. The last light of day had just about faded from the sky, and the full moon was rising, half revealed in scudding clouds. He couldn't imagine why anyone would be riding away from the city this late in the day. Nor were there any boats in port right now. Whoever the riders were – it sounded like more than one horse – they were coming here. He waited, listening to the sound of a pair of barn owls in the beech trees behind the house.

The two riders, silhouettes against the twilit sky, were obviously

Roman. One of them had a crest of horse hair jutting above his helmet, a fashion among the troops that was fading in Rome. He wore a heavy cloak over his shoulders, and a sword, worn on his left, gleamed in the moonlight. The centurion, Marcus Favonius. Wearing metal greaves on his shins. Not here on a social visit. As used to Romans and their way of life as he was, he still felt a prickle of apprehension at the sight of armed warriors. Whatever it was, this was not going to be good news.

"Tiberius!" The centurion hailed him as the horses reached the colonnade.

"Marcus Favonius, welcome. What brings you to my house so late?"

"Serious business," the centurion said, dismounting. "A cold evening! A cup of good wine would be welcome before we leave."

Two young servants hesitated in the shadow of the columns. Like all boys, they were curious about the late-arriving visitors. He beckoned to one of them.

"Hold the horses." To the other he said, "Fetch wine and cups and set them in the dining hall."

The second rider dismounted, a young tribune with his sword on the right hip as military custom dictated for his status. Togidubnus didn't recognize him. Favonius, like most Romans, was shorter than Togidubnus once he'd removed his helmet, but the tribune was shorter still. He indicated the Romans should precede him inside; the servant was setting cups on the table. The aroma of roast meat drifted in from the kitchen where the cook prepared a light supper.

The centurion waited till his cup was filled, raised it, and nodding a quick toast to Togidubnus, drank it down. He lifted his own cup and returned the toast. The younger Roman, like most tribunes obviously more aristocratic than his superior officer – one of the oddities of Roman military structure he'd never totally understood – glanced around the small, sparsely furnished hall with barely disguised disdain, but made no comment. At some point, the centurion named his tribune, Didius Octavius, but the man made little attempt to join the conversation.

He waited, his sense of impending trouble driving away his earlier hunger. These men represented military authority in Noviomagus, he civil.

A VILLA FAR FROM ROME

But he had no illusions which of them backed up that authority with overwhelming might.

"Wine warms the blood, my friend," Favonius said. "We'll need that before the night is done."

"What great business brings you here?"

"Gracila reminded me you're a king now, thanks to the emperor. And a king is just what I need to settle something that looks as if it might grow into a real problem."

"A problem the legion can't solve? Surely not."

"There you're wrong. Of course we could wipe the troublemakers out. The men would probably enjoy that! But I think Rome is better served when potential rebellions are dealt with by those who represent the very cause the troublemakers are agitating for."

He wasn't certain he'd followed that argument. "Who are rebelling? And why?"

The tribune made a derisive sound, covering it by raising his cup again when his superior frowned. In the silence that followed, Togidubnus was aware of a chill that wine couldn't dispel.

"Not necessarily Regni," the centurion said.. "That remains to be determined. I have word that one of Boudicca's captains escaped that final battle and is here in your territory, stirring the tribes to seek vengeance. I'm told he claims you're her relative."

"A distant relative," he said, controlling his rising anger. "I'll remind you that I fought with the Second Augusta against Boudicca –"

"No one's questioning your loyalty! In many ways, you're more Roman than I am. I never spent time at the court of the emperor as a young boy! But I'm laying out the reasons why we need you to accompany us tonight and calm these hotheads down."

"Tiberius," a voice said behind him. "I didn't know we had guests."

Antonia stood in the doorway, wrapped in a loose white sleeping robe, her hair free and flowing over her shoulders. He was suddenly aware of the way her small breasts pushed against the thin fabric. One of the servants hovered nervously behind her.

The centurion and the tribune stood up from the table.

"Have you instructed the servants to bring food, Tiberius?" she asked.

He noticed that she didn't take her eyes off the centurion, and Marcus for his part preened under her gaze. His wife. His house –

The recognition came with the instant realization that there was nothing he could do about it. The wine turned sour in his stomach.

"Thank you, Lady, but we took our meal earlier," Favonius said.

"But surely, you'll take more wine?"

"Unfortunately, Lady, not tonight."

He heard the note of regret in the centurion's voice, watched where the man's eyes went. A hawk eyeing a songbird.

" I hope we'll find another occasion?" she said demurely.

"I'm sure we will!"

She smiled at him, lowering her lashes. "I wouldn't want to delay you on your official business."

"Lucky man," Favonius said when she'd left the room. "You've got a pretty piece there!"

All the emotions of the last few days boiled up in him till he felt like striking out in his rage. Attacking the centurion was not an option, not if he wanted to live. This was how the fox must feel, trapped by the hunters. He would bide his time.

CHAPTER FOURTEEN

"I'VE PREPARED A LETTER FOR THE EMPEROR," Antonia said. "Will you take it to the dock and find a courier for it?"

Nikolaos looked up from the writing tablet he was using to teach Lucia her letters. "Do you think that's wise?"

The sky was dark with rain clouds, filling the room with cold shadows. The weather had been wintry for the past week and she was sick of it. She was getting to the point that she couldn't keep her mind on anything. It kept tumbling around from thought to thought.

"Ma," Lucia said. "Look. I can write my name."

The steady drumbeat of rain on the roof, the sound of the run-off cascading down into the water course that carried it away, the drip-drip-drip of leaks in this room or that. And the only rooms that were warm were the bath chamber and Tiberius's own bed chamber. She couldn't very well spend her days in either of them.

"Why shouldn't it be wise? It's much too cold here. We need a way to better heat the house. All I'm asking is a little money to do that."

"Have you spoken to your husband about this?"

She folded her arms and stared at him. He held her gaze until she looked away.

"Imagine having to wrap oneself in musty old blankets in one's own house to stay warm! This place is horrible. It's too small. The roof leaks. The hypocaust doesn't work properly. Everything stays wet, all the time. And I found mildew on the blankets."

Seeing the comfortable villa Gracila lived in with her family had been the impetus to writing the letter. Why should she suffer anything less than a centurion's family had?

Niko said, "It's a risk, reminding Caesar we still exist."

"I hate this place! And my child almost drowned here."

The Greek shook his head.

"But Niko – he doesn't know how bad things are here. He wouldn't want the child to suffer, surely? What harm does it do to tell him the dreadful situation we're in, so very, very far away from Rome?"

He took up the stylus and drew another letter for Lucia to copy. "Unwise."

"If you will just stop playing with Lucia –"

"We're not playing, Ma," Lucia said. "I'm learning to make the letters for my name. See?"

She laid the letter she'd been carrying on the table and put her hand on her daughter's hair, full of tangles. She combed it with her fingers. Her thoughts slid away from the task. Marcus, the centurion's name was Marcus Favonius. He was tall – almost as tall as Tiberius – and younger, too. Her heart pounded at the thought. She was so full of contradictory thoughts these days! She wanted to go home. She wanted to stay and learn more about the centurion. The centurion had a woman who'd been kind to her. The house was too small and cold to make staying attractive. It was the terrible climate affecting her, she was certain of it.

She remembered how the centurion's eyes had glittered in the lamplight when he spoke to her. He hadn't shifted his gaze away but stared at her boldly till she felt weak. He'd promised to come back. But he already had a woman. Her body felt oddly hollow, as if it didn't belong to her.

"I don't advise it," Niko said. "The emperor's a treacherous man."

"You never tire of telling me! But I didn't ask for something he can't give me right now. All I want is a little money to make some improvements here."

So many improvements would have to be made before this cold place was livable. But Tiberius was spending his money on a temple. If the roof was repaired, and the house warmer, then she could invite guests from Noviomagus.

"Have you considered your husband's wishes?"

"My father did the world a great disservice when he freed you!"

A VILLA FAR FROM ROME

Niko smiled.

"Will the emperor come to live with us?" Lucia asked.

"Of course not. And don't interrupt your elders!"

She hoped Nero was vain enough to respond to the flattery she'd sprinkled all through her letter. *Her hair is so golden and curly, like her illustrious father's!*

"Please, Niko. Take the letter to the port for me and pay a courier."

He set aside the stylus and the writing tablet he and Lucia had been using and picked up her letter. She'd folded the thin sheets, wrapping them in linen, then in soft leather for protection, tying the letter securely with a thong and sealing it with wax and her own seal, protection against the hazards of the journey and prying eyes.

Cold air, heavy as a blanket with the smell of earth and wet grass, flowed into the room when he opened the door. She shivered. A memory from childhood swept over her – warm rain spattering the hillside, her youngest brother, Titus, stomping through puddles, herself torn between the urge to join him and wanting to be the serious older sister, her next oldest brother, Valentinus, laughing at them both. She'd been eight years old at the time. What wouldn't she give to go back to those days?

* * *

Lucia filled her mouth with the overflowing spoon, a small one that the Regni cook indicated once belonged to Tiberius's sons. Antonia had never thought much about her husband having children of his own, though she vaguely remembered seeing a boy on the dock the night they'd arrived.

Lucia was always hungry. Growing fast, Niko said. She couldn't remember much about how fast or slow she'd grown in her own childhood. After the events that followed the ill-fated chariot races and banquet in Pyrgi, there'd been no more time for such childish concerns. She'd scarcely begun her monthly bleeding when she'd conceived the child; she'd had to grow into an adult almost overnight.

It was dark again – The days were so short this far north – and she had the house to herself. The centurion had taken Tiberius with them yesterday, and Gallus – who didn't like her – went up to Noviomagus every day. Niko would probably use the excuse of his errand to wander around the port. The Greek liked to learn things; he made a good tutor for Lucia.

The cook – she'd learned everybody called her Old Nev – slopped more porridge into the bowl. Antonia watched her work for a while. The kitchen, though primitive by Roman standards, was well-stocked. Partridges and hares were hung to cure in an attached cool room, with a wheel of cheese – a local variety and surprisingly tasty once she was used to the sharp flavor, and eggs also, baskets of rosy apples, freshly picked and stored for the coming winter. A young boy brought fish and oysters and mushrooms every morning. Olive oil imported from Gaul and malt vinegar made in the nearby village, onions and garlic, bunches of herbs hanging from the rafters – thyme and marjoram, sage, a clutch of laurel. She didn't lack for food here in the outpost of the empire, though the preparation was uninspired and she must teach the servants to do better. Maybe the young girl Tiberius had employed to come every day to help Old Nev would be easier to teach than the cook herself.

She should find something to occupy her mind while she waited for the emperor to summon her back home. Niko was right; it might take a long time before that happened. She could teach the Regni servants to cook properly, but that wouldn't be enough to take up the hours. There was plenty of open land around the house; she could organize a garden, grow her own herbs and vegetables. Would olives grow here? Or grapes?

She stood by the door, looking over the dark garden. Night here was so different from night at home where it was always warm, full of comforting sounds of nightbirds. She missed the cicadas' clicking song in the vineyard.

Old Nev straightened from the table, wiping her hands on her coarse-woven skirt. How old was the woman? She found it hard to read barbarian faces. There was no silver in the woman's hair yet, but her expression was bitter; she stared at Antonia, her mouth pulled into a thin line. She spoke a few words in what passed for language among the Britanni, then gestured with her hands, indicating the cooking hearth, mimed sweeping the kitchen, frowned at Antonia, willing her to understand.

A VILLA FAR FROM ROME

"Old Nev says what do you want her to do?" Lucia said, porridge dribbling out of her mouth as she spoke.

Astonished, she stared at her child. "How do you know that?"

Lucia busied herself with the bowl that was already scraped clean. "I don't know how, Ma. I just do."

Old Nev said something else to Lucia, and the child nodded, slipped down from her place at table and went out of the kitchen.

Niko would've hauled her back and made her ask her mother's permission. For a moment, she saw the changes living in this wild place would bring to all of them.

It was a frightening vision.

CHAPTER FIFTEEN

A HEAVY DRIFT OF LEAVES MUFFLED THE HORSES' HOOVES as they passed under a stand of mixed beech and young oaks. The full moon drifted in and out of the racing clouds and their breath trailed behind them. They rode fast, the centurion and his tribune hardly speaking. Togidubnus still didn't know where they were headed. They followed the Roman road west out of Noviomagus, and for a moment he feared they were going to the island in the marsh where Breca's family lived.

He thought of the old Druid's prophecy. So many hazards in his path to hold the chieftainship for his oldest son; so many ways for it not to happen.

As they reached the ford where he'd waited for the tide to turn a few days ago, they veered off the road and took a narrow track that headed up to the Downs, the chalk hills that rose behind Noviomagus. An owl hooted in darkness above his head.

"I sent men on ahead," Marcus Favonius said suddenly, slowing so his horse was abreast of Stormfellow. The horses cantered together, breath steaming. "Mars willing, there won't be Roman blood spilled tonight."

He sensed he was being drawn into some kind of trap where there would be no right action. Even a minor uprising, a beer fueled argument started by fools that inconvenienced the Roman settlers was potentially dangerous for a man with a foot in both camps. The vision he'd taken to Rome, weeks ago, of the tribes of Britannia thriving in peace under Roman rule was like the idle dreams of a callow youth.

Favonius pulled ahead again, kicking his horse to go faster, heading north and west. Far away, a wolf howled and was answered by another.

A VILLA FAR FROM ROME

Stormfellow's sides heaved, making heavy going of the way that rose beneath them; the old warhorse was no longer capable of such extended exertion. His nose filled with the smell of the horse and the wet earth under its hooves. After a while, he could see the ridge of a hill outlined against the unsteady moonlight. There was no settlement that he knew of up here on this part of the Downs. A shepherd's hut, maybe, or a tumbledown stone pigsty long abandoned. Or the smooth, turf-covered mounds that marked the funeral barrows of the Ancient Ones, older than his own people.

Above him in the crowded winter sky, Cernunnos blazed, the horned hunter of his people's tradition. When he was a young man first paying court to Breca, Arto had told him Cernunnos was his patron. Though he'd outgrown his childhood allegiance to the Celtic pantheon, no Roman god had ever been able to quite vanquish the hunter in his affection

His heart lurched. Somewhere up here on the hilltops there was a place the Druids held sacred, a grove of old oaks. And Yule was fast approaching with its own ceremonies and observances. The gods forbid Favonius was heading for the sacred grove! The Romans tolerated Celtic religious practice in their empire, mostly, he'd decided, because they didn't take their own gods seriously. But he knew how fine the line that practitioners of the old ways walked in this occupied Britannia.

They were very close to the boundary of his territory. Over the ridge lay the land of the Belgae, a tribe no bigger than his own, but no friend either, only an uneasy ally. One that had sided with the Iceni and the Trinovantes and lost when the Second Augusta crushed Boudicca's revolt.

The sacred grove lay somewhere ahead. Now he smelled wood smoke and saw the pale yellow flicker of flames ahead on the ridge. And men, clumped around it, huddling in their cloaks. Coming closer, he saw it was just an ordinary cookfire. Beyond it, a small ruined hut. Firelight struck a gleam from an unsheathed gladius. The men were legionaries, not Druids. Relieved he let out breath in a *whuff*.

The men looked up as their centurion rode into the circle of the firelight.

SHEILA FINCH

Just out of the firelight's reach, Togidubnus saw a man slumped against a tree trunk to which he'd been tied. The tribune, Didius, dismounted and strode over. Drawing his gladius, he lifted the man's chin with its tip so the light revealed his features.

"Do you know this man?" Favonius asked. He leaned in the saddle to watch Togidubnus's face.

He nudged Stormfellow forward. The prisoner was filthy, bedraggled as though he'd crawled through mud, his tunic torn and one shoe lost.

"Name yourself, Spy!" the tribune said.

The man looked up his expression sullen. "Ask him!" He tipped his head toward Togidubnus.

He shook his head. *Not Regni.* "I don't know him."

"Tarvos!" the man said. "Son of Hamesus."

Memory blossomed at the sound of the man's voice. The great queen – sorely mistreated. His own ancestors had come from the same land. *A distant relative.* Yes. But Boudicca had become an outlaw. Like his father and grandfather, he understood the wisdom of not opposing Rome. He remembered the clash and thunder of battle, the smell of horse sweat and horse shit, spilled blood, vomit – bodies of Roman and Iceni alike ground into the mud under the war-chariots' wheels. And he saw in memory this man's face, on the wrong side in the battle.

"How did you get away?"

"Not like a traitor, in triumph with our Roman masters!"

The tribune struck the prisoner hard across the mouth. Blood flowed.

He turned to the centurion. "What's the charge against this man?"

"We received word he was gathering a band of malcontents here to plan an assault on the garrison in Noviomagus."

"He's yours. Take him in."

"He's a Celt. I'm giving him over to you," the centurion said. "Examine the matter further and deal with him as you find just."

Planning to attack the garrison was treason. If he dealt leniently with the prisoner, he'd betray the Romans. If he dealt Roman justice on the man, he'd make mortal enemies out of the Belgae and probably his own tribe, too. The legion held the power; Favonius didn't need to demonstrate it. The centurion had arranged for him to walk into a trap.

"It's a Roman matter. You don't need me."

"The prisoner's a Belgae princeling," the centurion said. "You're the local power that should be taking care of stability in the region."

Why would Favonius do this? He remembered a warning his father had given him long ago, *No friendships survive a Roman agenda.*

The centurion smiled. "The emperor made you king, after all."

CHAPTER SIXTEEN

"THIS LETTER CAME FOR YOU," Niko said, holding out the thin tablet.

Antonia shook her hair free of the band she'd used to contain it while she surveyed the garden – such as it was. Yesterday's cold rain had beaten down the few plants she recognized, the ones whose late blooms she'd hoped to bring inside to enjoy. She held her hand out for the letter. Far too soon for an answer from Rome. Who would've written to her?

"The messenger brought it down from Noviomagus," Niko added.

She opened it. The handwriting was spidery, hesitant, as if its maker was not used to the work of putting ideas down on a tablet. Not a male hand. She tasted disappointment and relief together that the letter had not come from the centurion. That would be a dangerous game and she didn't know if she was ready to play it.

And not a pretty cursive, either, so not written by someone's household scribe. The spiky smell of the carbon mixed with gum arabic in the ink prickled her nose. She took the letter over to the couch and sat down. The message was brief.

To my dear friend Antonia Plautina, from an admiring and solicitous Gracila Favonia. Do visit this afternoon! Bring the child. We shall indulge ourselves in talk enjoyable to women!

The centurion's woman. Would he be there? The possibility made her heart race.

Tiberius had come home in the middle of the night after being gone a whole day. The clatter of horse hooves on the gravel path and harsh voices raised outside had roused her from sleep. He was either still sleeping or he'd gone away again. In any case, she didn't need his permission to go to

A VILLA FAR FROM ROME

Noviomagus.

"See to it that Lucia wears a clean tunic." She rose from the couch.

Niko looked at her steadily but didn't move. One of these days she'd have to find a nurse for her daughter. The Greek grew rebellious in the role, ever since she'd berated him for allowing the child to go out alone and nearly drown herself. But the native women didn't seem to want to work in Tiberius's house any more. They were more stubborn about it than the men. She suspected it had to do with the wife who'd been displaced. That was unfair, because it wasn't her doing. She'd have been content if the woman had remained, a kind of older relative, or even friend. It would be pleasant to have a friend.

"Oh, I'll do it myself!"

"Your daughter is hurting too," he said. "You should think about that."

* * *

Lucia was excited at the prospect of riding in front of her mother on Tiberius's sturdy little mare, Snowmark. For once, she didn't fidget as Antonia dressed her and combed her hair.

Unable to deal with Niko's stubborn refusal to continue in the role she'd assigned him, Antonia had found a young Regni boy cleaning the stable to accompany them. No Roman woman would go into town unaccompanied! The servant situation bothered her; it was almost as bad as the last days at the family estate in Pyrgi when everyone had been freed or let go.

Niko came back from the stable, leading the mare. He was frowning about something.

"What is it?"

"There's a door beside the main one into the stable. I think it leads to a storage chamber for hay or oats. It usually stands wide open. Today it's closed and heavily barred on the outside."

"What's that to me?"

He shrugged. "Perhaps we have a guest?"

"Fine way to treat a guest!" She allowed him to boost her up onto the mare.

She didn't want to be any more involved in the intrigues and strategies of her husband's life than she was forced to be. He handed Lucia up to her, and she kicked the mare lightly to move her forward. The Regni youth walked beside them.

A strong breeze blew in from the southwest today, carrying the sharp scent of the sea. The sky was mostly blue with patches of cloud, yet the air carried a deep wintry chill. She was glad for the good cloaks of Britanni wool Niko had purchased in Noviomagus.

She glanced at the fields stretching away from the house, seeing mud-speckled shapes of cattle, a lone Britanni, his own red-checked cloak billowing in the wind, minding the herd. They owned cows, Tiberius said, and apple and pear orchards, as well as many fields, fallow now, that would be planted with crops again in the spring. So they were her cattle too. She hoped no one would ever expect her to know what to do about them. Her father had bred horses, nothing as lowly as cows.

"That way, Mater," Lucia said. "Go that way. See the dolphins."

"Not today. We're making a visit."

"I want to see the dolphins."

"Hush! Maybe there'll be other children for you to play with."

"Do they have a dog?"

"What're you talking about?"

"Catuarus has a dog. And Beech pulled me out of the water."

"Catuarus?" She stumbled over the word. "What a dreadful name!"

"Not a dreadful name! Catuarus is my friend."

"Today you'll meet *Roman* children." She emphasized the word. It would be difficult bringing up a child to be Roman so far from Rome. Niko would have to continue helping! At least Greeks were civilized.

Men carrying heavy loads on their shoulders, others driving donkey carts, walked the road that led from the port up to Noviomagus. The men waved and Lucia waved back. They made the rest of the short journey in silence.

Her spirits rose as they passed through the south gate. Noviomagus

A VILLA FAR FROM ROME

was a small town, not that much larger than Pyrgi, but the buildings were recognizably Roman. She saw a group of legionaries marching down one street, red cloaks fluttering in the cool breeze. No sign of the centurion. She was annoyed with herself for these thoughts about the centurion, but Tiberius was old enough to be her father, and dull, and the prospect of year after year with him was frightening.

The youth led the horse to the centurion's house.

Gracila was delighted to see them, embracing them both as soon as they dismounted, drawing them through the atrium to an inner room.

"You must be hungry!" She clapped her hands to summon a slave and ordered food. "And this is the little girl?" She tilted Lucia's chin up to study the child's face. "Beautiful! Such eyes! Such golden curls– "

Gracila stopped suddenly and glanced at Antonia.

Of course she would've heard the gossip. Antonia had been here long enough to know that chatter about the affairs of others, especially those in high places, was just as rife in Noviomagus as it was in Rome. Anybody who didn't suspect whose daughter Lucia was had to be blind and deaf. It was a small matter. She didn't have to care about their opinion.

"You poor child," Gracila said. She took Antonia into her arms.

Gracila smelled of the little imported eastern lily, a perfume she remembered her mother had once worn. There were tiny lines at the corner of her eyes, again like her mother. Lines also bracketed Gracila's lips as if the mouth had been drawn down by sadness many times; her mother had those too. The woman was a courtesan – even with her sheltered childhood she could recognize that! – but Antonia clung to Gracila, wracked by an urgent homesickness.

Two children entered the room, the toddler she'd seen on her first visit and a boy about Lucia's age. They stood uncertainly in the doorway. A dark-skinned slave girl with a tray of dainty foods, small biscuits, olives and figs, and a pitcher of wine, hesitated behind them.

"This is Lucia," Gracila said to the little boy. "Caelius, take her and show her your animals."

The boy held out his hand, and Lucia went away with them.

"Delamira, take the baby with you," Gracila said, and the slave girl carried the toddler away.

"Now, we'll enjoy the food, and we'll talk."

"I envy you. You have so many servants."

"Oh! That's an illusion. I had to find a new girl when the previous one got sick and died of something I hadn't heard of before. It's quite strange. Marcus says some new legionaries joined the Augusta from Palestine and they were sick with the same thing when they got here. I hope the gods aren't punishing us for something! But enough about servants and soldiers." She drew Antonia over to a couch, not letting go of her hand.

"It's very kind of you."

"Nonsense. I need company or I shall go mad in this dreary climate. And it's good for my son to practice his manners. His father takes him to be with the army too much." She stopped and gazed at Antonia. "My dear, you're so far from home, but don't weep."

"You're far from home too."

"Tut! I'm older and I'm used to it. Far better than following the legion around in the north where the tribes are ferocious and it rains *all* the time! We're happy to be left in peace in this backwater – at least, I am. Marcus would probably prefer action, if you asked him. It's not easy to be at the mercy of the emperor's will. But now you've made your eyes red. First eat. I'll have the girl bring my cosmetics and we'll amuse ourselves."

Somehow, she managed a few bites of food, a few sips of wine while Gracila chattered on. It was comforting to let the older woman steer the conversation. The tensions and unhappiness of the past weeks dropped away and she relaxed. Responding to Gracila's questions, she told stories of her parents and the villa in Pyrgi, the grapevines on the hillside above the sea, the funny escapades of her brothers, how they swam like the fish and raced horses like the wind. But that reminded her of the fine stadium her father built the year the emperor came to take part in the horse races, and she was silent again.

Gracila patted her cheek and stood up. "Time to play!"

She went to the door where another slave hovered and spoke in a low tone. Gracila was soft and round as a pillow, but her movements were lithe and smooth as befitted her name. The girl returned with a tray full of marble pots, jars made of glass and alabaster, and bowls of scented water.

"Come," Gracila said. "Sit here in the light and hold this mirror." She indicated a bench by the window and handed Antonia a good quality polished bronze mirror with mother-of-pearl inlay on the back. She picked up a small brush that nestled between two jars, one of rosy cream, the other with a more golden hue like summer sun on wheat. "Now, which shall we use?"

She had never used anything other than a very light oil of the olive's first pressing to keep her skin smooth and give it a faint sheen. Her father had forbidden anything more showy. Whether this was because he'd thought her still too young, or because he didn't want her drawing attention to herself in her disgraced state, she didn't know. A little of both. She had no idea what most of the sweet smelling cosmetics were for.

But yes, she did know what they were for! They were meant to attract a man. Her heart pounded again.

"I shall choose for you." Gracila tipped Antonia's face back turning it a little from side to side, considering.

Gracila set about mixing elements, then stroked cream into Antonia's cheeks and up to her brow, finally dusting a fine powder over them. The cosmetics filled the room with the thick scent of roses and lavender and the more delicate scent of lilies of the valley. She picked up a boxwood comb set with tortoiseshell and teased Antonia's hair into curls around her finger using a thicker cream and arranged them on her brow.

"I had no idea there were so many things to choose from." Antonia breathed deeply of the flowery scents.

"This is just a selection, suitable for your young colors."

"How do you know to do all this?" She watched her appearance change in the bronze mirror that added its own rosy gold hue to her reflection.

"When I was younger, I was an entertainer – for lack of a better word

– and my city was built on fantasies. A woman learns fast in a place like Pompeii."

"Tell me what it was like to be in Pompeii."

"Oh, the living was fine! Streets of grand houses, and shops filled with everything a heart could wish for. The smell of bread baking from the shops, and meat roasting on spits. Beautiful people passing up and down the streets, and the sea sparkling where the streets ended. Musicians and jugglers and everyone enjoying all that the gods give us. I was born there, you know. My mother was an entertainer before I was born, but I never knew my father. Pompeii was a wonderful place to be a child!"

"Did you – I mean –" She felt her cheeks flaming. She wanted to ask *Did you meet him there?* But that would be a terrible violation of manners, considering what Gracila had just said.

"Yes, my dear," Gracila said gently. "Like everybody else with a couple of gold coins to rub together, the legions' best came to Pompeii to enjoy their free time."

Embarrassed, she tried to steer the conversation away from the quicksand it had stumbled into. "You're very good with the cosmetics!"

Gracila dabbed a spot of color on Antonia's lips. "When you aim to keep a young eagle like Marcus in the nest, you don't forget the little tricks." Gracila's face passed into shadow.

She realized in that moment that Gracila must be older than her centurion. "I'm sorry. I shouldn't have asked."

"I've embarrassed you." Gracila set the cosmetics aside and took both of Antonia's hands in hers. "What a poor hostess I am."

"Think nothing of it." Antonia admired her transformation in the bronze mirror.

"Tell me, have you never painted your face before?" Gracila lifted an eyebrow. "Surely your mother –"

"My father wouldn't allow it."

"Poor child!"

"He was very stern. Especially after –"

Gracila stroked her arm gently. "And you were very young, from the age of your daughter."

A VILLA FAR FROM ROME

"Twelve," she said. The word sounded to her ears like a stone dropping into a pool.

Gracila took both her hands in her own. They were both silent for a while.

"I should go," she said. "It'll soon be dark. Night comes so quickly, now that summer has passed!"

Gracila let go of her hands. "Take these cosmetics with you."

As if she'd been listening for her cue at the door, the dark slave girl appeared with Lucia by the hand and the older boy behind her.

"Ma," Lucia announced, breaking free of the girl's hand. "Caelius has a pony!"

"She is so taken by animals," she said, glad for a change of subject.

Gracila smiled. "You must come again and bring her so she can ride."

"I hope we will! And you must visit our poor little house."

"Gladly!" Gracila said.

Outside on the twilit street, the Regni boy held Snowmark's reins. They stood awkwardly together in the vestibule for a moment.

"Think of me as a friend." Gracila bent to kiss Antonia's freshly painted cheek.

"Thank you," she whispered. "I need a friend."

CHAPTER SEVENTEEN

HE SENT THE STABLE BOY TO FETCH A MILKING STOOL and waited in the raw cold outside the storage shed, now doing duty as a prison. The morning sounds of Snowmark and Stormfellow moving about in their straw in the next-door stable comforted him with their familiarity. He wasn't looking forward to a fourth day of wrangling with his prisoner, an exercise that would probably yield as little outcome as the previous visits.

Thinking over the futility of that first visit and the subsequent ones, he despaired of finding a solution that would appease both the Belgae and the Romans and not bring trouble on himself. He didn't have a lot of experience with prisoners; either he'd killed on the battlefield, or the Romans had taken those they wanted as hostages. This situation didn't offer such clear-cut choices. The charge of intent to create rebellion was probably trumped up, but it didn't matter.

The boy returned. He was the same age as his own son, Amminus; they'd been friends. He didn't remember the lad's name; he'd always relied on Breca for things like that.

He took the stool. "Remember to empty the pisspot today."

"He threw it at me yesterday!" the boy protested.

"We're not savages. We don't return ugliness for ugliness."

The boy scowled and pushed up the heavy bar that fastened the door. Togidubnus went inside.

He found his prisoner slumped on the hut's one stool, a chain around his ankle and fastened to a link on the wall, an empty bowl that had probably contained goat's milk on the floor by his feet, and a stinking pisspot in one corner. One window, high up, admitted a little light. The Belgi was short, dark haired and sallow skinned; like many Celtic males, he'd grown his mustache into a grey-brown waterfall that signified a

A VILLA FAR FROM ROME

warrior. The two tribes were not close relatives – and certainly not friends – but in the blood they were both Celts. Tarvos had fought with Boudicca, and the Romans would not forgive that even if Togidubnus was inclined to be lenient.

He set the second stool out of range of the captive and sat. "Talk. Give me a reason why I shouldn't have you killed."

"You aren't my tribe's chief."

"Perhaps not. But I'm your captor."

The man spat, narrowly missing his boot. "I don't make deals with traitors."

"We're at peace with Rome. The queen was a rebel. You were on the wrong side."

"My people will never be at peace with these invaders who occupy our land."

"Better make your peace with them. We have as much to gain from them as they have from us."

"Maybe they'll make me a *king* too?" The man's eyes glittered angrily in the light from the high window. "Kill me and be done with it. That's what your Roman masters want."

"It's not what I want. Help me resolve this problem."

The prisoner turned his face away in silence.

He hadn't really expected to break the impasse so easily. He was surprised that the Belgae hadn't learned of the capture of one of their princelings by now. Worse, that a neighboring chief was holding him. When that happened, the time for diplomatic solutions was gone. Pride and ambition would come into play, long-held jealousies and suspicions would surface, the peace between rivals would be shattered. And he had no doubt whatsoever that Marcus Favonius would bring the legion in and slaughter them all.

He went out of the shed and the boy secured the bar over the door.

He saddled Stormfellow himself. The wind was picking up and the air grew colder. He took the Roman road that led west toward Clausentum, leaving it where the track lead over the marsh to the land that was an island at high tide. Today it was ankle-deep in fog rising from the marshes.

* * *

Breca's uncle and her aunt, her mother's sister, had raised her when her own parents perished in a black fever that swept the countryside one winter long ago. She sat with the old Druid on cushions arranged around the fire in the center of the round house, spinning fibre from the mass of wool on a distaff. Firelight gleamed on the copper and silver torque around her neck and on her bracelets. He'd given them to her. Was that a good sign? He was hesitant to think it so. She glanced at him as he entered the house, then turned her eyes away.

He knew his presence was disturbing to them, but Regni traditions of hospitality over-ruled their distrust. They would hear him out, but whether they could help him was in doubt.

"Sit, Nephew," Breca's uncle said.

The house was warm from the central firepit, warmer than his own Roman house with its inadequate hypocaust. An obviously pregnant cat, fur mottled in the firelight, slept beside the pit. Finely woven wool tapestries covered the walls, some with elaborate embroidered hems in red and deep blue. Sleeping benches with heaped wool blankets followed the curve of the walls, and shelves above them stored pots and cooking vessels, some bronze, some ceramic with incised and burnished decoration. The house of Arto and Adraste was only a little bigger than others in the village, but its furnishings were better, befitting the high status of the Druid and his wife.

He glanced over at Breca and saw she'd been looking at him too. She looked away. This strangeness between them must not go on much longer. He tried to put his love for her into the look he sent her way.

The aunt came inside the house, her arms loaded with herbs she'd been collecting. She acknowledged his presence and brought him a cup of warm beer with honey. He was never quite at ease around her. Her name, Adraste, referred to an Old One, a war goddess that Boudicca herself had worshiped and to whom she'd sacrificed Roman prisoners. Sometimes, looking at the old aunt's fierce expression, he imagined the warrior queen's spirit inhabiting her. He'd always thought she'd be dangerous to offend;

now he wondered uneasily if he hadn't already offended by his ready adoption of Roman ways.

And Arto, named for the bear that roamed forests to the north, was a priest. If there were a solution to be found to his dilemma, it would be here – if they'd be willing to share it with him. He had no illusions about what they thought of his attempts to bring Roman ways to Celtic Britannia. But they were wise, and their counsel was more precious than gold.

Wind gusting over the roof sent a downdraft of wood smoke to fill the house. Arto coughed and Adraste offered him honeyed beer to ease his throat.

Catuarus was dispatched to bring more firewood. Togidubnus used the time to describe the events of the night on the Downs, between the land of the Regni and the land of the Belgae, where the Romans had captured a Belgae princeling who'd fought on Boudicca's side. He told of the days spent fruitlessly questioning the sullen captive. Telling the story in the Old Tongue lent it an almost bardlike, heroic quality, missing from the same story recited in Latin. Breca, he was heartened to notice, never took her eyes off him during the telling.

"The charge is a serious one," Arto said when he'd finished his telling. "Rome can't afford to turn a blind eye to rebellion. Why have they turned him over to you?"

"I've thought about that, Uncle, but I'm no closer to the answer."

The old Druid settled a heavy blanket woven in a green and blue plaid over his shoulders. His face was deeply lined in the play of firelight and shadow, but his eyes were sharp. "Obviously you can't kill him. That would invite war with the Belgae – something we haven't seen for two generations."

"He's unrepentant about his support of the queen. I suspect there are others among his people who are still sympathetic to that lost cause."

Arto shook his head. "The thunder of terrible events like that is heard for many generations. Who is to judge the rightness of the cause?"

He was uneasy with the question. The Druid didn't support him, fearing he was far too close a friend of Rome. The irony was that Rome thought he was too much a Celt.

"He wishes to die at your hands," Breca's aunt said suddenly.

"But why?"

"Tarvos is a minor princeling, second son of a second son," Adraste said. "He'll never gain power in the tribe. But he is a zealot, and a follower of the old ways. All that is left to give his people is his blood to water the seeds of war. And then he will pass through the veil of shadows into the spirit world, a hero."

Breca laid her spindle aside. "You have enemies among the Romans. You'll never be fully accepted as one of them, hard as you may try."

He gazed at her, the much-loved face showing new lines that only added to her beauty in his eyes. He said humbly, "What shall I do?"

"If Tarvos is a devout man – devout enough to lay down his life for his people," Arto said, "maybe there is a way."

The conversation stopped while Catuarus came in with logs for the fire, the dog at his heels. Soon the flames were leaping high again, the scent of burning pine wood filled the house, and his son sat leaning against his mother on the other side. Last year at this time, he remembered, his sons had been eagerly planning their part in the family's Yule celebrations in this very house. In his mind, he saw them dancing around the flaming log, laughing, their shoulders decked with oak leaves and holly berries. Now Amminus was far away. This year, the darkest day in the year would be echoed by the darkest day in his heart.

"You must celebrate Yuletide in the old way," the Druid said.

"I hadn't planned to!"

"Listen to my uncle's words, Togi," Breca said.

Her use of her pet name for him gave him hope. "I'll listen, my heart."

"You must celebrate Yule," Arto said. "If Tarvos is a guest in your house at that time, he can do you no harm, nor you him. That's the old way. Remember, he cannot refuse any gift the host gives him under the sacred mistletoe, including his pardon. In return, he must give you his oath of peace."

A VILLA FAR FROM ROME

"Whatever happens after that," Adraste added, "his blood won't be on your hands."

He hadn't followed the old traditions for many years, content to have them slowly fade away. But there was wisdom here; Tarvos was a traditional Celt, and this was a solution that might work. He wouldn't be forced to kill the man and thus make mortal enemies of the Belgae, and at the same time Tarvos would be bound by his oath not to make further war against the Romans. The thought of more war and bloodshed chilled him. Could he remember enough of the old customs to make this work? It wouldn't matter if he believed in them; it would be enough if Tarvos did.

"Rome doesn't care to interfere in Druid matters," Arto said.

"For now," Adraste added.

He stared at the old woman, wishing he could see what she saw of the future. Even he knew that Roman tolerance for the old ways wouldn't last for ever. That made his work even more crucial to the tribe that still hadn't fully accepted him as their king.

"Will you burn a Yule log?" Catuarus asked, his voice bubbling with excitement. "We'll come, won't we, Mother?"

Breca turned her eyes away and he knew not to push her. He might solve the problem of Tarvos that the centurion had set for him, but he couldn't solve the problem of Breca's estrangement until Amminus was safely home again.

His heart lifted a little when she rose to walk out with him. They stood by Stormfellow, stroking the horse to avoid looking at each other. The awkwardness of the moment felt like a wall between them. She sighed.

"You're doing what you think right, Togi. I understand that. Perhaps I'm wrong. Perhaps it's just my pride that stands in the way –"

"No, my heart, don't say that. You can never be wrong. It's just that I gave my word to the emperor to take care of Antonia. He gave his to take care of Amminus."

"And you trust this emperor?"

"I have no choice. I shouldn't have taken the boy to Rome. I thought

—"

She put her hands on his cheeks and drew his face towards her and kissed him. He held her close to his chest for a moment, breathing in her familiar scent. All would be well as long as he had Breca's love.

"You're a good man, Togi," she said, releasing him. "But even good men make poor decisions."

"Breca, I beg you to reconsider. Come back with me. We'll find a way. This other *marriage* – I hate to even say the word!– doesn't matter. It can't replace our vows."

"It comes from being raised by Druids." He heard the sadness in her voice. "But my honor doesn't permit me."

"I will never take the Roman girl to bed! I give you my oath." He was aware how desperate he must sound.

She smiled and stroked his cheek. "Do you think I doubted that?"

"Seven more months, my heart. Amminus will come home. I'll send the girl and her child away whether Nero wants them or not."

"We can be patient that long," she said.

CHAPTER EIGHTEEN

ANTONIA WAS SURPRISED WHEN TIBERIUS TOLD HER they were going to celebrate a Druid festival for the end of the year. Yule, he called it. He was always so eager to appear Roman! But whatever the day meant to him it would be a grand excuse to entertain. Tiberius didn't seem to want to discuss it further with her. Fine. She'd do her own planning without him and his long-faced doubts and hesitations. In the middle of this dark and depressing winter, it would be good to prepare a feast, call in musicians and invite friends. She started planning immediately. He hadn't given her much time.

She made two lists, one of household preparations that she'd give to the servants – Tiberius would need to persuade his servants to come back. Why couldn't he just order them to return? – and a second list of the guests. She walked along the colonnade to Tiberius's private room to find writing materials. He wouldn't be there. He'd gone up to Noviomagus again to watch them lay the foundations of the temple he was building before snow stopped the work. Just as well. She wasn't ready to discuss her plans with him yet; they would be her secret. Perhaps it would make him happy?

The first people she'd invite were Gracila and Marcus and their children.

The thought of Marcus in this house turned her bones to water.

Of course she'd do nothing to take him away from Gracila! But they weren't married – the law forbade a centurion from marrying. What harm would it do if she danced with him?

She had no idea how a Druid mid-winter festival was celebrated. Surely there'd be dancing? If not, she'd introduce the concept. What kind of musicians would she find among the barbarians? It was a pity she couldn't include Tiberius in her planning, but she'd make do without him.

Besides, she appreciated that he was keeping his pact with her and treated her courteously. So many problems, but it was a joy to solve them.

Coming out of Tiberius's room, she glanced through the narrow pillars of the colonnade and saw Niko crossing the inadequate garden. It was still so cold this morning that frost sparkled on the grass in the pale sunlight.

"How can you bear to be outside without a cloak?" she asked when he came toward her. "Greece is even warmer than Rome at this time of year, isn't it?"

"Not by much. But I'm getting used to this climate."

"I certainly am not. Where's Lucia? Isn't she at her lessons?"

"She worked for two hours at her reading. Now she's sleeping. Young children need their sleep."

She glanced at him, suspicious he was belittling her knowledge of child-raising in his subtle way, but his expression remained neutral. "Come inside. You're the scholar. I want you to tell me all you know about this Druid celebration called Yule."

He followed her into the house. "It's a mid-winter festival marking the solstice – the dying of the old year and the old god, and the birth of the new one with its new god."

"Two gods? Or two faces of one god? Like Janus."

"It's a mistake to use one religion to explain the practices of another."

She stared at him. "What a pedant you are sometimes!"

"Have you discussed this with your husband?"

"I'm going to surprise him."

"As you wish. Someone needs to go into the woods to collect certain plants that are traditional for a Yule celebration. Holly, ivy, mistletoe –"

"Ugh! Even I know that's a parasite and poisonous."

"Mistletoe is important. But it's not difficult to find."

"Just don't use a kitchen knife to cut it! We could all be sickened."

He ignored her. "It grows on the apple trees in the orchard."

"How do you know all this?"

"I talk to the servants. Most of them speak some Latin. Druid

A VILLA FAR FROM ROME

practices aren't written down, but they remember them. Some Druids include a blood sacrifice in their observance —"

"Stop!" She covered her ears. "I don't want to hear it!"

"The difficulty will be where to burn the Yule log. It's supposed to burn for twelve days to bring luck to the household. But unlike the houses of the Britanni, your house doesn't have a fire pit."

"That shall be your task, Niko. I have invitations to write."

* * *

Days of planning and preparation flew by. The women who came reluctantly to work in the kitchen baked till the house was scented with nutmeg and cloves, and others cleaned and polished till all the wood glowed. She hurried from one room to another, scolding, instructing, despairing it would all get done in time. Tiberius stayed away, apparently not noticing anything, leaving household matters to her. She wondered if he even cared.

On the day of the Yule festival itself, she waited in the house's doorway, ready to welcome her guests. The sky was overcast, the air cold, the sun hadn't shone all day. She wore a new tunic, woven with a blue and yellow pattern around the hem. Unlike Roman fashion, this tunic had long, loose sleeves, Britanni style. Under it, she wore another, plain tunic; she was grateful for their combined warmth, but she couldn't seem to get really warm today, no matter what she wore. She had a moment of envy for the Regni who had no hesitation in wearing woolen trousers under their tunics and fur-collared cloaks. She'd put on a new gold necklace and rings, and bracelets made of red and blue glass beads threaded with silver, treasures Niko had found for her in the market in Noviomagus. An hour spent with a bronze mirror and Gracila's cosmetics had finally satisfied her. But her head ached and her stomach felt as if it were full of tiny birds all panicking and fluttering their wings.

She couldn't stop her hands from plucking anxiously at her new tunic, smoothing it over her hips. How foolish to be nervous about a barbarian celebration! The house was ready for guests, the kitchen prepared. She'd had to tell Tiberius what she'd planned as the time came closer. He hadn't been pleased, but he'd surely change his opinion once the celebration began. The aroma of roasting meat and baked apples drifted from the kitchen. The feast wouldn't be as grand as those her mother set out for guests at the Saturnalia in the old days before they lost the villa, but she'd seen to it that it would be a bright Roman light in this dark Britanni winter.

How fine those old days had been! How wonderful her family's celebration of the Saturnalia at the end of the year! In her memory they shone as if they'd been etched on gold. The house filled with the scent of flowers and fragrant foods, roast suckling pig, sausages, fish in garlic sauce, figs and sweet dried plums! Her mouth watered at the memory. Pater distributing gifts to every guest who crossed their threshold; Mater, dismissing the slaves and combing Antonia's hair with her own hand.

"When will they be here, Ma?" Lucia danced with excitement. She had on a new white tunic with a blue sash, matching blue ribbons holding back her curls.

The glowing images were from the early days. Towards the end, there'd been no money for gifts or suckling pigs; the slaves were sold or freed like Niko. There was no going home again because there was no home to go to.

"Caelius!" Lucia cried, clapping her hands. "Perhaps he'll bring his pony. And Catuarus! He'll bring Beech – I just know!"

She glanced at the child. When she'd been that age, life had been one grand celebration after another. Poor child, to be excited about so little. Sometimes she resented Lucia, seeing the girl as robbing her of her own childhood, as if she were responsible! The day would come when they'd return to Rome, and she'd try to make amends.

Right now, she must attend to the arrangements for this celebration, in spite of the fact that she was starting to feel a little unwell. Excitement, no doubt. It would pass. She'd taken pains with the invitations not to over-emphasize the Druid aspect of the celebration while not ignoring them. Not that Romans were averse to celebrating the end of one year and the beginning of another, but she'd thought it best not to remind her Roman guests of the pagan roots of the feast she invited them to share. First on

A VILLA FAR FROM ROME

that list were Marcus and Gracila, but she'd made up a list of other Romans living in Noviomagus, as well as several leaders and officials among the Britanni. She wondered again if Tiberius's native wife would come – surely not! Lucia expected her son. If they should come, she would be cool and gracious, But she'd save her conversation for her Roman guests.

Tiberius and Gallus had gone out that morning to find just the right log to burn in the firepit that had been dug just beyond the colonnade. They'd returned dragging a sizable bough from an oak, and Tiberius had instructed Lucia in how to decorate it with pine cones and ivy strands. Niko had draped mistletoe on the bare branches of a young tree near the house. Snowflakes began to drift down, softening the contours of the winter landscape.

Tiberius set fire to the log. The flames rushed up, glittering on the Roman short sword he'd belted over his tunic. She stared at it; its presence made her uneasy. He wore no cloak or toga, impervious to the cold.

"Oh, *when* will they be here?" Firelight lit the dark evening, flickering on her daughter's face.

She laid a hand on Lucia's shoulder, quieting her and watched the road for her guests. She shivered with cold in spite of the fire's warmth. Niko noticed and fetched cloaks for both of them. They waited.

The first guest came through the snow on foot, long braids sparkling as the firelight reached them.

"Pudens Pudentinus," Tiberius said in greeting.

"A good Yule to you, my friend." Pudens bowed to Antonia. "Lady."

A servant led the man inside where hot wine waited for the guests..

The garden filled up with snow, and the hills in the blue distance turned white. The shortest day of the year was dying fast. It was past the time for her guests to arrive. Now she could also smell the mulled wine being prepared in the kitchen. For a moment, her stomach turned uneasily at the thick, spicy odor; her throat too closed on the very thought of swallowing. In spite of the cold, she was starting to feel too warm in the cloak. She loosened it around her neck where the sweat had appeared.

SHEILA FINCH

A small group, five in all, men and women who farmed Tiberius's land, emerged out of the snow. Another man, a minor official from Noviomagus, with his fat wife. The servant led them inside to take wine.

"Look!"

She gazed through the falling whiteness to where Lucia pointed. A lone figure on horseback approached. Her heart hammered in her breast. The stableboy ran out to grab the horse's reins. The rider dismounted and strode towards them

It wasn't Marcus Favonius.

Tiberius stepped forward to welcome a man she'd seen once before, the centurion's second-in-command, the tribune Didius Something-or-other. They stood together at the edge of the firelight talking. Darkness swallowed the garden beyond the fire's reach.

She drew Lucia under the protection of the colonnade's roof. The child leaned against her, silent now as if she too guessed the truth. No one else was coming. Her head hurt and she was close to tears.

The snow came down faster now, and Gallus had trouble keeping the log aflame. It hissed and spat as the white flakes struck it. What had happened to the merry party she'd planned? Shame brought heat to her face.

The tribune brushed snow out of his hair. "I could use a mug of that hot wine I'm smelling."

"Let me lead you to it, Tribune," Gallus said. "I could use some myself!"

"Wait." Tiberius held up his hand. "I invited you here to witness a ceremony, Tribune – a Celtic tradition. Gallus, bring the prisoner."

Her husband's voice struck her as cold as the snow on her cheeks. Didius stared at him, but Tiberius offered no explanation. She'd learned days ago of the prisoner's presence in the storage room by the stable, but not the reason for it. Obviously, it was very important to Tiberius. Now she thought of what Niko had said about Druids and blood sacrifice and wondered if he were mad enough to use his sword on the prisoner.

"Lucia, go inside!" She turned her daughter away from the fire.

"But I want –"

A VILLA FAR FROM ROME

"Now!"

Niko took the child's hand and led her into the house.

Gallus came back from the stable, leading a short man of middle years, chained, with unkempt dark hair and beard. They stood near the sputtering fire. Tiberius bent to the little tree and took the mistletoe.

"What's this?" the tribune asked.

"Celts have a custom," Tiberius said. He stepped closer to the man and Gallus released his chains. Tiberius held up the sprig of mistletoe in his left hand. "Friendships made and enmities forgiven under the mistletoe are sacred. Oaths taken this one time a year under the mistletoe are not broken. The worst of deeds may be pardoned under the mistletoe. Am I not right, Tarvos?"

The prisoner scowled at him, firelight playing over his dirty face. "I don't want your mercy!"

"I'm not offering mercy. I seek peace."

The snow came down in thick, wet flakes. She shivered and pulled the cloak tighter under her chin, her breath like a knife blade in her chest. Her throat hurt and she longed to go inside and go to bed, but that was impossible for the moment. She was afraid to watch but more afraid not to.

Tiberius spoke to the prisoner in the tongue of the Britanni, then switched back to Latin, for the sake of the tribune. "Will you join me in this, Tarvos, or would you forsake the ways of our ancestors?"

"Wait!" the tribune said. "I don't know what's happening, but –"

Tiberius stretched his right hand out to the prisoner. The prisoner hesitated, then slowly put out his own hand. Tiberius grasped it. His other hand held the mistletoe over their clasped hands.

"May Holly King and Oak King sanctify what we do here," Tiberius said. "I give you my pardon under the sacred mistletoe for whatever assault you have made on the peace."

"And in return under the mistletoe I swear peace to you," the man muttered, sounding as if someone was holding a knife to his throat.

Tiberius lowered the mistletoe and released his hand. "Now go!"

The man scuttled away into the darkness beyond the reach of the firelight.

"I don't believe what I just saw!" the tribune said. "You've just released a dangerous prisoner!"

"You are witness to my justice, Tribune. He was given into my custody to deal with as I saw fit. He is Britanni. I've dealt with him according to Britanni law. He is no longer a threat to Rome."

"You've released a rebel, a —"

"By Bacchus himself," Gallus interrupted."Never mind this King Holly and Father Oak business. I'm ready for that hot wine now! Let's all go inside —"

She realized the old man was trying to avert the conflict.

Didius held up his hand, silencing Gallus. "This has to be reported to the centurion immediately."

He strode through the snow drifts to the stable to retrieve his horse. Tiberius watched him in silence, snow piling on his shoulders.

"What shall we do now?" A fit of coughing took her by surprise, and it was a while before she could continue. Her head pounded.

He glanced at her. "What's done is done for good or bad. But you're shivering. Are you not well?"

She shook her head. "It's just very cold out here."

"We'll go in."

The Yule log had gone out, in spite of Niko's best efforts, smothered in the snow.

CHAPTER NINETEEN

[AD 67]

THE STABLE BOY CAME UP TO HIM with Stormfellow's saddle, and hovered by the horse's side, ready to assist. An icy wind fluttered the boy's cloak and the horse's mane.

Togidubnus waved the boy away. "Get out of the cold, lad. We've had enough sickness in this house."

The sky was full of racing clouds. Most likely there would be more snow flurries before nightfall, winter's last assault. He hoped that riding out to survey his herds would allow him to work through this bleak mood that had held him for too many days. It always lifted his heart to spend time with the men who tended the cattle that had belonged to his family since his father's day. It was still early in the new year, but some of the herd would probably be calving. The wheel of birth and death and birth again among the animals, the plain conversation of simple men around a good fire, these were pleasures he valued, a refuge against the storm of problems that plagued him.

He'd been angry when he'd learned Antonia had planned a Yule celebration without consulting him. He hadn't intended the occasion to be anything more than a ritual to command Tarvos's good behavior. He was angered when he learned she'd somehow made a list of people in Noviomagus to invite. That in itself was bad enough, but they'd shown their contempt by not coming, and that shamed him. Other than Pudens, a true friend, the ones who did come were trash who would have gone to Hades itself if there was a chance of free food and wine. Was there no end to the humiliation and scorn she could bring down on him? He'd given up celebrating Yule long ago. Certainly, he hadn't interfered when Breca took the boys to her uncle's house to keep the old traditions; he'd even accompanied them. But the old ways meant nothing to him. That was another thing he'd learned at the court of Augustus. The old gods were just stories, some kind of magical charm to keep the unlearned in their place.

Someone had obviously helped her do this. Not Gallus – he sensed the old man didn't like Antonia. The Greek? The man was devious, a cipher, like others of his race he'd encountered as a boy in Rome. Athens might've been conquered by Rome, but as far as he understood it, in their hearts the Greeks felt themselves superior to everybody else. But Niko had shown his usefulness when Antonia fell sick after Yule. He possessed knowledge of healing plants and herbs that matched Breca's Aunt Adraste's own – perhaps even surpassed what the Druid knew.

He mounted Stormfellow and the horse obediently started forward. There weren't many travelers on the road today. That was just as well. He was in no mood to acknowledge anyone, Roman or Regni. Before he reached Noviomagus itself, he would head off on a narrower track to visit a small cluster of houses where his herders lived, in the rich grazing meadows at the foot of the Downs. Signs of winter's end were everywhere, the tiny globes of snowdrops poking hesitantly through the still half-frozen mud, a bird flying past with twigs to make a nest. Somewhere in the fields, a fox barked, signaling good hunting for its cubs back in the den .

Angry as he'd been with Antonia, he hadn't wished her to suffer in her sickness as much as she did. Niko wouldn't let him enter her room to see her, but he'd stood by the door listening to her rasping breath, as if every mouthful of air was torture. She was burning up with fever, Niko said, ordering the servants to bring snow and ice from the garden to try to bring the fever down. The child had wailed when she too had been denied entry into her mother's chamber, but Niko was adamant. One night he'd felt sure she would die, fighting for every breath; he'd watched her through the door a servant had left ajar, thrashing about in pain on the bed, gasping for air.

Two days earlier, Gracila had sent her own slave to help nurse Antonia through her sickness; the girl was standing near the Greek, holding a bowl he'd asked for. He couldn't believe what he was seeing, Niko with a knife – holding it to Antonia's throat – the slave holding the bowl to catch

A VILLA FAR FROM ROME

the blood. Just as he was about to throw the door wide and enter the forbidden bedchamber, Antonia's body went slack. But she wasn't dead. He saw her chest heaving as air rushed in through the hole Niko had cut in her throat.

Whatever the Greek was, he was more than just a freed slave.

He thought about this as he rode, a light fall of snow dusting his shoulders, quickly turning to slush under the great horse's hooves. The Greeks he'd known in his boyhood year in Rome had been a proud lot; many of the freemen among them disdained taking Roman citizenship. He still found that hard to understand. The Romans tolerated them for their knowledge and their culture. The Greeks in their turn were scornful of Roman attempts at art, especially sculpture – which they said was a poor copy of Greek achievement. He didn't know if they were right; he had no skill at judging art.

A vivid flash of red against white bushes caught his eye. A lone robin out to find breakfast. Birds and trees, sheep, goats and wolves, the hills, the clouds and the stars in the night sky, these were the things he understood and valued. It was because these things were precious that he believed in cooperating with Rome to the extent of putting Rome's laws ahead of Celtic desires. He couldn't expect his people – or even his own family – to understand that immediately, but he must try harder to convince them it was for their own good.

Smoke stood straight up from the low roundhouse ahead. Hearing the clatter of Stormfellow's hooves on the packed earth of the path, a young man appeared in the doorway, his arm raised in greeting. He'd taken over his father's position when the old man grew too weak to work. Two hounds bared their teeth at the visitor, but dropped their heads when the young man raised his hand to them, sullen in their obedience. A red-cheeked woman – hardly more than a girl – came to take the reins. He'd known them since they were children. From the look of her, the woman was about to produce another child; one, a boy about the age of Lucia, clung to her skirt.

SHEILA FINCH

He walked with Colinus, keeper of his herd, to the nearby barn where the cattle about to give birth were kept, a noisy place full of the earthy stink of dung.

"Twelve should give birth in the next week or so," the man told him. His pride showed in the way he carried himself, his confident speech. Togidubnus appreciated that in his steward..

He inspected the cattle one by one, soothed by the feel of warm flanks under his touch, the steam of breath rising above each beast, the placid eyes that turned to watch him. Colinus commented on each one's good points. The herd produced good quality milk with thick cream that Old Nev would turn into the cheese he loved. Any excess – and there was usually an abundance once the grass in the river meadow came in thick in spring – would sell to the garrison in Noviomagus. The older cattle that no longer produced milk were slaughtered each year before the winter set in to save on the cost of feeding them. Much of that meat went to supply the legion too. His steward talked on, this many sides of beef, that many amphoras-worth of milk to be looked for once the cows had calved, the price the legion was willing to pay for good meat. The talk washed over him with the healing comfort of household prayer.

After the inspection was done and the accounting fully made of monies spent and monies coming in, they sat in the warmth of the fire in the tidy house, the old farmer nodding contentedly as his son talked to their king, a man both farmers had known for many years. The young wife served hot beer with honey from the bee-houses she kept nearby – a cup for each man present, a sign the gathering was in friendship not ritual – and roasted cakes heaped with thick dark cream from his cows. When he smiled at her in approval, she dimpled and laid a strip of smoky dried meat before him.

"A new thing for her," the husband explained. "They didn't smoke the beef in her family."

"Well done." He chewed the savory meat. "It's very good."

The young woman dimpled again..

Two more men came in from the fields and she served them too. The

A VILLA FAR FROM ROME

old man sat smiling toothlessly at the talk that flowed, the younger man's father who had been steward to his own father. He remembered the many times he'd sat in the smaller house that had stood on this site, accompanying his own father, listening to the talk about calves and milk yields, just as they were doing today. He felt at peace for the first time in many months.

He spoke to them of the temple he was building in Noviomagus, careful to emphasize that it would honor Sulis in her Roman garb for he knew they, like so many of the Regni, held onto the old ways.

"We don't get into town much," the young man said, carefully. "Calving time takes good watching. And after that..."

He laughed and clapped the man on his shoulder. "Once a year should keep our Roman friends happy."

"That's important, isn't it?"

"Yes."

Firelight sparkled in their eyes, and their ruddy cheeks spoke of the beer warmth in their bellies. His too. He was neither Roman nor Regni here, king nor warrior, just a farmer talking about his fields and his herds and the weather. But the look that passed between these honest people at the mention of Romans didn't escape him.

"Lord," his chief herder began hesitantly. The other men were quietly watchful over the rim of their beer.

"King, now," someone muttered the correction.

He held up a hand, staying them. "Speak, Colinus," he said. "We are men of the land here, freemen all."

"I would like to ask –"

He waited, his senses heightened by the man's obvious nervousness.

The young man swallowed another mouthful of beer, gained courage and said, "Will the legions stay in Britannia, do you think? Or will the land be ours again some day?"

He was silent for a moment, weighing his words. Then he nodded slowly. "Yes, they will stay. And yes the land will be ours – It already is. We are all Romans now, and all will be well."

But in his mind, he saw Tarvos's sullen face lit by the Yule flame. He'd think about what this might mean later; right now, he would enjoy the moment. He planned to ride through his tribe's land, doing what a chief must, listening to grievances and settling squabbles. Time enough to examine this undercurrent of unrest he sensed even in the house of herders who'd served his family for more than a generation.

CHAPTER TWENTY

ANTONIA LEANED FORWARD in the chair Niko had placed on the colonnade and allowed the young slave girl, Delamira, to tuck a blanket over her shoulders. Though the sun shone, the air was still cold. The garden she hadn't seen for several weeks was like a strange country with a frenzy of vivid spring growth in the trees and hedges, the new grass so green it hurt her eyes.

"It's still too cool for you to stay outside for long," Niko said. "You're not fully well yet. But a little fresh air will do you good."

A sudden memory of an odd, slightly gritty taste came to her mind. "What was that liquid you made me drink while I was ill?"

"Silver dust. A Greek remedy to prevent sickness from getting worse."

"How very strange!"

She touched the bandaged place on her throat where Niko had made a hole for her to breathe through. That was stranger still! The wound was sore but healing. Niko's potions made sure of that.

Somewhere at the far end of the garden, she heard her daughter's voice. Niko had been adamant that the child not come anywhere near her mother during her sickness. He had some odd notion that if she did, she'd become sick too, as if the sickness could just pass between them instead of when the gods so willed. That seemed like Greek superstition to her. How good it was to feel superior to arrogant Greeks for once! But she didn't deny that – counselor, teacher, now healer – the Greek was a treasure. She was lucky that he'd chosen to accompany her after the family's downfall.

Odd, that he hadn't wanted to go home to Greece when her father freed him. Given the opportunity, she'd go back to Italia any day. No wonder she'd fallen ill in this damp climate. Home crowded everything else out of her dreams, the family's villa on the hillside overlooking the sea, the rich perfume of the grapes at harvest, her mother contentedly spinning outside on a warm summer evening while her father spoke of affairs of the senate with her oldest brother, Julius, before he left to join the legion.. Sometimes, the longing to go home was too much to bear.

A small brown bird with red-capped head swooped over her, a twist of something white and furry in its beak. She watched to see where the nest was. It disappeared into a young tree just beginning to leaf out.

"Linnet," Niko said.

"How do you know so much about everything?"

"I make it my business to learn about my surroundings."

"Doesn't that grow tiresome after a while?"

He didn't bother to answer, and she hadn't regained enough strength to pursue the thought.

She'd been sick a very long time, the days and weeks blurring together in her memory. Vague pictures of Niko trickling broth into her mouth, her difficulty swallowing, the coughing that wracked her chest as if she would tear herself apart, the sound of Lucia crying because she wasn't allowed in the room, the rasping pain of trying to breathe with lungs on fire. She'd thought she was going to die. Somewhere in that haze, Gracila Pavonia had swept in, installing Delamira, the dark-skinned slave from Carthage, as Niko's helper. Once, she remembered seeing Tiberius peering around the door. Niko had waved him away.

"Where's my husband?"

"He rode out two days ago. Tribal matters," Niko said.

"Two days?"

"Some family squabbles that needed the king to settle them."

Surprised by his odd tone, she looked up at him. "That's odd, isn't it?"

"A Celtic king is the tribal arbiter."

"He thinks of himself as a Roman."

"The question is," Niko said, "do they think of him as one."

"Ma!"

She squinted across the grass and saw three blurry figures, backlit by

A VILLA FAR FROM ROME

the sharp sun, racing towards her. Her daughter, a boy child – and an animal. A dog?

"Ma!" Lucia threw her small arms around her mother in a fierce embrace until Delamira scolded and pulled her off.

She looked over Lucia's head at the boy. Older than Caelius. Red hair. Not Gracila's boy.

"This is your husband's second son," Niko said."The oldest, you'll remember, stayed in Rome with the emperor."

"What's he doing here?"

The boy scowled at her, and she realized he understood Latin. That didn't surprise her; his father had probably taught him a few words.

"Tiberius wants his son to be tutored."

The illness that had almost claimed her life had not completely faded, leaving her quickly tired. Conversation was stressful. "Tutored? By whom?"

"I can as easily instruct two as one," Niko said.

"A teacher and a healer too. What a surprise you are, Niko."

"Little surprise that Greece knows more about medicine than Rome."

He shooed the children away.

She closed her eyes against the sun's glare. "What was this sickness that almost killed me, Niko?"

"What do names matter?"

"You're the one who's interested in knowing things for their own sake. I just want to know."

"It's known as the 'leather sickness,' for what it does to the sufferer's throat."

"How horrible! But tell me –"

"No more talking. You've had enough excitement for today. Delamira will take you back inside."

* * *

It rained the next two days, but not the icy torrents of winter; these were the softer showers of spring, carried on the west wind, more heavy mist than downpour. With the shutters open to the garden, she smelled the sharp, fresh scent of grass and new leaves; yellow and white butterflies crowded the blossoms on the apples trees, and she heard the cuckoo call to its mate. The slave Gracila had sent to her was busy overseeing her food in the kitchen, but Antonia didn't want to wait to have the girl comb and arrange her hair. Niko was occupied with the children and Tiberius still hadn't returned.

The day called to her, sweet and mild. She felt well enough to take a walk by herself. She draped a warm Regni cloak over her shoulders – How thin she'd become! Bones sticking out all over -- But she was alive, and it was spring. She stepped outside. Under the blossoming trees, daffodils splashed the earth with gold, and at the edge of the grass that surrounded the house, right where a stand of oaks and elms held off the east wind, a patch of blue so brilliant it hurt her eyes. Shading her eyes as she came closer, she found a riot of tiny bluebells under the trees. She took a moment of pleasure in them. The flowers she remembered from her native land were bigger, splashier, but their colors and perfumes were no more beautiful than the demure blooms of this island so far from Rome. The sky too was different; Rome's sky was hot and brassy, a dazzling, burning blue, but here even the bluest sky was tempered by puffs of white cloud. The insight surprised her; she was growing accustomed to her new home. She might even come to love it someday.

A stranger was walking up the path from the sea, a Roman, by the look of his toga and high-laced sandals more suited to Rome than to rough Britannia. He was a short man with a well-fed look about him, carrying an armload of scrolls, and behind him a slave staggered under the weight of several lumpy looking bundles. Another, younger man followed, tall and thin, his skin dark as if he spent much time in the sun, his long nose showing the sudden turn down that betrayed his roots in the cities on the Nile. It wasn't unusual for people to come and go between Noviomagus and Rome, the road between the town and the small harbor led right past the house. but these strangers were heading to the house itself. The short man was obviously out of breath as if unused to such strenuous activity. Antonia stopped at the edge of the colonnade to see what they'd do. Surely this was a gift! Visitors from Rome would bring news and gossip, contact

A VILLA FAR FROM ROME

that she was starved for.

"You!" the man said when he became aware of her. "Announce my arrival!"

At first, she thought he must've aimed his command at the slave following him. But no, he was looking at her – glaring at her – as if she must be too stupid to understand.

"I don't know who you are."

"I am Septimus Severus." the short man said. "Your master will be expecting me."

She shook her head. Since her illness, she hadn't been quick with her thoughts, but this made no sense. "I don't think we –"

"A letter of introduction preceded me," he said grandly.

She glanced from the short man to the gloomy-faced slave behind him. The slave shook his head. "I don't think there was a letter ..." she began. Surely if Tiberius was expecting guests from Rome he'd have made arrangements?

"No letter?" Severus said. "Then it was lost at sea! Well, no matter. I'm here. Girl – go summon your master."

She felt as if he'd hit her. He took her for a slave! And what else should he think as she stood there, a skinny wretch with tangled hair in a barbarian cloak?

She caught the eyes of the younger man standing behind Septimus Severus. Was it her imagination, or had he actually winked at her? He smiled at her as if he had guessed the truth even though the older man hadn't. Her first anger gave way to a pricking of mischief.

"Please, sir," she said humbly, hiding her own smile, "step into the audience chamber here behind me, and I'll summon the house's owner."

"I shall require food and drink." He strode past her, scrolls rustling in his arms.

The slave stood on the grass, lumpy baggage at his feet. He shrugged at her.

"There'll be food for you in the kitchen," she said. "But tell me why you've come here? We weren't expecting visitors."

"He's the emperor's architect," the slave said, nodding in the direction of the now vanished Roman.

"And I'm his assistant," the younger man said. "Aron by name. Septimus Severus is here to build a villa."

"What do you mean?"

"The emperor sent him. To build a villa."

"A villa? But for whom?"

"For whoever lives here right now, I suppose," Aron replied.

She must be dreaming. She couldn't have heard that right. She'd written to Nero asking for a small sum of money to repair the failing hypocaust – and if they'd had a working one, she wouldn't have been so ill last winter – but a whole house? This was beyond dreaming! She'd been right about the emperor. Elation swept over her. Wait till Tiberius heard this news!

She remembered the pompous little man waiting in the audience chamber for "the owner of the house" and her desire to trick him returned. When Aron and Severus's slave had trudged off with the bundles towards the outbuildings where the servants slept, she pulled her cloak around her shoulders and entered the audience chamber.

"Good day to you, sir," she said.

He looked up from the bench he'd seated himself on and frowned. "I told you to fetch your master or mistress!"

"I did. I am Antonia Plautina, wife of Claudius Tiberius Togidubnus, and mistress of this house."

His mouth gaped open, but he shut it in a hurry and scowled. "I am not accustomed to being the butt of jokes!"

"And I am not accustomed to being treated as a slave. So we're even. I bid you welcome. My husband and I will enjoy hearing your plans for this house. But for now, I'll send someone to guide you to a chamber where you may stay."

It felt good to laugh after such a long time of being ill, but she stifled it until the door closed behind her.

* * *

A VILLA FAR FROM ROME

"I doubt your husband will take this well," Niko said when she told him.

Septimus Severus had been settled in the small room Tiberius used as a study to work on the house's accounts and records. One of the Regni servants was taking food to him as he wished to refresh himself in private. The Roman's expression when he'd realized he was speaking to the house's owner and not her servant caused her to double over with laughter, even now.

"Tiberius will be happy with a larger room to work in when the villa's built."

"I meant building a whole new villa. I didn't know he'd even considered it."

"Of course he'll like a larger villa! Why wouldn't he? He hasn't spoken much about it because he's so busy building the temple in Noviomagus."

Niko shook his head.

She lay back on her bed and allowed Delamira to arrange pillows for her head. Niko had insisted she needed to rest, even though she felt so full of energy right now. She'd never expected Nero's response to a simple plea for a little money to result in the presence of an architect and plans for a new villa. And a most interesting assistant, a voice whispered in her mind. Tomorrow, after Severus had rested, he would show her the plans.

Under Niko's instruction, Delamira brought warm water and tended to the wound on her throat. It was healing, just a little soreness remained.

"You have a healing touch, Delamira," she said.

"Thank you, Lady. I know a little. But not as much as Nikolaos."

She lay still, thinking things over. Of course she still wanted to return to Rome some day – it was her true home – but a grand new villa would make it easier to bide her time. Surely that proved the emperor held her and her child in favor? Once that news got out, the haughty Roman matrons of Noviomagus – all except Gracila, of course, it wasn't her fault – who'd snubbed her at the Yule celebration would be forced to show respect. This was a far grander outcome than she could have ever wished. The villa of her dreams, big enough and fabulous enough to entertain even the haughtiest visitors.

"There will be consequences," Niko said.

Delamira finished dressing the wound and fussed with the pillows; she turned to the window to close the shutters against the night. She waved the slave away.

"I think you're wrong, Niko. The emperor means us no harm. He may even come to visit us."

"Zeus forbid!" Niko said.

CHAPTER TWENTY-ONE

HE HEARD GALLUS BOOMING COMMANDS to the builders before he saw the old legionary. Dismounting, Togidubnus handed Stormfellow's reins over to a small Regni boy who was lurking at the edge of the site, hoping to earn a few coins. He'd been away for more than a week this time and was anxious to get back to the house and bathe, stroll in the garden, admire the new crop swelling on his apple trees. In his imagination, he smelled the blossom and heard the murmuring of the bees. It would be good to be home again. But there was time for a brief detour to Noviomagus to see how his temple was advancing.

The squabbles he'd encountered and settled on his journey – Somebody stole eggs from somebody else's chickens, somebody's son killed somebody else's goat, trivial matters blown up to proportions he wouldn't have thought possible before. He was disturbed. The undercurrent of discontent among the country people, and the ominous rumblings of discontent along his borders with the Belgae, concerned him. Something was stirring, and he didn't like the feel of it.

Boudicca's shadow still lay across the land and would have to be dealt with at some point. It was bitter irony that the warrior queen, so beloved of the Celts as a symbol of their freedom from the bonds of Roman occupation, had brought the full crushing fury of the legions down on them because of her hot-headedness. He knew they would never see it that way.

A lot would depend on how the Romans handled the routine problems of keeping the peace. Tact was called for in situations like this. Not a quality the Romans valued! Though he was reluctant to speak to the man, he should find the time to have a word with Marcus Favonius.But this afternoon, with the unusually warm spring sun sparking the nearby sea and larks singing on the Downs, he could take time to think about the day when this tribute to Breca would be dedicated.

The site for his temple was a very fine one, close to the center of Noviomagus. He could never have afforded to purchase it; how fortunate that Pudens Pudentinus had chosen to donate it. He picked his way carefully over piled stones and stacked wood, nodding at the master builder and his son, avoiding pits dug to hold the heavy upright beams that would in turn hold up the temple's roof. Workers brushed past him carrying loads of brick slung from yokes over their shoulders. He could see from the foundation lines and the beginning of walls how it was going to be when it was finished, and it pleased him. Grand enough to impress his enemies! The site rang with the roar of the blacksmiths's furnace and the sound of hammers pounding stone. Rock dust rising on the air made him sneeze.

Gallus stopped shouting and turned to talk to one of the tribe's Elders who had his back to Togidubnus. Coming closer, he saw the traditional braids and recognized Pudens.

"Well, what do you think?" Gallus said, noticing his approach. The Roman raised his voice to project over the noise. There was a bruise on the legionary's cheek, and his crooked nose was thicker than Togidubnus remembered. Fighting, he remembered now, was the old man's favorite pastime, second only to drinking beer and gambling.

Pudens turned also and lifted a hand in greeting. His white toga was covered in dust.

"It seems to be progressing well. Have you had any problems?"

"Only with lazy workers who stand around muttering among themselves, or think they should go home as soon as their wives summon them," Gallus said.

"It looks as if one of them took a fist to your face."

The old man put a hand up to touch his cheek carefully. "His face looks worse."

"One of these days, Legionary, you will pick a fight you can't win."

"If I could just have a few of the Fourteenth Gemina –"

"But you can't."

"Pity. We laid roads so fast the legion was traveling them before the mortar had set!"

A VILLA FAR FROM ROME

"Now we know the secret to Rome's conquests," Pudens said with a smile. "They have the fastest builders in the world."

"Right enough!" Gallus wiped sweat from his brow. "Want to look around?"

They picked their way carefully around the carpenters and stone masons, the workers stacking bricks or carrying buckets of iron nails. A grey donkey trudged in a circle, turning the paddles that stirred the lime mortar. Somehow, it had managed to tangle one hoof in a trailing rope. Gallus drew his short dagger – old, and judging by its nicked blade, much used – and cut it free. He indicated where sections of the temple were beginning to be recognizable, the courtyard, the inner sanctuary.

"How long do you think this is going to take?"

"As long as the gods send good weather, the main part could be done by the end of the year."

"That's fast."

"The centurion paid for extra workers to speed things up," Pudens said. "In addition to what the Guild of Smiths contributed. That way, Rome shares in the glory of the new temple."

"I don't like that thought."

"Consider it this way, my friend," Pudens said. "They rob you every time you take a breath – they take land that used to be yours, you pay them taxes, your very freedom is not yours any more."

"Dangerous talk," Gallus observed.

Pudens spread his hands. "Allow them to pay a little back."

He didn't like the idea of the centurion having anything to do with his temple, but there wasn't much he could do about it. Contributing to the building was a play for power. "You are a cynical man, Pudens."

Pudens smiled. "I pick my battles. When it comes to Rome, I believe some of the coins should trickle into my hands."

When he'd seen enough to satisfy him that this was going to be a worthy tribute to Neptune and Minerva, he stopped and accepted a cup of water that a thin young lad scooped out of a bucket. He too was now covered in dust like everyone else at the site. He looked forward to a visit to the caldarium at home, small but serviceable, the servant scrubbing off this rock dust with oil.

"You'll be wanting to get home to your other building project," Pudens said.

He frowned. "What's that?"

"I suspect you're not going to like it, Little Fox," Gallus said.. "I didn't want to be the first to say it. The emperor sent an architect to build you a new villa."

* * *

Antonia was in the garden talking to a short, stocky stranger when he rode up; her daughter played nearby with his son's dog. Evening shadows were dappling the grass under his apple trees where they were examining an unrolled scroll. The last rays of the sun bathed the walls of his house with a warm, creamy light, the color of daffodils in spring, and in one of the windows a servant had lit a lamp welcoming him home.

He stopped short. The courtyard was a dismaying jumble of planks and bricks, the new temple site in miniature. Worse – now he saw that one end of his house was gone. Workers, stripped to the waist, scurried about carrying buckets and pushing carts loaded with stones or mortar. Some of them were Regni– he knew them by sight – but the others he didn't recognize.

"Who gave permission for this destruction of my house?"

Antonia looked up at him. "The emperor is giving us a magnificent gift, Tiberius – a wonderful new villa!"

"Based on the beautiful building I designed for him in Rome," the stranger said.

"And who are you?"

"Caesar's architect," the man said proudly. "Septimus Severus."

"Think of it, Tiberius, a copy of Nero's palace here! Look at the plans."

"Nero's palace?"

"The Golden House," the architect said, drawing himself up proudly. "My design!"

A VILLA FAR FROM ROME

Images of gargantuan statues crowded his memory – mind-numbing colors – artificial lakes – gigantic halls with enormous glass ceilings –

"Why should the emperor suppose I would need such – such a vast – enormous –" Words failed him. He wanted to call the palace he'd seen in Rome for what it was: decadent, wasteful, monstrous – but prudence suggested his words might be carried back to Rome when this boastful little man returned.

"Why indeed!" the architect scoffed. "I suppose a barbarian would be content in a pigsty. But my emperor has decreed otherwise."

"My husband is Roman!" Antonia said.

The architect sniffed. To the Romans, Togidubnus knew, he would always be a barbarian first.

He turned to Antonia. "Why would the emperor even think we need a new house?"

"Why? Perhaps he wants this child – this *Roman* child – not to grow up like a barbarian!"

There was no way he could afford so grand a villa. "Did you ask the emperor to do this?"

"How can you think that?" Her tone was angry, but he saw the small spot of color start in her cheeks. "We can certainly use an improvement to the hypocaust – that's all I asked – no matter who's paying."

"Bah!" the architect said. "Not worth my time to come so far to repair a hypocaust!"

He would never believe that Nero had a kind thought in his mind, let alone the urge to build a palace for his unfortunate child. There was another purpose here, and he was afraid to think too deeply what it might be.

He shouldn't try to deal with this now, tired as he was by his long journey around his kingdom. It took a lot of energy to argue with a Roman – two of them at once here – but he couldn't let it go. "I did not give permission for this. I don't want to live in a copy of the Golden House. It will stop immediately."

"But the work has already begun, as you can see," she said.

"It won't be as big," the architect put in. "Obviously, that's not possible!"

"I can see that you've allowed the building where my bath house was to be destroyed."

"I suppose I could put together a temporary hypocaust," Severus said, his tone indicating how far beneath his dignity that would be.

"Please, Tiberius – *husband*. The old house is so small and uncomfortable – and cold."

He looked at her and saw that she was trembling. He remembered how sick she'd been, how close to the death that had claimed so many others. Even now, she was a shadow of the healthy girl he'd been forced to take as wife. He could see her sharp collar-bones, her stick-thin wrists, her ivory pallor.

But she hadn't thought it necessary to consult him.

Of course, he would have said no. There was nothing wrong with the house the way it was. And to build a villa with the emperor's money! That was a gift that would come with an enormous debt attached. Why was Nero doing this? If Antonia told the truth – and whatever her faults, he hadn't found her untruthful – all she'd asked for was an improvement to the hypocaust. How did that small request, however unwise, grow into a copy of Nero's greatest villa? At the very least, he was now deeply in the emperor's debt.

Was there to be no end to the indignities Nero would heap on him? Apparently not for as long as Amminus was his hostage.

"I'll send Delamira with hot water for you to wash," she said hesitantly.

The old owl that lived in his oak trees uttered its first soft evening call. He looked up at the trees. The bird – or its parents – had been here as long as this house, at least since his father's time. He strode away from Antonia and the architect, afraid he wouldn't be able to hold his temper much longer.

CHAPTER TWENTY-TWO

TIBERIUS HADN'T BOTHERED TO TAKE SUPPER with her and their guests last night. Antonia had made excuses, weak ones she knew the Romans didn't believe. It had been just as well. Septimus Severus had spent much of the meal boasting of the beauty of his design for the Golden House in Rome, and how he planned to reproduce it here in this odd little corner of Britannia. That would never have pleased her husband, and she had no doubt he would have been outspoken in his displeasure. Aron, the architect's young assistant, said very little, but from time to time she'd caught his deep-set eyes watching her.

It was raining again this morning, as she made her way to the kitchen to supervise the country people who every day brought eggs and milk, fresh fish and flour from the mill, and vegetables that the house's own garden didn't supply. She'd listen to Old Nev's plans for the dishes to be served – translated from the Old Tongue into passable Latin by one of the younger servants – and make changes as she thought appropriate given the Roman guests.

In spite of the rain, Niko had set off again for Noviomagus. He enjoyed his little ventures into town on small errands; often he'd be gone all night. At times like this, her mind flew back to the villa in Pyrgi, and the sound of her mother's voice in the kitchen instructing the slaves. In memory, the skies were always blue over Tuscany, the weather warm, the breezes scented with wildflowers, inviting the family to dine outdoors on the shaded terrace or under the grape arbors. Sharp pain stabbed her heart at the memories. Would she ever see them again?

She couldn't do much about Britannia's weather, but the architect could build some kind of bower outside where she could enjoy the few pleasant summer days this climate afforded.

SHEILA FINCH

"Are you not happy here?"

Startled, she turned in the kitchen doorway to see Severus's assistant emerging from the little room he'd shared with unused storage bins and crockery, his arms full of building plans.

"Why would you question me?"

He was a strange one, only a year or two older than she, too tall to be elegant, and thin as a willow sapling. The deep-set eyes and hooked nose were not attractive. And he didn't dress like one who'd spent his life in Rome – at least, not if the fashions hadn't changed considerably from what she remembered. The sleeveless tunic he wore over some kind of shirt hung loosely from his bony shoulders. The sandals laced up his calves in a most un-Roman way.

"I don't mean to pry," he said. "Please, accept my apology. I couldn't help noticing a certain sadness in your expression."

"Are you some kind of magician, sir, that you read my thoughts?"

He stared at the flagstones of the kitchen floor without answering.

She took pity on him. "I admit I was indulging in a moment of homesickness, so you were right."

He brightened at that, light coming into the dark eyes. "Where's home?"

"A little town on the Tuscan coast, Pyrgi. Perhaps you've heard of it?"

He shook his head, and his body wobbled as he did, so that she was hard put to hide a smile. How awkward he was! But that awkwardness was somehow endearing.

"Sadly, no. I was born in Palestine, but I was educated in Alexandria. My knowledge of Rome is limited to the building sites where Severus attempted to teach me to put stones on top of stones without them falling down – my Alexandrian education being rich in architectural theory rather than practice."

"I imagine you are a very apt pupil."

"And you are a kind lady."

They gazed at each other for a moment. "Are you hungry?"

"I'm not accustomed to eating much in the morning –"

"That might do for Rome, but here we need to prepare ourselves for a

A VILLA FAR FROM ROME

long cold day. And I'm under orders to eat heartily and frequently to recover my health."

She held the door open and they went into the small kitchen. Old Nev put platters of bread and cheese on the table, and poured milk.

"Tell me about the villa you will be building for me here. I hardly had time to absorb all the wonders of the Golden House. I can hardly imagine all that glory here!"

Aron set down his cup. He studied her face for a moment. "You do know why the emperor sent Septimus here?"

"Of course! I pleaded for a little money to repair the hypocaust, but the emperor is a generous man –"

Lucia chose that moment to tumble into the kitchen, wet hair streaming wildly over her shoulders, her cheeks rosy. "Ma! That man's banging down the walls of our house!"

The child was far too young to understand such matters. "Please, Lucia. Remember what Niko teaches you about how to behave in front of guests."

Lucia stared at Aron. The young man lifted his hand in salute. She turned and ran out of the kitchen as ungracefully as she'd entered.

"My daughter," she said when the sound of the child's passage died away.

She was suddenly embarrassed. Did he suspect anything? Her cheeks grew warm. Certainly Roman society would've gossiped about the events of that terrible banquet, but they couldn't know for sure. Would Aron guess why the emperor was giving her the gift of a grand villa?

"A beautiful child," he said, his expression unchanging.

There was something on his mind, she could see the shadow of it in his eyes. But she guessed it had little to do with the child. "What is it?"

"An emperor always has enemies – would-be assassins. This one has many. One day he might have to leave Rome before they kill him."

"But what has this to do with us, so far from Rome?"

"Exactly. Caesar may need a refuge if that dire day comes, a place where his enemies won't think of looking. Septimus is going to build it here for him."

Could that possibly be true? Would Nero some day need to hide here? "But why here, in such a faraway, primitive place? No one would choose to live here!"

"You've answered your own question, I think," he said.

CHAPTER TWENTY-THREE

THE BUILDERS STARTED WORK on the part of the house where the room Niko used to tutor them was. They would have to move somewhere else, Niko said. But where? He went off to see what he could find, leaving them siting at the table, their lessons in Latin grammar open before them. She could hear the men outside, talking, banging things about, and the man Mater said was in charge yelling at everybody.

"Catu," Lucia said. "Let's run away before Niko gets back."

"We shouldn't do that," the boy replied. "It's not a good thing to do to Niko."

"But I don't want to learn anything today."

"He was going to tell us about the great library in Egypt – and the lighthouse. I wanted to hear about the lighthouse."

Lucia pouted. Lighthouses weren't interesting. "It's too noisy in here."

"It's noisy," he agreed. "But where would we go?"

She put a finger to her mouth and thought for a moment. She hadn't thought about *where* because she hadn't really expected him to agree. "Take me fishing?"

He gave her an odd look. "I'd be beaten if I did that! The last time you went out on the water you almost drowned."

"We could take Beech. Beech wouldn't let me drown."

Catuarus shook his head. "No."

Tears spilled out of her eyes. "I never get to *play* with anyone."

"You know that's not true, Lucia. What about that Roman boy in Noviomagus?"

"I haven't seen him in months and months and months!" she protested. "Not since Ma got sick."

He made a face, his mouth all puckered up. She could tell he was starting to give in. "Please, Catu? Oh, please!"

He made a big sigh. "I suppose we could walk a little way, down by the harbor."

"Yes!"

"Just for a little while, mind."

"I want to see the dolphins again."

"I can't promise that."

She slipped off the chair and headed for the door. The tablet with its grammar lessons fell on the floor behind her.

"Hey – Wait!" He picked it up and replaced it on the table.

She was halfway across the grass between the villa and the road to the harbor when he caught up with her. He grabbed her hand. Beech, who waited patiently under the apple trees for him to finish his lessons every morning, got up and joined them.

The noise and confusion of the construction fell way behind them as they walked. The air was bright and warm and full of the perfume of flowering trees. Sparrows flew past, their beaks dangling worms for their nestlings. Thrushes sang in the hedgerows. Catuarus named them all for her. It was almost like having Niko with them.

But after a while it grew tiresome.

"Those are harebells over there, "Catu said, pointing.

"We have bigger ones in Rome."

He stared at her. "You do not!"

"Do too! Bigger and prettier. Blue ones and red ones and green ones –"

"There aren't any green flowers. You're making it up." He let go of her hand.

A small rabbit darted away from their feet. The dog eyed it for a moment but didn't give chase. A group of people on their way from the harbor to Noviomagus nodded at them. Their backs were bent under the weight of the sacks and boxes they were carrying. The day suddenly turned darker. None of it would be fun if Catu was angry with her.

"I'm sorry," she said in a small voice.

A VILLA FAR FROM ROME

He took her hand again and squeezed it.

She felt so happy her chest was tight. To ease it, she pulled her hand out of Catu's again and did a somersault on the grass.

There was a small ship moored at the dock when they reached it, but no dolphins out to sea. They stopped to watch its cargo being unloaded.

"Not as big as the boat we came on from Rome," Lucia said.

"Do you remember that?"

"Course I do! Ma was sick then too, all the way across the sea. Do you remember that boat too, Catu?"

"I don't want to talk about it."

"Catu!" She gazed at him, astonished to see his grim face.

"It's not your fault. But that was the day my mother and father couldn't be together any more. And we couldn't live in our home."

"You said you liked living with your uncle," she argued. "You said he knew a lot of really strange things – like magic."

"Druids don't do magic!" he said scornfully. "You don't know anything about it at all."

She didn't understand why he was so upset with her. She hadn't meant to make him angry. Why couldn't Catu and his family live in the villa with Ma and Niko and Tiber? When it was bigger they would.

"When I grow up," she said, "it can be your home again. And Beech's home too."

They walked past the dock across a rocky area to a small cove. The low tide had uncovered tide pools stretching out to deeper water. Several women and girls, skirts hitched up around their waists, knives in their hands, were bending over the pools. Further down, on a sandy strip, two women were digging with long forks.

"Listen!" she said. "Catu, they're singing!"

"Why not? People do sing, you know."

"What're they doing in the water?"

"Collecting shellfish, mussels and cockles, and maybe finding oysters."

"What funny names!"

"Well, they taste good."

"Can I do it too?"

Without waiting for his permission, she scrambled over the rocks toward the tide pools. The dog bounded after her. A girl who looked about Catuarus's age held out a hand to steady her as her sandals slipped on wet rock.

"Show me how?" she begged. "I want to find *mussels* and *cockles!*"

The girl raised her eyebrows and looked at Catuarus. He said something to her in his own language and the girl nodded. She gave Lucia a short, blunt-bladed knife and demonstrated how it was to be used to pry the shellfish off the rocks where they were stuck tight. It was hard work at first, but she got the way of it – you had to push the tip of the knife between the rock and the green grassy stuff the blue shells were sticking to and then wiggle it till they came free. The other women stopped working to watch her. Once the shell was free, the girl showed her how to make a fold in her tunic to be like a basket for carrying them. In a short time, she'd pried loose three mussels.

"I'm going to ask Old Nev to cook them for you, Catu," she said. "They can be your supper."

He laughed. "I'll go hungry if that's all I'm getting!"

The Regni girl took the knife back and slit open the two halves of the mussel shell, showing her how small the fishy part inside really was. But what was more exciting than the fish – which smelled as fresh as the sea – was the beautiful pearly colors of the inside of its shell.

"We'll keep the ones you find," Catuarus said. "I'll make the shells into a necklace for you."

She went back to work determined to get enough shells to make a big necklace. As she worked at loosening the mussels from the rocks they clung to, he talked to the girl who'd shown her how to take them. From time to time he called Lucia's attention to something he'd found in the tide pool – a tiny crab scuttling across the palm of his hand, a very small, spiral-shaped shell. Gulls flew over her, turning their heads down to watch what she did. Beech bounded in and out of the water barking in joy, splashing everybody. It was such fun!

A VILLA FAR FROM ROME

After a while, Catuarus said, "We should go now. Niko will be worried about us."

She started to protest that she wasn't ready to go home, but her back was aching a little from bending over, and she was very hungry. She counted her treasures. "Unus. Duo. Tres. Quattuor. Quinque —"

"Someday I'll teach you to count in my language," he promised.

The sun was past its highest point in the sky as they walked back from the sea, the morning long gone. When they came in sight of the villa, they saw Niko and Tiber standing outside, waiting for them. She could tell from their faces they weren't happy.

"I'm in trouble now," Catuarus said.

"You mother has been very worried about you," Niko said as they approached the men. "Whatever possessed you to run off like that without telling anyone?"

"I am ashamed of you, my son, that you would endanger this child!" Tiber said.

"Oh – But Catu didn't! I wanted to go ...." She broke off, knowing they weren't going to listen to her.

Tiber gripped Catuarus by the shoulder and turned him away from the villa. "Home!"

Niko took her by the hand, but she pulled away from him, spilling the mussel shells on the grass, and reached out to touch Catuarus.

"Catu," she said. "I'm going to marry you when I grow up! And nobody's going to stop me."

Chin tilted skyward, she marched into the villa, Niko trailing behind.

CHAPTER TWENTY-FOUR

THE NOISE THE BUILDERS WERE MAKING gave Antonia a headache. She lay on the couch in her room, a cold cloth on her head. The summer morning was warm, no hint of a breeze, the garden too full of dust and noise to be restful. Already, they'd pulled down a large section of the old house, leaving the family crowded into a small space. When Tiberius was home he complained it was a great inconvenience. Lucky for them both that he spent so much time in Noviomagus.

The chaos and confusion prevented her from thinking straight this morning. She needed to think about what Aron had told her. The villa would be glorious once it was finished, especially since Nero wanted it to be a copy of his Golden House! It would be more than she could have dreamed of. But it wouldn't be hers, if the emperor came to live in it. An emperor in exile was still powerful, and her wants and wishes wouldn't count for very much if that happened. He'd find the villa not big enough for both of them and send her away.

"Ma!" Lucia tugged on her arm.

"Not now, Lucia.."

"Ma, look what Gallus made for me."

Her daughter held up a carved wooden doll, the length of her fore arm. It was crude, by the standards she'd known as a child, but the arms and legs had been pinned so they moved.

"Very nice, but please –"

"Can we make a tunic for her to wear?"

Lucia's face was shining with excitement. Such little things it took to make a child happy, she thought. "Tell Delamira to make one."

"I can't find her."

"You haven't looked."

A VILLA FAR FROM ROME

Lucia pouted but left the room. Antonia closed her eyes and thought about Rome.

A few moments later – had she drifted into sleep? – she heard someone at the door and opened them again.

"Guest," Old Nev said, one of the few Latin words she'd mastered in all the months since Antonia had arrived.

She sat up, hands flying to her hair. She wasn't prepared to meet guests.

"It's only me," a familiar voice said behind Old Nev.

"Gracila?"

The Roman woman, dressed for riding in boots and cloak, came into the room carrying her small girl. "I'm pleased to see you recovered from your sickness Antonia."

"I'm so happy to see you! It's been far too long. Please, sit down and Delamira will fetch food We have to pantomime everything to Old Nev – "

"Thank you, but no." Gracila set the child down. "We won't stay long."

"I wish you would! I've missed you."

"How is your throat? I heard that your Greek magician did something terrible to it – but you are well now?"

"Magician indeed! I might well have died without his knowledge."

She displayed the healing scar to her friend's examination. She became aware that Gracila wasn't smiling.

"Oh, my dearest friend!" She held her hands out to Gracila, drawing her down onto the couch beside her. "What can it be? Tell me."

"The sickness was particularly hard on the very old and the very young. Like Caelius. Some didn't live."

"But – not Caelius? Not your son?" She read the unwelcome answer on her friend's face. "No. Oh, surely no!"

"Marcus is taking it very hard. He adored his son."

She put her arms around Gracila and let her friend weep. This was devastating news. Whatever could it have been that took the old and the young but let her survive? She remembered Gracila saying something about legionaries joining the Second Augusta from Palestine, and the young slave who'd hung around them and died. Caelius was the same age as Lucia. What terrible fate had the gods sent that struck soldiers and small children – and why? She should make a special sacrifice to Minerva in the new temple to safeguard her own child..

"I've come to say goodbye," Gracila said. "I'm going back to Pompeii."

"Of course. You need time to heal from such a horrible loss."

"No. You don't understand. Marcus is sending us away." The tears were gone; she spoke calmly. "We were never married, you see. The legion doesn't allow ... Well. With Caelius dead, he doesn't see the point of keeping us here. His son was everything to him."

"But the little one – your daughter. She's his daughter too!"

"You know how it is, Antonia. He wanted a son."

"But what will you do in Pompeii? How will you survive?"

"I'll do what I was doing when I met Marcus, I imagine."

Gracila spoke casually, but she sensed the well of despair under the calm words. For the first time, she saw the bitter lines around Gracila's eyes and mouth, the grey that twisted through her dark hair, and realized that in Marcus's eyes she was too old to bear another child for him. It was unjust, but she knew that was the way of a Roman man.

"We have to leave now before the bad weather sets in," Gracila said. "Once the winter storms come, the sea captains won't be so eager to make the crossing."

"Tiberius should talk to Marcus. Tiberius could make him change his mind."

"I think you saw at Yule how little power your barbarian king wields with Rome."

"But he's a Roman citizen too –"

Gracila shook her head. "Besides, I think Marcus has other plans."

* * *

After Gracila had gone, Antonia went to find Tiberius.

A VILLA FAR FROM ROME

He was sitting at a small desk in the original part of the house where he used to conduct the affairs of the tribe, a room he'd threatened the builders to leave out of their plans for destruction. The servant who'd been lighting oil lamps against the late afternoon shadows went away. He was still angry that the emperor was paying to build a new villa for them. *"And what will we owe him for this?"* He'd rejected her answer that the emperor wanted a good life for his daughter. How angry he'd be if he ever found out the real reason Nero was building this villa! Minerva defend them from having to face that day.

Tiberius looked up from a letter as she entered, his expression distracted as if he didn't remember who she was. Then clarity returned and he inclined his head politely to her.

How old he looked in the lamplight! His face had retreated into new lines and creases, and surely his hair had whitened since before her illness? Something stirred in her at the sight of this new vulnerability she saw in him, not love, certainly, but a form of caring. If her life had been changed by Nero's actions, she realized how much his had too.

"Tiberius, Gracila Pavonia is going back to Rome. Marcus has sent her away. Why would he do that? What can it mean?"

"You know his son didn't survive the sickness."

"I do now. But how does that explain anything?"

"I think the centurion has plans to advance his status."

"How does sending Gracila and his daughter away help with that?"

"She wasn't his wife –"

"That I know! *The legion doesn't allow –*"

"Lady," he said patiently. "I'm not your enemy. You don't need to fight me all the time. This is Roman law."

She wanted to argue, but he was right, and an argument might lead to things slipping out that she'd regret. "I apologize. But how could he have plans that mean sending Gracila away? It doesn't seem just."

"This isn't easy on any of us."

"I'll miss Gracila!"

Instead of replying to that, he said, "What will happen now to Delamira?"

"What do you mean? Gracila gave her to me."

"There are no slaves in my house. Those who serve here are free."

"Then I'll free her! What difference will it make?"

"Good." His expression softened. "I understand being here isn't easy for you."

"Thank you."

Before Septimus Severus arrived with the plans to build a grand villa, intended for Nero to inhabit, as she now knew, she'd been resolving to do better in the position the emperor had consigned her to. She couldn't do anything about the politics of Rome – and nothing would come of it anyway. But she could take control of her own life, starting now.

"You were busy. I've interrupted you. Is there something I could do to help?"

He looked up at her, surprise showing in a frown that he quickly hid. "I'm seeing signs that disturb me." He held up the document he'd been studying when she came into the room. "A messenger just delivered this letter from the garrison in Noviomagus. A call for more taxes to fund the legion and pay for our 'protection against the predations of hostile tribes.'"

"Which hostile tribes?" Determined as she'd been to be of help, this sudden sharing of his concerns surprised and confused her. "I didn't think Rome had trouble with anyone here right now."

"Nothing beyond the ordinary day to day squabbles and grudges," he agreed.

Pull yourself together! she scolded herself. Here was a chance. "I may not be very schooled in government, Tiberius, but I learned a few things in my father's house. Centurions are not responsible for collecting taxes or raising them."

"Not in Rome, certainly," he agreed, laying aside the stylus he'd been using to make notes. "Not even in our larger cities that have a *procurator provinciae.*"

"I don't understand this. Doesn't Rome fund the legions?"

"Normally. But the emperor has just committed a significant amount of money to build a magnificent villa here. Don't think Marcus Favonius hasn't noticed that."

Were the two things connected in reality? She understood without the need for him to explain, that how real the connection might or might not be would hardly matter if the centurion suspected it. If Aron was right, the money was not for her sake or Tiberius's, but that would hardly matter to the centurion feeling the loss of support for his troops.

"I imagine this exercise in wielding power is the centurion's first step in demonstrating his worthiness to be promoted to higher command," he added. "I don't know how far his ambition stretches."

"What are you going to do about it?"

"I can do very little. I'll ride out again tomorrow."

"But you have so recently returned –"

"I must take the news of these taxes to the Regni myself. They won't be popular. I'll start with the farmers and merchants close to town, before the weather changes. If we're blessed with a good summer, I'll venture further away. The sooner this gets done the better."

Relief swept over her. He'd be far away and too busy to think about the real reason Septimus Severus had been sent to build the new villa. If he knew that, she couldn't be sure he'd be able to contain his anger, with possibly terrible consequences for them all. She turned her attention to her own anger at the centurion for sending her friend Gracila away. Such a short time ago she'd harbored daydreams – She understood that her view of the centurion had been that of a moonstruck girl. Now she saw him in daylight.

She left Tiberius at his desk before he could see the warmth she felt spreading across her face.

CHAPTER TWENTY-FIVE

THE MEETING HE'D PLANNED WITH SHEEP-HERDERS didn't start well. He hadn't expected it to be easy, but sullen silence was harder to deal with than argument. There was always a certain amount of friendly rivalry between cattle folk as his family had traditionally been and sheep folk, but he sensed a more serious undercurrent here. He'd spent several days riding from one argumentative group to another, sullen with grievances.

The herders sat in a circle around the fire which the wife of the chief among the herders had built against the chill that arrived with a heavy rain, and the small house was thick with the smell of burning peat and unwashed bodies crowded together. An honest smell, one he much preferred to the perfumes Antonia had been wearing since her visit with Gracila. He knew most of them by sight if not all of them by name; he'd always made it his purpose to know his own people. The chief herder, he remembered now, as the older man gazed across the fire at him, was the brother of Epilus who'd become his enemy on the Council of Elders. They shared the same hooded eyes full of barely concealed aggression.

A young woman brought him the cup of wheat beer. Acknowledging his rank, she left it with him instead of waiting for him to drink then passing it on to the next man. He thought of Gallus and his love of Celtic beer; for himself, he would've preferred a Roman wine.

"This is no easy sacrifice I ask of you." He gazed in particular at the younger men, the ones he knew were most resistant. "It sounds much more heroic to take up knives and cudgels and defy the Roman tax collectors. But I would remind you of the lesson Boudicca learned, that the legions have swords and far-flying arrows and catapults hurling iron balls and battle chariots. I saw this myself. We Regni – farmers and herdsmen and craftsmen – stand to lose our lives in futile rebellion."

A VILLA FAR FROM ROME

He thought of the potters he'd visited yesterday, a woman and her two daughters, too busy to give him their undivided attention, their stolid, expressionless faces sweaty from the heat of the kiln. He remembered the earthy smell of wet clay that caked their fingers. Life was hard, the mother said, stoking the kiln fire, since the death of her husband three years ago. They showed him the pots they were making, and he praised the delicacy of the vessels, the intricate patterns of the decoration, the smooth glaze. They spoke of the wonderful new road the legion was building that would eventually link Noviomagus with Londinium, giving them a much larger market for their pots. No pleasant task to bring the potters the news, but it was his duty. Hot-headed as any man, they'd rebel and reach for the knives before anyone had a chance to stop them. And the Romans would massacre them. He bought a pretty jug for Breca from them, thought again and bought another for Antonia, stowing them both in the saddlebag on Stormfellow.

After leaving the women, he'd sheltered for the night in a pig-herder's hut, the man – hardly more than a boy – obviously unable to pay whatever tax he was assessed now. Remembering, he sighed. So many stories like that.

"As your leader, a friend with your well-being at heart," he said now to the sheep-herders, "I urge you to consider that the way forward is to cooperate with the Romans, to learn from them whatever good there is to be learned."

He tried to catch the eye of each of the men in turn, reinforcing their tribal unity with him. Several of them refused to meet his eyes – not a good sign. They didn't share his opinion of the benefits of Rome. Some of them had probably been supporters of Boudicca's cause, more popular in the countryside than in the towns. And they would remember which side he'd been on.

The chief herder's round-house was almost as big as the one Breca's uncle had built on the island. The small settlement of two family houses and a rectangular building to house the unmarried younger men had been built high on the Downs with views that stretched all the way from the sea almost to the border with the Atrebates. A ditch around the houses held in the settlement's chickens. A brown and white stallion, half wild by the look of it, cropped the grass inside an enclosure; he'd noted that the boy who took Stormfellow's reins didn't put him in the same enclosure as the other horse. Hundreds of sheep stood patiently on the rolling pasture land, enduring the rain, their unshorn backs dark and sodden.

It was a lonely, windy life up here, away from the market center in Noviomagus, the public baths and the new arena. These herders weren't even close enough to other Regni villages for companionship. He wouldn't be able to stand it for long himself; he'd grown too accustomed to Roman amenities. But he'd lived like this in his youth, in his grandfather's house, and again when he'd traveled with the legions. A hard life produces hard men, and hard men are difficult to convince they should pay more of their small wealth in taxes. He understood their reluctance.

"We see far up here," the chief herder said, breaking a long silence. He was an old man with long white hair in braids; when he narrowed his eyes to look at Togidubnus through the smoke, he was the very image of his brother Epilus. "We'd know if anyone tried to breach our borders. We've seen nothing that calls for extra defensive measures."

Several of the men nodded at that.

He understood how thin they found the Roman excuse of defense against intruders. He was inclined to agree with them but for the memory of the Belgae prisoner, warrior in Boudicca's lost cause and stubbornly hostile to the Roman settlers. They'd made an agreement under the mistletoe to keep the peace, and a good Celt would keep it. But what if there were more like him, angry younger sons chafing under the twin restraints of lack of power in their tribes and Roman rule? When he'd been a young man, he'd been full of fire too. If he hadn't become convinced that the only sane path for the tribes' future existence was cooperation with Rome, he might've been that rebel the centurion had captured.

"What do they plan to do to us if we can't raise the money?" a man with a long scar on his face demanded. "Take away our flocks? I'd like to see a legionary herding sheep!"

A VILLA FAR FROM ROME

There was laughter at that. They were sheep-herders, not warriors. But they were also quick-tempered Celts, not given to listening to logic at the best of times.

He sipped the beer, then passed the cup on, wishing they'd added honey to it the way the folk down on the coast did. Bees didn't thrive up here on the windy hillsides where a rough grass grew and few flowers other than clover. He realized he knew nothing about bee culture, and should learn.

"Rain's stopped," a thin, pinch-faced young man, the chief herder's son, announced. "You should leave now."

He couldn't let the deliberate incivility pass. He stood, aware of the resentment in the young man's eyes. "Do not suppose that peaceful words mean weakness."

"Shouldn't our *king* defend us against thieves, even if they are Roman?"

The chief herder rose to his feet too, upsetting a platter of dark bread and sheep cheese. He struck his son on the cheek. "You will not insult our king under my roof!"

The men were all looking at him, waiting to see how he would react. Most of them – the older ones – showed by their expressions their disapproval of the young man's disrespectful words. But not all. He hadn't chosen to be made king, nor did he use the title, but the damage had been done the day Nero bestowed it on him. There was no right action for him here. He turned abruptly and strode out of the roundhouse – a breach of courtesy that signified his displeasure.

The old herder followed him. They stood looking out over the wet Downs, now sparkling in a shaft of sunshine. The smell of wet turf, wet wool and air as sharp as crystal filled his nose. Somewhere up high, a lark began to sing, and in the distance he heard the call of the cuckoo. Soon, full summer would be here and the cuckoo would fall silent, her work planting her babies in other birds' nests over for the year. Much like Nero had planted a bastard in his nest, he thought. A girl, splashing through puddles in her bare feet, brought Stormfellow to him.

"Forgive my son," the old man said.

He looked steadily at the old man, Epilus's brother. How far could he trust this family? "Forgiven."

"The young ones are restless and hard to control."

"Understandable." He hoisted himself onto the horse's back. "But a dangerous attitude to encourage. Rome is powerful, and not given to tolerance for rebellion. See to it that you keep your young ones under control."

The old man patted Stormfellow's neck and went back inside.

* * *

Two more groups of herders, one with a mixed herd of sheep and goats, were all he could manage to visit in one day. He was getting too old for this sort of extended surveying of his territory; his muscles complained and his bones creaked. But he felt an urgent need to carry the news himself and not allow his folk to be ambushed by the arrival of the tax collector accompanied by legionaries. He knew too well how Rome dealt with those who opposed her will.

There was time for one last visit on the way home, a group of salt farmers whose huts clustered together in a shallow valley where a wide stream made its way to the sea. He summoned up his remaining energy and urged Stormfellow forward.

The sun was low over the Downs as he rounded a bend in the road and saw the steam ascending from the boiling pits on a rise above the sea. Drawing closer, he identified the large flat-bottomed settling tanks that held sea-water in the first stage of salt extraction. The fields around the tanks were bare, their trees having long ago been felled to fuel the fires. Which was harder, he pondered as he approached, toiling over kiln fires or salt-water boiling pits, or tending sheep in winter on the exposed Downs? By what stroke of fate had he avoided these heavy lives to be born into a chief's family? His own problems became less burdensome when he contemplated the lives of his people. His hope had been that by adopting the laws and the advanced knowledge of the Romans, his people would come to live better lives. The Romans in their turn would benefit from the

A VILLA FAR FROM ROME

grain, cattle, wool and silver the island had to offer. Now, he wondered if the exchange could ever be truly balanced.

The salt farmers were more vocal in their reception of his news. Six of them stood by a deep cistern that held the salt-laden water on the first stage, thick-armed men who wore very little in spite of the chilly late afternoon. They didn't offer him hospitality of any kind. Instead, he was assaulted by questions about the demand for more money and arguments that they were already paying more than their fair share.

"They need our salt," a fat, middle-aged man with red cheeks and bulbous nose that betrayed his love of beer complained. "If we didn't provide it, their meat would rot on the way to Rome! Let them remember that."

"Aye," another man agreed. "We're free men, not slaves to be worked to death."

"What if we all refuse?" a third asked. "What could they do?"

He shook his head. The garrison at Noviomagus was small, but he had no doubt the Romans could quickly bring in enough troops to smash a revolt. He'd seen Roman power at work crushing Boudicca, and she'd been better prepared to face them than any of the farmers and craftsmen who'd found his news so unwelcome. Acceptance of Roman rule had to happen. Better for the Regni that it happen peacefully and not by the sword.

"It's not right that our king should support the Romans over his own people!"

He left them arguing behind him and headed home.

He was worn down to his bones by the past frustrating days carrying the unwelcome news. Stormfellow was tired too, plodding patiently along the narrow road that led back to Noviomagus. The sky darkened in the west, only a few purple streaks left to show where the sun had been, but the air was still warm. Any other time, he would've derived great joy from his visits. Nothing was more satisfying to him than observing the trades of shepherds and potters and farmers, learning the wisdom that didn't come from books. His father and grandfather had taught him that he owed it to the people he ruled to understand what their lives were about. Until now, that had not been a burdensome task.

Was he doing the right thing? He was certain that cooperating with Rome was the path of the future, but his people didn't understand. Some of them saw it as betrayal. His mood darkened as he rode on. Even his own Breca had seen it as betrayal. And why should she think otherwise? She had been banished from his house as much as Gracila had been banished from the centurion's. Though it had been Nero's doing, not his own, hadn't he accepted it?

The way passed through a copse of young elms, in shadow as daylight slipped further away. Even the birds whose chatter he'd been aware of all day had quieted with the approach of evening. In the distance, he thought he heard the sound of a horse whinnying, but it was only the wind rising to stir the branches of the trees. Few people came this way; he had the road to himself. He'd heard the occasional story about thieves lurking amongst these trees, waiting for unwary travelers, but he discounted them. A thief might have to wait a long time and then encounter a poor man with nothing to steal!

For a moment, a sliver of doubt entered his mind. Perhaps he should have accepted Gallus's offer of accompanying him. He hadn't seen the need. Yet a friendly voice would be welcome right now.

Darkness fell over the wood. The moon had not yet risen, but the horse knew his way home. He doubted it would really come down to outright revolt. The Regni would argue and propose outlandish schemes to avoid paying the increase the centurion wanted. A lot of words would be wasted on threats and boasts and scorn for Roman citizens, but they'd find a way to do it. That was the Regni way. And in the end, they would know the benefit.

As long as the Romans restrained themselves from their tendency to think every argument should be overcome with the blade of a sword.

The back of his head exploded with pain and his vision went black. Pain raced through him like fire. He tried to grab for the reins which had slipped from his fingers but his hands were no longer under his control.

Another blow, this one to his shoulders. He struggled to draw his

A VILLA FAR FROM ROME

gladius. Hands grasped his leg. Stormfellow reared up, whinnying in fear. He slashed with the blade at an attacker he couldn't see. He felt himself being dragged off the horse –

His last thought was regret that he'd never see Breca again.

CHAPTER TWENTY-SIX

Antonia sat at Tiberius's desk in the one part of the old house that hadn't been demolished yet, looking over a page of plans Severus had given her to review. She needed to be of some use here, and if she couldn't help Tiberius with his problems, at least she could supervise the construction of the villa – she'd made a determined effort not to think about its eventual destiny. But that was proving harder than she'd supposed.

It didn't help that somewhere in the house somebody was singing – if you could call the peculiar wailing *singing*. The horrible noise was causing her head to pound.

She didn't like to admit she couldn't understand architectural drawings and was waiting for Niko to come and explain them to her. At this time of the morning, the Greek would be busy with the children's Latin lessons or something, but she'd sent him a request, and he wouldn't ignore that.

The weather was finally warming – thank the gods! – and the rain that had settled over the island for ever had blown away. The sky was the clear, bright blue of summer, unsullied by the winter's smoke haze of kitchen fires. Through the window came the sounds of workmen hammering and sawing, the occasional high-pitched oaths that the architect indulged in when things weren't going his way, and the deeper, slower replies of his assistant, Aron.

"Your husband didn't return last night," Niko said as he entered the room.

She was irritated by the Greek's lack of formality. Of course, he wasn't a slave to bow and grovel when he came into her presence, but she could still hope for a small sign of respect. She was a queen, after all. What an odd thought that was! Obviously, she wasn't ever going to get that level of respect from him.

A VILLA FAR FROM ROME

"Is that meaningful? He's often gone for days on tribal matters."

"Gallus expected him at the temple site this morning. There are decisions he needs to make."

"What can I do about it?" She gritted her teeth. Whoever was making that appalling wailing needed to stop before her head burst. "Niko, find out what that noise is."

"It's only Delamira singing."

"No wonder Rome destroyed Carthage if that's what their singing is like!"

"Do you know what settlements your husband planned to visit?" Niko was sorting though documents on the desk, obviously searching for something.

"What are you looking for?"

"A book of animal stories in their original Greek that I ordered to be shipped here. I thought the children could benefit from them.

"You're teaching them Greek now? Lucia can't even read Latin fluently yet!"

"Now is the time."

She made a face to express her displeasure and returned to the previous topic. "What makes you think Tiberius would discuss his plans with me?"

"Because you're his wife."

"You take liberties, Niko!"

"Perhaps I do, but you do yourself no good by such displays of arrogance."

There were moments when she suspected Niko would treat her like a child no matter what she did. Why did she tolerate him? She needed him; there was no other she could turn to, especially with Gracila sent back to Rome.

"You have no right to scold me, Niko. You have secrets of your own. Don't think I haven't noticed your little excursions into Noviomagus that last until well into the night."

He straightened up from the desk, a book in his hand. "Your father made me a free man. I don't have to ask your permission."

"Oh – of course not!" She was suddenly full of apprehension. What would she do if he left her? "I'm sure Tiberius will be back soon."

Though how could she be sure? Things went more easily between them now, since her long illness, but she was ever aware of the shadow of the Regni woman that came between them. Courtesy would do; she didn't need him to love her.

At least, Delamira's dreadful singing had faded and the room was quiet again.

"I want you to look at these drawings, Niko. Severus has proposed a change in one room. Tell me what you think. Is it a good idea?"

He took the scroll from her and unrolled it, laying it out on the new table Tiberius had bought from a shipment that came from Italia recently. It was a pretty table, a dark, carved wood with a rather lovely pattern of grain, and she'd been delighted when a porter carried it in. It surprised her that Tiberius actually thought about such things as the objects surrounding him in his own home.

Niko studied the plans for a moment. "A villa the size this one's going to be will need the expanded kitchen facilities he's drawn to feed all the visitors who will surely come."

"Is that what those funny symbols mean? Kitchens?"

He gazed at her without answering.

"Of course I understood that! I just wondered –"

"If they were going to be located in a convenient place," he said smoothly. "Yes, I think so."

"You think I'm still a child, don't you? As if I know little more than Lucia."

His expression softened. "To me, you will always be that little girl running through her father's villa, hair streaming out of its ribbons, one sandal lost in the garden somewhere."

She laughed. "We were playing 'Catch-Me,' my brother Valentinus and I. His games always got us into trouble with Pater, but he always shielded me from blame."

A VILLA FAR FROM ROME

"I remember how you chased the chickens in the courtyard too."

"I was gathering eggs! Oh, Niko, if only we could return to those days. Are you ever homesick? I don't mean for Pyrgi."

"I don't spend much time thinking about Greece."

She heard more in his flat tone than the words conveyed. She was certain there was some secret hidden in his past, before he'd been captured in some rebel skirmish and enslaved.

The door banged open and Septimus Severus strode in, so secure in his position as Nero's favorite architect that he never needed to ask permission. The man was hard to like, but he was building a beautiful house for her so she held her tongue. Behind him, hesitating in the doorway as if uncertain of his welcome, she saw Aron.

"So?" the architect demanded. "Have you considered the plans? What do you think of them? Are you satisfied? The kitchen facilities will suit you?"

His rapid fire questions didn't really leave room for her to present her own ideas – if she'd had any. She felt sure he wouldn't have listened in any case.

She handed the rolled plans back to him. "Yes. I'm pleased."

"Of course you are," the architect said. "After all, I built the magnificent villa for Nero. This shares many of the same features. How could it not satisfy you?"

None of the dust of tearing down the old house or building the new ever seemed to cling to the short man's tunic. His dark hair was always impeccably oiled and curled on his head – some of it trained to curl across a spot where the scalp had begun to show through. His overbearing arrogance intimidated her today.

"I'm satisfied. But could we discuss the new garden some time?"

"I'm an architect, Lady, not a digger in the earth!"

"I could find diggers and planters too for you in Noviomagus," Aron said softly. "And plants."

The architect glared at his assistant. "The only space for a garden is where the apple trees are now."

"Those are your husband's apple trees," Niko put in.

"Old, hardly bearing any fruit, and what does grow is shriveled."

"Leave my husband's apple trees. We'll find somewhere else for a garden. But what I'd like is a grape arbor."

"Ridiculous!" the architect snapped. He led the way out of the room, motioning for her to follow him,

The plans for the villa were grander than she could have hoped for or even imagined. When it was finished, he showed her, there'd be four long wings in a square around a wide grassy space that could contain columns and statues or fountains, even a flower garden if she insisted. The east wing, facing the road from Noviomagus to the sea, would have a wide entrance hall, just like the one she'd entered when she first encountered the emperor in Rome – without the enormous statue of Nero, she hoped! The audience chamber would be in the west wing, and very grand. The south wing would face the sea beyond another garden, a better vista than even Nero's house on its hillside could boast of. Not that it would all be completed this year – or even next. Severus insisted he was an architect, not a magician. He lacked the expert builders and carpenters he'd had access to in Rome, not to mention skilled craftsmen to lay the mosaics. Some materials would have to be imported from Rome, and who could say how long that would take?

Severus went on and on with his complaints, and she retreated into her thoughts. Lucia had asked if the emperor would come to visit them. Her heart pounded. In the end what happened here would have nothing to do with her, she thought. If events in Rome grew so dire –

But that might never happen. No sense wasting thought on it.

After a while, she allowed herself to daydream about the villa itself. Surely it would be complete – and magnificent! – by the time Lucia was grown. An attractive dowry when she came to marry. But of course, they'd have gone back to Rome long before then. A shadow passed over her heart at that, a feeling her old nurse had called an owl's feather dropping on her tomb, a bad omen.

She had a growing need to do something here, to be more than the

A VILLA FAR FROM ROME

wife Tiberius had been burdened with, unschooled and unskilled. There was something she knew, a skill she'd learned at her father's side, even when he didn't know he was teaching and wouldn't have approved if he had. She knew how to make wine. And if she didn't have grapes — which in any case would take several years before she could harvest them — she could use other fruit. Walking in the garden at the point where the beech trees grew, she'd noticed bushes still full of blackberries. Tomorrow she'd gather all she could find, then she'd summon Old Nev and together they'd make blackberry wine. It would be a productive way to fill the time.

She realized suddenly that Severus had finished lecturing her about his building plans and gone away. Aron was still in the garden, staring at her. Flustered, she smoothed out the folds of her tunic. But it wasn't a hostile stare, rather it proclaimed that they shared something between them that others didn't, the verbal abuse of Septimus Severus. She smiled at him, and he smiled back and went away.

Just as she was about to go inside, she saw Gallus coming down the road from Noviomagus, leading an animal. Puzzled, she watched as he grew closer. It was a donkey, an old one, judging by the white muzzle and the slow, shambling gait. Gallus stopped and raised a hand in greeting.

"I'll just put this one in the stable with the horses," he said.

"It's a donkey."

"Yes. She'll do fine with them."

"But we don't need a donkey — especially an old one."

He gazed at her. "I thought the little one would like to ride. This old girl's not much good working on the building site any more — they're bringing in a young one to replace her — but she'll make a gentle playmate for a child."

"You'll have to ask Tiberius about this when he returns."

The old legionary nodded. "Plan to. But Little Fox likes animals."

There was a rebuke hidden in there, she thought, but before she could reply Lucia came running across the grass, followed by Tiberius's boy and the boy's dog.

"Ma! Ma!" Lucia cried. "See what Gallus brought!"

The child petted the old creature who lowered her head to have her ears scratched. The boy hung back a little way, shy around her as always, and the dog bounced all around the children's legs.

"...not today," Gallus was saying to the children. "She needs a few days to rest and get better –"

"Is she sick?" Lucia asked.

"She's old. Worn out with work."

"But she'll get better?" the boy asked.

"If you take care of her. Give her lots of good food. Next week, maybe, you can take turns riding her. You need to be good to her."

"Oh, we will!" Lucia promised. "What's her name?"

"I don't think she has one. The builders called her 'You!'"

"We're going to call her 'Gallusina' aren't we, Catu? Because Gallus gave her to us!"

The boy frowned. "I think a name in the Old Tongue would be better."

Lucia was crooning in the donkey's ears, not listening. "Gallusina! Gallusina! We like you, Gallusina!"

"That's enough chatter!" It came out sharper than she'd intended.

Her daughter's face reflected her confusion. She laid a hand on Lucia's shoulder, softening the hurt. *It's not the child's fault!* Memories of her own childhood with horses had flooded in, but she must learn to let that go. It was like poison in her heart.

"Gallus, I need to speak with you."

The children went inside. Gallus waited with the donkey.

"Do you know where my husband went?"

The old warrior shook his head.

"I worry that his return is so delayed. Could something have gone wrong?"

"I offered to go with him – a spear to guard his back, if you like," Gallus said. "But he said these are his people and they're not at war, and he doesn't need protection."

"Do you think he does?"

A VILLA FAR FROM ROME

Gallus shrugged. "The legion taught me that everyone with authority does."

"I want you to look for him, Gallus. I have a bad feeling about this."

The old legionary nodded. "I'll leave right away."

CHAPTER TWENTY-SEVEN

SOMETHING – SOMEWHERE SOMETHING – BUZZED WITH PAIN. He tried to think about that but couldn't seem to keep the thoughts from floating away like bubbles in the surf.

Hurting – very bad –

It came to him suddenly that it was he who was hurting. An explosion of pain in his head followed the recognition. How long he lay like that before the pain subsided to a level he could manage, he didn't know. Time didn't exist in this country of suffering he found himself inhabiting. He was lying on his side, his right arm pinned beneath him. Gradually, he became aware of other places on his body that were injured: shoulders, one leg below the knee, arms. Fingers of the free hand stuck together.

He wiggled them, and was rewarded with another explosion of pain higher up his arm. This time he realized the stickiness was his own blood. He lay panting for a while. At least, the fingers had moved, so they were still attached to his hand and his hand to the rest of his body, though there was obviously a problem somewhere along the arm between his head and his hand.

His eyes, too, were stuck shut. But now he understood what the problem was. Cautiously, he moved the fingers of his free hand again. This time he was ready for the pain and it wasn't so bad. Slowly he brought his fingers up to his stuck eyelids, and very carefully slid them along the cheek bone, trying to dislodge some of the blood. It was warm, not crusted, which meant a head wound was still bleeding. He managed to unstick one eye and opened it.

Darkness. But not quite as complete as before he'd opened the eye. Trees above him, black branches spreading against the lighter blackness of a sky full of stars. He tried to remember what had happened.

A VILLA FAR FROM ROME

He'd been on his way home. Where he'd been and what he'd been doing remained sketchy. But he was lying in the dirt somewhere in a woods. On the way home. The road to – *Noviomagus* – the word entered his mind, and with it a flood of memory.

Somebody had come up behind him and attacked him. More than one, most likely. He hadn't seen who did it. Had they meant to kill him? Were they disturbed before they'd finished the act?

Desperate men sometimes lurked in a forest to take money from unsuspecting travelers. The Romans were unable to completely stop that. But not in this part of his kingdom. And he'd had nothing on him worth taking. Even his horse was old –

Stormfellow.

He managed to get the other eye open, and moved his head. Fire raced through him. He stopped to catch his breath. Tried again.

Listen! He strained to catch the rustle of a cricket, soft passage of a mouse on the way to her nest. No sound of his horse. Stormfellow never wandered off on his own. Once, he'd lain in dirt much like this after a battle, knocked off his horse by one of Boudicca's warriors. When he'd come to his senses, he'd found Stormfellow quietly cropping grass beside him, oblivious to the sounds of battle not far away.

"Storm – " It came out as a croak – his throat felt full of dirt – and much too soft to carry far. He tried again. Nothing. The old war horse was either gone, stolen, or dead.

He closed his eyes again at the realization he wouldn't get very far without his horse even if standing and walking became possible at some point.

At least his mind was now a little clearer. He would think it through, find the pattern.

Someone had attacked him. Someone who'd followed him. He didn't doubt he had enemies outside the tribe. Inside, too? He thought of the hostile reception he'd received as he took the unpopular tax message to the salt farmers, the goatherds, the sheep-herders.

He remembered the hate in the eyes of the chief herder's son when the father struck him. He remembered how Tarvos had scowled at him and how the tribune had struck him that night high on the Downs, drawing blood. Twice now a spirited man had been shamed for opposing him. Nothing good would come of that. The Regni, like all Celts, were a proud people, fierce in their loyalty. Woe to the king who lost that loyalty.

The proper ceremonies were never performed. Some of the Regni denied he was their king.

Exhaustion overcame him, stopping further speculation. He fell into a fitful sleep filled with snatches of bad dreams – Amminus at Nero's table – Breca turning her head away from him – Arto sitting in his little fishing boat with a half-drowned child in his lap – only it was Catuarus he held, not the Roman child.

When he awoke, the sky had lightened to grey, gold and pink streaks in the east showed where the sun would soon appear. Wood doves made their mournful song, and in the trees overhead the branches were full of rustling, chirping life. Apart from a thunderous headache, his mind was fully restored to him.

Someone had attacked him. Not to kill. But to what purpose? To leave a message, a warning?

He sat up with great difficulty, stopping several times to let the pain subside. Even that wouldn't have been possible last night. Something tickled on his brow and he put up his good hand to feel what it was. His fingers dislodged a small brown beetle that had discovered the drying blood.

It was cold in the tree shadow. He'd lost his cloak and was shivering. He felt the urge to sleep creeping up on him. He knew he couldn't allow himself to fall asleep again.

Now he saw the trail of crushed grass and scuffed dirt that showed where he must've been dragged off the road to be left partly hidden under the trees. Whoever had done this to him hadn't wanted him to be quickly discovered by any other travelers going up to Noviomagus. Still no sign of Stormfellow. No clue a horse of any kind had been in this place under the trees. The saddlebag with his gifts was gone too.

A VILLA FAR FROM ROME

He didn't think the injured leg would take his weight, so walking was out of the question. He ran his good hand cautiously down the length and decided the bone was broken. Moving it caused fire to streak up his leg to his hip and started his head pounding again. Well, he'd crawl back to the road. But first, he'd rest a little to gain strength.

After a while, he roused himself. The sun was high overhead now. In spite of the care he took, positioning himself on all fours, the injured leg and shoulder screamed with pain. It became difficult to think coherently. His head pounded. But he refused to give up. Slowly, inch by inch, one good arm and one good leg managed to drag the rest of him out from the shelter of the trees to the edge of the hard-packed dirt that formed the narrow roadway. He collapsed, sweat pouring off his brow, nauseous.

The sun warmed him a little, and he closed his eyes to rest again.

He must've drowsed off at some point. He became fully awake when he realized that what had disturbed him was a human voice.

"Looks like you had a bad night, Little Fox," Gallus said, leaning over him. "Let's get you home."

CHAPTER TWENTY-EIGHT

SEPTIMUS SEVERUS WAS GIVING workmen directions about where to unload the fresh supplies that had just been brought up from the port. Afternoon sun struck a gleam from the bald spot on his head. Unconcerned with the dramas of the house, the architect went about his work as if nothing had happened. Of course, Antonia knew, in his mind nothing that wasn't about him or the villa he was building mattered. Aron trailed the architect around the unfinished walls and the outlined rooms, stooping a little to bring his head down to the level of the smaller man.

She might as well have been one of the servants by the way Niko had ordered her out of the room when Gallus brought Tiberius home yesterday. Admittedly, she'd shrieked when she'd first seen him, covered in blood, his clothes torn and muddy, and only half conscious in the old man's arms. But what woman wouldn't have been shocked to see her husband in that condition? That was yesterday, and now the sun was well past its zenith, and still nobody had told her anything yet about his condition. At one point earlier this morning, Gallus had emerged to send Delamira to Noviomagus for an ointment Niko needed. Delamira was her servant, but Gallus didn't ask her permission. Now here came the girl carrying a package – running, the girl never went anywhere slowly. It tired her to watch!

There were two men following her on horseback. Romans. Marcus Favonius, and the tribune, Didius.

The centurion wore no cloak, so his bronzed arms were bare in the summer sun. Her heart pounded wildly. Of course the centurion had come to see Tiberius. Nothing strange about that – Tiberius was king here and Marcus, as the representative of Rome, would be concerned with what had happened to him. But wasn't it odd that he'd come himself this time instead of sending his tribune the way he had at Yule? Both men dismounted and walked across the grass to her.

She was immediately ashamed of herself for the thought, with Tiberius lying wounded in the next room, yet she couldn't stop the shiver of excitement that ran through her at the sight of Marcus. Sunshine turned his bare head to molten gold. He was taller and more bronzed than she remembered from that night he'd first come to the villa, his legs sturdy and muscular in their sandals. She couldn't help it if she thought he was as beautiful as a god. An uncomfortable thought entered her head: *Once, you thought of Nero that way.* She dismissed it.

"Lady." The centurion bowed his head politely. "Have I been informed correctly about your husband's unfortunate condition?"

"Yes. He – I – I think – He was attacked." She was furious with herself for stumbling over her words like an ignorant girl, but her mind was whirling.

Marcus smiled, and she knew he'd taken note of her confusion. Heat crept into her cheeks.

"May I enter and visit him?"

"Niko's with him – our Greek servant. If Niko allows ...."

She stopped. How childish she must sound!

The centurion apparently decided to let her retain her dignity. "Of course," he said solemnly. "I wouldn't wish to intrude. But are you certain you can trust the Greek?"

"What can you mean?"

He shrugged. "You must know he's *cinaedus*, like most Greek men. Untrustworthy. I'm sad you have no better man around to serve you."

She stared at him, not following his argument. Both men smiled broadly at a joke she didn't understand.

"Well," he said. "There are more important matters right now. This attack on your husband is of concern to Rome. The sooner we get to the bottom of it, the better."

Delamira, who'd gone straight into the large bedchamber in the newly built wing of the villa with her package now came back out again, followed by Gallus. The girl's face was set in an exaggerated mask of grief, and for a moment Antonia thought Tiberius might have succumbed to his wounds and died. Seeing the two Romans, one of whom had recently been her master – she glanced at Antonia, then hurriedly backed out of the room again.

"Centurion," Gallus said. The old man's tone was flat, polite, one Roman citizen to another and no more.

"You were the one who found him?" Marcus asked. His voice was equally cold, the authority dealing with underlings, she thought.

"Yesterday, Centurion, when he didn't return as expected. He'd been beaten and left by the road, east of here. Apparently he was on his way back from the salt farms down by Bright Water's Mouth. No sign of who did it."

"Do you have any thoughts on that?" the tribune put in.

"No."

Something in Gallus's tone and behavior jolted her out of her own confusion. The old legionary's dislike of the centurion and the tribune was so obvious it bordered on the insulting.

"I wish to question him briefly," Marcus said.

"He doesn't remember much about what happened, Centurion."

"Open the door."

Gallus stood back – reluctantly, she saw – and allowed the centurion to enter the bedchamber. Didius, the tribune, remained in the antechamber.

"Gallus. Is he – will he –" She was afraid to put her fears into words less the fates mock her and the fears became reality.

"If it's possible to pull him through, your Greek friend will do it," Gallus said. "We'll just have to wait."

Her legs felt as if they'd turned to water and she sought a bench to sit down. Of course she didn't want Tiberius to die! That was not what she wanted at all. Tiberius was a good man.

"Are you well?" Gallus asked. "Your face is the color of a pitcher of milk."

"I'm concerned for my husband," she said with as much dignity as she could manage.

A VILLA FAR FROM ROME

"As are we all," the tribune said smoothly.

There was something distasteful about Didius. She couldn't put a name to it, but she disliked him. He might have high-born and important relatives in Rome – all who held that office did – but he reminded her of a snake in her father's garden. She distracted herself with domestic concerns.

"Gallus, could you tell a servant to bring refreshment for the centurion? I don't know where Delamira went."

Gallus went away. The tribune paced to the door of the bed chamber and stood as if on guard.

Time passed sluggishly. The tribune continued to stare at her. She struggled to control her emotions. So much had happened to her in the last few years, so much turmoil and upheaval. So many tears shed and so few moments of happiness.

"Stupid!" she scolded herself aloud and immediately covered her mouth in embarrassment.

"Excuse me?" Marcus stood in the open doorway again, half-smiling.

She was about to dissolve into idiocy under the force of his vividly masculine presence. Annoyed with herself, she stood up. "Are you leaving, Centurion?"

"Marcus." He held his hand out. "Antonia."

She struggled to control her voice. "Did you get the information from my husband that you came for?"

He shrugged. "He's in bad shape and not much help. His attackers were probably rebels. *Britunculi.*"
‘

She flinched as she recognized the derisive term Romans used for the tribes of her husband's country. She didn't react to his outstretched hand. He came closer and lifted one of hers.

"But it's you I'm concerned about, Antonia."

She wished he wouldn't use her name. It wasn't right. It reduced her to a subordinate. "Me?" Her voice squeaked.

He stroked her cheek with his other hand. "You."

This was what she'd wanted, wasn't it? But what if Gallus came back into the room – or Niko? She realized Marcus didn't care about other men's opinions.

"You're a pretty little thing," he said.

She gathered her self-control enough to reply. "Centurion, my husband lies in that room behind you – possibly dying."

"So?" He sounded puzzled. "You think we should wait until he does?"

Behind them she heard the tribune's half-stifled laugh.

It was as if someone had emptied a pail of icy water over her. Her confusion vanished, replaced with anger.

"I think you should leave this house now, Centurion."

She tried to pull her hand away but he held fast.

His expression hardened. "I would remind you – "

"Delamira's with the little one. Don't know where Old Nev is. Here's all I could find in the kitchen."

Relief swept over her at the sound of Gallus's voice. "Thank you!"

He held out a plain earthenware jug filled with clear liquid she was certain was water. The old man's contempt couldn't have been more obvious.

Marcus released her hand. "I'm leaving now."

Gallus glanced from one to the other. She felt certain he knew what had happened here. Had he overheard? Her cheeks flamed again.

Marcus strode out of the villa, followed by the tribune. After a moment, she heard the sound of their horses's hooves on the gravel path.

"That man has a black heart," Gallus said. "You shouldn't trust him."

"I don't."

"Good."

She felt suddenly tired, as if the conversation with Marcus had been hard, physical work. Yet at the same time, something had lifted from her spirit. This was what life was really about, always struggling to find the right action, not always the thing that gave pleasure. Her father had thought so. Men she admired like her father and Tiberius made that the rule in their lives. She wasn't a child any more, lamenting the loss of her innocence. She would try to do the right thing too. Dear gods, let Tiberius live!

"We have more guests," Gallus said, glancing out at the garden.

She turned. An old man with shoulder-length grey hair and a boy were coming across the grass, stepping carefully past the construction materials littering the path. She recognized Tiberius's son.

With them was Tiberius's Regni wife.

CHAPTER TWENTY-NINE

WHEN THE CENTURION HAD TAKEN HIS LEAVE, Niko squeezed water out of a cloth, then laid it on Togidubnus's hot brow. The water was cold and aromatic with the herbs he'd sent Delamira to procure.

"Lie still," the Greek said. "You've suffered a *quassatur* and need time to recover."

"The leg hurts worse."

"Broken bones are easily set, if they're a clean break. And cuts and gashes can be stitched. Bruises heal with time. Heads too, but you must limit movement."

There were many matters he should be taking care of. Marcus Favonius hadn't stayed long, but he'd grasped the centurion's concerns about the signs of rebellion growing in the region and his own responsibility for maintaining order among his people. If war broke out, Rome would hold him responsible. He needed to be up and doing something, not lying prone like a suckling lamb.

Niko held a cup to his lips and dribbled a bitter liquid into his mouth. "This will help with the pain."

He made a face. "Must physic taste so foul?"

"The gods need their amusement."

"What is this poison?"

"A brew made from the bark of a willow."

He closed his eyes. The headache made it difficult to think about the problem for very long, but he had to try. He felt Niko replacing the damp cloth with another, lapping it over his eyes too this time, and was grateful for the coldness. The thudding pain in his head subsided a little.

"Tell me how you know so much about healing."

The Greek was silent for a moment. "I was a physician once. I traveled to the island of Kos to learn from an old Jew who knew more than Hippocrates, the school's founder."

He frowned, instantly regretting it; furrowing his brow brought the headache back. "Why are you so reluctant to reveal your skill? Surely, it would've gained you great advancement in Rome?"

"Someday I may tell you. Not now."

He heard Antonia's voice outside the door, more than one person answering. The door opened.

"Nephew."

He recognized Arto's voice and opened his eyes. Behind the old Druid he saw Catuarus. And Breca.

"We came to satisfy ourselves you were ... that you would recover from your wounds," Breca said, awkwardly.

He saw how she avoided meeting his eyes, and knew instantly how ill at ease she must feel in this villa that already reflected great changes from their small home. He wanted to take her hand in his as if she was the one who needed comfort, but his arm refused to obey his mind's command to move and the moment passed.

"You will recover, won't you, Father?" his younger son asked.

"Of course he will," Niko answered for him.

Thinking was difficult through the haze Niko's potion had brought on. With effort, he lifted his hands and the boy took one. After a moment, Breca took the other. He closed his eyes again. He was hazily aware of Arto and Niko discussing the potency of the herbs the old man had brought with him. Niko had once remarked that the Druids too had a knowledge of herbs that evaded the Romans.

"Never fear, my son," he said. "I'll soon be well again."

"Be patient, Catuarus," Breca said. "Your father needs rest."

"This is a time of danger for our people." The old Druid glanced down at him. "The way through isn't clear to me."

"I'm old enough now to fight beside you, Father," Catuarus said.

Breca hushed the boy.

"But I am! I can do many things now. I caught fish for you this morning in the channel. Two fat plaice. Just the kind you like."

He tried to reply, to reassure the boy, but their voices receded as the physic Niko had given him took over.

"Fish will be good for him, Catuarus," Niko said. "But now he needs to sleep."

He wanted them to stay, especially Breca. He heard his son start to protest as Arto took him out of the room. Breca still held his hand. He didn't want her to leave.

Niko said softly," You may have a brief moment with him."

He heard the door close behind the Greek. "Breca –"

"I'll come again, Togi. Now, please rest."

"My heart, it must be said –"

"I know. Hush."

He felt the brush of her lips against his brow and his heart burned with love. She released his hand. Then suddenly he slept.

CHAPTER THIRTY

THE OLD REGNI WHO'D ACCOMPANIED TIBERIUS'S NATIVE WIFE came out of the bed chamber with the boy. The old man looked gloomy, but the boy's expression touched her heart, stricken as if he thought his father was already dead. Poor child, so young to have such worries! She remembered what it had been like to be so young and not understand the dangerous currents of politics surrounding you. One day, the wave breaks over your head and you're drowning.

"Please stay. I'll have Delamira bring food and drink."

The old man shook his head, but the boy brightened.

"Yes, please, Lady."

His Latin was almost perfect, Niko's doing.

Delamira, who'd been hovering at the edge of the room, went to find refreshments. They waited in awkward silence.

"There's a storm coming," the old man said at last. "This house stands at the center."

He had more of an accent than the boy, making his Latin harder for her to follow. For a moment she thought he spoke of the weather – not unlikely for a storm to disrupt the season's mildness in this silly climate. But she saw from his expression he meant something worse than thunder and rain. Now she remembered a scrap of gossip Niko had relayed to her: Her husband's first wife had retreated to live with her uncle, a Druid priest.

"There wasn't time to exchange names when you arrived," she said. "I'm Antonia Plautina –"

"I know who you are." There was no impoliteness in his tone, just a depth of hidden meaning that stopped the retort on her lips. "I am Breca's uncle."

"Arto," the boy said helpfully.

"Arto, and – " She hesitated, then remembered what Lucia called her friend, "Catuarus. Be welcome to –" She was about to say *my house* but caught the words back in time. She felt the blood rising into her cheeks and was annoyed. It *was* her house.

"You are not to blame here," the old man said as if he heard her thoughts. "Your fate was controlled by another. As was his."

She stared at him. Something about this grey-haired Regni reminded her of her father – not his appearance, certainly, but his air of quiet authority. It undermined all the defenses she'd built over the last year. It was as if he could read what was in her heart.

Breca came out of Tiberius's room and stood hesitantly, as if she were unsure what to do. Catuarus went to his mother and put his arm around her. Antonia hesitated too, not sure what she should say. She'd thought about this moment, how she would be graceful and welcome Tiberius's first wife to the house, even what topics they would talk about. But now the moment was here she was tongue-tied.

Delamira hurried into the room.

"Lady," she whispered in Antonia's ear. The girl's eyes were bright with excitement at all the commotion in the villa. "There's a messenger here to see the king! He says he has a letter from Rome."

A man in a sailor's cap stood behind the girl.

"He may be sleeping. But Niko will decide." She was tired of having to deal with so much.

Delamira opened the door to Tiberius's chamber, seeking Niko. Another servant stood in her place, carrying a pitcher of wine and another of water. The woman, a Regni that Tiberius had persuaded to come back to work for them, hadn't asked permission to use the best serving ware – blown glass with swirls of emerald and ocean blue, brought at great cost from Rome. The contrast with what Gallus had brought to serve the centurion was shocking. For a moment she was ready to strike the woman for her impertinence. But could the servant be blamed for wanting to honor Breca who'd once been her king's wife?

They were none of them to be blamed. Some malignant god had set up this situation and now laughed at their pain.

She took it upon herself to mix water with the wine in a cup for the

A VILLA FAR FROM ROME

boy while the servant served Breca and her uncle.

The emotions of the moment vanished, leaving her hollow and shaking. She couldn't trust herself to speak. Instead, she sat down and held out her own cup to the servant, and when it was filled she gulped it down. Warmth ran through her body, and she felt the urge to laugh at the preposterous story her life was spinning.

"Thank you for taking care of Togidubnus," Breca said.

She wanted to jest, *You think I was going to let him die?* but realized that was the wine talking. She hadn't eaten all day and it had gone quickly to her head. The only other time she'd drunk so much so rapidly was the day at Nero's banquet table. Then as now, she realized, she drank to hide from things out of her control. She glowered at the Regni woman, wanting to be angry, but seeing in a rush of understanding the lines that marked Breca's face. She was a thin woman, at least a head taller than Antonia, her dark hair streaked lavishly with grey, but she held herself as upright and proud as if she carried a warrior's heart in her breast.

Antonia formed the words carefully. "He was badly injured, but Niko will look after him The Greek is very skillful."

"His head's wounded," the boy said anxiously. "But he's going to live, isn't he?"

"Yes, Catuarus, we'll make sure of that." Poor child, his fear touched her heart.

"He will be needed," the old Druid said. "But which side will he take? There will be an uprising among the tribes. Rome will not be tolerant. The result will be war. This house will not be spared the bloodshed. You must take your child and leave."

The warm sentiment she'd felt a moment ago vanished. *He wants me to leave so the woman and her boy can move back in!* Well, they might be in for a surprise in that case, if what Aron had told her was true about Nero's plans for the villa's future. But what if the old Druid was right? What if the attack on Tiberius was a sign of things to come? Terrible things. If the tribes rose against Rome they would be crushed.

"There's always unrest amongst the tribes isn't there?" She spoke lightly, as if her words could themselves hold back the darkness she feared might be advancing. "The Belgae are jealous of the Regni." She thought hard to remember the names Tiberius had used for the local tribes. "And the Atrebates distrust everybody..."

She broke off, aware how pitiful her argument must sound to them.

Arto put his hand on the boy's arm and steered him towards the door. Breca turned to follow.

"Wait." She didn't know what she was going to say, only knew there was something in her heart she must say, even if there was little she could do about it. "I'm sorry for what has happened." Such a lame apology. And for what? It hadn't been her idea. But all the same, she needed to say it."Visit him whenever you wish."

"Thank you," Breca said.

"I don't wish to be your enemy."

"Never that," Breca said.

CHAPTER THIRTY-ONE

HE STARTLED AWAKE AGAIN AT THE SOUND of a tap at the door, a voice.

"A messenger from Rome to see Lord Tiberius. He says he has a letter."

"He's resting," he heard Niko reply.

Whatever it was, he needed to deal with it. "I'm awake, Niko. Let the messenger enter."

A small, wiry-looking man with a sailor's cap on his head came in carrying a letter. "I was given this to carry to Tiberius Claudius Togidubnus,"

Even at several paces, he recognized Amminus's hand in the address – the boy was no artist with his letters! "Give it to me!"

His hand shook so much that it took a while to disentangle the letter from the strings that bound it and hold it to the light to read.

To my most honored and beloved father, Tiberius Togidubnus, from his most obedient eldest son. Oh, how I wish I could see you again, beloved father, and my mother! I am well, but I dream of home. I will not write more. Your loving son, Amminus.

"Niko. I have to get up – I have to go to Rome."

"You aren't well enough to travel. Perhaps in a week or two –"

"Now! My boy – I need to bring him home."

He became aware of the messenger still in the room, twisting the sailor's cap in his hands, his face cast in gloom. "Someone will pay you for your trouble. Niko, find a few coins – "

"Not that," the man said.

"What is it?"

The seaman looked at the floor.

He said impatiently, "If you have another message for me, give it!"

The man shook his head. He looked as if he were about to burst into tears.

"Now, man!"

"The day after the lad wrote this letter, he ..." The sailor broke off.

The air in the room suddenly turned to ice, and voices– his own with them – retreated down a long corridor. "He what? Speak up, man!"

The man studied the floor. When he spoke, his voice was so low Togidubnus strained to hear. "He died."

The pain in his head had obviously distorted his hearing. "What're you saying?"

Niko laid a warning hand on his shoulder.

"I don't like having to say it – but – "the man stammered. "Forgive me, Lord. He's dead."

"Explain what you mean by this!" He struggled to get up, head pounding, but Niko held him down.

"Don't blame me, Lord!" the seaman said, his voice filled with panic. "I'm only the letter carrier! It seems there was an accident–"

"An *accident*?"

"I don't know any more, I swear it! It's all I was told."

"An *accident*, you say?"

"They – the boys at court - were practicing with swords – playing. In the courtyard." The man was trembling, his voice cracking. Sweat stood out on his brow. "It shouldn't have happened. An unfortunate slip –"

"*Who* told you this – this *lie* about my son?"

"No lie, I swear it." The man's face was white with fear. "The emperor's own servant – Satrias the dwarf? I know him well! He's from my own village, see? He liked the lad – Satrias was his friend at court! Satrias came to my room the night before we sailed and gave me the letter. He told me."

There was a wild roaring in his ears and his heart felt as if it were crushed under his ribs. His son. Amminus –

Dead.

No, that couldn't be. His injuries meant he had misheard.

He saw from the expression on Niko's face that it was true. He struggled to free himself of the Greek's restraining hands but was too weak.

A VILLA FAR FROM ROME

The seaman hurried out of the bedchamber. He collapsed back onto the pillow.

Amminus. Dead.

Hadn't he made the proper sacrifice in Neptune's temple? Why had the gods allowed this to happen? This was punishment for not truly believing.

"Drink this," Niko said, pushing a cup against his lips. "Now lie back. You mustn't continue to stress yourself. You've caused your wounds to bleed again."

"Niko –"

"We'll talk about this tomorrow."

"Now!" But his eyelids grew heavy.

After a while, he felt Gallus's breath on his face. He opened his eyes and found the room deep in evening shadow. The old man was leaning over him. He struggled to get up, get his legs off the bed. His limbs didn't obey him.

"I have to go to Rome, Gallus." His voice came out in a whispery rasp. "I have to find out what happened – I have to kill whoever –"

Gallus eased him back down on the bed. "When you are well."

"I'll kill him, Gallus. I'll kill Nero himself –"

"Hush. We'll talk about what's to be done tomorrow."

He tried to argue, but there were no words for the torrent of grief inside.

"I can't bring the boy back to life, Little Fox," Gallus said. "But I'm going to make a start to break this curse you seem to have fallen under. I'm going to find out who did this to you, and then I'll kill them."

CHAPTER THIRTY-TWO

LATER, AS THE VILLA FILLED UP WITH EVENING'S SHADOWS, long after the sailor had come back out of the chamber and left, Antonia found Gallus watching her. She set down the book she'd been trying to read, essays by a newly popular philosopher in Rome that Niko had thought she might benefit from reading.

Of all the people around Tiberius – Roman or Regni – Gallus disturbed her the most. His dislike of her might as well have been announced by a sign around his neck. She wondered now if he went so far as suspecting she'd had something to do with the attack on Tiberius.

"Is Tiberius sleeping? Shall I go in to him?" How childish she sounded to herself, almost as if she were asking this old warrior's permission.

"Let him sleep. Niko gave him a potion. His pain is too much to bear right now."

"His pain? But I thought Niko –"

"Some things even your Greek friend can't mend."

"But he will recover?" The boy had asked that too, she remembered.

"Of his body's wounds, yes."

"What does that mean?"

Gallus's own face contorted with pain.

"I will hear it, Gallus. I am his wife."

The old man said reluctantly, "His oldest son won't be coming home from the emperor's court."

"Amminus?" That was his name, wasn't it? "I don't understand."

Gallus shook his head. "Not for me to say more."

He left the room. What could he have meant by those words? Many barbarian kings sent their sons to court in Rome. Some were little more than hostages – had Amminus been one? – but surely even Nero would treat them well. She'd never heard of one wanting to stay. But what if that wasn't his own idea?

She needed to hear what Niko had to say about this.

Opening the door as gently as possible so as not to disturb Tiberius if he slept, she motioned to Niko who sat in shadows by the bed.

He said softly. "You can do something for me."

"What is this news about Amminus? What has happened?"

"He received terrible news about his son. Amminus will not be coming home. Not ever."

"Niko! What happened?"

"He'll tell you more when he's ready. But I need you to go outside – down to those grey-green trees with the long trailing branches by the stream. You know the ones I mean?"

"The willow trees? Whatever for?"

"I need you to cut some bark. I've used up my supply and his pain will be worse when he wakes."

She stared at him. "Why can't you do it yourself?"

"Because he might wake while I'm away."

Too astonished to argue further, and heavily burdened by the news she'd just heard, she left the house.

The stream that meandered across the garden, between piles of rubble from the demolished part of the old house and the lumber stacked to build the new villa in its place, finally reached the sea at the bottom of a little cliff. It wasn't far from the house, but the grove of willows that had spring up on the stream's bank sheltered her from the sounds of the villa, so that she might have been several miles away. The wind had dropped as the twilight's first stars appeared in the pale sky.

The bark wasn't as easy to peel off the tree as she'd expected. She tried one tree after another, never managing to separate more than a finger's length in any of her attempts. Stupid not to have stopped by the kitchen for a knife before coming here. Her fingers were sore from contact with the tree and she'd broken two nails already.

"Let me do that for you."

She spun round to find Severus's apprentice had come up so close she almost stumbled against him. He put out one of his long arms and caught her shoulder, but he held her away from him as if he too wished to avoid contact.

"I didn't hear you coming."

He shook his head. "My fault. But may I ask what you are doing?"

"Trying to peel off some willow bark for Niko who wants it for some reason."

"It's a pain physic," he explained. "He'll make a potion and give it to your husband to make him sleep."

"How do you know that? Are you a physician too?"

Aron gave her a shy smile. "Even apprentice architects learn a lot of useful things in Alexandria."

He took out a small knife and carefully peeled a long strip off a branch near the main trunk of the largest tree. There was a calm gentleness in his movements that invited trust. A sharp contrast to his ungainly body.

"Hippocrates taught, 'First, do no harm,'" he said. "Centuries ago now, but still a good precept to follow."

"How like Niko you sound!"

She became aware of tears, and dabbed at them impatiently, but the tide of grief that had been building overflowed. The last days at Pyrgi – her father's suicide – exile to this cold place – the loss of her only friend, Gracila – the fear she might lose Tiberius – her growing understanding that Amminus – the pale young boy at Nero's banquet – was dead.

Aron sat down with his back to the oldest tree and drew her down beside him, letting her head rest on his bony shoulders. "There now," he said, patting her arm as one might soothe a fretful child. "There now."

She hadn't meant to speak of these things, but his was a comforting presence. The hurt of years began to tumble out. And finally, she told him about Lucia's birth. He didn't comment.

"I shouldn't have burdened you," she said at last.

The sky had darkened, a sliver of new moon came out and the

resident owl spoke. They sat for a while longer, his arm a comfort about her shoulder.

At last, he stood and helped her up. "You'd better go inside. Niko will need the willow bark."

She nodded, suddenly ashamed of her childish weakness. "You are kind, Aron. Thank you."

He turned away quickly, but she'd glimpsed the flush that rose into his cheeks.

CHAPTER THIRTY-THREE

THEY SAT UNDER AN OAK TREE, silently sharing an apple left over from last year's harvest and watching Beech chase yellow butterflies. Those that were on the trees now weren't ready to take. There wouldn't be any apples to harvest this year, Niko had told them, if the architect had his way about cutting the trees down to make way for a new wing of the villa. So they were making this one last.

"Look," he said. "See that bird floating way up there? Not moving its wings? That's a kestrel."

"How do you know what it is?"

"Listen to its cry – *'Kee, kee!'* That's how you know."

She listened, and heard the plaintive sound the bird made.

"The kestrel is a hunter."

"What does he hunt?"

"Little things. Rabbits, mostly."

"I wish he wouldn't hunt rabbits, Catu!"

"Finish your apple," he said.

Mater told her yesterday that they'd soon be able to move into some of the rooms in the new villa. The workers made a lot of noise and there was a lot dust everywhere. Just looking at them made her feel hot.

The new donkey, Gallusina, still wasn't strong enough for them to ride, Gallus said. There was a clutch of daisies in the grass a little way off, enough to make a daisy chain for Gallusina's neck. She'd have to remember to come here tomorrow and pick them. It would be good to do something nice for the little donkey, but making a daisy chain didn't seem like something she wanted to do today.

"Can we go down to the sea again?"

The boy shook his head. "Better not. The grown-ups are all acting like bees when you overturn the hive today, and I don't want another whipping."

"Why would you overturn the hive?"

"Not a *real* hive! It means they get angry easily. But I just remembered something."

He stood up and fished in a pocket of his breeches and Lucia watched with interest. He didn't dress like Romans did in tunic and toga. She thought his breeches that fitted tight around his ankles looked better for climbing trees and scrambling over rocks than what she had to wear. His funny hair looked as if it was on fire in the sunlight. She liked it.

"I promised you this," he said, holding something out to her.

It was a necklace, five blue and green pearly shells strung on a knotted cord. The mussels she'd pried off the rocks herself.

"Here, let me tie it round your neck." He knelt beside her to fasten it.

"That's the best present ever!" She turned to him, put her arms around his neck and kissed his cheek.

He pulled away and made a show of whistling for Beech to come to him.

"Why is your face red?

"Because – I don't know! Because it's hot in the sun."

She thought about that for a moment. Catuarus had just celebrated his tenth birthday. She knew this because Niko had taught them what Roman boys did to celebrate their tenth birthdays. She hadn't paid attention because it sounded boring. She thought his red face meant he was worried. Her own face got hot sometimes just before she cried.

"Don't worry," she said, putting her hand on his bare arm. "Niko's taking care of Tiber."

The dog came up to them, panting, and swiped both their faces in turn with her long wet tongue. Across the lawn, the man who'd come from Rome to build the new house shouted at the workmen. Delamira came out of one door and went back in another, carrying blankets.

"Those are bad words the architect used," Catuarus said. "Don't you ever repeat them!"

"You know so many things, Catu."

"Soon you will too," the boy promised.

"When I'm six I'll be old enough to go down to the water and see the dolphins and nobody will stop me."

"Even Gallus wouldn't bet on that! Anyway, you can't just order the dolphins to appear. They do whatever they want out there, and sometimes you don't see them for a long time. You were lucky."

"I wish I were as smart as you."

"Not smart enough to help my father when he needs it," Catu said. "There's going to be a war. My uncle said so. And Gallus thinks so too. Between my people and your people."

"What's a war?"

He looked at her, scowling. "It's when people fight with each other. And you and I won't be able to be friends."

"But I don't want a war."

"They won't be asking you. Or me. My father will try to stop it, if he gets well enough."

"I want to always be your friend, Catu. I like you."

"I like you too – most of the time. That's why I made the necklace for you."

She touched the smooth shells at her neck. They were warm in the sunshine. She remembered the day he'd taken her to see the women looking for shellfish in the sea, the way the waves tickled her bare feet, the smell of the shellfish when the woman opened it for her. "Let's promise to always be friends, you and me and Beech."

The corners of his mouth turned down and she thought he really was going to cry – but boys didn't do that.

"I wish my brother were here. Amminus would know what to do if there's a war."

"I miss him too," she said.

That made him laugh. "Silly! You don't even know him."

But he folded his arms around her and gave her a hug, and she knew everything would be all right.

CHAPTER THIRTY-FOUR

BRECA HAD VISITED HIM SEVERAL TIMES since he'd been wounded, bringing fresh shellfish and mushrooms from the island. For a long time he hadn't been able to eat them, but she'd worked in the kitchen with Old Nev to make a broth which she'd patiently spooned into his mouth. As he healed, they'd taken to walking in what was left of the garden at sunset, her hand fast in his, watching the yellow ball descend through layers of red and purple cloud over the misty Downs. Autumn was settling early this year across the land and every living thing responded by ripening, softening, slowing down Somewhere at the edge of his trench-scarred garden, a nightingale began its melancholy evening song.

He couldn't keep it from her much longer.

"There's something on your mind," she said, as they came within sight of the sea, wearing its evening indigo like an emperor, the setting sun laying a path of gold across the calm surface of the water.

"My heart –"

She came into his arms and he kissed the top of her head, breathing in her beloved scent. Today, there was sweet heather mixed with the muskiness of wood-smoke. He wanted to hold on to this moment forever, to believe in the possibility that things would come right in the end.

"I know you well enough to know you're carrying pain that has little to do with your injuries."

The words dried up in his throat and he lost his nerve. "I'm just tired tonight."

"Don't lie to me, Togi," she said sharply.

He turned his gaze on a small sailboat heading lazily back through the channel from a fishing expedition. The boat rode low in the water; the catch had been a good one. "Truth is, I don't know where to begin."

She was silent for a moment. "It's Amminus, isn't it? He's not coming home for a long time yet? Perhaps...." Her lip trembled. "Perhaps never?"

He thought of trying to soften the blow, but there was no way to do it. He owed her the truth in this as in everything else they shared. "There was an accident. I don't know more than that."

"What do you mean, an *accident*?"

"They – the boys at court – were at play – he didn't live."

She stared at him. "Amminus is dead? My son? Dead?"

"Breca –"

"It was the emperor's doing. Nero is a monster and a murderer!"

He started to say they couldn't be certain, but that wasn't right.

She overrode his words. "May he and his house be cursed! May his food turn to poison in his mouth, his bed be a bed of knives. May the wind cut his flesh to the bone! May the wild dogs and the wolves dig up his grave and scatter his bones! May his spirit find no rest –"

He folded her in his arms, smothering her fury against his heart. When his own tears came, he let them roll down his cheeks as if he'd been a woman.

* * *

Remembering the bitter scene as clearly as if it had been yesterday – though it had been a month ago – he put his elbow on his desk and rested his brow on his palm. A king didn't have the option of a long recovery; those whose lives were in his hands expected him to serve them with his justice. The man standing in front of him droned on with his complaint. The fifth this morning. This man was a goatherder with a very small flock. He told the truth that he could hardly afford the assessment he had now; higher tax would possibly send him and his children into starvation.

He'd let it be known he'd hear grievances again, once a week in this audience room. There was a time when the complaints would've been neighbor against neighbor over fruit taken off somebody's trees, or missing lambs presumed stolen without evidence. Once in a while, somebody wanted him to discipline a half-grown son who was going wild. Anything more serious or complicated, he referred to the Council of Elders. The mood here today was different.

A VILLA FAR FROM ROME

His head felt as if it were stuffed with spider silk, and the headache that had plagued him ever since he'd been attacked on the road, skulked around in the corners of his mind like the would-be assassins who'd caused it. The broken bones and the wounds had healed under Niko's skilled hands, but the headaches and the moments of feeling far away from whatever was happening around him remained. Time, the Greek had told him, only time could heal his head. The other wound, the one that had ripped his heart out of his breast, he doubted that would ever heal.

"..... on my behalf?"

He came back to himself, realizing he'd been asked a question and should reply.

"I'll consider your complaint."

He had enemies on the Council who would like nothing more than to make a case that he wasn't taking care of his people, and at the same time he wasn't enforcing Roman law.

The goatherder's expression betrayed his dissatisfaction with the answer, but he left. The next man stepped up with his grievance. Togidubnus happened to know this one was prosperous, a merchant making his money supplying olive oil and fish oil from Rome and wine from Gaul to the garrison in Noviomagus. The man could afford the higher taxes Marcus Favonius had decreed. But rich or poor, both despised new taxes. Justifiably. It was legal for Favonius to demand a new tax, but not surprising the people would complain about it.

Through the open window, the sounds of the architect shouting at his laborers drifted in to him. They were digging a new channel to re-direct the course of the little stream that crossed his land. It had to be moved, the architect insisted, in order to make way for the land to be drained so another wing of the villa could be built. Romans, he decided, were seldom happier than when they were subduing the land, re-arranging it to fit their grand purposes. They derived pleasure from building straight roads, instead of meandering paths that took in the beauty of the countryside as the Regni's paths did. They built walls to keep some people out and other people in, aqueducts that marched across the land bringing water where no rivers flowed – Well, he conceded, that last one was probably a good idea. But they didn't know the birds that fished in that little stream they were diverting, or the trees that bent over it, or the sound of its voice as it rippled over the stones in the bend in its path. The stream would be ordered into a new pathway, and the villa would expand. And perhaps Antonia would be happy.

The merchant muttered something about the Regni. He forced his mind to pay attention. That was the third or fourth time the man had mentioned the tribe by name. *"My people, the Regni...."* Togidubnus, king of the Regni by Roman fiat, was not to be counted one of *My people*.

He stared hard at the man until the merchant dropped his eyes.

"As king of the Regni, and a Roman citizen – as are you, my friend –" The merchant wouldn't have acquired his lucrative contracts to supply the Roman troops unless he too had become a citizen. "I took an oath to enforce the law and protect the people equally."

The merchant went away without further words.

His anger rose in his throat till he could taste it. "No more petitions."

He rose and the men still waiting to speak to him shuffled out of his way, grumbling under their breath, as he left the room. He needed to get away from the noise and the confusion of construction of this gaudy copy of an imperial palace that he neither liked nor wanted. The constant bickering and complaining of all the people around him sickened him.

The autumnal garden was chilly, most of the leaves were off the trees and few birds chirped in the thickets. He walked under the bare branches till the construction dwindled behind him, his thoughts tumbling in his mind, his stomach full of acid. Before this, he'd always been able to glean comfort from the land, enough to sustain him through troubled times, but there was little solace to be found here today.

Emerging from the grove into an open space of grass studded with clover where a few bees still droned, he came face to face with an old stag with a broken antler. They stared at each other for a long moment, unafraid, both kings in their own realms.

"Good day, Lord Sailetheach." He slipped easily into the Old Tongue

A VILLA FAR FROM ROME

to greet Cernunnos's animal. "One wounded warrior salutes another. Go on your way in peace."

The stag lowered its head as if in acknowledgment, then moved unhurriedly away.

If only Breca would consent to come back. The ache he felt for her was a wound that wouldn't heal. He missed her wisdom and her steady way of dealing with the unhappy people who brought their grievances to him day after day.

Remembering that moment when he hadn't been able to shield her from the truth, he stared at the sea. He was a strong man, but it had unnerved him to hear Breca curse. He would never be clear of the memory of her tear-stained face, or her silence after that outburst. It had been his wish for Amminus to be educated in Rome that had caused the boy's death. She had every right to hate him for it. But she held her anger against him in silence, and that was his punishment. If so, he would bear it. He wouldn't allow his pain to stop what he must do, even if his people didn't understand. Even if Breca didn't understand. Even if he himself was beginning to doubt he understood.

Still feeling the sting of Breca's sharp words as if they had fallen on himself as well as Nero, he turned back to the villa. The day was winding down toward night, the birds flying home to roost. Coming toward him on the path he saw the Greek tutor with Catuarus and Lucia.

"A little late to start an outing?" he said.

Niko stopped. "The right time, I think."

"We're going to look at the first stars of evening, Father!" Catuarus said. Excitement shone in his eyes. "Niko will name them for us. He's going to teach us where to look for them rising at different times in the year so we can navigate safely."

"I know one already, the first star," Lucia said. "It's called the... the – What is its name, Niko?"

"What are you teaching these children? Certainly something more than Latin grammar."

"I'm teaching the boy to be a king someday, with a king's knowledge."

He let them pass. Once, he would've shared with his son the same Celtic lore he'd learned as a boy. Now it took a Greek tutor to do it.

One man had remained under the colonnade after the other petitioners had left, a sallow-faced fellow with eyes of different colors, one brown, one amber. He should remember that. A sour stink to him. He couldn't place the man. Too much of his memory was still ensnared in his clogged mind! Time would heal, Niko said – But he didn't have time.

"A word with you?" The man put out a hand as if he would physically restrain him.

He stopped and stared into the man's odd eyes. The man withdrew the hand.

"I have news," the man said, his manner now respectful.

"Tell it."

"Two young men – sons of a sheep-herder living up on the downs – were missing for several weeks. They've been found – at least, their bones have."

He remembered the man now, a copper miner who lived just outside Noviomagus. A troublemaker. "A sorrow for the father, indeed. But what has this to do with me?"

"The knife that did the killing was found under one of the lads. Apparently, he struggled with his killer and fell on the knife that had taken his life." The potter held a knife out for him to see, his expression half eager, half cunning. "Looks like a Roman dagger, doesn't it? Perhaps from a legionary?"

Frowning, he looked down at the knife, the setting sun's rays coloring the blade crimson. He'd seen that blade with the telltale nicks on its cutting edge before. It was dull, lacking luster from lying in the earth, but he recognized it instantly. A half remembered conversation when he was delirious with pain surfaced out of his clouded memory. A promise to avenge.

"Why bring this to me?"

"I thought you would want to know."

If the man thought the killer was a Roman, he should take the knife to the centurion. It wouldn't take too long to find the owner. But the man had brought it to him. That could only mean one thing: he suspected who the knife's owner was, and who that man's protector was. But to acknowledge that he understood this would put him in debt to a man who couldn't be trusted. The man knew Gallus was his friend. Whatever he did at this point would be dangerous, for Gallus and for himself.

"It's a legionary's *pugio*. But there are many legionaries in Britannia, with many knives. Shall we examine all of them to find out who has lost his? And what if a thief stole it from its rightful owner – used it in a thwarted attempt at thievery with the young sheep-herders?"

The man refused to meet his gaze. He wasn't fool enough to think the matter was closed. The copper miner expected to be paid for bringing the knife. But one payment would lead to many.

"I don't pay for information."

The miner lifted his head and gazed at Togidubnus. He very deliberately opened his fingers and dropped the knife on the newly laid mosaic floor of the anteroom.

"Clumsy of me," the man said.

There was danger here in every word, every action. One misstep and Gallus's life would be forfeit.

The copper miner left.

"I could ensure you aren't bothered like that again, at least until you're fully recovered," Niko said.

He turned to see the Greek physician leaning against a pillar in the evening shadows, arms crossed, observing.

"Back so soon?"

"Clouds blew in from the sea, blocking the stars. We'll try again tomorrow."

"It's my duty as their king." He felt an illogical need to explain himself to the Greek. "I listen to all grievances. Sometimes, I act."

"Our philosophers would approve. They've spent the last couple of hundred years thinking about how to govern."

"I thought Rome had settled the question?"

"Only to Roman satisfaction. There are several forms government may take. Rome seems to favor the tyrannical."

He was intrigued. The Greek physician was a strange man, but always thought-provoking. "And what path do you see that I should follow here?"

Niko gazed at him, his expression serious. "You may not have the chance to choose. But if you do, remember a king's authority should be based on more than might."

He shook his head. "You speak in riddles, friend."

"The rock on which you build your kingdom must be the love of knowledge, not the sword."

"I see how well that served Greece against the Roman Legions!"

But even as he mocked, he remembered the joy he'd known as a small boy, so proud to recognize that the tiny, grey eggs speckled with olive he'd found on the Downs belonged to the skylark pouring out her song high above. Yes, as a king to follow him, his son would do well to gather knowledge.

How odd to mean Catuarus, not Amminus in that thought! That wound in his soul would not be healing for a long time to come.

* * *

"There you are, Tiberius! You haven't forgotten, I hope?"

Antonia dressed for an outing, fine cloak over her long white tunic, her hair piled high in elaborate curls that must've taken Delamira hours to accomplish, jewels at her ears and throat, stood in the doorway of his bedroom.

He reached for a robe to cover the nakedness he slept in. "What might I have forgotten?"

She sighed. "You forget so much since you were injured. This afternoon your temple in Noviomagus is to be consecrated."

"But it's not finished." He remembered that much. The wound to his head still caused forgetfulness as well as headaches, even though many weeks had passed since the attack.

"Of course not. But you decided – after the priests consulted you – that it was far enough along to consecrate it."

A VILLA FAR FROM ROME

"Ah." Yes, he did remember that now. The inner sanctuary, the high altar, the courtyard where the worshipers would gather were ready. He felt the urgency of having a functioning temple as soon as possible, even if the work wasn't completed. Autumn would draw down to winter before very long. And Pudens, his lone supporter on the council, had advised haste to forestall more criticism.

"The children are ready to accompany us," she said. "They wait for us outside."

Antonia went away.

A temple to Minerva and Neptune. In Breca's honor. That had been his plan long ago, in more innocent times. He closed his eyes against the troubling memories.

CHAPTER THIRTY-FIVE

ANTONIA STOPPED IN THE COURTYARD to read the inscribed panel, newly installed, on a wall of the unfinished temple. Weeds sprouted in little points of gold and pale green along the foot of the wall. Afternoon sunlight illuminated the carved words:
NEPTVNO ET MINERVAE
TEMPLVM
PRO SALVTE DOMVS DIVINAE
EX AVCTOITATE TIBERI CLAVDI
TOGIDVBNI REG MAGN BRIT
COLLEGIVM FABRORVM ET QVI IN EO
SVNT DE SVO DEDERVNT DONANTE AREAM
PVDENTE PVDENTINIO FILIO

Collegium fabrorum –The Guild of Smiths. What had they contributed to the temple of Minerva and Neptune other than a lot of useless advice Tiberius had complained about? At least it recognized Tiberius as "Great King."

Catuarus was pointing to the inscribed words and reading them aloud for Lucia. The child clung to the boy's side, suddenly shy in the midst of a crowd of strangers thronging the temple for its consecration. Lucia was too dependent on him for companionship, but there were no more Roman children her age or rank in Noviomagus since Caelius died, and Tiberius would never have allowed her to bring a young slave into the house as a companion for her daughter.

"Come." She pulled her palla around her shoulders as a sudden breeze chilled her. "We must go in."

Tiberius had gone ahead to confer with the priests. He was in a foul mood today and she was just as glad not to have to make conversation with

A VILLA FAR FROM ROME

him. A group of Regni men and their wives hurried past, next a Roman family with their servants. The lesser folk must stay outside in the chilly courtyard. The courtyard was filling with both Roman and Regni families, but among them were several Regni women alone. She couldn't decide whether she found it scandalous for a woman to travel alone as Regni women often did, or whether she envied them a freedom denied to her. A little of both.

A hand touched her arm and a voice asked, "Here alone?"

Marcus's tribune – Didius Something. She gazed pointedly at his fingers on her arm and he withdrew them.

"My husband is inside, Tribune."

"Leaving his pretty little wife to fend for herself?"

There was something false-seeming about the man's narrow face.

"Excuse me." She took a step away.

She looked around for Niko and found him in the shadow of the opposite wall, his dark head bent to speak to a young, fair-haired legionary. Sensing her gaze, the Greek removed his hand from the younger man's arm and stepped away. She waited as he came over to her.

"Neptune is an odd choice for the first great temple in Noviomagus, don't you agree?"

"Consider that this is an island." Niko shepherded the children through the main arch of the temple. "We are beholden to Neptune here more than to Jupiter."

"I will never be truly at home here!"

Her chances of returning to her birth land were small and getting smaller with each passing year spent in this island. Yet the ache to go home remained. Just to be careful, she waved a priest over and gave him some small coins.

"Sacrifice for me to Minerva," she said. "And Niko – for once teach the children the customs of Romans!"

A line of legionaries marched into the courtyard, berry-colored tunics, shiny mail cuirasses, bronze helmets suggesting several hours of work bringing them to this high parade standard. They were young men, hardly older than herself, but there were a few hardened faces among them. Some had faces as dark as Delamira's. Mercenaries, she guessed, joining Rome's legions to do better than they would have done in their own poor kingdoms. They passed through the doorway into the temple.

She ushered the children after the soldiers.

Gallus was inside, talking with a Regni man who wore his grey hair in long braids. The old legionary acted proud of himself today – new toga, shiny new sandals, and a gleaming new dagger in his belt. He reminded her of a rooster strutting across the courtyard in her father's home, something she hadn't thought of for a long time. Appropriate, considering his name! She'd hated the bird because it attacked her ankles She hadn't seen much of Gallus for the last few months while he was in Noviomagus overseeing the building of the temple, which was just as well. If the gods allowed, he'd move into town permanently when it was finished. The thought of him in her new villa was not appealing.

Tiberius came out from an inner chamber with the long-robed priests, her tall husband towering over the shorter, fatter Romans, and the ceremony of consecration began.

Remembering the bad-tempered rooster made her homesick again. There had to be some way she could go back to Italia for a brief visit. Surely the emperor would allow her that? He might've been dangerous for her at one time, as Niko warned her so often, but that was years ago! Lucia had been hardly more than an infant in Niko's arms, and now she was in her eighth year and growing tall.

She remembered what had happened to Tiberius's son at Nero's court. Well, they wouldn't have to stay in Rome itself. She could look for Gracila in Pompeii. There certainly was nothing left for her in Pyrgi, yet the longing for sunlit hills plunging wildly down rocky slopes to the blue sea and a climate where it didn't rain every other day wouldn't go away.

The incense the priests were burning stung her eyes. Their chanting made her sleepy. Niko put out a hand to steady her when she swayed on her feet. She didn't care about the gods, in any case; they hadn't done much for her when she'd needed them. But it was never wise to openly question their power. She should ask Severus to be sure he planned a prominent alcove in the new villa where the household gods could be displayed and honored.

"Where are they?"

She blinked at the boy beside her. He rarely spoke directly to her. "Who?"

"My mother. My aunt and uncle," Catuarus said. "I don't see them. Niko, can you see them?"

A sudden flurry of wings startled her. In honor of Minerva, the priests had released a captured owl. It flapped past her head and out the temple's great door to land on an unfinished wall in the crowded courtyard. It paused there, blinking in the sunlight.

"That's a good omen," Niko murmured. "It didn't leave Minerva's temple right away."

The owl launched itself off the wall and vanished beyond it.

She shuddered, the nightbird's presence threatening somehow. "Whose custom is that? I thought we sacrificed birds in Roman temples."

"Nobody kills Minerva's owls," Niko said.

"We're lucky they don't release fish for Neptune!"

"Where are they? I can't find them," the boy persisted.

She gazed at him, a younger version of his father, his hair a darker red but almost as tall.

"Well, perhaps –" she began.

She saw Marcus Favonius, splendid in his centurion's white ceremonial robe, his hair curled and gleaming with oil, standing by the altar, surrounded by his favored legionaries. His tribune stood beside him. The man was staring at her. Catching her gaze, the tribune opened his mouth and his tongue came out. Shocked, she looked quickly away.

Tiberius had invited all the important families in Noviomagus to a feast after the ceremony, in the newly finished banqueting room at the villa. Marcus too. Would they come, or would it be a repeat of the embarrassment of that Yule celebration so long ago? Would that rude tribune come too? He'd have to watch his manners in her own home with her husband present.

It was hard trying to concentrate on the ceremony. The priests droned on.

The ceremony ended at last and people drifted out of the temple. She waited inside with Niko and the children for Tiberius who was talking to Marcus. At least, Marcus was talking and Tiberius was listening. Probably urging him to continue the work that had got him almost killed. Tiberius was right about that: No one wanted to pay more tax than they had to, and insisting on compliance with a harsh law was causing unrest, possibly threatening rebellion at some point. If Tiberius accepted that role, he would be in danger.

Tiberius came down the shallow steps from the altar and took her arm, putting his other arm around his son's shoulder. His face looked old to her today, and set in solemn lines, not the satisfied expression she would've expected on this occasion. Building the temple meant as much to him as enlarging the villa meant to her. It was the strangeness of the Celt in him, always mournful, unsatisfied, one foot in the past. Time had showed her that he was a good man, but no matter how long her life with him might be, she knew she'd never completely understand him. And it wasn't in her to love him.

They walked in silence through the temple courtyard to the street where a small carriage waited for Antonia and the children. A boy held the horse's reins, another held the grey stallion with a long mane that Tiberius purchased from Gaulish horse-traders at the last fair to replace the lost Stormfellow. Catuarus climbed in and held out a hand. Niko lifted Lucia up.

Tiberius helped her into the carriage. "The guests will reach the villa before you do."

She frowned at him. "You're not coming?"

"I ride out immediately with the centurion and a party of legionaries. The tribune will have control while we're gone."

"Tiberius! Surely it can wait for one day, at least?"

He shook his head. "This is becoming a dangerous rebellion along the border with the Belgae. It needs to be stopped, fast, before the winter weather sets in."

"Are you well enough to do this? This is different from collecting taxes."

"My duty as a Roman citizen includes helping Rome keep the peace."

"But you're not dressed for a battle."

"I have my sword. I'll borrow the rest from the garrison."

They gazed at each other for a long moment, so much unsaid dividing them.

She sighed. "Guard yourself, Tiberius."

He gave the horse a light slap and the carriage moved forward..

CHAPTER THIRTY-SIX

THE LEGIONARY RIDING AHEAD OF HIM THROUGH the sleeting rain didn't have a chance. Togidubnus heard the battle yell. He saw the flash of blue-daubed skin as the Celt dropped out of the tree and sliced open the Roman's neck. The man's startled scream. Bright blood gushed, splashing the terrified horse as its rider slid down its side to the mud. The attacker too hit the ground, curled his body and rolled away into the thick ferns under the trees. The horse galloped away.

His own horse snorted and stumbled, avoiding the fallen man. Two riders ahead reined their mounts and half-turned to see what had happened. They were assaulted by two more battle-painted Belgae dropping out of the arching trees that formed a tunnel over the narrow path that left Clausentum.

Blades rang against bronze helmets. Yelling, ululating men rushed out of cover and attacked the Roman line, their voices pitched to strike terror in Roman hearts.. Above the noise of attackers and panicked horses, the centurion shouted orders to the riders coming up the path.

The trumpet sounded the battle call "Spears up!"

He tore his gladius out of its sheath.

A face appeared beside his saddle, nostrils flared, eyes red with fury. A female Belgae face. A knife slashed perilously close to his cheek. He parried it with his bare arm, knocking it sideways. The woman's expression darkened in hatred when she recognized that the rider she'd attacked wasn't a Roman. Blood arced up as her knife caught his horse's shoulder. Through the red mist he saw the shadow of a raven passing overhead.

The gods of battle gathered here. He was fighting Boudicca all over again. The gods condemned him to repeat the mistakes and suffering of the past.

A VILLA FAR FROM ROME

The woman screamed in his ear. Blood lust took over and there were no more thoughts. He slashed at the attacker and she disappeared from sight.

He moved through the din and the confusion, hacking left and right with his gladius, his horse slipping in the mud, the jarring connection of Hispania's best steel with bone, a silent space in the din of battle all around him. Deep anger rose in his throat, a scream for everything that was wrong in his land, Roman treachery, his own stubborn tribe, his family. The smell of blood, horse sweat and dung, and the acid smell of men's fear filled his nose, intoxicating him. He yelled again and buried his gladius in another rebel's throat. The body fell away and was trampled under his terrified horse.

Just as suddenly as it had begun, it was over. Roman discipline prevailed. The squad stood fast against the attackers, war paint no match for men armored in leather and iron. There had been eight in the attacking group, all dead, including the woman. Two Romans had lost their lives in the ambush in addition to the first to fall. Three more were wounded. He himself had taken a deep cut on his forearm. He hadn't felt it. Eight, he thought, only eight yet so much damage! He dismounted, found water and washed his horse's wound. Stormfellow's replacement had a lot to learn about battle, though he'd been the best the Gaulish horse-traders had offered.

This morning, they'd gone door to door again, searching for rebels and finding none home. They'd been fighting like this for more than a week, farther and farther away from Noviomagus, on the borderlands of the Regni and the Belgae, and it was always the same. The unrest that had begun as a revolt against new taxes was turning into full rebellion. They could have used more than the hundred men the centurion had brought with him.

The centurion rode up, his face flushed and bruised where he'd taken a swipe from a blade, sweat pouring off his horse's flanks, blood that was obviously not his splashed over his tunic.

"Are you wounded?" Favonius shouted. "Can you still ride?"

He shook his head. "A flesh wound."

"Good! We'll regroup and ride on to Venta Belgarum. I want to reach the camp before nightfall. I've sent a message for more troops!" The centurion veered away.

The Belgae borderlands were always a hot point on the map. And Venta was deep inside the tribe's territory. But there'd be hot food and medics in the camp, a cot for the night instead of the cold, hard ground, and the chance to add another squad to replace their losses. The rain that flooded the land they fought on stopped, and the low sun of early evening struck a million red sparks on the trees and the tired men's armor. A barn owl flew low over his head setting out on its nightly hunt. He felt the air moving over his brow as he watched the bird.

There were no good omens for him here.

Exhaustion flooded him. The borrowed armor, made for a younger, more slender man, chafed his skin. His bones ached. He remounted his horse.

* * *

The next two days repeated the pattern as they hunted for rebellious units in the hilly no-man's-land between the two tribes, uneasy allies in the best of times. They'd needed the extra support of the fighting men they'd picked up at Venta. The attacking groups, eight or ten – sometimes as many as twenty – blue-daubed men and sometimes women, were as likely now to be Regni as well as Belgae, though they were deep into Belgae territory. They materialized out of thin air. He didn't think about what was happening. It was better that way. The mind shut down, but the body remembered its early training and knew what to do.

Marcus Favonius was a savage warrior. He took no prisoners, but before dispatching them to Hades' kingdom – hardly more than youths, most of them, and not schooled in Latin – the centurion had Togidubnus question them in the Old Tongue. Recognizing him, one of them spat in his face. A legionary ran the boy through with his spear.

At least there was no more rain to slow them down.

The third night out they camped in a small copse full of fallen leaves.

A VILLA FAR FROM ROME

The orderly in charge of food served a meal of dark bread over which they drizzled olive oil, a little hard cheese, and some dried fish. The orderly's young helper made his rounds with a jug of watered wine for the tired men lounging around the fire. In the sky that had faded to purple like the hem of an emperor's toga, the Evening Star appeared.

The weather was turning cold, but the centurion had stripped off his armor and now wore sandals and a tunic, loosely belted and reasonably free of mud and grass stains. He strolled among the men, moving easily as if he hadn't ridden all day, exchanging words with them. He stopped and gazed down at Togidubnus.

"I sense a distaste for our work."

"My opinion doesn't matter."

"Your Britanni are a cunning lot, and they don't always give up their secrets. But we need whatever information we can get."

He would've called the Britanni fools, not cunning, for risking war with the legion, but he didn't feel like replying.

"This uprising seems to be inspired by the work of someone we know," Favonius said. "Someone whose loyalty you assured me was firm."

He'd suspected Tarvos, minor princeling of the Belgae had broken his sacred oath given under the mistletoe. *If he is a devout man*, Arto had said, at that long ago Yule. But who could be relied on to be devout these days? The old order was breaking down; oaths taken in the name of Celtic gods couldn't hold any more. The Roman gods had taken away their power. The tribes didn't accept the message that cooperation with the Roman occupiers of what had been their land was to be tolerated. They didn't believe that it would ultimately be to their advantage to submit. Did he himself still believe it? He'd gathered shreds of this truth from prisoners he'd interrogated before Favonius killed them, words uttered in bitterness and bravado that he kept to himself and didn't translate for the centurion.

"We've found no evidence of his hand in matters so far."

"So far," Favonius repeated. The centurion walked away.

He sat cross-legged on the damp earth, watching a trail of ants going about their business. He looked down at the wedge of dark bread in his lap but wasn't hungry. He accepted a cup of wine when it was offered and drank it down quickly, hoping to put out the embers of a headache that had troubled him all day and now threatened to break loose. The wine only made things worse.

He felt disconnected from the earth, lost, adrift under a black sky. The dark river of blood and death that men set out on seldom flowed toward peace. What would it mean for his dream of the future of Britannia if the tribes wouldn't keep the peace even in this small, relatively settled part of the island? What would it mean to him and his family? The fates sent troubles so thick upon each other's heels there was no time to think about them. But even the fates, goddesses though they were, grew tired, just like old warriors.

Overhead, the Bear marched across the night sky. Someday, there'd be time to build the dream up again. If he lived that long.

He was an old man. He wished he were home.

Tomorrow, he knew he'd kill again.

CHAPTER THIRTY-SEVEN

"IT CONTINUES THROUGH THIS ROOM to the next."

Severus pointed out the path of the new hypocaust under the floor. Behind his shoulder, Aron gazed solemnly at her. She was glad for his presence; Severus was so overbearing.

"And through this archway here, we come to the large heated bath chamber and the cold plunge. It will be very convenient when it's completed. The servants' wing is just beyond. Don't fail to notice the fine work of the masonry vaulting over your head."

She glanced up. The architect wasn't exaggerating; the stones had been worked till they resembled lace brought back to Rome from the conquest of some Gaullish tribe or other. Stray beams of pale sunlight filtered through the unfinished windows, dappling the work.

This misty morning was the first time he'd let her inside the almost completed wing. He hadn't discussed the plans, so she'd had no chance to offer suggestions or make her wishes known. She was certain that was intentional. They picked their way carefully over the unfinished floors. Aron held out a hand to help her at one point where the floor was uneven. He gave her a shy smile.

Good to know the villa was going to be warmer this winter than the last, once the furnace was going and the floors were warmed by the hot air. There was frost on the ground in the mornings, and the nights were becoming cold. For a moment, she thought of Tiberius, somewhere a long way away, fighting rebels. Was he cold too, wherever he was? Surely the legion carried good supplies of blankets for the soldiers?

From outside, she heard the shouts of the workmen, and an overseer issuing orders as a new shipment of supplies came up the road from the port.

SHEILA FINCH

Craftsmen who'd been brought from Rome to work on the villa were laying the mosaic floor in a black and white checkered pattern. Another thing she hadn't been consulted about. The emperor had one just like it, the architect said, ending the discussion before it could begin. Was he like this with all his clients, or did he simply find her young and provincial?

One feature she found particularly pleasing was that the interior walls had been painted in bright colors, panels of yellow and red and a beautiful blue like the sea. The colors lifted her spirits. A big new villa needed lots of new things to furnish it, and though much could be purchased from local craftsmen, in her opinion the best still came from Rome. She would furnish the villa with the elegant things this design called for, silver serving dishes, and beautiful colored glass, books for Lucia.. She could even deceive herself into believing she was back in Rome.

"Notice the use of locally obtained blue-white limestone, and the imported white marble from Carrara. How they blend well together. You must appreciate the difficulty here of working at such high standards so far from Rome! And of course, the fine tesserae being used for the floor mosaic. No expense has been spared for materials or craftsmen."

The marble was smooth and cool to the touch. It came from a quarry up the Tuscan coast, and that was a nice thing to think about. She liked what she saw, the bright colors on the walls, the mosaic patterns, but she wished Severus would at least make a pretense of consulting her about the plans, even if he ignored everything she said. She was realistic enough to know he would do whatever he wanted in any case, but it would've saved her pride.

"Outside," the architect said, "you will have noticed the colonnaded terrace between the house and the garden area. When it is finished, it will connect all four wings of the villa and serve for protection from the rain. The emperor is very fond of touches like that!"

"Sometime soon, I'd like to speak to you about a grape vine in the garden."

He ignored her. The smell of still-drying mortar and not-quite-dry paint wasn't unpleasant, but she was eager to fill the rooms with the perfume of flowers. She could almost imagine the warm, rich smell of

A VILLA FAR FROM ROME

ripening grapes.

"We are laying out site marks for the three other wings that will enclose the garden –"

"Do we really need the villa to be so big?"

The small man drew himself up proudly. "I build not for you alone, Lady, not even for the emperor, but for the centuries to come. The entrance hall alone will amaze all who gaze upon it! The alcoves lining this hall will contain the finest sculptures carved from the finest marble all imported from Rome. The emperor, who has impeccable taste, picked the designs out himself. Nor have I forgotten your request for a place of honor for your own divine patrons."

"Let's speak about the garden. Besides hedges and flower beds, I want olive trees –"

He stared at her as if he thought she'd suddenly gone mad. "Olives and grapes won't grow in this climate. And if they do, they'll produce small, sour fruit."

"Even so. I want them."

Severus concluded his tour without another word.

Aron said in a low voice, "Don't be concerned. It will be big, but it can't be as big Nero's palace in Rome. That's almost a city in itself."

He hurried after the architect.

The new garden she planned would be full of color and perfume, but for now the old garden was a ragged thing of stalks, brown seed pods and withered leaves. Yet here and there a brave flower defied the end of its season by flaunting its red and gold banner in the gloom. There might be enough for one small vase for her room. The stems were too woody to be easily snapped; she looked around for a gardening tool. In a shed next to the stables she found an old, rusting knife, forgotten on a bench, and picked it up. It was heavy in her hand, the kind of short dagger legionaries wore in their belt, a pugio. She ran her thumb carefully down the blade's edge. This one had obviously been left out in the rain to grow dull and its blunt blade was badly knicked. Still, it would do for her purpose.

"Be careful, Lady. A rusty blade can poison the blood."

She turned to see Delamira, her expression concerned. The girl was a good worker, not sullen or conniving as many of the slaves she remembered at the villa in Pyrgi had been. A conversation she'd had with Tiberius a while ago came to mind.

"Delamira, would you want to go back to Carthage?"

The girl looked at her as if she thought the Roman woman had gone mad. "How would I do that, Lady?"

"Oh, I don't know. I was only wondering."

"I had an infant in Carthage, when the Romans took me. I don't know what happened to him."

"You don't look old enough to have had a child!"

"As old as you, Lady!" the girl said sharply.

She was startled by Delamira's tone. "I'm sorry. I didn't know."

The girl's hands flew to cover her mouth. "I shouldn't have said that!"

She'd turned Tiberius's words over in her mind a dozen times. Why not act now? "Delamira. I'm going to prepare the papers to free you."

"Lady?" The girl gaped at her.

"I don't want you to be my slave any more. Do you understand?"

"Are you not satisfied with my work?"

"Yes, of course I'm satisfied!" This exchange was almost stupid enough to make her regret her impulsive words. But she saw Delamira's eyes were wide with hope. "Come to me tomorrow and I'll have them for you."

She didn't want to wait to hear the girl's expressions of gratitude. Instead, she went back to her task of looking for late-blooming flowers to brighten her room.

Aron was working on something by a half-finished wall. He looked up as she drew near.

"Some grape varieties might do well here," he said. "We could try."

"Without Severus knowing?"

He smiled. "He's not as observant as he thinks he is. I have a cousin on my mother's side who lives near the foothills of the Alps. He grows grapes, and that climate isn't anywhere near as warm as Rome. I'll send to

A VILLA FAR FROM ROME

him for some hardy cuttings."

"You're very kind."

To her surprise, the young man's face turned red. His embarrassment softened his bony features and made him seem even younger than she'd first realized. He was hardly much older than she herself.

He helped her find several blooms in autumnal colors. They worked in silence, and she sensed he was as reluctant to speak as she. Once their hands brushed against each other's and both apologized at the same time. He moved a little distance away to prevent it happening again, but her hand still tingled from his touch. In a little while, he excused himself and went away.

She returned with four sprays of flowers to her own chamber, one of the rooms the builders had worked on first. She set them in water, sat on the side of the bed and unlaced her sandals, thinking about Aron.

CHAPTER THIRTY-EIGHT

TIBER HAD BEEN GONE FOR AGES and nobody knew where he was or when he'd be back. Mater had shut herself up in her chamber. And even Niko had disappeared. They sat waiting for him in the little room where they did their lessons but he didn't come. Only the man from Rome who was building the new villa was still around, but he was busy. Besides, she'd found out that he didn't like children.

The day was too beautiful to waste sitting indoors.

"Let's go out and watch them move the little river," she suggested.

"Septimus Severus won't like that," Catuarus said.

"We'll stay out of his way, Catu."

"I don't think so."

She pouted. "We haven't been anywhere since that day we had to get dressed up and go to the new temple. And that was boring!"

"You're a Roman. You have to like the temple. Besides, we're supposed to be learning things."

"You can teach me more names of birds and trees."

"The only birds still around here are the doves and house sparrows, and you know those. The rest are frightened of the construction noise and the mess."

She folded her arms stubbornly and glared at him.

He sighed. "All right. We'll go outside. Where do you want to go?"

"Somewhere I've never been."

He thought for a moment. "You didn't like the temple. What if I showed you a *real* sacred place?"

Her eyes widened. "Can you do that?"

"Of course. Get your sandals on and we'll go. We'll take Snowmark because it's too far for you to walk."

A VILLA FAR FROM ROME

"And my shell necklace!" she said, running to get it.
* * *

She rode in front of Catuarus on Tiber's gentle brown mare, Snowmark. Gallusina, the donkey Gallus had given them, still wasn't strong enough yet to carry even one of them on a longer journey, Catu said. His arms were around her waist, holding the reins. Beech loped along beside them. The pale sun warmed their backs and a few lone bees droned by, gathering a late harvest, Catu told her. They followed a wide track away from the villa that slowly narrowed between still-flowering hedgerows.

"Hawthorn," he identified it for her. "And that's cow parsley flowering along the ground below the bushes. And those butterflies? They're called chalky blues because of their color."

"What's that bird?" She pointed at a small brownish bird that had been sitting on the track ahead of them and shot straight up into the air as they approached uttering a squeaky chirp.

"Meadow pippet," he said.

"It went straight up in the air!"

"Huh. You should see the skylark do it. She goes higher. And sings better!"

She turned her head so she could see part of his face. "How did you learn about so many things?"

"My father taught me. This is our land, he says, and we must take care of it."

"Birds sing. Delamira does too. But Ma never sings."

"Never?"

She thought he sounded as if he didn't believe her.

"My mother could sing to you sometime, if you like."

"Oh, I would like!"

Then he changed again, as if he were sorry he'd said anything. "Just keep holding on tight so you don't fall off! I don't want to have to keep getting down and helping you."

At a rise in the land, the trees and hedges opened up and she saw the sea, blue as the glass bowl from Rome that Ma used for best. A flock of brilliantly white seagulls wheeled over the water. And there would be dolphins under the waves.

"I like it here, Catu. I want to take care of it too." She leaned back against his chest.

After they'd been riding a while, they came to a place where the land was marshy, full of reeds and the glint of little pools. It smelled like the sea. He told her that when the tide was high the path disappeared, and most people waited to cross over to the island so they wouldn't get their feet wet. The tide was running out when they arrived; they could safely continue. Snowmark's hooves made squelchy sounds as she moved. Beech ran from side to side in front of them splashing through the puddles.

They rode past a group of the round, wooden houses that the Regni lived in. She'd seen some like that before, nearer the villa, but this was a whole village. Children came to the doorways to peer at them, and one or two women. Catuarus didn't stop Snowmark or say anything, even when a small boy waved at him, but he waved back. As they approached the largest house in the village, an old man in a long grey robe came to the door and Catuarus stopped.

She'd seen that old man before. He'd pulled her out of the sea when she'd been looking for dolphins and the waves knocked her over. She pulled on Catuarus's sleeve, but he wasn't paying attention to her.

"Uncle," Catuarus said.

"Catuarus," the old man said. "You've brought us a visitor."

"I want to show her the holy place, Uncle. Where Sulis is."

They spoke in the Old Tongue which she was getting good at now. The old man came all the way out of the house and laid one hand on the horse's rein. He gazed up at her. She thought he was scary-looking, wearing some kind of heavy neck ring made of silver and copper and set with black shiny stones. But she wasn't afraid of him. He'd saved her life. Nobody said anything for several moments. The old man nodded.

"It is right action, Nephew."

"Will she speak to us?" Catu asked in a hushed voice.

"We don't command Sulis. The goddess chooses her favorites."

A VILLA FAR FROM ROME

"Ma says Sulis is just the old name for Minerva," Lucia said. She was following the exchange very well, missing only a word here and there. She was proud to be able to take part in the conversation.

For a moment she thought she'd angered the old man. His brow wrinkled, his lips set themselves in a thin line, and he stared at her. She shrank down on Snowmark's saddle, trying to disappear. He said something rapidly to Catu that she couldn't follow at all. Catu looked away and fidgeted in the saddle. What could the old man have said to him?

Catu's uncle smiled. "The child is right. The goddess has many names. Sulis will be glad to have you visit. She's chosen you."

"What did he mean, Catu?" she asked as the old man went back into his house and they rode on.

"He thinks you're all right – for a Roman!" Catu sounded sulky.

She thought about that. If he thought she was all right – for a Roman – But what had he said before that?

"Why were you angry? What did he say to you?"

"I wasn't angry! Maybe a bit ashamed that I didn't think of it earlier."

"But what –"

"He said I shouldn't forget you're Roman and you could be in danger. Some people around here don't like Romans very much right now."

"But you're Roman too," she argued.

"No! My father and I are Roman citizens. Not Romans."

She felt his anger and didn't push him to explain the difference. "How could I be in danger, Catu?"

"Stop asking so many questions!"

They entered a thicket of trees and Catu forgot his anger. He pointed out a place to her where they could gather hazelnuts some day. They came to a stop in front of a low grey stone building with three sides. Catu slipped down from the mare, then helped her. The doorway was just a little bit taller than he was. If Niko were with them, he'd have had to stoop to enter. Beech lay down beside Snowmark with her nose on her paws to wait.

Catu took her hand and they went inside.

"It's not a very big temple," she said, when her eyes adjusted to the dusk inside.

"Not a temple. This is one of the special places where we come to talk to Sulis."

"I didn't mean it's not nice in here." She took a deep breath. It smelled like the herbs Old Nev used when she was cooking.

He pointed. "That's the altar where people put offerings to the Maiden. Flowers and fruit and stuff."

She took a step closer. There was a heavy drift of leaves on the stone, as if nobody had been here in a while; they crumbled to dust as she ran her fingers through them. The smooth stone under the dust was warm to her touch and just a bit tingly, like running her hand over prickles. She felt something hard and closed her fingers around it.

"I found something." She held her hand out for him to see.

"A comb. Made for some lady's hair. That's silver – all tarnished now. And look here." He scratched dirt away from the hair-piece, revealing a small, soft stone, dull orange in color. "Amber."

"What's it doing here?" she wondered.

"Somebody made an offering to Sulis, I suppose."

"Do you think I can keep it?"

He shook his head. "You'd better put it back. It belongs to Sulis now. Somebody gave it to her so she'd do something good for them."

She replaced the comb. Then she had an idea. "Can I leave one of the shells from my necklace? Would Sulis like that?"

When he nodded, she slipped the cord off her neck and held it out to him. He unknotted one shell from the cord and gave it and the necklace back to her.

"Do I have to say anything?"

"You say it in your heart. Sulis hears."

She closed her eyes and placed the shell beside the silver comb on the altar.

He whistled for Beech. He didn't say anything for a while after they got back onto Snowmark's saddle and made their way off the island. The western sky was filling with clouds and a cool breeze sprang up, ruffling the

A VILLA FAR FROM ROME

reeds in the marsh.

He said in a gruff voice, "What did you ask Sulis for?"

"It's a secret." She remembered he'd made the necklace for her – four blue-green shells left now – and relented. "I asked for us to be best friends for ever."

He grunted.

That made her nervous. "Everything's going to be all right, isn't it?"

"You Romans!" His voice softened. "Things aren't always all right. Sometimes the good things go away and bad things come in their place. My people are used to that. And then sometimes, if you're lucky, things go right again. That's just the way the world is."

Was that good or bad? She didn't understand and didn't like to ask him.

"We forgot to ask your Ma to sing," she said, twisting on the horse's back to look at him.

He began to sing in his own language. It was hard to follow, but it was very pretty. Sad too, it made her want to cry. The mare stepped quietly along the path. The rhythmic rise and fall of the warm horse under her was soothing.

"My uncle told me to be sure to get you home before dark," Catu said when the song was over.

She fell asleep against his chest on the way back.

CHAPTER THIRTY-NINE

A COLD WIND RATTLED THE WINDOW SHUTTERS, waking her. She lay, eyes still closed, reluctant to wake. The blankets were tangled, half on the floor. She shivered. The air in her room was like ice; the furnace hadn't been working reliably since the workmen had laid a new route for the heat to flow. If Tiberius were here, he'd speak to the architect about that. She opened one eye to the grey light of early afternoon.

Troublesome thoughts flooded her mind. Tiberius had been gone for over a month and nobody – not even Didius, the tribune left in charge – knew where the centurion and his men were or when they'd be back. Gallus, who heard all the gossip in and around Noviomagus, had no information. There was a problem developing, Gallus had told her, a revolt among the tribes that had started with the new tax but hadn't stopped there. Tribes that had distrusted each other far longer than Rome had been in Britannia, were joining forces.

Even someone as little interested as she in politics could see that war would certainly not be good for the Roman community in Noviomagus. Encouraged by the peace that had seemed to be holding, and the grand design visible in Tiberius's villa, several of the leading families had announced plans to build their own villas outside the town. An uprising would put an end to that. The centurion had no choice but to crush the rebels, Gallus said. She knew the old legionary would have given much to be fighting along with Tiberius.

At least the old man knew what he wanted to do. She, on the other hand, was unmoored, like a boat floating aimlessly out to sea with no clear journey ahead.

The Celtic celebration of Yule was only weeks away, but she'd learned her lesson that first year. This Yule would slip by with no celebration. She'd

A VILLA FAR FROM ROME

been here long enough that Rome was no longer a constant ache in her heart, but she would never be entirely at home here.

"Lady," Delamira said in the doorway. "A stranger stands at your door. He asks for you."

"Tell him the king isn't here." There was a steady stream of people needing Tiberius to arbitrate their disputes. "And it's too late in the day to come seeking him, even if he were!"

"He asks for you by name, Lady."

Not a petitioner. She sighed. "Bring him to the audience chamber. I'll receive him there."

When the girl had gone to fetch the stranger, Antonia stood up. There was barely enough light left in the day for the bronze mirror to reveal her untidy hair; she shoved the unruly locks under a comb and pinned them securely. Would there ever be a time when the early darkness of winter night in this island no longer fretted her? She'd thought she was doing better, accepting if not embracing her life here, but Aron's talk of grapes had unsettled her again. She pulled on a woollen robe.

A stranger was an inconvenience but also offered the possibility of distraction. Who might it be, asking for her not her husband? Since Gracila's departure, she had no friends here. She was afraid to spend too much time with Severus's assistant for fear of the feelings that might develop between them. A sign she was growing older, she thought. When she'd first been charmed by the golden-haired centurion, she hadn't worried about such things.

She went down the colonnade, shivering in the gusting wind, to the reception chamber, past the high arched alcove where she'd placed a small statue of Minerva. Voices from the kitchen told her preparations for the evening meal were underway. She heard the architect, venting his usual sour mood on the workers, and glanced to see where he might be so she could avoid him. The low sun pushed through tangled clouds, raising deep shadows on the trampled lawn and torn up garden of the old house; it would soon be dark again; he'd have to let the workers go for the day. Even

SHEILA FINCH

Severus couldn't work them all night, though sometimes she suspected he'd like to.

The Roman stranger waiting for her in the gloomy audience chamber was young, a year or two older than herself, in a legionary's tunic but with his sword on the left and wearing the distinctive helmet with its protective side flaps and transverse crest. A centurion. There was something oddly familiar about him.

The centurion narrowed his eyes at her, recovered his manners and bowed his head.

"Good day to you, Sir, and welcome," she said politely.

"You are the Lady Antonia Plautina? Of Pyrgi?"

She had the strong feeling she ought to know this bronzed stranger. But she didn't know any centurions other than Marcus Favonius, and it was difficult to see his face under the protective helmet. "I am the wife of Claudius Tiberius Togidubnus, king of the Regni."

"Antonia," he said, removing the centurion's helmet and setting it on a side table, revealing his complete face. "Don't you know who I am?"

She stared at him. "You are – But you can't be!"

He laughed and seized her hand in both of his. "Yet I am. Your own brother, Valentinus."

"How you've changed!"

"Military life will do that to a man!"

Valentinus, second oldest of the four Plautinus children, Valentinus who'd taught her to ride and wrestle, and later as the golden days of childhood faded behind her and the family's fortunes declined, taught her own little daughter to swim.

"I can't believe this! What're you doing here? A centurion?"

"Believe it," he said, folding her in his embrace. "I'm to join the Ninth Hispana in the north at Eburacum, but I have official letters to deliver to the garrison in Noviomagus first. I have two days here."

"The soldiers are out in the hill country somewhere, putting down rebellion, the centurion and my husband with them. I don't know when to expect them."

"I can't tell you how I worried what had happened to you after you

A VILLA FAR FROM ROME

and the Greek slave left Pyrgi," he said. "We had no idea you'd gone to Rome! It wasn't until one of Pater's old friends in the Senate who sponsored me for the legion found out for me where you were."

"I couldn't stay home any longer. Not after Pater died – because of me."

He nodded soberly. "Mater and Titus went south after the villa was sold. I think Mater had relatives in Herculaneum."

"They are all well? Mater? And little Titus?"

"Not so little Titus now! Yes, they are in good health. More than that, one may only trust the gods." He rummaged in a leather bag he'd been carrying and pulled something out. "Here. It's from Mater. She wanted you to have it."

Hesitantly, she took the little silk purse he held out to her. Mater had hardly been speaking to her when she left Pyrgi. What would she be sending? She opened it, eyes on her brother for some explanation but getting none.

Inside was a small gold ring set with a garnet, the stone etched with a picture of a hen and her chicks, a treasure she'd seen her mother wearing in happier times.

"She sent this for me?"

"Well, I can hardly wear it, can I?"

"I don't understand –"

"What is there to understand? She knows how much you liked the chickens at Pyrgi."

"I thought –" The rejection she'd harbored for so many years was too painful to put into words.

"That she blamed you for what happened? I think rather that she blamed herself for not preventing it. She'd kept you out of Rome since your tenth birthday, away from the emperor's eyes, but it wasn't enough."

"I'll treasure it for ever." She slipped the ring on her finger. Tears filled her eyes. "Valentinus, I need to know. Why did any of this happen?"

"Why did Nero decide to ruin our family?" There was bitterness in his voice. "You were too young to know. Gaius Antonius Plautinus, our father, was a powerful opponent in the senate. Nero feared his influence. A visit from the emperor and his full court to a senator's country home – with a demand to enjoy chariot races in a stadium built specially for him – That's not something anyone can refuse, even though honoring it pushes the richest family deep into debt. You, little sister, were just a moment's entertainment, just as Mater feared you might someday be."

She'd tried to convince herself the emperor cared for his child if not for her, but she'd known the truth in her heart for a long time now.

"But he's building this villa for us, Valentinus." She was trembling now, so that it was hard to get the words out.

"I should think it's obvious why. It's not meant for you at all! He planned a refuge for himself, for the day that he knew would surely come when his enemies dethroned him. The emperor may have been many things, but fool wasn't one of them."

A palace to hide in, like an animal gone to ground, in the far-away rainy Britannia. She knew this, but she kept trying to believe in her little dream that Nero intended it as a gift for his daughter.

"And you yourself?" Valentinus asked. "This barbarian king treats you well?"

"Tiberius is a good man. He's been kind to me and to Lucia."

"Then I won't have to fight him."

She saw he was smiling. "Now I remember how you used to tease me!"

"Yes, I was your favorite brother."

It was best that she put thoughts of the emperor and his motives out of her mind. "And Lucia's favorite uncle. She'll be so happy to see you."

"And I to see her."

"I'll send for her in a while. But you must be tired after that horrible journey – and hungry. Will you eat a little before resting?"

"Some wine would be good," he said.

Hand in hand they wandered from the audience chamber down the colonnade where the bright blue and yellow paint on the columns wasn't yet dry to what would be the smaller of two dining rooms when the next

A VILLA FAR FROM ROME

section of the villa was completed. Here, lamps spilled a warm yellow light, chasing the gloom. She saw Delamira hovering and sent her to bring refreshments. Valentinus's slave followed Delamira.

The wine arrived in an earthenware pitcher, the slave carried a platter of olives and cheese. She sat with her brother at the table and poured his wine herself.

"I'm so happy to see you." She handed the cup to him. "But you've changed so much. Tell me what it was like to join the legion?"

"Hard training, day after day, snow, shine, or rain, month after month. It makes a man out of a boy. Marching, fully armed, mile after mile on an empty stomach, hardens the spirit as well as the body. The legion becomes your mother and father, your family."

She thought of Marcus and Gracila, how "family" had been lost to the legion's demands. "I hope the contubernium the centurion took with him into the field will be back soon, so he and my husband may meet my handsome brother."

"That's a small force to take if the rebellion is serious," he commented. "But I can't wait for them to return. I must arrange for a messenger to ride out to them."

"Tell me news of Rome, Valentinus. I'm starved for gossip."

He set down his cup, his expression somber.

"What is it?"

A servant came into the room and trimmed the lamps, the oil sputtering and smoking before the flame steadied and grew bright. Valentinus waited till the servant went out again.

"The news is grave. The emperor has taken his own life."

Stunned, she stared at him. "Surely not?"

"Either that or somebody took it for him. Believe whichever story you like. Rome is afire with both versions."

"Nero – dead?" She saw his face clearly, as she'd seen him that time in the Golden House, the tumbled curls and puffy cheeks, the sharp, bright eyes of a bird of prey. He'd commanded her fate with the carelessness of a boy playing with sparrows. How could he be so suddenly gone from her life?

"Rome is on the brink of civil war," her brother said. "It isn't at all clear who will be the next emperor. The city is in chaos. The Second Augusta's commanders must be notified."

"Noviomagus Regnorum isn't the legion's fortress, Valentinus. We're a Civitas here, but the legion's command is two days' march away. How could this dreadful news affect us?"

"The gods forbid the legions take sides! Yet it's happened before. " He took up his cup again and drank. Her own was untouched. "My task is to get the message to whoever has command here. He'll send it on. Other messengers will carry it to the Second Adiutrix in the west, and I'll carry it myself north to the Ninth."

They were both silent, considering this. What did it mean for herself and Lucia? After a moment, she said, "When did this dreadful thing happen?"

"A month ago. Maybe two. I lost track of the days on that cursed voyage. We had bad weather the entire way – worse once we passed the Pillars of Hercules."

She could sympathize with that. But Nero dead! The child's father who'd sent her into exile. She could go home now in safety.

As if her brother knew what she was thinking, he said, "Don't think about bringing the child back to Rome. With the emperor dead, the succession is in question. An heir to Nero – even a girl who could be married off to one competing party or the other – would be a dangerous addition to the situation."

Was that truly what she wanted , to return to Rome? Once she had, but now the matter didn't seem so clear. "I must think about this."

"Don't speak of this with others yet, Antonia. At least until I see which way the legions pledge their loyalties."

She studied the dark shadows under his eyes and new lines on his brow. "Another night's delay for the message won't matter. Rest here tonight, Valentinus. You can ride into Noviomagus tomorrow."

He gave her a dark look under furrowed brows. "Guard yourself, sister. Bad times are coming."

CHAPTER FORTY

THEY CAMPED AGAIN OUTSIDE SORIODUNUM, in a small clearing in the woods on the border of Durotriges territory. They'd been out for so long he'd lost track of the days. His joints ached with oncoming old age, his throbbing head a reminder of the wound he received from unknown attackers in the woods outside Noviomagus. He had trouble remembering things, such as how to buckle his horse's harness, and this morning for a moment he'd been unable to read the words on a map a legionary shared with him. Such moments passed quickly and he was able to continue, but they worried him. What he wouldn't give to have Nicolaos here to heal him again!

Some days, there'd been time for him to ride ahead into a Belgae village or a settlement of the Durotriges, a chance to engage the Elders in urgent talk, a chance to persuade them, as fellow Celts, to see how useless it was to oppose the Romans, how the way forward for Britannia lay through peaceful cooperation. *"How is cooperation possible with a slave master?"* one grey-bearded Belgae Elder demanded. *"I say kill them all and finish our kinswoman's work!"* Everywhere he'd heard this echo of Boudicca's challenge. But they were doomed if they clung to that! He began to see more Regni in the rebel groups, recognizing them by the distinctive weave of their plaid cloaks. His own people were joining other tribes in increasing numbers. Stubborn fools! Fiercely independent like all Celts.

As he had been once.

This afternoon, grey and wintry, they'd been joined by two contuberniae from a fort near Vindoclada, and the men camped together under the stars. The newcomers brought cooks who prepared mutton roasted on a spit in addition to the usual bread and hard cheese. He should eat, but his stomach churned at the smell of the meat cooking. He couldn't rid himself of the image of the two ravens that had descended out of the empty sky to pick over the dead on yesterday's battlefield.

Favonius held council that night with Valerius Vericus, centurion of the Vindoclada units; he sat with them in the firelight. The uprising they'd encountered so far was spotty and uncoordinated, awaiting a spark to inspire it. Vericus spoke of rebellious groups raiding outlying settlements and small Roman posts, then retreating deep into these forests. At the moment, the uprising could go either way, the commanders agreed; better, therefore, to crush it completely now. Favonius argued that they should not wait for support from one of the main forts in Isca Dumnoniorum or Glevum; since both lay so far from here the fight might be over before troops could reach them. The man's obvious hunger for blood turned his stomach as much as the smell of the meat cooking on the spit. He listened to the two without comment, oddly disconnected from the group and their strategies tonight.

He'd never been this far west of Noviomagus. The plains sweeping west toward sunset held a history older than the Romans, and older even than his own people. A long-forgotten race had once lived here, leaving tall standing stones as mute witness. Not even the Druids knew for certain who the Ancient Ones had been, though he knew they sometimes used the massive stone circles for their own rites.

As the moon rose, the talk around the fire dwindled until finally the centurions went to their beds and the rest followed. Unable to sleep, he sat huddled in his cloak, staring into the embers until the moon started its journey down the sky again. Try as he might, he saw no way forward for him. Loyalty to Rome, something he'd never questioned before now, had brought him to this. He was killing his own people by collaborating with Rome. Stubborn and rebellious the tribes might be, but how was this not betrayal on his part? He couldn't find an answer, and the question remained in his heart like the lump of undigested mutton in his stomach.

Next morning, the weather had changed for the worse. Heavy clouds pushed in from the north-east, threatening heavy snow that would put an end to battle. Both centurions issued orders for their men to eat hurriedly, then load up the baggage and be prepared to move out. Before long, both sides would need to withdraw and return home until spring made battle possible again.

The next two days passed in a haze of snow flurries, noise, confusion, blood and exhaustion. Each day brought clashes with rebels who were better prepared than he'd expected, and fierce as Celts always were. This had begun as a revolt against the new taxes, although by now they were far beyond the area Marcus Favonius could claim to control, but it had gone deeper than that almost from the beginning. Sometimes he thought he was fighting with the Fourteenth Gemina again. The screams, the blood, the ravens picking at bodies in the snow were the same.

A boy appeared beside Warrior's flank, knife in hand , his face a mask of anger. A Regni, hardly more than Amminus's age, about to bury a dagger in his thigh. He parried the blow with his leather-shielded wrist.

It had come to this. He was fighting children from his own tribe.

"Go home! I don't want to kill you!"

The boy clutched at Warrior's reins, screeching curses, his eyes wide and filled with hate.

"Stay alive, you idiot!" He yanked the reins, trying to move the horse out of reach. The boy clung to Warrior's long mane with one hand.

"Go home! Damn you!"

The boy screamed at him. The dagger plunged towards the horse, catching its neck. He saw the bright red beads of blood. Warrior staggered, squealing.

His vision darkened.

He ran the boy through with his gladius.

* * *

Fighting over for the day, the prisoners were slaughtered as Favonius ordered, their bodies hung on trees as examples to others who might be thinking of rebelling. He withdrew from the other men and sat near the horses, his back to a tree. He couldn't remember details of the day. That was just as well, but he'd always been clear-minded about battle strategy and this lingering confusion in his head disturbed him. One thing was clear to him: He'd killed a boy of his own tribe. A boy, no more than his own son's age. He was no better than Nero.

A shout from the camp's sentry roused him. A man galloped into camp, drawing up in a cloud of snow. He slid down from the saddle, took out a rolled up letter from where it had been tucked into his tunic, and looked round for the centurion. The man was sweating as much as his horse, evidence that he'd ridden at speed for a long distance. Favonius strode forward; he took the letter the messenger offered and the two stood talking. Togidubnus heard their urgent tones, but not what they were saying. He closed his eyes, tiredness dragging him down.

"Vericus! Tiberius!"

He dragged himself to his feet and turned to Favonius. Vericus came over.

"News from Rome." Favonius held up the letter. "The emperor is dead. Killed by his own hand – or by the hand of a very crafty assassin who made it seem so."

"Nero gone?" Vericus queried. "And who is to succeed?"

"That, my friend is in question. The city may be on the brink of civil war."

Vericus laughed. "As if that has never happened before on the occasion of an emperor's death!"

Nero dead. Amminus too. There was no contract now to honor. His first thought was of Breca. Nothing to prevent him taking her back as his wife. Longing surged through him. What would become of Antonia and the child? Nothing would prevent them from returning to Rome. Good! But alone. Unprotected in a city filled with the chaos and unrest that followed the violent death of an emperor. Did he hate her that much? He needed Breca to hold him, help him know what to do.

His head pounded.

"The question is, which legions will support which candidate?" Favonius said.

Vericus nodded somberly. Backing the wrong candidate would be disastrous, as several legion commanders and the men they commanded had learned in the past.

This news was already old when it reached Britannia's shore. By now the struggle for the imperial throne could well be over. And who could guess the ultimate winner, or his plans? It was hard to accept that such distant events could alter the path of his life.

"How does this affect us here in Britannia?" Easier to think about Britannia's large needs than his small ones.

Favonius looked thoughtfully at him. "For the present, not much. Perhaps not at all. We'll wait and see how the situation develops. But I should leave for Isca Dumnoniorium tonight to consult with the legion's command."

Vericus nodded. "I'll return to my base."

"The men need rest," Togidubnus said. "Two days non-stop fighting has wearied them. I'll take them back to Noviomagus tomorrow."

"They may rest tonight," Favonius said. "And the decurios will bring them in the morning."

He glanced at the centurion, fastening his belt as he prepared to ride out, flaunting his virile youth, fresh and ready even after a hard two days of fighting.

"You won't need to creep out of camp ahead of us again, Tiberius, trying to warn your kinsmen. Don't think I haven't noticed."

The man was smiling confidently again, teeth showing sharp as a wolf's.

CHAPTER FORTY-ONE

LUCIA HADN'T FORGOTTEN HER FAVORITE UNCLE. She was chattering non-stop right beside him as he sat on the bed, pulling on his boots in the guest sleeping chamber. Antonia stood in the doorway, taking pride in the freshly painted frescoes of the guest room, the bed , the chair made of fine wood decorated with ivory that had been brought over from Rome, the chest where the blankets and feather-stuffed pillows were stored, the mosaic floor with its black and white pattern that Severus said was the current fashion in Rome.

Life in this remote island was beginning to be bearable, but she could never forget the city of her birth. The old pain had subsided, but the small, dull ache remained. Odd that now she had a new problem, going back to Rome might be possible.

She noted the mud her brother's boots had tracked in yesterday, smearing the new floor. One of the Regni servants would be by to clean it up soon.

"Old Nev has food prepared for you, Valentinus. You mustn't go up to Noviomagus without eating."

Hazy morning sun shone through the window, but Niko had warned her to expect snow by nightfall. The garden was mercifully quiet for once, except for the song of a robin.

Valentinus looked up. "No time to eat. This is legion business."

"How long does it take to eat a little porridge?"

"I'll eat up at the garrison."

"I hope they can prepare food as well as Old Nev can now that I've taught her the Roman way!"

"You said you'd take me riding, Uncle," Lucia said. "Last night you said it would be like the times when I was little and I rode in front of you."

"Later, little one."

A VILLA FAR FROM ROME

Lucia's mouth puckered. "But, *when?*"

"Hush, Lucia. Your uncle has something very important to do first." In the old days, Valentinus wouldn't have let anything stand in the way of pleasing his little niece.

"I must carry this message to the garrison command," he added. "It can't wait."

She understood that Nero's death was important news to the legions here in Britannia. A change in the emperor on the throne in Rome might affect them in ways she couldn't begin to guess at. Legion affairs were complex, not something a mere woman could be expected to understand. The memory of Gracila came to mind again, sent away because she no longer fit with Marcus's plans in the legion. The legion didn't deal kindly with women.

It wasn't trivial news for her and her daughter either. She'd spent the night thinking about the implications of Nero's death for them, and the warning Valentinus had given her about possible peril for the child. He knew Rome and its conspiracies better than she ever would – but surely there might be some way? At the moment, the problem was smaller, more local. In the happy days of her childhood in Pyrgi, Valentinus would never have broken a promise to a child.

"I need to make arrangements to sail with the next ship going north, whenever that is," Valentinus said.. "With winter just about here, and the wild seas around this island, I can't take a chance. I need to leave as soon as possible,"

She gazed at him. "You said you'd been granted two days, Valentinus."

"And this is the second." He stood up and reached for his red cloak which was draped over the back of the new chair. "Be grateful, sister. At least now this villa is truly yours."

She didn't know what to say to him. The legion had changed him from the loving brother she'd been so happy to recognize yesterday, the boy who'd been full of plans to have fun, plans that never left her out even when her oldest brother thought she was too young, or "just a girl," and balked at taking her along. Valentinus had always been her teacher, her playmate, her defender. Today he was all cold centurion; she didn't recognize him.

"Please?" Lucia begged.

Valentinus fastened his gladius, the sword glinting in the wintry sunlight streaming in from the garden. "There might be time on my way back, after I've delivered my message."

He strode out without another word, leaving the door open. Cold air blew into the room, carrying the scent of smoke from the furnace where one of the servants had just stoked the hypocaust.

Lucia burst into tears. "Ma! He promised!"

"Well," she began, but she didn't have a good solution to offer. "In any case, Lucia, Niko will be looking for you to do your lessons soon."

"Niko gave us a day to play because my uncle was here."

"Go find Catuarus. And Beech. They'll play with you."

"Catu's going out on the boat fishing with his uncle today. And you forbade me to go anywhere near the water again." Lucia's cheeks were smudged with tears.

"Certainly not in winter!"

She wanted time to herself, time to think about this change in her brother and what that meant. But the child's unhappiness touched her. Her brother's presence had brought back memories she'd long forgotten, of being small and disappointed because adults broke their promises, or when Julius cut her out of their games because she was too young. It was cruel of Valentinus to treat Lucia that way, no matter how important his message. Nero was long dead now. What difference would a couple of hours pleasing a child have made?

She knelt down and put her arms around her daughter, drawing her close. The floor was slowly warming as hot air from the hypocaust circulated beneath it.

"We'll find something to do, Lucia. Perhaps I could play with you?"

How oddly right it felt, to have the child in her arms! It had never been Lucia's fault that her mother's own childhood had been so abruptly

A VILLA FAR FROM ROME

ended by her birth. The family's declining fortunes were not Lucia's responsibility either. That had all been caused by Nero's desire to ruin her father, a man he'd seen as an adversary in the senate. It had taken her a very long time to acknowledge this, years of pain and resentment, and the loneliness of exile. Her small daughter had paid the price because she hadn't been able to love her the way a mother should. Hadn't Niko told her Lucia was suffering? She hadn't believed him. Surely it wasn't too late? It couldn't be too late. But what if it wasn't in her to be the mother Lucia needed?

The little girl's sobs were turning into hiccups. "What would we play, Ma? Do you know any games?"

"Certainly I do."

But at that moment she couldn't remember one. The realization was uncomfortable. She felt as if she stood on a lonely path, facing a crossroads. Neither option invited her with shelter or good weather. But she must go forward.

"Nobody wants us here, do they?" the child said suddenly. "Nobody has time for us. Except Catu. And he doesn't have time today either."

Aghast, she held Lucia at arm's length and gazed at her tear-stained face, seeing for the first time the signs the child was growing into girlhood, no longer the innocent, carefree infant she'd been when they'd left Pyrgi. "That's not true, Lucia. Niko likes us – "

"Niko doesn't count. He has to like us."

"Tiber is good to us too –"

"But he's not here!" the child objected.

"No more of these tears. I know what we'll do. Let's dress warmly and go down to the sea. We can ask Old Nev to give us some bread and cheese to take with us. Would you like that?"

"Yes! I like the sea. But what will we do when we get there?"

She hugged her daughter tightly again and kissed her tear-stained cheek. What would they do?

"We'll look for dolphins, of course."

CHAPTER FORTY-TWO

HE WOKE FROM HOURS OF TROUBLED SLEEP to find a plan in his mind. The weather was bitter cold. He sat up and laced up his boots.

The decurios were rousing the men, preparing them to march out, their breath steaming in the air. He didn't eat with them, instead stuffing a hunk of bread into his saddlebag and throwing it over Warrior – the name he'd chosen hadn't had the desired effect, the horse was skittish in battle – and left the camp before sunup.

Two hours fast riding brought him to the empty plain where the standing stones waited, one circle inside another of enormous blue-white columns, and both surrounded by the familiar type of ditch and earthworks he knew all over the Downs. The sky was vast and streaked grey with high clouds; too cold for snow today. A sharp wind whipped his hair against his face. A robin sprang up from a bush as the horse approached, and a small flock of sparrows chided him from the turf.

He passed through the protective earthworks, the ditch and mound, dismounted outside the first stone circle and hobbled the horse. The blue-grey stones were enormous, the outer ring set in twos with a joining stone on top. Near the center was an altar stone. Wondering at the size of this structure, he paced out the ring at its widest part. Who built this? Not the Celts. And why? It had been here since before Time itself. He had no better ideas than the Druids; the place guarded its secrets well.

He ran his fingers over uneven surfaces, icy to the touch, listening to the voice of the wind through the archways. The stones gave off a faint perfume, the smoke of long ago burnt offerings, and a hint of the far away sea. Completing the circle, he walked it again. And again, his mind empty of thought, only sensation. The horse stopped grazing to gaze through the archways at him as he passed. The hazy sun was at its highest point for the day now, still low as the year turned toward solstice, and the sky had blown

A VILLA FAR FROM ROME

itself sharp and clear as glass. His legs grew tired, but he ignored them and walked the circle again. It felt right to do this.

Overcome with sorrow he'd been keeping at bay for too long, he sat down abruptly on the turf. Tears flowed. He opened his mouth and the sounds of his pain poured out. The pain assumed a name: *Amminus!* Then another: *Breca*. Lost to him by his own actions. All his fault. His throat ached. His tunic was wet with tears. He couldn't stop. All the years he'd held in so much grief. He was drowning.

A shadow fell across him. An old woman dressed in a tattered homespun cloak stood looking down at him, hair the color of the stones themselves hanging loose and tangled over her shoulders. Her eyes were grey, set in a deeply lined face. She rested her weight against a wooden staff as tall as she was.

"You are sick." Her voice was surprisingly deep for one so aged. She spoke the Old Tongue, but with an accent to it that he couldn't place. "Heal yourself or you will die."

"Not sick, Mother. Weary is all."

"The soul is sick. Regret. Guilt. A king should not burden his soul with such poisons."

How could she know? "I don't claim that title, Mother."

She brandished the stick at him. "You may hide from yourself, King. You cannot hide from me. Get up!"

He did as he was told, seeing how long the shadows were now that stretched from the standing stones across the grass. The air was rapidly growing colder. The sparrows had fallen silent. There were no roads or settlements within a day's ride from the stones that she could have come from.

"Your soul is in danger, King."

He shook his head; either she was mad or he was. Yet at the same moment he experienced the confusion of her words, he was filled with longing to be whole again. "You're right, Mother. I'm weary in body and soul. I can't find healing."

She shook the stick at him again. He had no doubt she'd strike him with it if the idea took her, and she was probably stronger than she appeared.

"Let it come out," she said.

"I've killed my own people. And a boy – a boy like --" He couldn't go on.

"A boy like your own son."

She nodded at him, but there was little compassion in her face. He didn't deserve compassion from others when he couldn't find any for himself. How would he find healing?

"If you would be healed, King of the Regni, you must spend the night here, in the Stones' embrace. But not clothed like that."

She was right that he'd be better off camping here overnight and returning to the legion in the morning. But the legion had moved on, leaving him alone with his decisions. He looked down at his clothes, rumpled, grass-stained and mud-stained, damp with sweat and his tears. Blood along the hem of his cloak. Not his blood.

"I have no other garments, Mother."

"Fool!" she scolded. "You think the Stones want your Roman abominations?"

What harm could there be in doing as she ordered? Druid ceremonies sometimes called for the body to be naked, and Celtic warriors often went into battle even in the depths of winter unclothed except for the paint. He'd done so himself in his youth, before he went with the legions. Yet he would've wagered she wasn't a Druid, not even a Celt. He thought again of the stories of the Ancient Ones in the dawn of time who'd raised these blue stones.

He was dreaming.

"You know better than that!" she said, her voice scornful.

Her way of knowing his thoughts jolted him. He drew his gladius and laid it carefully on the ground. She kicked it away, out of reach. A moment, then he removed his cloak, his leather wristlets, his sleeveless leather jerkin, the rows of iron ringlets clinking, his tunic and his boots. Without his armor, he felt light enough to blow away.

A VILLA FAR FROM ROME

"You stand there in a loincloth like a baby?"

Anger stirred in his breast, but he silently unwound his loincloth and dropped it beside the other garments.

Her sharpness turned suddenly to mother's milk. "Now, King of the Regni, you complain that the rites were not performed in your ascent to kingship? I will perform them."

From under her cloak she produced a small stone jar containing a greyish paste and went about daubing it on his brow and cheeks, his naked chest and his groin. The paste had a fishy odor, and his skin prickled under the touch of her fingers. He felt the shapes she drew like lines of fire, and somehow he knew they weren't the symbols Celtic warriors drew on their skin when they went into battle. As she anointed him, she crooned in a low voice, words in a tongue he'd never heard before. One last touch to his tongue, like fire in ice, racing through his limbs, sending his thoughts whirling. Then she was done.

His blood pounded through his veins, yet he knew it was right action for him to allow this.

She stepped back and gazed at him. "Now you are ready."

"What am I to do?"

Her mouth gaped and she stared at him as if he were an idiot – which was how he was feeling. "Stay here with the Stones until dawn. Keep watch. You must not sleep!"

"I put no trust in rituals, Mother. The gods are no friends to me."

"Good." She nodded sagely as if he'd spoken great wisdom. "I shall return at dawn."

She hobbled away, leaning heavily on the stick.

His first thought was to wipe off the fishy paste and put his clothes back on. But hadn't he come here to find – something? Even if he didn't know what that something was. He could think of it as a penance, his own small act of suffering for the grief he'd caused in his life. He could accept that explanation for what he was doing here.

His stomach rumbled and he remembered the wedge of bread in his saddle bag, still on Warrior's back, outside the circle of stones. As if it knew he was thinking of it, the horse whinnied. He was strangely reluctant to walk outside the meager protection the stone circle offered to get the bread. He would go without. It wouldn't be the first time, on a campaign, that he'd traveled on an empty stomach.

He rubbed his upper arms briskly, the wind attacked the plain with knives of ice as the sun sank. His breath smoked. Fool, she'd called him, and maybe he was, to entertain the ramblings of a crazy old woman. He thought again of Amminus, dead in far-way Rome. He would do this in penitence.

He started briskly walking the circle again.

Daylight faded into twilight which in turn became dusky purple, then the indigo of a winter night. Stars came out, crowding the sky, the Bears both big and small, the Seven Maidens, and from horizon to horizon the great arcing wash of that white river that Druids called the River of Souls but that looked to him tonight a vast net full of silvery fish. He remembered leaning out over his father's small boat at night under the stars, a lad, younger than Catuarus was now, marveling at so much light reflected in the darkness of the sea.

What was a puny human in the face of that, even a king?

An owl hooted, and far away wolves howled to each other. Finally, truly exhausted, he lay down on his back on the grass in the middle of the stone circles and watched the winter star patterns wheel slowly overhead in the moonless sky. The warmth of his body released the peculiar smell of the paste she'd used on him. He found that he didn't mind it.

He was aware of his own breathing, the rise and fall of his chest. He felt as if he were going out of himself, but at the same time, everything around – stars, stones, night birds and wolves – flowed into him.

He must not let himself sleep.

The next moment, darker thoughts tumbled through his mind. The battles he'd seen in his life, the blood he'd shed, the Regni boy he'd killed – his own son's age. He was overwhelmed with sorrow for his lost son – lost because of his stubborn pride – lost because he'd wanted his son to grow up Roman.

A VILLA FAR FROM ROME

The gods must truly want to see him suffer.

He no longer believed in the gods, Roman or Celtic!

And even if they did exist, they didn't deserve his worship. If they'd cared at all about mortals, they would have let Amminus live. For Breca's sake he'd gone through the rituals and the observances, but the Druids too deceived themselves. The world was as it was and full of evil. It didn't take the existence of gods to explain that.

A sudden experience of emptiness, the absence of gods, swept over him. A vast nothingness more terrifying than divine rage could ever be. The anger of gods was a finite thing, but this absence was infinite. Tears filled his eyes, a longing to return to the innocent days of his childhood when he had believed in something bigger than himself. Is this why he was doing as the old woman ordered, pretending to believe in some empty ritual? He was a failure as a king and as a man if he found comfort in pretense.

When he moved his head, dizziness struck him.

He looked down suddenly from a high point. The Stone Circles were below him, small as river pebbles. He stretched his arms wide to the sky and opened his mouth, but he had no words.

He woke, stiff from lying on the icy ground, but oddly, not cold. He opened his eyes and gazed at the stones; they glowed in the darkness. Rising over the horizon he saw Cernunnos the Hunter, his own emblem.

Then he was floating again, high above the world. He saw all things as if it were a book opening before him: The Ancient Ones, here in the islands long before his own people. The coming of his people. Now the Romans marched along their roads. And after them ...? He could see the blood-soaked roads of Time, and coming down them wave after wave of conquerors, settlers, farmers, fishermen, priests, soldiers and slaves. He saw the flames of battle, heard the cries of terror, the songs of victory, he smelled the blood. On and on into the blackness of a future not even a Druid could dream of.

He was helpless to understand Time's march, let alone stop the torment. Tears streamed down his cheeks. This time he opened his mouth and roared words in a language older than his own Old Tongue, words he didn't understand but knew in his heart.

The sound of a bell aroused him.

He sat up. His eyelids were stuck to his cheeks; he scrubbed them free. The morning star, the Herald, rose in the east announcing the sun; the sky turned from grey to pink like the inside of a fish's mouth. His own mouth felt full of sand, but other than that, he felt – not quite young again, but somehow renewed, like a child waking from a deep sleep. And oddly, in spite of the dusting of snow on the grass inside the Stone Circles, he didn't feel cold.

The chiming sound came again. Puzzled, he looked around for the source. The old crone was back, standing by one of the blue stone pillars. An owl perched on one shoulder. A wolf, as old and grizzled as she, sat at her feet. She drew back her arm and struck the stone with her staff. The stone rang like a bell.

He laughed. Wolves docile as dogs, tame owls, stones that were bells – Nothing surprised him now. A great surge of well-being coursed through him.

"It pleases me you find it funny, King," the old woman said.

"I mean no offense, Mother."

"Of course not. Laughter is right action here." From somewhere under her cloak she produced a cup of water and gave it to him. A ray of sunlight struck it, turning it to liquid silver.

He took the cup from her and drank. It was pure and cold like starlight.

"What happened to me last night?"

Now it was her turn to laugh. He was astonished that she laughed like a young girl, silvery and sweet, like the sound of running water over river stones. He saw her now in her green-robed aspect as a young Maiden, the flowers of spring in her long, golden hair. His heart knew who she was.

The owl flew off to perch on top of one of the stones.

"You will listen to what I have to say, King. Your name will be forgotten in the river of Time. The Celts will vanish from the land along with their Roman masters and those that will come after them. Many conquerors will take this land, only to lose it again in time. All things are one in the eyes of the Eternal.

"Yet you have many lessons for your tribe, many difficulties to guide them through. And your seed will take root and grow in your place, and you will nourish them. You will lead not by the sword but by the words."

"My seed?" He looked down at the poor shriveled thing that was his manhood, blue as woad in the cold morning. He sensed the wolf was eying him and felt the urge to cover it with his hands.

Again, the girlish laughter. "You have already begot your heir, King."
She turned away.

"Wait, I beg you. Tell me who you are. I ask humbly."

"You know my name," she said.

He knew that he did.

She walked lightly out of the circle in a dazzle of morning sunlight. Her figure dwindled slowly, the wolf trotting at her heels, until he could no longer make her out from the frost-spangled grass on the plain. High overhead, a hawk circled.

In spite of the fitful night's sleep, there were no stabs of headache waiting to ambush him. Surely it had been a very strange dream!

He knew better.

He pulled on his tunic and laced his boots. His gladius was not with them. He looked around and catching the glint of the sword's blade at the foot of the altar. He bent to pick it up. About to secure the gladius in his belt, he stopped, gazing at the nicks and scratches on the blade, the dark bloodstains.

Not by the sword.

He turned back to the altar stone and laid the sword on it.

CHAPTER FORTY-THREE

VALENTINUS HAD TOLD HER HE PLANNED TO LEAVE for Eburacum as soon as possible, taking a supply ship that would sail north up the coast of Britannia while the weather was still reasonable. He'd go straight from his visit to the garrison in Noviomagus to the port to make arrangements. Niko had taken the children into Noviomagus.

Antonia was restless, full of half-imagined plans and desperate hopes. What if she didn't go back to Rome, but sought her mother's home on the coast in Herculaneum? The path to her future wasn't clear.

This late in the year the garden had no flowers, and the bramble hedges had no more berries. She would decorate the rooms the Celtic way, with holly. The blood red berries would glow in the lamplight this evening. She threw a cloak over her tunic and went back to the shed to find the old pugio she'd used before. The weather was cold, threatening snow. The holly branches were tough and hurt her hands as she held them; she should have looked for gloves. The blade was too dull for the task and heavy enough to tire her hand. She considered giving up on the idea.

"Let me help you."

Startled, she turned to see Aron wearing woolen leggings and a heavy quilted jacket, Celtic in design. "Thank you. But I can do this by myself."

She spoke more sharply than she'd intended. But she didn't need the complication of allowing him into her life any further.

"I don't wish to intrude," he said. "I only offer out of friendship."

The clumsy jacket enhanced his awkwardness. And how odd his thin face was made by the contrite expression he wore! Yet there was something about him more real than she'd found in most other people around her, and a kindness in his eyes if only she'd allow herself to accept it. She'd needed a friend since Gracila went away.

A VILLA FAR FROM ROME

She didn't need something else to complicate her life.

"I don't need your friendship!"

"My apology for any misunderstanding." He gazed at her for a moment, as if reading her deepest thoughts. "I have work to do. Good day to you, Lady. I won't bother you again."

Immediately, she regretted her words. "Aron – I –"

He was out of hearing, his long legs taking him quickly across the frozen ground. Whatever her difficulties, she would face them on her own.

Ivy grew on one side of the old part of the house. It would add a splash of color to liven the darkness of the season, but it lacked the pretty berries she wanted to brighten the winter-dark rooms. Further from the villa, the holly trees were younger, their boughs not so tough.

The solitude of the barren garden soothed her; she put Aron out of her mind and thought only of the plants she was seeking. She went deeper among the little trees. The sound of the architect scolding his workers and the banging and crashing of the work faded behind her. Severus was particularly bad tempered today because he feared winter would shut down all outside work for several weeks.

Aron will be kept busy today– She closed the thought of him out of her treacherous mind. She wasn't a silly girl anymore, yearning after every young man she saw. She'd turn her mind to other things.

Thoughts troubled her. She was glad to have her brother here, but his treatment of Lucia had been a shock and a disappointment. Once the reunion was over they'd had little left in common. It bothered her that there was still no news of Tiberius or when he would return. Her brother thought the campaign to subdue the rebellious Britanni would stop for the winter soon. But when?

The trees here might be a newer growth, but their green limbs were almost as hard to cut as the older branches. Fatigued, her hand sore from gripping the knife's hilt, she sat down to rest on fallen log, out of sight and sound of the builders. The stream ran too fast to ice over in all but the most fierce winter; the water was thick with watercress. She could harvest some for Old Nev to use. She set the holly branches and the dagger on the ground beside her.

Something scuffled the dead leaves, drawing her attention. A long-eared hare stared back at her, then vanished. How good it would be to run away from the thorns and knots of life, like the hare bolting to its hole! The tales Valentinus told last night about the emperor's growing madness, the orgies, the assassinations, confirmed what Tiberius and Niko had always believed but she'd resisted. The emperor had never been capable of loving his child. In her deepest heart, she'd always known that truth, but it had been too hard to accept.

Something cold and damp touched her arm. The dog that followed Tiberius's son around looked up at her as if asking a question, its tail swinging to and fro.

"The children went into town with their tutor. I don't know when they'll be back." How stupid she felt to talk to a dog! "Shoo. Go away!"

The animal lowered its tail and went away.

A chill gust of wind made her shiver, and she pulled the woolen wrap closer. Which was worse? If she did ignore her brother's warnings and went back to warm Italia, how would that affect Lucia? The child was Roman, growing up like a barbarian in this island. Yet she had been much too young when they left to remember anything. Going back would be difficult for her. And Tiberius? He was a good man, but they were much too different in birth and character to ever make a real husband and wife. Besides, in his heart Tiberius had only one wife. She could only guess at what his obligation was to Nero, but surely the emperor's death had now set him free. Nothing to worry about there.

And for herself? What would she be going back to? She had no home to return to. The country villa with is vineyards in Pyrgi was gone No family – It was a fantasy that her mother would welcome her back with a young child to reduced circumstances in Herculaneum. And her only friend Gracila, who'd been forced back into her old life in Pompeii. How could Gracila be expected to help when she couldn't help herself?

She was a woman on her own.

A cluster of crows on the branches over her head started an argument,

A VILLA FAR FROM ROME

cawing noisily and jabbing at each other, wings flapping. Dead leaves fluttered down, landing on her lap, with them a dusting of frost. She stood up, gazing into the distance where the road wound up from the port past a few outlying Regni houses. Smoke rose lazily from the chimney of the hypocaust of a newly built Roman villa.

It was so hard to decide what to do.

Two figures, Regni, by the look of their heavy clothes. carrying sacks over their shoulders and leading a donkey cart headed up the road to Noviomagus. Another, a Roman on horseback, came south. The light had changed, the clouds were lower, the wind dropped and the air took on the sharp-edged smell of snow.

Italia would seem as strange now as Britannia had when she first arrived. Was it resignation to fate, or growing wisdom, or just aching tiredness after the years in exile that made her hesitate to make this decision? She was coming to respect this island with its wild moods and dark woods, its animals and birds, even the quarrelsome crows. Was respect enough?

A few flakes of snow drifted down, settling on her cloak. Time to go back to the villa. She stood up and adjusted the wrap to cover her head.

"Not so fast!"

A hand grasped her arm, holding her in place. She gasped at the violence of that touch. The tribune Didius had come up behind her.

"We missed your company at the Saturnalia celebrations in town." He smiled at her, all teeth and sour breath. "I thought you might be lonely without your barbarian here."

"Tribune. Please remove your hand from my arm." The man might be the son of a senator, but his manners were lacking.

Didius stopped smiling. "When I'm ready to, girl."

"I order you to!" How dare he take such a liberty? He must be drunk.

His eyes glittered. "You *order* me? Emperor's whore. Concubine of a barbarian king. You think you can *order* me?"

Ice flooded through her veins and her knees went weak. "Let me go at once – or I'll summon help!"

"And who will come?" He stroked her cheek with one finger as if they were lovers.

Who would hear if she cried for help? She was out of sight of the villa and her voice wouldn't carry far. Why had she been so quick to send Aron away? She jerked, trying to get free.

He hit her across the mouth, sending her stumbling. Pain flamed across her jaw. This couldn't be happening to her again! She would've fallen except for his tight grip on her arm.

"Keep your mouth shut, whore. I'll tell you when I want it open."

He twisted her arm, forcing her down. She screamed for help. He slapped her again. He knelt over her, his other hand pulling her tunic, out of his way.

The crows had fallen silent. Somewhere a dog barked.

Memories she'd long-forgotten flashed through her mind – the emperor's peppermint breath, his weight on her body. Surely this was a nightmare. Warm taste of iron blood at the corner of her mouth where he'd struck her told her it wasn't. His breath was hot and rancid on her cheek. She squirmed under him. Kicked her feet, trying to dislodge him. He was too heavy.

He hit her a third time. Her head snapped back against the icy ground. For a moment, the world went dark. Pain blazed through her.

The dog barked again.

No – I can't – I won't –

"No!"

He forced her legs apart with his knees. He clamped his mouth over hers, silencing her. She struggled – got her mouth free – sank her teeth into his lips.

"Bitch!" He hit her again.

She turned her face away from him as she could. He was much too strong for her. She felt as if she were going to die. Snow fell on her face.

No! She wasn't twelve years old this time. She wasn't going to give up without a struggle. There must be something she could do.

Memory flooded in. *"Not like that, silly!" Valentinus said. She was eight and*

A VILLA FAR FROM ROME

he was ten. They were rolling around on the grass in the hills above Pyrgi, a wrestling game. "You can't beat me by resisting me. I'm a boy. I'm too strong for you."

The memory of her brother's voice gave strength. She worked one hand free from where it was trapped under him. Didius grabbed her hair and forced her to face him again. Her scalp burned as clumps of hair came out in his hand, but her hand was free. She scrabbled fingers in the dirt and leaf mold, searching the ground under the trees. It must be somewhere here! She felt the prickle of holly leaves. *Gracious Minerva – help me!* His rancid body smell nauseated her – sweat and stale wine. He was heavy as a sack of lead. It was starting to snow. Despair rose in her chest.

There. The pugio –

She touched the sharp tip. Just out of reach.

"Stop struggling or I'll kill you, whore!"

Somehow she managed to shift her body under him, enough for her free hand to touch the old knife's blade this time, her fingers rasping along the rusted edge toward the hilt. But she couldn't move. She couldn't get a purchase on the knife. The snow fell faster now.

She felt the warmth of his manhood on her thigh, wet, sticky, snaking its way. She'd sooner die than let this happen again!

She gathered her saliva and spit into the tribune's face.

He pulled back to hit her again and that took some of his heavy weight off. She managed to reach the knife. Fingers suddenly slippery, she turned it to point up. She felt a sharp prick on her palm and adjusted her grip. He lunged again. The blade slipped sideways, nicking his skin but not entering. He grunted but was not put off. Now he was struggling to enter her. She clenched her fingers on the knife's hilt, bracing it against the hard dirt under her, straightening it to point upward. Waiting. She forced herself not to resist.

This time when he lunged, she felt the sudden giving way as the blade entered his abdomen. He screamed – arching away from her, She clenched her teeth and put all her strength into twisting the knife in his flesh. He slid off. The knife tore out of her hands. Hot blood spurted over her thighs, her exposed hips.

He floundered, gasping on the ground beside her, then went still. Sickened, she closed her eyes against the thought of what had happened.

"Lady! Lady! Do you hear me? Are you all right?"

It took effort to open her eyes. Gallus leaned over her, holding out his hand to help her sit up. The dog was beside him, stiff, panting. She trembled so hard it was difficult to see. She looked down at the tribune's body –

The knife – Scarlet blood against white ground – Blood on her own hands and legs.

She doubled over, retching, but nothing came.

"Are you all right?" the old legionary asked again.

Her voice caught in her bruised throat and came out in a whispery croak. "He would've taken me."

"Did he – " Gallus began.

"No! He tried...." The thought was too raw to finish.

The old man looked at the bloody pugio still in the tribune's stomach. He leaned over and pulled it out. He stared at it for a moment, frowning, then threw it deep into the thorns under the trees. He knelt beside her and tenderly wiped blood and saliva off her face and hands with a corner of his cloak.

"Gallus – I killed him."

"Hush. He shouldn't have laid hands on Little Fox's woman! I should've been here to protect you. I should've been the one who killed him!"

She tugged her tunic over her exposed knees. Tears flooded now, and the old man wiped those away too. She was shaking violently. He took off his cloak and wrapped it around her shoulders. He pulled her to him and rocked her as if she'd been a little child.

"What're you doing here?" Her voice came out as a whisper.

"I met Niko and the children in town. He wanted to visit his young legionary friend. I offered to bring the children back – "

"Surely they're not here?" The children mustn't see her like this!

"No. It's all right! They're inside. Delamira's getting supper. I heard the boy's dog barking like the beast had gone crazy and came over to see what was happening."

The dog barked once as if it agreed with this.

Realization set in. "Gallus – what have I done? What will happen to me now?"

"I'll say I did it. He over-powered you – and then I came along –"

"I can't let you take the blame!"

" A tribune – a senator his father! They'll exile you, Lady, if they think you did it! It won't matter he was trying to rape you. You're just a woman. How would you survive if they send you away?"

The snow came down steadily; she couldn't stop shivering. She looked at the tribune – already half-covered in a white pall. He deserved his death. But Gallus would be in terrible danger if they ever suspected him.

"Marcus Favonius will have you killed," she said.

"I'll pull the body under the trees. The snow will hide it. That'll give me some time to make a better plan."

"Go away at once, Gallus. You must!"

The old warrior smiled at her. "Don't think about it any more."

Hearing the sound of voices, she turned. Several men were running towards her.

One of them was her brother.

CHAPTER FORTY-FOUR

CATU PUT HIS ARM AROUND HER SHOULDERS and she leaned against him. They were hiding among the branches of an old yew tree on the far side of the garden, high enough to watch the confusion but hidden. A light snowfall made a gauzy curtain between them and the figures at the end of the garden. Nobody would be looking for them, even though it was now way past the time for the evening meal.

"You're trembling," Catu said.

"I'm not."

"I can feel it. But it's all right to be scared."

"I'm not scared." She swiped at the tears on her cheeks with the edge of her tunic. "I'm just cold. And this branch is scratchy."

"Well, I'm scared of what they're going to do to Gallus."

They'd returned from their visit to Noviomagus about an hour ago, with Gallus instead of Niko because their tutor wanted to stay in town and visit a friend. When they reached the villa, nobody was home, but they'd heard Beech barking wildly – and Gallus told them to stay indoors while he went to see what it was. She'd wanted to see what was the matter. She went straight outside after Gallus. Catu followed her.

They'd been in time to see something dreadful – her mother fighting with a man on the ground in the snow. Then Gallus arrived and they couldn't tell what happened because he had his back to them. But when he turned, he was holding a dagger and there was blood on the old legionary's clothes. She didn't understand what had happened.

She sniffed back tears and snuggled closer. "What are they doing, Catu?"

Catu shook his head.

A lot of things had happened next, so close to each other that she was confused. Catu had insisted they needed to hide up in the tree. He'd given her a boost up, climbed above her and pulled her the rest of the way up into a fork of the tree, as far as the branches allowed without breaking under their weight.. He said they could see and hear from up in the tree, but unless people were looking for them, no one would see them.

What did it all mean? Even from a distance she could see that her mother was crying and her clothes were dirty and bloody too. Then Uncle Valentinus came striding across the snow from the direction of the sea where she and Catu had gone that day to hunt shellfish. He was very angry – yelling and waving his arms – Servants ran from the villa to see what was wrong, Delamira with them. Gallus was standing there in his bloody tunic. It was snowing hard. More people came and Uncle Valentinus looked as if he was giving orders. Two men grabbed Gallus by the arms. A third ran off and came back a moment later with a length of rope. They tied Gallus's arms behind his back.

She didn't mean to let it, but a sob came out.

"Hush!" Catu said. "They'll hear us."

"Do something, Catu! Help Gallus!"

"What can I do?" he said. "I'm just a boy."

Delamira led her mother past the tree where they were hiding. Lucia held her breath, but they didn't look up. Her mother's face was dirty too. She watched them go into the villa.

Uncle Valentinus wasn't shouting any more, but his voice still sounded angry. He was waving his arms around as if he was giving orders. Now they could see the man lying on the grass was wearing a soldier's tunic.

"Gallus is legion," Catu whispered in her ear. "The legion will have to deal with it, whatever it is."

He took his arm away from her shoulder. "Stay here. Don't move and don't make any noise. I'm going to try and climb further out on one of those big branches so I can see better."

He wiggled away from her, across two more branches till he reached a large one that stuck way out and slid over that. Without his arm anchoring her, she was scared to move, so she clung to the scratchy bark. After a while he slithered back.

"What is it?" she whispered. "Catu, what happened?"

"The man lying on the ground is the tribune. I think Gallus killed him."

* * *

They waited till the men and Gallus had gone before climbing down from the tree. Catu swung his legs over the branch and slid down. Reaching the snowy ground, he held up his arms for her and she dropped into them. They didn't speak.

Lamplight twinkled in the villa's windows. Shadows stretched across the snow. It was very cold. They didn't go in; Catu said it would be better to watch through the window into the room where Tiberius did his special work. Uncle Valentinus and the men holding Gallus were still talking, but they couldn't hear the words. They'd seen one man set off running up the road to Noviomagus, and he hadn't come back yet.

Now there was an argument. She couldn't make it out properly, but she thought her uncle won because everybody stopped talking and looked at him. The men who had tied Gallus's arms led him out of the door and off somewhere.

"What are they going to do with him?"

"You expect me to know everything. Well, I don't! But I'll tell you one thing. It's not good for Gallus."

She understood that he wasn't really mad at her. He was just as scared as she was. "We have to do something, Catu. They're going to hurt Gallus."

"There's nothing we can do."

She was shivering hard now. "We need to tell Niko. He'll think of something."

"He stayed in town. You know that."

"Niko knows how to do everything. Fetch Niko!"

He looked at her for a moment. "I know where his friend lives. In the garrison."

"A lot of people live in the garrison," she said, feeling smarter than

A VILLA FAR FROM ROME

Catu for once.
    "Well, I know his name too. But I'll have to hurry. It's getting dark."
    "Be careful, Catu," she whispered.
    "And you stay out their way while I'm gone!" he ordered.

CHAPTER FORTY-FIVE

DELAMIRA COAXED HER TO SIP THE WARM GOAT'S MILK laced with honey. She didn't want to eat or drink anything, but the girl insisted it would help. She lay back on the couch, and Delamira wrapped a blanket over her.

Valentinus was pacing the room, arguing with a man she'd never seen before, Roman by the look of him, a sea captain. Her brother stopped mid-pace and turned to her.

"Did you encourage him?"

"Valentinus!"

"Well – did you?" His voice was harsh. "Why else did the tribune come here? He knew your husband was away."

"You insult me. You, my brother who should be my champion!" She recognized that part of her anguish came from the secret desire she'd once held for Marcus. If this attack was a punishment sent from the gods for those daydreams, she'd brought it on herself. Yet it was unjustly cruel of immortals whose own stories were filled with deeds of lust and jealousy and revenge to pour out so much pain on one who was only mortal.

"I'm trying to arrive at the truth," Valentinus said, his voice cold.

"No," she said in a whisper. "I don't know why he came here."

The room was quiet for a moment. Long-faced, Delamira padded about lighting the oil lamps.

Valentinus stopped pacing. "Get out!" He slumped in a chair with his back to the girl.

Delamira made an evil face at the back of his head before leaving the room.

"There's no arguing the old man did it," Valentinus said. "That was a Roman dagger we found in the undergrowth. No doubt whatsoever it'll turn out to be his! This is a terrible matter. And I must take charge of it in the absence of the centurion."

"Best to handle it right away," the other man agreed. He was leaning against a wall, his face in shadow. "If a story like this gets out – a Roman tribune makes a secret visit to the wife of a barbarian king, then is murdered by a rogue legionary – who knows what reaction that'll cause? I've been in these parts a while. A story like that? You need to quash it fast!"

"Legion discipline calls for a tribunal in a case like this. But the garrison in Noviomagus is small. Are there enough tribunes here?"

"Too bad you didn't stick your own dagger in his ribs when you reached him. You had it out."

"Are you challenging me? You think I wouldn't have done it?"

She listened to them bicker, growing more disturbed. She wasn't ready to let Gallus take the blame."Valentinus! Didn't you understand what I said? The tribune was trying to rape me – he might even have killed me – I had to do something –"

"Act swiftly now, centurion," the man advised.

"*I* did it!" she shouted at them. "Not Gallus – *I* killed him! He would've raped me otherwise."

The men ignored her.

"The guards I sent for should be here soon." Valentine rested his head in his hands. "They'll carry him up to the fort tonight. Best to get that done in darkness. I don't know if the man has friends here. I'll have to take charge. I'll make my decision how to proceed by morning."

"Valentinus, Brother. Please listen!" The brother she remembered from childhood was not so churlish. She put a hand on his arm, her wounded palm stinging at contact.

He brushed it off. "Say no more about it, Antonia. This is legion business."

"It's *my* business too! I killed the man who was trying to rape me!"

"Would you want your husband to hear the unpleasant details?" the sea captain asked. His voice was oily. For the first time she noticed how his tongue squirmed around in his mouth as he spoke. "What would it look like? A secret meeting while your husband was away –"

"This is best for you, Antonia," Valentinus said. "I'll try to spare you from the shame this time."

She wanted to scream at them, but a woman's rage had no power here. The worst of it was, she knew his assessment of the situation was right. She had nothing to gain by forcing her confession on them. They needed a scapegoat to show off their power. They would kill Gallus anyway.

"Lady." Delamira stood in the doorway. "Soldiers – four of them."

"Good," Valentinus said. "We'll get this taken care of quickly."

* * *

She couldn't sleep. She huddled in a wool blanket in a chair, watching the ghostly snow falling past her window. She couldn't eat a bit of the meal Old Nev had prepared, but Valentinus had consumed his food with the appetite of a wolf. The sea captain hadn't stayed, claiming his need to return to the ship in preparation for sailing on the dawn tide. Valentinus had announced his decision to stay in Noviomagus to oversee the trial of Gallus.

The four legionaries who'd come in response to her brother's summons brought news of the centurion and his men. The patrol had returned that evening, but Marcus wasn't with them. He'd gone on to the headquarters of the legion, carrying the news of Nero's death to the legions's commander. They expected him tomorrow. Her husband hadn't returned with the men either. Her mind shut down, leaving her hearing words, and even answering questions when asked, but not able to hold their meaning for long.

Valentinus came into the room from the colonnade, letting in a blast of cold air and a swirl of snow.

"I'm going up to Noviomagus. In the absence of the centurion, I must stay here and take command. The killer must be sentenced and executed immediately as an example to others."

"Can't this wait till Tiberius returns?" He at least would listen to her.

"This concerns the legion, Antonia. No one else."

A VILLA FAR FROM ROME

"Tiberius fought with the legion –"

"No."

She saw that he was wearing a leather cloak over his armor as protection against the snow. And what about Gallus? Would they provide a cloak for him too? She knew they wouldn't.

"He's an old man, Valentinus," she said. "Show mercy."

He went away without answering her.

Exhaustion finally took her down into fitful sleep that was broken by ugly dreams. In one, she turned from killing Didius and raised the knife against her brother.

Some time later, a noise in the room startled her. Niko stood by the chair she'd slept in, one hand on Catuarus's shoulder. The boy looked ragged with tiredness and fear. They were both covered in snow.

"I brought Niko to help," the boy said. "But it's too late!"

"We passed them on the road," Niko said. "They didn't see us hiding in the bushes."

"What could you have done anyway? Valentinus will see that he's put to death."

"My father won't allow them to do that!"

"Your father won't have any say in this, Catuarus," she said. "It's a Roman matter."

He stared at her. She could see he was trying to make sense of something he'd never had to think of before. He and his father were Roman citizens, but not *Roman*.

"Will they be merciful to him?" the boy whispered. "I wouldn't want Gallus to suffer."

CHAPTER FORTY-SIX

"ROMAN JUSTICE IS MANY THINGS, but never merciful," Togidubnus said.

Nobody in the room said anything. Antonia looked wan. Niko had given her a potion to help her sleep but it hadn't worked yet. The Greek hadn't added anything to the discussion. The children crouched in a corner; he knew they feared he'd send them away if they made a noise; he let them stay. Food and a pitcher of wine stood on a low table, but nobody was hungry.

He'd made good time coming back from the Stone Circles, any faster and he would've injured Warrior, but the early winter night had closed in before he reached the villa. Even if he'd known, he couldn't have been here sooner. Yet he felt guilty for not preventing the attack from occurring.

A king should not burden his soul with such poisons.

A dream. All that had happened in a dream. This – Antonia's anguish, Gallus's danger– was real.

"Gallus was trying to save me, Tiberius," Antonia said in a small voice.

Her voice caught in her throat. For a moment, he had the idea there was something else here, something she wasn't telling him. He sensed she'd been about to, but the children had come into the room and she'd fallen silent. He saw tears in her eyes and took her hand. He noted that she flinched slightly. He'd never showed her such an intimate gesture before. He should have. Regrets and guilt. Poison in the way of right action.

Niko stood up from a stool by the door and caught Antonia's hand as she pulled it away. He stared at it.

"I tore it on some brambles when I was looking for berries," she said, avoiding Niko's eyes.

Niko went out of the room. In moments he was back with a small vial. He took Antonia's hand again and anointed it with an unguent that gave off a sweet, herbal smell.

"We have to help Gallus." His son's voice was quavery.

"You must do something, Tiber," the little girl said. "Don't let them hurt Gallus."

"What will happen to him?" Antonia asked. "My brother isn't persuaded by tears or begging."

He glanced at the children before answering, the girl getting tall now, his son with hair redder than his own used to be. It wasn't good for a child to grow up before its time, but that option had closed when they'd first become involved. A long-forgotten memory surfaced, a scene along the Appian Way that he'd witnessed as a boy on his first trip to Rome: Prisoners lashed to wooden crosses and left to die a slow death in the hot sun. A warning to others. Gallus would be tortured first.

"Nothing good or merciful," he said, and saw Antonia's stricken expression.

"But you're the *king!*" Catuarus insisted.

He was diminished in his son's eyes. A wave of bitterness swept over him. His eldest son lost, his wife estranged. Antonia attacked. This was his reward for dreaming of a path forward for Britanni and Romans together. Better he'd died with Boudicca opposing them! He'd made a silent vow in the Stone Circles to lay down his Roman sword, not take up arms again in the Roman cause, but to accept his destiny as protector of his people. Yet he was helpless to aid his own family, or Gallus – who might as well have been family – in his time of need.

"There's one last thing that can be done," Niko said. He went out of the room.

"I'm deeply saddened this happened, Antonia. If I'd been here –"

"If you'd been here, Tiberius, it would've happened at another time."

"Go, see to it that Warrior is well taken care of," he said to the children. "He worked hard today. Take apples from the kitchen. For your donkey as well."

"But it's dark outside. We go to bed when it's dark!"

His son stroked the girl's arm, hushing her.

"Go to bed. I'll do it."

The child set her mouth firmly. "I'll take an apple to Gallusina first."

The children scurried out.

There was so much that should be said, but no words to say it.

* * *

Niko came back after everyone except Togidubnus was sleeping. A pale sliver of moon was rising over the ragged silhouette of the villa's just started east wing, now sparkling with snow. He went out onto the colonnade to speak to him. The Greek was holding a slim bunch of feathery plants with small white flowers that looked to him to be something the local sheep herders called cow parsley.

"Not too hard to find, even in snow," Niko said. "It grows everywhere, especially damp, shady places."

"What is it?"

"The one last thing to be done."

"What do you intend to do?"

"I can't prevent Gallus's death. Neither can you. Once Roman justice gets underway, there's no stopping it. But I can prevent his suffering." The Greek fingered the stems cautiously. "I'll need to make up a potion. After that, the utensils I use must be smashed or buried, never to be used again."

"A physician who knows how to kill – painlessly?" His own shameful powerlessness to save a man who'd been his friend goaded him to add, "You've done this before."

Niko stood motionless, his hands holding the poison plants. "My past is none of your concern."

"Forgive me. I spoke in pain, not malice."

"Hemlock is very powerful. He'll sink into sleep and not wake again. In Greece it's used for humane executions."

He understood what Niko wouldn't say: The Greek physician had first-hand knowledge of this. Had there been some cloud over his own practice? Perhaps that was why he'd been reluctant to return to Greece when Antonia's father had freed him. Whatever the man's reason might be, it was not his concern. "How will you get it to him? How can you hope to pass the guards?"

"I have a friend, a legionary who performs guard duty tonight."

He'd heard the gossip about Niko's young friend. "This will be dangerous. The chances of discovery –"

"Do we have another choice?"

They went into the kitchen, deserted at this hour. Two oil lamps cast flickering shadows on the walls, shedding enough light for Niko to work. He watched as the man carefully laid the plants on a stone cutting board with a depression in the middle meant to catch blood and meat juices. Niko took out his own bone-handled knife and sliced the stems into small pieces. He wrapped the blade in a piece of sacking from the rubble the builders left outside. Carefully holding the wrapped blade, he used the bone hilt to crush the stems. A thin trickle of sap ran out into the depression, less than would fill a small wine-cup. Tilting the stone board, he gently poured the liquid into a small glass phial which he stoppered and put away in the pocket it had come from.

"The stone didn't absorb the poison. But to be safe, it should be buried deep in the earth where no one will find it."

"I'll take care of it." He was tormented with grief for Gallus and the knowledge of what Niko was preparing.

"My knife I'll clean in the flame." Niko took the glass shade off one of the oil lamps, turned up the flame and held the blade in it, turning it back and forth till it blackened. The sacking burned next with an oily smell. Then he put the knife away. "I'll leave immediately."

"Take a horse. Take Snowmark – she'll be fresh."

The Greek nodded and headed for the door.

This wasn't right. "Wait. I'll come with you."

"You're too conspicuous, Togidubnus. You can't be seen wandering around a Roman fort after dark. I'm already known – *cinaedus*. Tonight that will be my disguise."

He didn't recognize the Latin word at first, then it came back to him.

SHEILA FINCH

A man who slept with other men.

"I won't come back here afterwards," Niko said. "I don't think that would be wise."

No, probably not. Niko was known in Noviomagus. It wouldn't take long for someone in authority to suspect his hand in the old man's death. He held his arm out to the Greek who clasped it. He knew they would never see each other again. "Goodbye, my friend."

After a while, he heard the clatter of a horse's hooves in the darkness.

"May whatever gods you believe in go with you."

CHAPTER FORTY-SEVEN

TIBERIUS SPRAWLED ASLEEP IN A CHAIR in the anteroom where he'd spent the night, a sign, if Antonia had needed one, of the gravity of the situation. The fate of Gallus hung over everything. The villa was silent and deserted; the building itself seemed to be holding its breath, all normal household activities suspended. She too was finding it difficult to breathe, weighed down by so much pain. She took her cloak and went outside.

Yesterday's snowfall had coated the dead leaves still on the trees, giving them back a semblance of beauty the skeletal branches had lacked. The sky was clear of clouds but colorless too; the air had the bite of more snow to come.

There was nothing anybody could do to help Gallus. Her stomach knotted at the thought. Her own brother was the key, but he was the one who'd been most bent on punishing the old man. Little that Tiberius could do in a legion matter. And even if Marcus were to return suddenly, she couldn't imagine him in his mercy releasing Gallus. Marcus, the man who'd sent his faithful companion and his own daughter back to Rome because he'd wanted an heir.

Her heart turned to stone and her body seemed not hers any more it moved so sluggishly. Who could help? Niko did his best with his potions, but nothing would ever remove these scars from her heart. She was surrounded by people but had never been more alone in her life. It was as if she walked in a daze through a desert, too dried up even to weep.

Action would help, but even there she found nothing. The garden which she'd begun cultivating so carefully was deep under snow. She hadn't discovered anything else to occupy her time since she'd been here. She should have tried harder. There must have been something she should have been doing as the wife of the king of the Regni, something that would serve to occupy her mind at this moment when she didn't want to think. She might have been able to do well, helping Tiberius take care of his people, but she'd never accepted her life here as permanent. Now it was too late. What a waste!

The architect saw her and waved for her to come over to where the first wall of the new wing was beginning to rise out of the heaped snow. The self-important little man, bundled up in cloak and scarves, was oblivious of the turmoil in the villa. And he apparently thought himself too grand to interrupt what he was doing and come over to meet her.

As she approached, Septimus Severus rustled a sheaf of papers at her. "Contrary to my orders, my assistant sent to Rome for trees and plants for the gardens. They'll be here in time for spring planting. None of them will thrive in this foul climate – especially the grape vines!"

She watched his breath rise milkily on the cold air, loathing this fussy, overbearing man. "But you'll plant them?"

He glared at her. "I was commissioned by the emperor to build this villa on the same plans as the palace I built for him in Rome, and that is what I've been doing. If I had found anyone here with more knowledge of building than myself, the emperor's chief architect, I would've been glad to listen to them. But that is all finished now."

The villa obviously was not finished. She waited for him to go on.

He took a deep breath first."The terrible news has reached me! How can anyone expect me to continue my work when my patron is dead?"

"When there's no one to pay for it, you mean?"

His face went crimson. One of the workmen nearby, obviously overhearing her words, grabbed his tools and scuttled out of the battle zone. At the other end of the snowy garden, Aron bent to some work, ignoring her. Had he heard what had happened? Of course he had; gossip traveled as fast as lightning. Did he care? If only she hadn't been so quick to send him away!

"I am the emperor's servant, Lady," Severus said haughtily. "I shall work till the money I've been given is gone."

Who would pay for the villa's construction now, she wondered. Would it ever be finished? Did it even matter after what had just happened?

A VILLA FAR FROM ROME

She felt like a jug that had been drained to the last drop, yet someone kept pouring, hoping.

Fighting with Severus – annoying as he might be – was not what she needed to do. But what was it she needed to do? She must find something or she'd dry up and blow away in wind like a dead leaf. She turned her back on the architect and examined a pile of colored stone, waiting to be broken into chips for another mosaic floor. What patterns had he decided on? Yet another detail he hadn't thought worth consulting her about. The depth of his scorn for a woman's opinion was obvious. That was the way she'd been raised; men scorned to listen to women's opinions.

"What design will these stones make?"

"What design?" He rustled the plans ostentatiously. "Ah. A cupid. And a gorgon head – very popular floor designs this year in Rome! Another geometric design with strong perspective built in. Very fine! And – ah – Pegasus."

The thought occurred suddenly, and she knew instantly it was right. "I'd prefer a dolphin in one of the rooms."

"Dolphins are *not* in the plans."

She turned to face him. "Put one in."

"I will not be treated like this!" Severus threw the plans down, sputtering with outrage. "I shall return to Rome immediately!"

"As you please." She walked away. It felt good to get her own way for once; the pain of recent events that burdened her heart lifted, if only for a moment or two. In any case, it had only been a matter of time, once the money disappeared, before Severus left Britannia.

At the far end of the garden, Severus had indicated there would one day be a *triclinium* like the one her father had caused to be built for her mother, where she and her guests could dine outdoors in summer under an arbor of vines. The ground had been cleared to mark its position, it showed dark against the thin snow here under the shadow of tall trees, but no structure had been started. She sat down on a stone bench under the colonnade's roof. The memory of the *triclinium* provoked nostalgia, but this time she wasn't overwhelmed by homesickness.

Aron had disappeared. High overhead, a flock of birds made their way south – so much later than the rest of the migrating flocks. Their calls drifted down to her. Would they be safe? Perhaps they'd land for a while in Pyrgi. She wanted to believe that.

She needed someone to talk to, someone who wouldn't think she was going crazy, someone who'd understand without the need for her to put it all in words. Another woman. But there was no one since Gracila had gone back to Pompeii.

Drawing her cloak about her shoulders to fend off the cold wind that had suddenly sprung up, she went back into the villa. Her bones craved warmth; her heart, she thought, would never be warm again.

CHAPTER FORTY-EIGHT

"It's my fault," Catuarus said. "If I hadn't kept wishing she'd go away so my mother and father could be together again, none of this would've happened."

They were throwing sticks for Beech to retrieve. It was something to do so they wouldn't have to think about what was happening around them. It wasn't working.

The dog bounded through the snow like a hare. The late afternoon sun was shining, but it was still cold, and she was glad she'd grabbed up her cloak for once. They were lucky Niko hadn't been around to see them go outside to play. She wondered for a moment where he was.

"That doesn't make sense, Catu."

"I must've angered the gods."

"Why didn't they punish *you* instead of Mater?"

"I shouldn't have let Gallus come back with us when Niko wanted to stay in town."

"That's silly!"

"I feel so guilty."

She put her hand in his. "Don't. It isn't your fault."

"I don't know what to do to make it right."

She was learning something: Men and boys always wanted to *do* something. As if they could move the world! She didn't share this way of thinking. She fingered the shell necklace he'd made for her; she wore it every day. The pretty blue shells, so smooth under her touch, soothed her.

"I know someone who could make Ma feel better," she said.

He threw the stick again for the panting dog. "Who's that?"

"Your mother."

"Do you really think so?"

"Ma liked to talk to Gracila. I think she'd like to talk to your mother."

He gazed at her for a moment, thinking. She knew it was because he didn't want her to think he followed her ideas just like that. She waited patiently.

"It might be worth trying. I don't know if she'll come here."

"Let's find out."

They'd make the journey to the island faster on horseback. But inside the dim stable they found Snowmark gone. Tiberius's new horse, Warrior, was so big he towered over them both, and that scared her. The other horses were either too old or not used for riding.

"It's either Warrior or walk," he said.

"Can you handle him?"

"Of course I can!"

"Then let's do it."

* * *

Catu's mother was outside the roundhouse on the island, stirring something in a large pot over a fire. She looked up as the big horse came down the path. She had a cloth tied round her head to keep her hair out of the steam, and her cheeks were pink in the heat of the fire. A big grey and black cat wound its body around her ankles, hoping to catch a drop of liquid from her big spoon.

"Lucia's mother needs you," Catu said, dismounting from Warrior. He helped Lucia down.

Breca gazed at them in turn, saying nothing, and returned to stirring the pot.

"She's very sad," Lucia said. "Something bad happened to her."

"Did she send you?" Breca asked.

"Oh no! We just thought – Well, I thought – "

"I think it's a good idea, too," Catu said.

Breca didn't ask them anything they would've had a difficult time answering. She moved the pot off the fire. "I'll get my cloak."

They waited. Lucia would've liked to go inside the roundhouse to see what it was like, but she thought it might be rude to ask Catu to take her. Breca came back out, a brown and red plaid cloak over her shoulders. She'd

A VILLA FAR FROM ROME

taken the cloth off her head, and her braids hung free down her back.

"Warrior is strong enough to carry us all," Catu said.

"Wait," his mother told him.

She took a small pot with a cover over to the fire and ladled something out of the larger pot into the smaller one, and covered it. There was a handle attached to the pot for carrying.

When she was ready, all three climbed onto Warrior and began the journey back to the villa. The tide was coming in when they reached the ford, and water splashed around the horse's hooves but didn't slow him. The sky was filling up with clouds; Lucia knew enough about the weather by now to know that meant there'd be more snow by nightfall. She heard Catu whispering to his mother, telling her what had happened. There were things she would've liked to say or ask, but she thought it best to keep them to herself.

They got back as the sun, mostly hidden behind clouds, slipped below the hump of the Downs behind the villa. Delamira came out at the sound of the horse's hooves. The Master Tiberius had gone up to Noviomagus, she told them as she helped them dismount, and Niko was still not back. The Lady Antonia had moped about all day, not even bothering to eat.

Breca looked at the villa where no lights burned. "Set out lamps," she said to the girl. "And fetch bowls from the kitchen."

Delamira ran to do as she was told. They went inside to the warm room Tiber used to receive visitors, because there were more chairs and benches for sitting in this room than any other. Breca set the covered pot on Tiber's big table where he wrote his orders, took off her cloak then helped Lucia with hers because it had caught on her shell necklace.

After a while, Ma came into the room. Lucia went to her and put her arms around her. Nobody spoke. Catu helped Ma sit in one of the chairs, and Delamira brought bowls and a ladle and served the stew Breca had made.

Ma waved the bowl away when Delamira offered it to her.

"You must eat," Breca said. "It will restore your strength."

Lucia sniffed at the steam rising from her own bowl – fish and garlic, she could tell those two smells. Different kinds of fish. Her stomach rumbled with hunger.

"Oysters and mussels, crab meat. And white flatfish too that Arto brought home this morning. Onions and mushrooms, cabbage and white beans," Breca said, naming the most delicious things Lucia liked to eat..

"It's very good, Ma!" Liquid dripped off her spoon to run down her chin.

Ma allowed herself to be persuaded to eat a few spoonfuls. After they'd eaten, Breca told Delamira to help Lucia and Catu go to bed, Lucia in her own room and Catu in one of the new rooms built for guests where he often slept.

But Lucia knew she would never sleep. After Delamira left her room, she clutched a blanket around her and crept back to the candle-lit audience room where Ma and Breca were talking in soft voices. She didn't know where Tiber was.

"… bring trouble to whatever family I live in," Ma said. "My own in Pyrgi, yours –"

"Hush, child. We don't control our fate."

"The gods hate me."

"I doubt that. You've been the victim of terrible men with power."

"And I've hurt the only men I've met who weren't terrible and powerful – Gallus and Tiberius!"

Lucia thought Ma's arguments were hardly much different from the one Catu had made earlier today, *it's all my fault,* and probably not much truer. She wanted to hug Ma and comfort her, but sensed Ma would not be happy to know she was hearing any of this.

She huddled in the dark by the doorway and tried to concentrate on what they were saying. She hoped that she'd learn something that she and Catu could do to help. The villa was very quiet, Delamira and the Regni servants who lived there had gone to bed. It was colder now since the fire that kept the hypocaust going was allowed to die down at night and she was very glad for the blanket. She didn't understand a lot of the things Ma and Breca said, and her eyelids were getting heavy.

Clasping her precious shell necklace, she fell asleep by the door.

CHAPTER FORTY-NINE

HE DIDN'T WAIT FOR THE NUBIAN GUARD to announce him into the planning room. The Second Augusta's quarters in Noviomagus were nowhere near as large and well-equipped as the legion's permanent camp in Isca Dumnoniorum, but even here the atmosphere was redolent of the military power of Imperial Rome. He strode past the Nubian and stood in front of the long table where two centurions were studying a map. Marcus Favonius had returned; the other centurion must be Antonia's brother, Valentinus Plautinus. Behind them, the banners and vexillums bearing the legion's emblems, Capricorn its birth sign and Pegasus, were displayed against the wall. The room was over-heated and stuffy.

Both centurions were in full uniform – red tunics with leather greaves, armored cuirass over padded vest – and both wore their swords. Favonius wore ceremonial wrist bracelets, signifying recognition of his bravery in battle. Their distinctive helmets with tall horsehair crests sat on the table as if waiting for their owners to pick them up and ride out to do battle. A ray of sunlight from the high, narrow window fell on them, striking sparks.

He knew it was a display of power, all for his benefit. He was supposed to feel intimidated. The legionary who'd brought the summons at dawn had told him Favonius was back. Now he wondered briefly how the change of command from Plautinus who'd held it temporarily had gone. Judging by the two scowling faces in front of him, not to either's satisfaction, and they hungered to take it out on him.

He too had dressed carefully for this confrontation. Over a blue tunic, embroidered by Breca long ago with clan symbols in silvery thread, he wore a green and blue plaid cloak, fastened on one shoulder with a large gold brooch decorated with coral, and his finest dark wool breeches. He'd put a gold and silver torque around his neck, and on his wrists silver cuffs that rivaled Marcus's own. Coming in before the sun had risen, Old Nev had painted the ceremonial blue circles and swirls on his bare arms. His own Celtic sword rode at his hip in place of the Roman one he'd given up in the Stone Circles. If what had happened to him there had been a dream, it had been a wise one.

The scowl on Favonius's face deepened. "You've gone tribal."

"I have never been otherwise."

"You were pleased enough before this to be Roman!"

"And now I'm pleased to remember I'm King of the Regni." Time to claim his rightful title.

Valentinus Plautinus broke in impatiently. "Get to the reason you were summoned!"

"I wait to hear the reason." He kept his tone courteous.

The centurions glanced at each other, and he wondered if they'd argued previously over who would deal with this matter. He could guess what this was about and wasn't going to help them.

Favonius cleared his throat. "I was sorry to learn of the attack on your wife."

He inclined his head, acknowledging the centurion's "sorrow," feigned though he knew it was. Favonius had never shown any sign of caring about the status or well-being of women.

"It was a criminal act, and one that should have been dealt with under Roman law," Favonius said.

"I heard that the man who was arrested was hot-headed and didn't wait for Roman justice to take its course."

The centurion's face darkened with anger at that reply, but before he could reply, Plautinus spoke.

"The wretch would've been dealt with in his turn, according to the law. But we've received word from the guards this morning that he was found dead in his cell."

"Ah. The gods like to surprise us. But why should this be important to me?"

"He was your friend," Favonius said.

He didn't intend to let them intimidate him, but this was treacherous

A VILLA FAR FROM ROME

territory."We fought together with the Fourteenth Gemina when I was hardly more than a boy."

"You brought him with you from Rome to be the overseer of the temple building."

"Legionaries are skilled builders. Gallus had put in his time building roads, walls and bridges with the legion. A temple was a small assignment for him to oversee."

"What do you know of his suspicious death?" Plautinus demanded. "No wounds on him, no weapons found."

"The cell's locks weren't breached," Favonius added. "Yet somehow, someone must've found a way in to the prisoner. Or will you expect me to believe in sorcery?"

Niko had done what he'd planned. He prayed the gods would recognize this act of mercy and help the Greek get away. He studied Antonia's brother. Young, full of his own importance, eager to make a name for himself and advance in the legion. Much like Marcus Favonius. Both of them felt cheated out of a prize. He could imagine the terrible death they would've planned for Gallus, a bloody spectacle in the new arena in Noviomagus.

"If the legionary was locked in a cell, and properly guarded, isn't it possible the gods were kind to an old man and took him in his fright?"

Plautinus pounded his fist on the table. "You know that's not what happened!"

"He was a prisoner in your custody. The responsibility for his safe-keeping lay with you."

He watched both centurions process the implications of this. Rome was not kind to officials – especially military ones – who didn't live up to their responsibility. Technically, Favonius was in charge here, but he'd been away and Antonia's brother had taken over. Neither would want to admit they'd allowed something to happen on their watch to a prisoner who'd killed a tribune – one who probably had an influential family behind him in Rome.

SHEILA FINCH

He was taking a risk by reminding them of their own jeopardy here.

"I intend to investigate this to the fullest," Favonius said. "You can be certain of that!"

Favonius gestured to the guard who'd been lurking in the doorway and the man went away. Plautinus looked down at his helmet on the table, his fingers fussing with the plumes, suddenly anxious to be done with the matter. A slave entered with a tray and three goblets of wine.

"We won't speak further of this now," Favonius said. "Valentinus Plautinus must leave to join his command in the north while the weather holds."

The centurions each took a goblet. Togidubnus left the third on the tray untouched.

He saw that Favonius took note of this breach of customary manners, but the centurion made no comment. Instead, he walked round the table where the intimidating helmets sat and laid a hand on Togidubnus's shoulder.

"We're going to stay close to our base here, my friend," he said. "Commander's orders, till we see what happens with the situation in Rome. Besides, the weather's turning foul – no hope of the men riding out again until the year turns. One day, I believe this land of Britannia will be more Roman than Rome itself! But in the meantime, I want you to continue your persuasion of the citizens to pay their taxes. There's still too much complaining and resistance. It must stop!"

He controlled his rising anger and gazed steadily at the centurion's hand until the man flushed and removed it.

"Collecting coins from poor farmers and sheep-herders is not a king's concern. I suggest you find a Roman soldier to do Roman work."

Favonius looked as if Togidubnus had struck him. "Is this a declaration of war against Rome?"

He allowed himself a small smile. "I'm no fool, Favonius." But the pretense of friendship between himself and the Roman command would never be the same after this. He couldn't predict the effect of that change, only knew it had been inevitable.

"It's insurrection –"

A VILLA FAR FROM ROME

"Name it as you will." He left the room without waiting for their reaction.

* * *

The early night of winter had fallen and owls were calling as he left the town, sheltering behind walls built by Roman legionaries like Gallus. Snow dusted the path, not enough to slow him. The winter patterns glittered overhead, Cernunnos always a personal encouragement.

He wasn't too worried that his rejection of the role Rome would like him to play – submissive client king – would lead to excessive oppression of his people. The garrison here wasn't strong enough to flex its muscles at his tribe's expense. Too much depended on Regni cooperation and Regni supplies. There'd be minor retaliations, Favonius wouldn't be able to resist venting his frustration. A few malcontents like the sons of the sheep-herder had been would be rounded up and flogged. But Rome had better things to spend its gold on than making an example of one tiny Regni kingdom so far away from Imperial power. He was no Boudicca, to his shame, but that might save his kingdom. Especially now, with a succession battle for the throne in Rome. Britannia had long been the stepchild of the empire, the site of bloody battles from time to time, but not in as much danger from Roman power as kingdoms closer to Rome that offered greater rewards.

Yet he walked the dark path back to his villa by the sea with a heavy heart. The dream of the bright years to come when the best of Celtic and Roman traditions, knowledge and laws would meld into one glorious nation had been destroyed. The future was not bright, it was dark.

In his dream-time inside the Stone Circles, the Lady had prophesied, *The Celts will vanish from the land along with their Roman masters.* She hadn't told him he would be an agent of that downfall. His heart filled up with darkness.

She had anointed him, and that must suffice.

CHAPTER FIFTY

THE TWO WOMEN STOOD UNDER THE COLONNADE watching the pale sun struggling against the cloud wrack in the east. Antonia breathed in the cold, salt breath of the sea. Tiberius had still been gone when she rose this morning.

A sudden beating of wings overhead, and she looked up to see a flock of white gannets, wintering on the island, heading out to sea to fish. An owl flew silently past, going home to rest from a night hunting. Such little things, but they were large in meaning. She remembered a time when she'd been scornful of Tiberius's great knowledge of all the plants and the beasts in this country, or even Niko's desire to learn about everything around him.

The road from the port to the town was empty at this hour. In the distance, a trickle of smoke rose from a house where one of the villa's farmers lived, a woman rising early to light the fire and prepare the first meal of the day. A cock crowed.

Something was growing in her heart, like a small sapling just planted that would someday grow into a tall vine and bear fruit. At its root was the knowledge that she had killed a man. Granted, a man who would've killed her if she hadn't been quicker than he. And Gallus had given up his own life to protect her. The gods would demand a reckoning, just as they had of Nero who'd taken away her childhood. But that was a long time ago, and she was stronger now; she'd face whatever the Fates sent.

"Togi is well," Breca said after a long silence. "I would know it in my heart if he weren't."

She glanced at the tall woman, marking the strong profile, the determined set of her mouth, the proud gaze. She should have made a friend of her long ago. But of course, that would never have been possible until now when shared sorrow brought them together.

A VILLA FAR FROM ROME

A new thought occurred. How well these people spoke Latin, even accented. And Lucia spoke their language as if it were her birth tongue. Could she have done the same if she'd tried? She'd been taught to read and write as a girl. Beyond that, she could spin and weave – though she suspected not as well as Breca's people. She'd learned about grapes and making wine at her father's side, though she hadn't had the chance to use that knowledge with her own grapes. How much more of her life was she going to waste in clinging uselessly to a past that hadn't treated her very well?

"I think I might have done better here, if I'd put my heart into it."

Breca turned to her, her expression showing surprise, but she didn't comment.

"I should have made an effort to see Tiberius's side of the situation – and yours. I saw only my own exile, a place I didn't want to be. I should have tried harder."

Yet as a woman, who would've honored her choices? Who would've let her make decisions?

Breca touched her arm. "Don't waste your time on such thoughts. Togi and I are old enough to know how fate gives none of us a choice. You had so much taken away from you."

"You did too. And you lost a son."

"The fault is not on you. The emperor was an evil man."

They were both silent for a moment, the villa behind them and its occupants still. The architect had packed his belongings and gone down to the port to take passage back to Rome on the evening tide. Aron hadn't been with him, but she didn't know where he was. It was too late for that to matter now. Much too late.

"I was unkind to Tiberius – arrogant – laying my unhappiness on him. And my being here has caused you great pain."

"We have a saying in my tribe," Breca said. "The past cannot be unwoven, but the future's patterns can be laid on the loom."

"I never tried to learn the Old Tongue. Even my daughter can speak it now."

Breca laughed. "Now you're looking for ashes to cover yourself! Lucia is young, she learns easily."

"In my heart I'll never be anything but Roman."

"You are a Roman-Britanni. One of the first."

More birds were awake now; she watched a flock of field sparrows wheeling overhead in search of breakfast. A robin perched on a heap of the builders' stones and began to sing. The first tint of pale yellow stained the sky where the sun would appear. There was a stark beauty to the bare trees, the snow-covered land, the sky full of birds. It had taken her such a long time to recognize it.

"Why don't you hate me, Breca? You have cause." She felt the hot tears rising and was too tired to control them.

"And what good would that do? Would it erase that day when you lost your childhood? Would it bring back my son?"

Breca's arms enclosed her, and she felt the kindness and warmth of the woman.

In the distance, a dog barked.

"That's Beech," Breca said, releasing her. "Shee must've seen Togi on the road."

Clutching their skirts, they both ran up the road where a figure trudged toward them. Tiberius wore Regni garments, fine ones at that. She'd never seen him dressed in anything but Roman tunic and toga. When they reached him, Breca threw out her arms as if she would embrace him, then hesitated, glancing sideways at Antonia. He took her hand in his.

"Gallus has evaded Roman justice," Tiberius said. He took Antonia's hand too, not letting go of Breca.

Her heart stopped. "What do you mean? Has he escaped?"

He shook his head. "Not from his cell. But he's free."

"I don't understand...."

Breca gazed at him. "Are you in danger because of this, Togi?"

"No, my heart. But we'd do better not to speculate about it."

"We won't speak of it ever again," Breca said.

Antonia didn't doubt that however Gallus had cheated his fate,

A VILLA FAR FROM ROME

Tiberius had a hand in it. A few days ago she wouldn't have thought this, wouldn't have thought it necessary. Now, knowing her brother as she'd come to know him, she understood it was better to keep secrets from him. It was a bitter thought. She was full of them this morning.

"We'll go inside and I'll make a meal for us," Breca said. "Help me, Antonia."

Why not? The villa was a symbol of Nero's tyranny and it had affected all of them. Two women who should be enemies preparing a meal together flew in the face of Nero's malevolence.

The children were awake when they went inside, both of them throwing themselves at Tiberius as if he'd been gone for weeks, not just a day. She followed Breca into the kitchen while the children entertained Tiberius with their chatter. Unused to the new kitchen, Breca needed help finding bowls and cooking pots.

"I like it that the kitchen's so spacious," Breca said politely.

"Severus had even grander plans for the rest of the villa," she said. "Or should I say, the emperor had plans."

Maybe they'd never come into being, now that Nero was dead. Severus had told her he was building for the ages to come; perhaps the plans had a momentum of their own and would continue without Severus or Nero or herself.

Together they made a boiled wheat porridge on the raised hearth, adding honey and raisins and a few dried berries the children had collected from the winter-blasted brambles around the villa. There was bread too, baked yesterday, and a little goat cheese, no meat or fish today – a sign, she thought of the darkness and confusion that had settled over the villa . They carried the plates and the steaming bowls in together and set them on the table. The sun's rays hadn't reached this room yet; golden light from the oil lamps pooled over the table and the family seated at it; even the shadows in the corners of the room were warm and comforting.

"Ah! I almost forgot."

She went back to the cool cellar and retrieved the small earthenware jar she'd used for the crushed blackberries. "It hasn't had time to ferment as much as it should, but this is the first wine made here."

The dark red liquid smelled of late autumnal sun on warm brambles, still more thick juice than wine. Eyes half-closed, she breathed it in, then poured each of them a small portion, the children too. There was just enough for each to have a mouthful. Lucia made a face but the others showed their pleasure.

After they'd eaten, they sat comfortably in the warm room; the servant had lit the fires that ran the hypocaust.

Tiberius's boy asked suddenly, "Where's Niko? Won't we do lessons with him today?"

When Tiberius didn't immediately answer, she knew what her father's former secretary had done. A physician clever enough to save lives as he'd saved hers and Tiberius's could also take them if he wished.

All her life, Niko had been there, slave, servant, companion along the way, tutor – but never friend. There had always been something hidden about him. What came clear to her now was that just as Gallus had put his life in danger for her, Niko had put his in danger for Gallus. And Tiberius had somehow done the same for Niko.

Lucia climbed into Tiberius's lap and snuggled against him. Antonia was about to scold her daughter when she caught his eye. He shook his head and she held her tongue.

"Let's say that I sent Niko away on business for me," Tiberius said. "We may not see him for a very long time."

"What business, Father?" the boy wanted to know.

Breca held a finger to her lips. "We won't talk about this, my son. Not ever. You'll have to study your lessons by yourselves for a while."

A shaft of sunlight had crept into the room while they were eating, washing it with light as creamy as the milk that arrived in the pail each morning. Country things, she thought, sometimes they were more lasting than the stones of a seaside villa that could fall into neglect, destroyed by the tides of politics. The boy left his seat to squat on the warm floor beside his father; he picked at a crust of bread in his hand.

"There's something I must say," she said.

A VILLA FAR FROM ROME

Until this moment, she hadn't realized the decision had been made. It had been hers to make for a very long while now, but she hadn't had the experience to know that. Now, she'd come into her power, even if her first action would be one of renunciation.

The longer she put it off, the more chance her resolve would weaken. She looked at them, Breca sitting beside Tiberius, Lucia in his lap, Catuarus at his feet. A family.

"I've made a decision."

Tiberius frowned as if he guessed what she would say. "Should the children hear this?"

"Yes."

They waited to hear what she would say, the children's eyes bright with happiness that they were all together. In that moment, she knew she loved them all and how hard it would be to give them up.

"I'm going back to Italia."

She heard Breca's sudden intake of breath and saw confusion on the faces of both children.

"You mustn't make this decision lightly, Antonia," Tiberius said, his voice gentle.

"I don't make it lightly. I've given it much thought. I wanted to go home the day I first set foot off the boat! Even building a grand new villa didn't help. What just happened to me –"

She broke off. She knew if they sensed she was wavering in her decision, they'd try to talk her out of it. She couldn't allow that. To give herself time, and to allow her heart to stop racing, she took a sip of the blackberry wine. There was only one drop left in the cup.

She tried to find the right words so that they wouldn't feel it necessary to argue against her. "Both of those things – the exile, this villa – were somebody else's decisions. Nero's. Even Gallus's decision to take the blame for killing Didius. This one is mine."

"Antonia –" Breca said. "Why are you doing this?"

"With the emperor who exiled me dead, there's nothing to stop me going home."

"Ma," Lucia said hesitantly. "Why isn't this our home?"

CHAPTER FIFTY-ONE

CATUARUS TOUCHED HER ARM, and Lucia knew he was trying to comfort her.

She wasn't going to be distracted. "This is our home, Ma!"

"But your family in Rome," Catu's mother said. "I thought your father –"

Ma had been looking hard at her. Now she turned back to Catu's mother. "I'll find my mother and my younger brother. Valentinus told me where they are."

"You don't have to do this," Tiber said. "This house is yours. For as long as you want it. I'll give orders that a separate wing be built for you, if that would please you."

Ma shook her head. But did that mean *No, we won't leave* or *No, we're not staying?*

Catu's mother said, "Hush, Togi. Let her make her decision."

She saw the little smile that came on her mother's face, a pretend smile really.

"I don't want to go to Rome!" she said in a loud voice.

The grown-ups were getting too far away from the real problem. This was home. They didn't need to go anywhere. Everybody ignored her. Catu pushed some of his uneaten bread and cheese over to her. Food wasn't going to make her feel better. It was very quiet in the kitchen for awhile. She liked the kitchen. It was warm and comfortable, and she could still smell the rich, sharp smell of the blackberry wine Ma had made. It smelled better than it tasted.

"I'm not going to change my mind. Tiberius – *Togidubnus* – you've been fair to me. I haven't always been fair in return. I free you from all obligations Nero imposed on you. Take your true wife back."

She didn't understand all the words Ma used, but she did understand that Ma's mind was made up. They were going back to Rome – a city she didn't remember and didn't want to see!

Catu stood up, his face all wrinkled up as if he were going to cry. "You can't go away!"

"I don't want to go, Catu!"

"Little one," Ma said – and she was astonished. Ma had never called her *little one* before! "I can't stay here, and I can't leave you behind."

"Won't Rome be dangerous for the child?" Tiber asked softly.

"Please," Catu said, "Don't take Lucia. Beech will miss her if she goes!"

"So will you, Catu!" she said indignantly. "You'll miss me too." But that's the way boys were and she forgave him immediately.

Ma looked as if she were ready to cry.

Catu's mother put her arms around Ma. "You could leave her with us for a while. Till you see how things are. We'd take care of her like our own."

Now Ma really was crying! But she needed to think about what Catu's mother had said. She could stay *here* – like one of their own. "Yes," she said. "Oh yes! Please!"

And Catu said it too, "Please!"

"I don't like to think of you returning to Rome all alone," Tiber said. "It's not safe."

Everyone was quiet at that.

"Not alone," Ma said, her voice sounding shaky. "I'll take Delamira with me. She wants to go back to Carthage."

"Not alone," another voice said.

She spun on her toes and saw who was standing in the doorway. The funny-looking man who'd been Severus's assistant. What was he doing here in their kitchen?

"I came to take my leave," the man said. "I'm going back to Rome. There's no more work for me here. I couldn't help overhearing. I'll be honored to accompany them – if the Lady finds my offer acceptable."

She was getting very good at knowing grown-ups left some things unsaid. There was something here that the man hadn't put into his words. She wasn't sure what it was, but she caught a very odd look that passed between Ma and the man.

"You're very kind, Aron," Ma said in a soft voice. "I accept your offer."

Everybody was hugging everybody else – she herself got squashed in Tiber's arms – and just about everybody was crying. Well, not Tiber.

Later, when Ma went off to pack her things for the journey, and Delamira took them out of the room, Catu whispered in her ear.

"What was that all about?"

"I'm staying here. Ma's going back to Rome."

"I know that! I meant with that man who used to help Severus?"

She whispered back. "I think Ma likes him, Catu."

"She didn't look as if she liked him!"

"That's because she doesn't know it yet."

Catu wrinkled up his face. Boys weren't very good at understanding things.

CHAPTER FIFTY-TWO

CATUARUS WAS PLAYING A GAME WITH THE YOUNGER CHILDREN, leading them in a leaping dance around the blazing log. Togidubnus watched Colinus's son making serious if clumsy efforts to copy him. It had been Breca's idea to revive the old tradition of inviting his tenant farmers and craftsmen to observe the Yule. Not a Roman celebration such as the sad occasion Antonia had planned so long ago, but a feast for family and friends. A sudden flurry of snow caused the fire to spit a shower of sparks into the air like falling stars. The children squealed, as happy as piglets.

The cattle herder, cup of beer in hand, sat to one side, watchful that his son not commit offense in his king's house. Four sheep-herders and their wives, and one of the women potters stood in a loose line, waiting for Old Nev to fill their cups, firelight playing over their faces. The old woman had grumbled at being pressed into service as server as well as cook, but he knew she was well pleased.

"Good to see you in good spirits for once."

He turned to see the man with long grey braids who had spoken. "Pudens Pudentinus, my only friend in Noviomagus, welcome."

"Hardly your only friend," Pudens replied. "But I hope to be a good one."

"I'm going to need friends in the days to come."

"I came to bring you some news – though whether you will regard it as good or not remains to be seen."

They stepped back a few paces from the throng around the fire, strolling along the colonnade to where construction of the new wing of the villa ended and the ground was marked out for the next to rise – which now would probably not happen. At least, he thought, for as long as he had anything to say about it. Here, they stood a while in silence. The death of Nero and the resulting chaos over the throne, the growing rebellion of the tribes, the enemy he'd made in Marcus Flavonius all promised a difficult year to come. Maybe many years to come. But the decision he'd made to accept his role as leader and defender of his tribe above all else – including, especially, Rome's ambitions in Britannia – gave him a sense of peace that he'd lacked for many years.

"So, give me the news and I'll weigh whether it's good or bad."

"The Council is understandably cautious about what they see as your new-found Regni enthusiasm," Pudens said. "But they'll come around. Pilus isn't eager to stir up more trouble after what happened to his nephews."

"I won't take part in any more killing. I allowed myself to be used by Rome without knowing it. A tool in their expansion of empire. We were a free people. We will be so again, though not as we are now. The world is changing, Pudens."

Pudens nodded. "The Romans have a saying, I believe. 'It took more than a day to build Rome.' It won't be defeated in a day either."

He laughed. "Rome's power will vanish one day, but Britannia will prevail. I have it from a very good source. But none of that is news to either of us, Pudens."

Pudens nodded. "The Council seems to have forgiven you for ascending to kingship of the tribe – Yes, yes, I know! It wasn't your idea. Now, wiser heads have suggested that it might not be such a strange idea to pursue uniting the neighboring tribes under a strong king. As you have certainly proved yourself to be."

"You are speaking of your own opinions here, of course."

"Others agree. We believe a time is coming when we will need a great king to make a stand." Pudens ran his hand over a section of new wall, still rough and waiting for the plasterer's art. "And a great king will need a suitable palace to receive ambassadors, a place to impress friends and enemies alike."

"What're you saying?"

"The council has agreed to supply the money to complete this villa on the plans the architect drew up for it."

Before he could answer, Breca came up to him and slipped her arm in his. The scent of wood-smoke was on her clothes, and her cheeks were pink from the fire. He put an arm around her shoulder.

"My heart, will you be happy here in this Roman villa? What if it were to be the size the architect planned? If you aren't happy, I'm not happy."

"I grant you it's rather more elaborate than I would've asked for," she said. "But I'll accept it as the gift it is. We have a family to raise in it now."

"Well said!" Pudens nodded at Breca. "I think we see eye to eye on this. Our role is to preserve and advance the peace, and take care of the Regni entrusted into our stewardship, as difficult as that may turn out to be. For as long as it takes."

"And for as much money as you can make?"

Pudens smiled. "I see no conflict between peace and commerce."

Shrieks of excitement drew their attention. Catuarus was now leading the old donkey with the small child of the cattle herder on her back.

He thought again of Gallus; the old legionary was never far from his thoughts for long. Gallus was the example of what was best in Roman society, fighter, builder, loyal, brave –

He turned his head so Pudens wouldn't see his eyes fill with a woman's tears. Yet there was no shame in admitting the loss of such a good friend. Nor of Niko either. He would let their memory be a lamp to him in whatever darkness he might find himself surrounded by in the years to come.

* * *

The Yule log burned down to embers, servants banked the small glitter of fire with ash, and Atto slanted a reed wind-break to shelter it from snow that would put it out too soon. Breca's aunt and uncle would stay the night in one of the new bedrooms in the villa. The guests had gone home, and a servant had put the children to bed. As a special Yule treat, Beech was allowed to sleep inside by the bed they shared.

The new house sighed as it settled into the night as an old house would, like a hen sheltering her chicks. He nodded at the comforting thought. He joined Breca in the bedroom where he'd slept alone for so

A VILLA FAR FROM ROME

long. In the soft amber light of the one oil lamp, he watched her unpin her long hair, admiring the thickness of it and the sheen as it tumbled down over her slim shoulders. She fumbled with the clasp on her dress.

"Let me do it."

She turned to him, smiling. The room was warm in the rich shadows, and his fingers thrilled at the feel of her bare skin. Her scent was the familiar lavender under smoke from the Yule log. He put his arms around her, wanting to prolong this moment.

"It's been a long time since I've seen Catuarus so full of joy," she said.

"Yes. He's happy to have his companion here."

"Antonia made the right decision. Though I don't doubt it broke her heart."

"I just hope –"

She put a finger on his lips. "We shall raise her as our own."

He was silent, thinking of the words Arto had spoken when he pulled the Roman child from the sea, words he hadn't wanted to hear. *And you will nourish them*, the Lady said in his memory. Even though his own name might vanish in Time's river.

"They were born for each other, Togi," Breca said.

She put out the lamp and drew him down onto the bed and curled herself into the shelter of his arms, pulling the fur covers over them. He could see stars through the unshuttered window. Or were they in his mind, his heart so full of joy? He heard the old owl hoot, once, twice – Sulis's bird – and he smiled. The worries and vexations of the recent days settled. Yet one thought persisted, troubling him. He'd shared everything with Breca before and could do so again.

"What is it?" she asked, sensitive to his mood before he even spoke.

"Something bothers me about the luck of Gallus arriving just in time and saving Antonia."

"She saved herself, Togi. He took the blame for her."

"She told you this?"

"She didn't need to. I knew it the moment I saw her."

He kissed her brow, her cheeks, her lips. "You were always the wisest of us all."

"With the Lady's help," she said.

He pushed himself up on his elbows and gazed into her dark, Druid eyes that he'd always believed saw beyond the veil. "I had a vision – a dream while I was away with the legion – an experience at the Stone Circles."

He felt her nod, waiting.

"A lady. Old, but somehow young too."

"Sulis."

"Yes. I think so. She foretold my future. Our future as Regni."

Breca put a finger on his lips. He knew she didn't need to hear more. It had been a long time, too long, without the comfort of this woman who knew him without being told..

Her fingers caressed his chest, slowly, deliciously sliding down his body till he shuddered with pleasure. Kingdoms rose and fell. The gods were not always smiling. What mattered was a moment like this when a beloved woman's heart beat close to her man's.

"Arto says the spring will come early this year," she murmured.

"Come closer and let me show you how spring is already causing something to grow."

She laughed and pressed her lips on his.

He closed his eyes and entered her.

"My heart," he said. "My dearest heart."

A VILLA FAR FROM ROME

EPILOGUE

[The Villa, AD 130]

THE OLD WOMAN PAUSED, leaning on her cane, silently gazing at the mosaic the workmen had just finished laying on the floor of the big dining room in the north wing. Her eyelids drooped. She was so still, the young man who accompanied her wondered if she'd fallen asleep on her feet. Not surprising, given the warmth of the summer afternoon and her age.

"Avi?" he said softly, using the pet name the children had always called her.

The old woman stirred and widened her eyes. "I wish your grandfather could've seen that mosaic. He loved the dolphins too."

Relieved, the young man said, "If you'd like to sit down, Avi, I could find a chair."

She waved his concern away. "It was all because of dolphins that I first met his family, you know."

He'd heard that story many times; all the children had. How little Lucia, fresh from Rome, had almost drowned in the sea, only to be rescued by their grandfather's uncle. And the dog. She never let them forget the part about the dog.

"Yes, Avi," he said. "A great pity he couldn't have lived a little longer to see the dolphin mosaic. It's very well done."

"I talk too much of the past," she said suddenly. "I want to hear of your adventures. Tell me about Rome, and – where was it you went? Athens?"

"Alexandria, " he said. "I'll fetch a chair first."

They went out into the garden, enclosed on three sides now by the completed wings of the villa, the fourth wing marked out and ready to rise someday. Gardeners were tending to the grape vines that grew on the trellises along one side that was sheltered from the wind. His father would send the fruit into Noviomagus where vintners would crush it and make wine. It was a good wine, though a little thin when compared to the wines of Rome or Alexandria. A flock of gulls flew overhead, arguing noisily, their plumage brilliantly white in the sun. The old woman watched them go.

When she had settled herself in the chair, she sighed. "Alexandria. How Niko would've liked to go to the great library! He spoke of it often."

"It is indeed a very great library, Avi," he agreed. It was easier to keep the talk on the library than on someone who had apparently once been her Greek tutor. She lived so much in the past these days. "Scholars come from all over to use it."

"We never saw him again, you know. Nikolaos. We thought he must've gone back to Greece. But tell me about Alexandria."

"Thousands upon thousands of books there, on every subject you can imagine, Avi. And teachers and philosophers. Prophets on every corner of the city. Always a lecture or a speech somewhere."

"Prophets? I don't wish to hear about prophets. Or the gods they boast about. The gods were never very kind to my family."

She dismissed the thought with another handwave, the bright gold ring that had been his grandfather's flashing in the sunlight on her middle finger.

"There's a famous lighthouse in the harbor, too," he said.

But she was done with the news about Alexandria. "We never saw my mother again, either. My dearest father – Tiber, I called him – who adopted me after she left, traced her to a town on the coast near Pompeii where she had relatives. But a year or two later the mountain erupted and destroyed everything. Houses, people, all gone. My father couldn't find out anything, not even whether she'd been there when the disaster happened."

Dismayed, he said, "But you were still very young when that happened!"

A VILLA FAR FROM ROME

"Oh yes, but I had Tiber and Breca, your great-grandparents. And my heart, my Catu." She leaned forward and gazed at him. "You were named for him, you know."

"Catuarus." He nodded. "He was a good man. I'm sorry he's gone, Avi."

"You look like him when he was your age. So handsome! My proud Celt." She sighed, as memory overtook her again. "Catu and I had a good life as children. Tiber was a great leader of the Regni. Togidubnus was his true name, of course. He defended them against the Romans. Not by the sword! He said he'd foresworn the sword. But he was strong in his will, and just, and after a while the Romans saw that too and made him governor."

The young man had heard most of it before. All the grandchildren took it in with their mothers' milk. But he realized he hadn't thought about it quite like this. How young she'd been when her mother had abandoned her here! He'd never understood why this had happened and hesitated to ask. His older sister, Julia, who liked to know everybody's secrets, hinted there was a scandal involving an emperor, but he didn't believe it.

"We've had many years of peace, thanks to Tiber," she said. "And my Catu who followed the path he laid out for us."

"Yes, Avi."

"Someday, you will be the one to lead your people, another Catuarus."

"Oh, but my father – and his brothers –"

"You, Catuarus," she said firmly. "And then I will give you his signet ring. It has his name on it, you know."

He didn't want to hear about staying in Noviomagus as king of the Regni – or governor, or anything else to do with the boring work of governing. He was a scholar by nature, not a soldier like his brother Gaius, or a politician like his cousin Lucullus. Yes, Lucullus would love to live here in the villa where they all grew up and be a Great King! What he himself wanted most to do was return to his studies in Alexandria. The library called to him with a most sweet song.

"Tiber used to say that one day a great nation would live here, not just

Regni and Romans, or even Belgae and Trinovantes or the Brigantes in the north, but others from far away over the sea. And not just Celts. Our family must be strong to lead them."

She fell silent after that and he thought this time she'd truly fallen asleep. He sat on a low garden wall beside her, careful not to disturb. After a while, his mother came out with a blanket. She put a finger to her lips and gently placed the blanket over the old woman's knees. It was a warm afternoon, but old people's blood runs chill, his mother always said. She went back inside, leaving him with his grandmother. He was his Avi's favorite grandchild, after all.

They sat in the humming of bees as the sun slowly slipped away over the great humps of the Downs behind the villa. Like dolphin backs, he always thought, or the whales that went by in the wild water between Britannia and Gaul.

It was because of all the stories she'd told him over the years that he wanted to be a scholar. He saw clearly now where that ambition had come from. But even if he were to fulfil her wish and live his life here as king of the Regni, that would be a long way off. His father was still a strong, healthy man.

He put his big hand over her small one, feeling the bones below the fragile skin. He'd stay for as long as she lived , which he sensed wouldn't be so very long. The library could wait till she went to join her beloved Catu.

AUTHOR'S AFTERWORD

In 1960, a workman cutting a trench across a field near the Sussex village of Fishbourne, came across what turned out to be previously unknown Roman ruins. This discovery by itself wasn't surprising as the countryside around Chichester is full of the evidence of Roman occupation. But this find turned out to be surprisingly large – and very puzzling. Archaeologists have only been able to excavate a small portion of the enormous Roman villa that backhoe struck; almost three-fourths of it lie under a main road and a housing estate and can't be accessed. But from what we can study, we can see this was no ordinary Roman family dwelling. Not only is it the largest such villa found anywhere so far away from Rome, it also seems to have been built in the style of Nero's own *Domus Aurea* in Rome.

Who could it have been built for? We've learned that construction took place between AD 65 and the end of the Third Century when a huge fire destroyed the whole structure. In between those dates, the villa came to possess beautiful mosaic floors (including "Cupid riding on a dolphin"), advanced under-floor heating systems, elaborate bath chambers, and public meeting rooms, and fine gardens. It was obviously far too grand a home for any of the petty officials, Briton or Roman, who were in that corner of Britannia at the time. So who was it built for and who lived there, almost two thousand years ago?

A few clues have emerged. A name, "Tiberius Claudius Togidubnus," appears on a plaque commemorating the building of a temple to Neptune and Minerva in Noviomagus Regnorum (today's Chichester) calling him rather grandly,"Great King in Britain." But as far as we know, Togidubnus was a very minor Celtic king who once fought with the Romans against the uprising of Queen Boudicca; there is a scattering of references to him in contemporary Roman chronicles. Was this splendid palace given to him as a reward for his loyal service? It's possible, but we really don't know.

What we do know is that the Emperor Nero became increasingly concerned that he was surrounded by political enemies, and that his life was in danger. Under those circumstances, it might have been prudent for him to consider building a "bolt-hole" in a remote corner of the Roman Empire. (Being Nero, of course, he'd send his own architect to supervise a glorious building.) We may never know if this is what happened or not, but it's certainly a possibility. In any case, Nero never had the chance to use his hide-away, if that's what it was intended to be.

And in 1995, a gold signet ring turned up in the garden close to the palace, inscribed "Tiberius Claudius Catuarus," most probably a son of Togidubnus.

In telling the story of this magnificent mystery house, I've tried to stay with the historical record as much as possible, inventing details and actions only when history is silent or not yet totally understood. At times, when the needs of telling a story competed with current scholarly speculation, I reserved the right to make small changes.

Some of these characters, Togidubnus himself, for example, the Emperor Nero, the emperor's architect Septimus Severus, Catuarus, Pudens Pudentinus, are real people; their motivations and intrigues are a product of my imagination.

ABOUT THE AUTHOR

Sheila Finch is the author of eight science fiction novels and numerous short stories, including the collection of first contact stories, *The Guild of Xenolinguists*. The lingster story, "Reading the Bones," won a Nebula. A non-fiction book about the intersection of science fiction with mythology, *Myths, Metaphors, and Science Fiction* appeared in 2014. She taught science fiction and creative writing at El Camino College, CA, for thirty years and at workshops around California.

CPSIA information can be obtained
at www.ICGtesting.com
Printed in the USA
FSOW02n0909200117
29860FS